A WIZARD'S DREAM

Cover design by MairaIris

fiverr/mairis23

Map design by Muhammad Abdul Momin Arju

fiverr/rubioaas

To the Artists

Whose canvasses
craft whole worlds out of imagination

Whose melodies
imbue those worlds with heartfelt emotion

Without you
this work would not have been possible

CONTENTS

PREFACE

The writing of this story has been a deeply personal journey for me. As I continued to write, it shaped me in return, calling on me to express emotion as much as I could, something that I've struggled to do in my daily life.

To this end, I've personified the world in which the story takes place. The land herself – from the tiniest dewdrop to the largest summit – has emotions, motivation and agency. When you see a masculine mountain or a feminine river, please bear in mind that this was done intentionally.

I've changed my writing style too, striving to give it a poetic flow, to express as much emotion through it as I could. I've bent some grammar rules in the process, but hopefully not so much that it makes reading a challenge.

This has resulted in an unconventional story, hopefully a truly memorable one.

ACKNOWLEDGMENTS

I'm indebted to the many people who have given their time to help improve the story. Their input – from minor remarks to book-wide critique – has shaped it into what it is here.

In order of appearance:

Johann Mynhardt

Kyle Trehaeven

Sancia Jularr

Linda Thomsen

Lee-Anne Wilson-Smith

Harikrishna Rengaraj

Audrey Lewis

Rick Waugh

Diana van der Westhuizen

Diana James

Simon Graeme

Allison Filiatreault

Jen O'Keefe

Sammi Fetterhoff

Joane Luesse

Randy Bisig

Rari Rajesh

Ellie Storm

Christopher Belmont

Tori Kelly

Amari Omehia

Rick Obo

David Stenton

Lockart Lowe

Cyrus Turner

Cole Buckon

Edwin St. George

Alex Hughes

Georgina Catto

Paul Willis Trammell

Mary Sedwich

Shanil Misra

Indira Misra

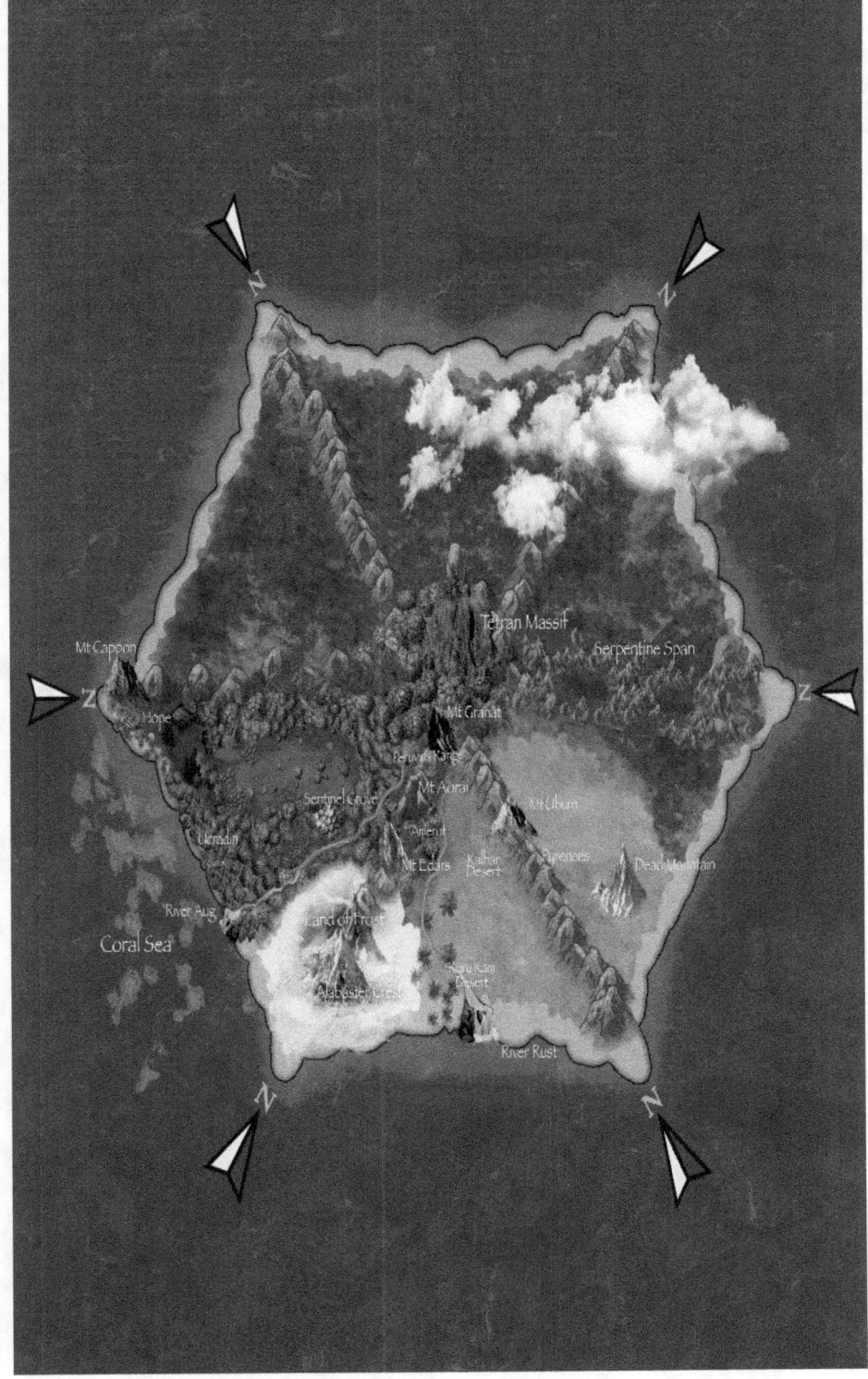

PROLOGUE

An elderly woman appeared at the edge of the clearing. A loose tunic made of desert leaves flowed freely across her broad frame. Wrinkled skin mixed with rusty stone comprised her face, betraying the many cycles she had seen. She stood there for a moment, her gaze sweeping across the busy dell.

The youngsters quietened down at the sight of her, transfixed on the unfamiliar figure standing before them. They dashed to their seats, leaving their gathering places by the twisted trunks of withered trees. The last seat filled before the stranger could complete her walk and take her place in the centre of the glade.

She stopped in front of an ancient tree stump weathered and split by the harshness of the land. The children sat in a semicircle around her. A broad smile spread across her face at the sight of them – a ragged bunch from a remote corner of the land, the kind that thirsted the most for her storytelling.

"Good morning," she greeted the class.

"Good morning," unrehearsed voices, subdued and enthusiastic, sounded in response.

"My name is Rukha. I'm your substitute teacher."

"Did you come to tell us a story?" asked a little girl from the front row without a hint of shyness.

The yearning in her voice brought a smile to Rukha's face. "I have indeed. A very particular story, from our ancient past. Do you know which one?"

Silence followed, though shaking heads and shrugging shoulders did little to dispel the sparkles of wonder in the children's eyes.

"No? I'm going to tell you about the wizard Asja. Asja the Dream Seer. Have you heard of her?"

A low murmur spread through the class, the children whispering to one another, their wide eyes beaming with excitement. Still, they held back from sharing with the new teacher, except for a little boy whose face grew a mischievous smirk.

1

"She could see people's dreams while they were sleeping?" he burst out.

Rukha's hearty laugh wrapped the class in a warm hug. "No, my child. The dreams she saw were altogether different. Intricate, not easy to explain. It'd probably be best if you waited for that part of the story. I think you'll understand then."

The boy nodded, still sporting a face-wide grin.

Rukha stood back to size up the class, proud of her ability to make them feel at ease. Their little hands shot up, impatient for the teacher to look their way and let them speak.

"She was a wizard who could travel to the stars!"

"I heard that she was a shapeshifter who could change her appearance at will. Sometimes she looked like a dwarf and sometimes like a mur."

"Didn't she stop the war between dwarves and goblins?"

A warm feeling washed over Rukha as the class came to life, the children recalling the tales they'd heard with growing ease and sharing them as if to outdo each other at painting a portrait of an ancient sorceress whose stature could rival Ama herself.

The legends had been kind to Asja, Rukha knew, embellishing her later achievements with abandon and flair while neglecting to recall the troubled past of the dwarf she used to be.

As if her wizardly deeds alone said all that mattered about her life.

As if her inner triumphs were not heroic enough to be worthy of a tale.

"What if I told you that Asja was once an enemy of our people?" Rukha asked.

The children's sharing came to an abrupt end.

"And not just any enemy, but a formidable adversary at that!"

Her gaze drifted into the distance as she made herself comfortable on the dry tree stump in front of the class. She closed her eyes, recalling the many people and events from Asja's time – and long before – that weaved into the story she was here to tell. A tale of a savage world far more barbaric and brutal than that of today. In that world, her people and their allies had many foes, but none instilled greater fear than Asja the Dream Seer.

GOBLIN RAIDERS

With a thunderous crack, Vagran's feet touched the ground. A few steps later he came to a stop, his enormous wings fully outstretched to help break the fall. A grimace of pain betrayed the force of the landing, lessened only by the giant bird's delicate frame.

With his wings still open, the thunderoc brought a talon to his chest. Asja climbed onto it from among the feathers, a long stick and a travel bag strapped to her back. She jumped off the talon when it reached the ground and scampered a short distance, bending down as she went to scour the muddy surface.

"The tracks lead into the river," she said.

"Cowards!" Vagran spat out in frustration, sparks flying from his mouth and eyes. He wanted to face his quarry out in the open, on the dwarf side of the shallow river.

"Wait!" cautioned Asja, still studying the tracks. "There are some large footprints here. I don't know who they belong to, but it's definitely not goblins."

She reached out and touched one of the smudges nestled inside a footprint. A dark liquid smeared her fingers. She brought them to her nose.

"Blood."

A shot of charge coursed through Vagran's body at the sound of the word. His eyes focused on the sprawling river who blocked their way, even though she was easy to ford at the end of the cycle, before fresh water poured from the mountain.

"They crossed here," he boomed. His gaze shifted to the dense forest rising beyond the channel.

"They must have. We're too late."

Vagran looked back at the grassy rolling hills populating the dwarf land. Hunting down a band of goblin raiders on open ground would have been easy. A forest was an altogether different proposition. Her dark, foreboding depths looked decidedly uninviting to a creature of the sky. But he doubted he could track them from the air amongst the dense foliage.

"What do we do now?" asked Asja. "Hunt them in their own land?"

Without saying a word, Vagran spread his wings, grabbed her with his talon and lifted her back to his chest. His wing feathers donned an azure hue, shimmering softly in the mountain breeze as he lunged across the river and into the goblin land.

The sombre trees stood dead still, tall and unwelcoming. He zeroed in on the path of broken branches and stomped shrubs who littered the forest floor; goblin companions had their own difficulties navigating through the woods. He pressed on, stepping over roots of trees with giant steps and ducking under tall branches with his wings folded tightly by his side.

The makeshift path veered to the right. Vagran groaned in frustration, his feathers sizzling with a build-up of charge. The forest had just started to thin out, soon to be overcome by the desert sands – the goblins' home. He ached to see the sprawling dunes on whose naked skin the goblins couldn't hide.

The twisting path followed the meanderings of the river instead, and of the thick forest who accompanied her. The thunderoc turned the corner and followed, as determined as ever to hunt the raiders down.

A low branch blocked his path only to buckle under the pressure and send a cracking noise through the quiet wood. He moved on as quickly as he could, knowing that he wouldn't have time to plan an attack, and had to be prepared to spring into action at the first sight of their quarry. His eyes arced at the thought; he was ready.

Sudden pulling on his chest feathers distracted him from his thoughts.

"Someone's ahead!" whispered Asja, just loudly enough for him to hear. He stopped dead in his tracks, his eyes peering into the tall wood. "Put me down and wait here."

She snuck ahead into the thick brush. Vagran hugged the forest floor, keeping quiet, not moving, with only his head up and alert, trying to discern what his friend might have seen or heard, or sensed in a way he did not understand. She soon returned, visibly shaken.

"Goblins?" his voice sizzled.

She nodded. "At least thirty, in the dell ahead. They must have joined a hunting party camped there. And two giant brutes whose kind I haven't seen before. They have the dwarves… from the village… they raided…" her voice cracked before she could finish. She took a deep breath to gather herself. "We can't wait. We must attack now."

"How?" the single word sparked out of him.

She looked back in the direction of the camp. "I'm going back to the clearing. I'll lie in the bushes and wait. You circle around and attack them from the other side. They will run towards me when they see you approach. I'll do the rest."

He stared at her, his beak open wide. "They will overrun you..."

She shook her head with cold resolve. "They won't."

Her confidence was slow to rub off on him. Has her magic grown that much since they'd parted? Curiosity washed over him again.

"Do you know what to do?" Asja pressed.

A proper reunion would have to wait. Vagran closed his beak and blinked his acknowledgement. He rose to his feet and headed for the river, carefully stepping around trees and shrubs, his wings still hampered by the dense brush. Asja made for the glade, her rucksack strapped across her back, the staff now firmly in her hand.

Vagran emerged from the thick shrubbery in full view of the river. He leapt forward and surged over the water, his outstretched wings spanning the channel, carrying him downstream at treetop height. He saw a large gap in the forest come and go before making a wide rising turn to surge high into the sky, gliding above the tall woods on the other side of the glade.

Campfire burned in the centre of the clearing. Scrawny creatures milled about, cleaning fresh carcasses, eating a roasted one, tending to two others hoisted over the flames. Ragged tents circled the troop, spears and bows resting on their sides. A tranquil quality permeated the scene, as if they expected no retaliation from the dwarves in the immediate aftermath of their raid.

The roc tilted his wings for a dive. Some of the creatures stopped what they were doing and pointed at him, grunting loudly and gesturing wildly, their sunken eyes squinting at the sight. He drew his wings close, concealing his size, gathering speed as he went. Then his wings burst open, breaking his fall, and with a surge of charge to the beak open wide, he shot a bolt of lightning at the ground below.

The flash struck the closest goblin, singeing his flesh and flinging him across the ground. The others just stood there, their mouths agape and lips unmoving, frozen at the sight. Then they scrambled for their weapons, breathing in short, hurried gasps, the whites of their eyes bulging in terror.

Two arrows swished and surged for the bird, but flatlined and dropped short of their mark. Vagran unleashed lightning in response, striking a bowman before he could flee. The other dropped his bow and, with his back to the thunderoc, ran headlong for the cover of the trees. His comrades followed, abandoning their weapons that proved useless against the thundering bird, racing through the camp to escape the attack with their bare lives.

Two large creatures came out of the tents to follow the goblins in their flight. Thick wooden clubs swayed in their hands. They struggled to keep up, their heavy frames made of flesh and stone. *The brutes!* Vagran thought, remembering the large footprints Asja had found in the mud. He flew closer and discharged upon them, striking one in the back, making him stagger before the second bolt brought the creature down.

A lone figure emerged from the shrubs to stand in the way of the fleeing mob. Vagran watched as the goblins closed in on her, too close to strike them down without risking injury to his friend. His eyes arced, his plumes changed colour, and he sped down towards them, forsaking the safety of the sky.

Asja raised her staff, pointing it at the advancing horde. It smoked and smouldered before a blistering inferno erupted from its tip. It swerved left and right, engulfing the goblins nearest to her. Razed where they stood, they uttered barely a sound, only charred flesh remaining from the flame. The inferno poured forth, torching the others, consuming their hair and clothes as she set them ablaze. They dropped to the ground and rolled in drawn-out agony. Others turned to escape, burning as they ran, only to stumble on the tents that got in their way.

The club-wielding brute emerged from the blaze. He raised his cudgel at Asja, yelling in fury and pain, his fur covering on fire, one hand seared by the burning wood. A protective bubble enveloped the girl, its lucid surface concealing its strength. The cudgel came down with tremendous force, slamming into the shield – forging a dent in its side – only to recoil, broken in two. The monster stared at the crippled weapon, as if oblivious to any pain.

With the club spent, Asja released her shield to stand in clear sight of the towering brute. A bolt of lightning shot out from her staff, striking the beast squarely in the chest and thrusting his burning body onto the grass.

A gentle tremor reverberated through the ground as the thunderoc landed amidst the carnage. His eyes strained to see through the smoke. All he could make out were burning bodies squirming in the grass before falling still, overcome by the flames. Asja slowly emerged on her own, walking cautiously with her staff in hand. She stopped when she saw her avian friend take a step closer through the thinning smog.

"Are you hurt?" Vagran asked.

She shook her head and pressed her body against his lowered beak. He let her hug him, the charge draining from his feathers as they fluttered with relief.

He raised his head through the smoke-filled glade, searching for signs of movement. His eyes locked onto a lone figure running for the trees offering shelter beyond the open dell.

"One escaped!" his voice sparked, his wings flinging open.

"Let him go!" Asja's yell caught him midstride. "He can tell others what happened here today. Perhaps then they will stop their raids and let us live in peace on our side of the river."

He abandoned his pursuit and took a moment to survey the camp. Smouldering tents and singed bodies lay scattered across the ground, carcasses strewn around the campfire, weapons lying in disarray, their owners burned beyond recall.

The carcasses by the campfire caught his attention. Unlike forest animals, they had a distinctly humanoid look. The closest one was disfigured, one leg lacking flesh, cut away with a knife to reveal the bone. The other remained intact, sturdy and short like that of a dwarf.

He recoiled at the sight. He closed his eyes in a desperate attempt to wipe the foul image from his mind. He'd grown up among dwarves, the only people he had known. Roasting them over a fire was unthinkable to him. He knew the savage nature of goblins, but never expected them to use their enemies for food.

The rising column of smoke betrayed their assault some distance away. "We must go," he said, remembering that they were in goblin land now.

He turned around. Asja was standing by the razed tents, staring at the dead goblins that got entangled in them. He called to her, but she didn't respond. Only when he nudged her did she look at him, her gaze clouded and distant. The look stayed with her even as he lifted her with his talon to bring her to his chest for the flight home.

REUNION

Campfire performed her lively dance in the cool evening air. Her spirited movements enlivened the outlines of the nearby trees, casting animated shadows over the surrounding fields. The sloping hills remained safe from her gaze, illuminated only by the distant denizens of the night sky.

Vagran had no use for the heat of the fire. The charge that coursed through his body sufficed for his needs. He settled down some distance away and just watched her perform, enjoying the flaming show. Asja had sat closer to better appreciate the sputtering warmth before getting up to join him, grateful that the day's proceedings were finally drawing to a close.

Vagran. The adolescent thunderoc lying peacefully by her side. She hadn't seen her childhood friend for so long, she couldn't even tell how long it had been. They had gone their separate ways out of necessity and probably wouldn't have stumbled upon each other here had it not been for the dwarf village sending plumes of smoke high into the sky.

She observed the village from a rocky outcrop on a nearby hill. The houses stood lit by pyres now that the closest skylight had vanished from the sky. Not the flames started by the goblins who had ravaged them earlier in the day, but ones started by the villagers themselves, as a part of their farewell to the close ones they'd lost. Vagran had recovered them from the goblin camp. Now they rested atop the burning heaps, together with the eight slain in the village itself – small children and two women who had stayed behind to watch over them while the others had left their homes to tend to the harvest.

Asja didn't know them. Before coming to their aid, she had only seen this region from high in the sky. They were fellow dwarves to her but not friends or kin. She could not sincerely share in the deep mourning for their loss. Ending the threat of further raids – at least for now – was the most valuable contribution she and Vagran could make.

"I've missed you," she whispered while stroking the tender skin just beneath his beak. He closed his eyes as his feathers fluttered with delight, a satisfied growl rumbling from his throat.

"You found the wizard?" he remarked once the rubbing had stopped.

Asja thought back to the circumstances of their parting and the uncertainty that hung over it. So much had happened since she'd last shared with her friend. "Yes, I did. Just like my vision said I would. More than one, actually."

The bird communicated his approval with a gentle blink. "I noticed."

"They did teach me a thing or two." Her gaze fell on the staff that had come to her on their last journey, one she could barely use before the wizards showed her how.

Then her smile faded. There was more to her magic training than learning to shield herself from attack or unleashing fire and lightning. It had left a raw wound she wasn't ready to divulge, not even in the company of her best friend.

She changed the subject. "Tor told me that you'd come by the house looking for me?"

Vagran blinked in response.

"You're a good friend." She beamed in gratitude.

"I was worried about you."

"Well, you don't need to worry anymore. I found what I was looking for, so I'm back now. For good," she reassured him. "And you? What did you get up to after I left you in the Land of Frost?"

"I looked for my people," the words sputtered from his mouth.

"Your people? You mean other thunderocs?"

He blinked after a long pause.

"You know, I've always thought of you as one of a kind," she admitted. "Did you find them?"

His eyes brightened from a sudden build-up of charge, then sizzled and arced in anger. "They are not friendly!"

The bitterness of his response caught her off guard. She understood now why he had come back to the dwarf lands. Her enthusiasm for his people waned just as quickly as it had come.

"Perhaps the two of us aren't meant to be with our people." She reached for the warmth of his feathers again, her eyes damp and her tone sombre. "At least we have each other."

His gaze fell back on the village. The fires had started to die down, though still offering enough light to illuminate the square. Most of the mourners had returned to their homes. Only an elderly dwarf and an adolescent still lingered by, sitting with their backs bent and shoulders slumped.

"What now?" The thunderoc stared at Asja, as if challenging her to decide what she'll do with her life now that her training was over and she was free to go and do as she pleased. She lowered her eyes, avoiding his gaze, still feeling a pang of regret for having left her childhood friend to go in search of the wizards.

"I want to go to Amerot," she finally said, steering clear of any thoughts of the distant future. "A gathering of the clans will soon take place there. I want to tell them about the goblin raids."

"They know."

"They know of the raids, but not how serious they've become. They are much more frequent now, and goblins aren't raiding alone anymore. The clans must understand that they can't leave the border villages to fend for themselves."

She paused before revealing the main thrust of her thoughts. "Would you take me? I'd never make it there in time without you."

His eyes brightened again, but instead of arcing, the sparks glowed and fluttered playfully across each iris. He blinked and pressed his neck into her arms. She held him as tightly as she could, grateful that her travelling companion was once again by her side.

The campfire withered to glowing cinders. Asja shuffled under her blanket, but sleep eluded her. Her mind kept returning to the smouldering ruins of the forest camp and the remains of goblins and the two hulking brutes that were strewn across the ground. Charred bodies, scorched hair, singed flesh. Grimaces that vented their final agony. She wanted nothing less when she saw the dwarf carcasses being readied for the fire. Now she couldn't let them go.

She snuggled up to her friend in the dying heat of the embers before drifting into a restless sleep.

AMEROT

Vagran stretched his wings as far as they would go. His lightning body floated on the air currents with natural ease, but it was the rhythmic flaps of his enormous wings that let it soar through the open sky. When it came to mastery of the heavens, thunderocs and pyrerocs had no equal.

He flew above the mountains on his northward journey along the Peruvius Range. The lesser peak of Mount Croms slipped underneath. The capacious foothills skirting the mountain rose and fell in haphazard fashion. The summit's broad reach more than made up for his short stature.

Out of the pervasive clouds, beyond the murky hills, rose the first stone guardian. His twin peaks, like nervous periscopes, betrayed the presence of the mountain hiding in the shroud. The fatter of the two ended in a crater, with grassy cover climbing up his sides. The thinner peak stood aside, a towering umber column of grim bare stone, defiant in his solitude.

Water and steam gushed from the crater, but only the steam escaped her confines. She rose into the sky to form a pure white cloud who hung over the mountaintop and filled the cone with her pristine presence.

Vagran pierced the middle of the cloud, revelling in her warm softness. He looked down at the sound of giggling coming from his chest to see Asja's hand reach out and sample the silky veil.

As the clouds thinned out, the southern Ural face came into view. Vagran gazed at the two walls of rock who spread out across the land like earthy waves frozen in mid-surge, barely visible in the faint light of a faraway sun. They hoisted twelve summits upon their shoulders – the heart of the Peruvius Range. It was a landscape he had only ever seen at night, mindful of the dwarves' fear of his kind, before the border clashes brought him out in the light of day and urged him to act.

Mount Aorai rose amid the summits, the Urals' highest peak, his skin grey and wrinkly, deep lines etched into his sides. Mounds of gravel and stone huddled at his base, scrubbed from the peak by unrelenting wind and rain. The curved spine exposed a mount who'd seen too many cycles to count, and was starting to yield to his own advancing age. The tip lay flat, having been blown off more than once by skylights too hungry for the freedom of the sky. It made Vagran wonder for how much longer the aging powerhouse could continue lighting the Ural skies.

But his target was not the Urals' highest peak. That honour fell to a prominent hill at the mountain's base. Mount Cougal, as he was known. Dwarves did not usually bestow the title on mere hills. This one had earned it by housing their most iconic settlement and the sole location of their clan gatherings – the picturesque town of Amerot.

Like his oversized companion, Mount Cougal stood adorned by steep sides and a flat top. But the top was grassy and fertile, and the cliffs much too short to forbid access. Rocks who protruded through the compact foliage gave the hill a picturesque ceiling. Dwarves shaped them – grew them until they acquired a hollow interior and gaps through which to enter – until they were deemed fit to serve as homes.

Stone houses littered the hilltop. Houses that nourished the creepers growing on them and houses made of bare rock. Some that afforded spectacular views of the valley below and others that only looked upon the towering silhouette of Mount Aorai. Homes that could barely shelter a solitary dwarf and a hall spacious enough to host a gathering of all the clans.

Vagran touched down on a grassy field on the southern edge of the hill, behind a line of trees, free of the people to scream horror at the sight of a giant bird landing in their midst.

"I will come back for you when the clans leave," he promised his friend after she'd disembarked. Then he faced the cliff end and took off again, vanishing into the breadth of the night sky.

Asja watched him depart, then set her gaze upon a stately hall illuminated by crystals at the edge of the town.

KINRUM HALL

Asja snuck into a marble hall, its interior hidden from view by the dense darkness of pre-dawn. It would fill with people when the clan gathering got underway — leaders of dwarf clans from across the Peruvius Range — but for now it stood empty, its imposing walls sheltering no one.

The scant light who entered the oval room had come from distant suns. He crept in via the porous dome to cast faint patterns onto the stone floor. A crystal ceiling, Asja now knew. She'd never seen anything like it as a child and remembered staring at it in wide-eyed wonder. She'd returned to it now, eager to see its dance with the luminous rays of light and the motifs they would paint all across the floor. Only the light was not yet ready. She leaned against the wall, closed her eyes, and waited.

A gentle tremor jolted the foundations of the hall. The walls grumbled in protest but remained unmoved. The rumble charged higher up Mount Aorai's top until he exploded in a violent roar at his very tip. A sun emerged from the open mount and shot up into the sky, burnishing the mountainside as he gained height and flooding the crystal ceiling with a lavish column of light.

The dome erupted with a dazzling display. Crystal fragments glittered and sparkled, brightening until they glowed luminescent white, overwhelmed by the sudden intensity of the skylight's glare. Unable to contain it within their structure, they let it spill onto the floor, turning bland stone into countless hues directed and dyed by the dome's crystalline frame.

Asja gasped at the sight she'd only seen once before, watching dwarf history replay before her eyes in the open space of Kinrum Hall.

Peruvius Mountains rose from the floor, sustained by the playful light projected through the dome. Floating specks appeared in the sky above them. Each grew a form — a winged body of a dragon, roc or some other beast who lived and thrived on the mountain range.

As the sun continued his upward journey through the sky, so did the domed crystals redirect his passage onto the floor, animating the beasts' wings and propelling them through the land. The landscape itself shimmered with their motion as if constantly reanimated into solid stillness.

The beasts dominated not only the sky, but the surface too, preying on creatures large and small and stomping or incinerating whomever they deemed a threat. Dwarves, like ants, milled about the lowly foothills, hiding underground until the skies cleared, too terrified to scale the exposed mountain slopes.

The range grew and shifted with the motion of the sun till nothing could be seen but a single mount – the solitary silhouette of Mount Granat, the northernmost tip of the Peruvius Range. He harboured a cave on his southern slope. A projection of a dwarf scaled the entrance with an oversized axe strapped onto his back. He vanished into the hole, only to emerge with clothes singed and torn, wielding the axe whose blade still spat and sizzled. He opened his mouth as if to yell, proclaiming his triumph over a vicious beast – the terror of these lands.

Asja remembered staring into the dwarf's eyes as a child, wanting to be him, impressed beyond words by his singular feat of courage. He was the first dwarf hero to be immortalised in a legend. Mogar the Wyvern Slayer, as he came to be known. His later demise at the clutches of wyvern Scintilla only added to the valour of this accomplishment.

The legend spread.

Heroes from other clans took up the challenge. Ostrig the Mighty snuck up on Zaymud Basaltic and slew him in his sleep, freeing his clan from the terror of the skies. Zunek the Crafty set a trap that snared and mortally wounded Beiris the Ignited. The pyreroc later died from her wounds, but not before expelling her last breaths to incinerate her captor. And Grim the Sly snuck up to and broke a ferrite's egg, then skilfully evaded the pursuing dragon, only to follow the path of destruction to a smouldering hole in the ground that was his home, pried open and razed by the dragon's raging wrath.

Asja stared at the scarred earth left in the dragon's wake that was projected so vividly onto the Kinrum floor. She could picture the devastation inside Grim's home, lightning breath pouring mercilessly through the yawning breach until it wholly saturated the interior of the cave.

It was a different world then. Dwarves' lives were savage and short.

And yet, there was something about it that had captivated her. Their foes were enormous and deadly, but clear and uncomplicated. Their own heroic deeds were courageous but straightforward. It was a simple struggle for survival. They knew what they had to do for their people to thrive, and they went ahead and did it despite tremendous dangers and personal cost.

In a way, she saw herself more in the early warrior heroes than in the runemages who followed – hoping that she, too, would someday earn her place in the legends among them.

The first of the mages was the archon Aorar. No one knew who he was or where he had come from. Part legend, part myth, he wielded axe and staff with equal prowess. He was not truly a mage for he stared down the beasts better than any warrior could. But he did show the dwarves what could be done with runes, and he set the example for the mages to follow.

The first one who did was Metallus. He did not invent metallic enchantments, but he did pioneer their use on an unprecedented scale. Patches of ore who dwelled beneath the mountains' skin turned to iron on his demand. The skin herself followed suit, as did the rocks and plants she nourished. Only water remained unchanged by the dwarves' runes, pouring out of the mountains through metallic vents and turning their surface to psychedelic rust.

Then came Iskri. Her childhood brush with a lightning bolt guided her work as an adult mage. The armour she crafted from runic tourmaline could withstand a direct hit. When augmented with olive peridot, it could also resist all but the most intense dragon blaze.

Armed with iron weapons – now in ample supply – and protected by enchanted armour that shielded them from the beasts' breath, even the more cautious dwarves rose up and joined the fight. What was once the province of the audacious and the foolhardy became the joint concern of them all.

Again, like ants, they emerged from their burrows and dotted the countryside whenever the giant beasts vacated the skies above. They gathered supplies, set giant traps, and harassed them in their sleep. And they persevered at their crusade until the last winged speck that had once circled the mountains vanished from sight, never to return.

The War of Inheritance was won.

With the beasts gone, what had been a warrior-like culture led by legendary heroes at the outset of the struggle morphed into an industrious one led by common folk by its end. Gone were the days of high adventure, of exploring high peaks and steep slopes and facing the dangers that awaited there. Gone were the times of the visionary and courageous few lighting the way for the many.

What took their place was the gathering and moulding of the riches of the mountains – the countless crystalline gems they nurtured in their depths and released upon discharge. *Fruits of the mountains*, they came to be known, the great promise of the Peruvius Range that the dwarves' ancestors had fought so hard for, and that their descendants who'd settled there claimed as their own.

The gems came to life on the Kinrum floor with the receding motion of the Mount Aorai sun. The more arcane among them even shone and sparkled with their own inner light.

The display had awed Asja the first time she'd seen it as a child. More than anything, she'd wanted to become a mage and dedicate her life to mastering the secrets of the precious stones. Asja the adolescent, however, had trained with wizards from faraway lands. She still admired the beauty of the stones, only now tempered by the knowledge of their limitations.

She breathed deeply and walked through the kaleidoscopic projection in the centre of the hall. It remained animated for a while longer, displaying the richness of the dwarf culture that was touched by the stones in so many ways. But Asja's attention returned to the goblin threat that had driven her to come here to seek an audience with the clans.

A gathering of the clans would commence once the Mount Aorai skylight had traced his journey through the sky. Despite her youth and lack of standing among mages and clan leaders alike, she remained committed to the mission she'd set for herself and her thunderoc friend – to bring back the heroic days of old, and banish goblin raiders from Peruvius Mountains once and for all.

CLAN GATHERING

Asja stood up, gripped the staff firmly in her hand, and walked quietly to the centre of the hall. She looked around at the people assembled there — representatives of the dwarf clans, independent mages and runemages, and even elf guests. The intensity of their collective gaze felt too much to bear. She turned and faced the delegation from her clan, faces she'd seen before, people she knew well.

"I'm Asja of the Peridot clan. Thank you for letting me speak on our behalf even though I was not chosen to represent us," she began, reciting a well-rehearsed speech, looking at Uronam, the leader of her clan, whose open face and warm eyes helped steady her nerves. "I was not home when you left for this gathering, not that I would have been included in the delegation anyway. But something important has happened since you left that I have to raise before this assembly."

Uronam smiled and nodded in approval, though he already knew what she was going to say — she'd sought the clan delegation out beforehand and told them what she'd come here to do, seeking his support, which he readily gave.

"A day before I left for this gathering, a goblin raiding party attacked Darum village in the foothills of Mount Edars alongside River Rust. There were more than thirty goblin raiders, and they were accompanied by two large savages, twice their height and many times stronger. They killed all the dwarves who hadn't gone out to the harvest, and they set their houses on fire before retreating back across the river.

"Rusthold village just south of Darum was attacked two days earlier. Magescar village at the southern end of the foothills a day before that. These are just the most recent raids. There were many others that I haven't mentioned. They've become very frequent over the past few cycles, and far more deadly than they used to be.

"We can't leave the border villages to fend for themselves anymore. Their counterraids are no longer enough. They need the help of our whole clan, and our clan needs the help of all of you. We have to find a way to keep goblins and their desert beasts out of our lands, and we have to do it soon."

With those words, Asja ceded the floor, though she remained standing in the middle of the hall, ready to respond to any questions on the matter she had raised.

A nervous murmur spread through the assembly. The clan representatives animatedly spoke to each other with hushed words delivered with great fervour. When the congregation quietened, Galen – the leader of the Garnet clan – spoke up.

"If your report is accurate," he began, his gaze bearing down on Asja until she looked away, "then we must act, and act quickly. The Garnet clan is lucky to border elf lands to the north and west. We have no enemies at our doorstep, no one who may be watching and waiting to take advantage of our absence.

"When we return, we will hold a gathering to tell our people of all the discussions held here and the decisions made. We will encourage them to travel to Mount Edars and take their weapons, tools, food, and anything else we may need to fight off the goblins. I'm sure many will come."

Galen sat down again, indicating that he had finished speaking, inviting others to have their say. Other Garnet delegates patted him on the shoulders and nodded vigorously, voicing their support for his offer of aid.

Uronam quickly rose in response, before the doubt cast on Asja's words could be left to linger. "What Asja says is true," his deep voice boomed through the hall. "We spoke before this gathering commenced. Goblins have long raided across River Rust, but the latest attacks have grown frequent and deadly. We must mobilise to protect our villages along the eastern border."

Norgt stood up next, his gaze switching between Uronam and Galen. "We of the Topaz clan share your good fortune, Galen. We too will be sending volunteers to help at the border. We live closer than the other clans, so you can count on us to be there before they arrive."

"It is time we put a stop to the goblin menace! We have let this problem fester for far too long," a member of the Citrine clan delegation blurted out, to widespread shouts of approval and banging against the stone.

Asja stood quietly in the centre of the hall, moved by the kind of reaction she would have expected from the dwarves of old, the ones who'd banded together to drive out the dragons and other flying monsters from the Peruvius Range. Clearly, their spirit had lived on to this day, even if the dwarves had moved away from heroic pursuits in favour of farming, making tools, studying runes and moulding stone.

"Looks like you could use our help," offered Lennolene, a prominent elf druid, a guest at the gathering. "Most of our tribes live far away, so any help from them will be slow in coming, but those of us who are here can help right now. We can grow sentinels to secure the border until the volunteers arrive."

"Not all of us can stay," Evindal corrected her. "Some must return to their tribes to give their people news of the gathering. On the other hand, this will give them a chance to spread news of your struggle through their lands. Even though the distance is great, some of our people will surely come to your aid."

A rumble of appreciation rose through the hall.

"If only Ilyasah were still with us," lamented one of the druids, "he'd give you all the help you need."

A chorus of voices sounded in support, surprisingly strong for their small number, the elves paying homage to the greatest hero from their legends and myths.

Not to be outdone, Norgt quickly retorted, "And if Aorar were still with us, no help would be needed."

The whole assembly exploded in banter over whose legendary hero was the greater, unwilling to give in to their allies and friends even as they stood for the same cause.

"You should take the news to humans as well," Lennolene suggested to the elves once the commotion had died down. "They may also be willing to lend a helping hand."

"Humans?" wondered Obalin, the head dwarf runemage. "How worthwhile would their assistance be? They have no ability or even desire to learn magic."

"Perhaps, but they did torch mur towns and drive their people into the sea," said Lennolene. "And we both know just how potent mur magicians can be."

Asja's eyes widened at the mention of the mur. Their magicians had been a thorn in the side of humans, elves and dwarves ever since the war. She didn't want her adoptive people to learn of her mur origins, even if she were an outcast who knew precious little about the people of her birth. She did her best to look inconspicuous and uninterested, which wasn't easy while standing in the middle of the hall.

"I only asked because Asja mentioned those large savages raiding with the goblins," clarified Lennolene.

"Asja, can you tell us more about these brutes? What did they look like?" asked Galen of the Garnet clan.

"They were... twice the height of goblins, perhaps a little taller, but hunched. They were made of both flesh and stone, with flat heads and thick necks. Big teeth sticking out. They wore hardly anything... rags really. Each one wielded a wooden club. When they moved, they were slow, but heavy and very strong. I don't know whether they could talk. All I could hear were grunts."

"You heard them grunt?" A look of surprise filled Galen's face.

Asja nodded.

"Did you see them raid?"

"No. Vagran and I rushed to Darum when we saw the smoke coming from the village, but we only got there after the raiders had left. We went after them and hunted them down on the other side of the river. That was where I saw the beasts."

"When did you say this happened?" asked Norgt.

"At the end of the last Aorai cycle."

The brow on Norgt's forehead furrowed in confusion. "The new Aorai sun rose just yesterday. How is this possible?"

"It took us a whole cycle to travel here," a woman from Asja's delegation spoke out.

"Vagran brought me," responded Asja. When she saw the puzzled expression on Norgt's face, she quickly added, "Vagran is a thunderoc."

Blood drained from the clan leader's face. He just stood there in stunned silence.

"Thunderoc?" Galen voiced what Norgt could not. "I thought we'd eradicated those flying monsters from our lands!"

Asja expected the reaction. "Vagran is a child of the mountain. My parents raised him. He is my friend."

The clan leaders couldn't hear her. They rose from their seats, their delegations rising behind them, and vented their unease to anyone who'd listen. The council degenerated into a morass of bickering. So engrossed were they in their furore that they didn't see Uronam walk to the centre of the hall and take station by Asja's side. But they couldn't ignore the fullness of his voice when it cut through the bustle and clatter.

"Silence!" he boomed. He waited for the clan leaders to face him and acknowledge his right to speak before continuing. "The thunderoc has never threatened anyone by the Edars Mountain. He is no threat to you."

"So you say," Norgt recovered his voice.

"Not only is he not a threat," continued Uronam, "but an invaluable ally. How do you think Asja was able to hunt down and slay the entire goblin raiding party supported by those brutes? By herself?" Uronam's gaze wandered from one clan leader to the next.

The elf Evindal bolstered his words. "Thunderocs are deadly foes. Their speed across the sky is legendary. If you have one on your side, you'd be fools not to use him."

"Can he even be used?" Galen scoffed at the idea.

"He is my friend, not my pet," Asja responded. "But we do help each other."

It was an uncertain response, but enough to cause Galen to settle back in his seat, deep in thought. Uronam took the opportunity to propose a bold new idea, the thunderoc not as alien to him as he was to the other clans.

"Would Vagran be willing to fly over the Kalhar Desert and scout out the goblin settlements within reach of the border? It would help us to know where our enemies lie."

"One enemy to scout out others?" sniggered Norgt.

"Not only that," Uronam resumed undeterred, looking straight at Asja, "but what other creatures can be found by their settlements? You've told us about those brutes who raided with them, but there may be others, stronger or more numerous, also helping them."

Asja only stared at the leader of her clan, grateful for his support, not anticipating his acceptance of Vagran after their rejection of him as a child. She gazed around the assembly to see silent faces, even a nodding head here and there, their roaring opposition to the thunderoc's presence now having faded into silence.

She could barely believe the turnaround that Uronam's presence and words had brought about. Not only was her warning heeded, she might play a vital role in eliminating the goblin threat and restoring peace to the dwarf lands. It may have been thanks to her friendship with Vagran rather than her own merits, but she knew that she could prove her worth given the chance. Perhaps even follow in the footsteps of the dwarf heroes of old. Her face lit up as an opportunity she'd longed for all her life, denied to her many a time, suddenly felt within reach.

She opened her mouth to respond when the voice of the head runemage Obalin rumbled through the hall. "If the thunderoc is willing to help us, then you should get him to scout Chromatic Hills. There is no place I wish to see more."

Asja's brow furrowed in confusion. "Chromatic Hills?"

"Do they even exist?" asked Uronam.

"You doubt Ferev's word?" Obalin challenged him.

"No one knows how far into the desert Ferev had gone nor what he had seen there, and he didn't live long enough to try again."

"True, but what he described with such fervour shouldn't be dismissed. If we can fly there, we must!" He opened his arms, as though begging the clans to honour his request.

His conviction was not lost on them. One by one, the clan leaders and their companions nodded in agreement. Uronam was the only one to offer a word of caution. "We must protect the border first. Only then can we afford to send the thunderoc elsewhere."

Obalin acquiesced.

"What are Chromatic Hills?" Asja whispered to Uronam, remembering the name from a legend she'd heard but unable to recall more.

"Hills beyond the Kalhar Desert. They are so rich in exotic crystals that they have no steady colour. Hence their name."

"Can you convince the thunderoc to travel there?" Obalin pressed. "If the place is real and true to Ferev's words, we must know."

"Why? It is not our land," replied Asja.

"It doesn't matter, Asja. Goblin savages have no use for such things."

Her bewilderment intensified. The request was so far removed from the struggle to quell goblin attacks that she didn't know what to make of it. She looked from one runemage to the next and saw something in their eyes that made her wonder about their intentions, as if their sudden acceptance of her avian friend had more to do with his usefulness to them than changing attitudes towards the beasts of old.

She thought she understood the importance of crystals to her people. They'd become indispensable even in a home as isolated and modest as her parents' was. But to fly into their enemies' lands in search of them?

Words of refusal sat on her tongue. The opportunity to show the dwarves her worth threatened to wither with them. In desperation, she turned to Uronam.

"This is a heavy burden to place on someone so young," he spoke to the assembly. "We should give Asja more time to consider the request. I suggest we adjourn this council for today. We all need time to ponder the grave matters that she has raised."

Uronam's words provoked nodding heads and rumbles of accord. The hall disintegrated into a clamour of shuffling feet and chattering voices as it started to empty. Uronam placed his hand on Asja's shoulder, nodded, and smiled. She looked at him with gratitude, thankful to be able to rely on his support one more time. Then she turned to leave, her steps heavy with the predicament the runemages and clan leaders had placed her in.

REMINISCENCE

Asja took a deep breath of moist mountain air. The air inside the hall had felt oppressive, suffocating even. She set out into the spacious courtyard that sprawled across the hilltop. A hefty stone – shaped like an altar – protruded from the ground some distance away. An elf standing near pointed at the crystals arrayed on its surface, engaged in animated conversation with two dwarf mages. Others had gathered around tables sprinkled across the courtyard, gems of all colours and sizes displayed on them.

She was surprised to see the rune crystals shown so openly. The mages usually practised their craft in the privacy of their chambers, away from prying eyes. She remembered the days she had spent as a child secluded in Obalin's study. Before he became the head runemage. Before he deemed her unsuitable despite her tremendous talent evident even at that age.

Seeing the crystals rekindled the feeling that the title of a mage lingered within her grasp. That the mages were letting her show off her skills in defence of the border as the first step to welcoming her among them. She shook her head. That goodwill rested on her fulfilling their request in return, using those skills in ways she'd rather not.

How would travelling to goblin lands help to keep them at a safe distance? How would stealing gems from them help to diffuse the conflict? It made no sense. The whole reason for her bringing the matter before the assembly was to enlist other clans' help in keeping goblins out of dwarf lands.

The parting words of the wizards from faraway lands played on her mind. She wouldn't heed their warning then – that dwarves were not whom she thought them to be. Dwarves were her people, who looked like her and had adopted her as one of their own. She'd dreamt of becoming a dwarf mage, to lead and serve them as best she could.

She hadn't departed from the wizards on good terms, the memory of their parting staying an open wound. But seeing what had transpired within the assembly, she could no longer suppress the idea.

What if the wizards were right?

24

She shuddered at the thought, trying to dismiss it before it could grow and gnaw at her bond with the only people she knew.

She walked on through the courtyard and across the jagged hilltop all the way to the western edge of the hill. The sheer drop revealed a valley who spread out before her, her forests, rivers and distant peaks illuminated by the dying light of a distant sun. Her own home lay to the south, well beyond any peaks she could see.

She saw the graceful contours of Mount Edars in her mind's eye. A thirsty lake who drank up all the waters who flowed from his eastern flank before releasing them into River Rust. Green hills who rolled gently across the land, and a modest house of mossy stone that oversaw them.

She saw a little girl who bounded from it with a smile on her face – a memory of a carefree existence she had as a child, with no inkling of what her life would someday become.

LAMENT

With a dull whooshing sound, a surging wave crashed onto the deck. He raced across the slippery surface – colliding with barrels and beams and people – before making his exit at the bow. There were no loose objects left to dislodge. Thick ropes tied the barrels of food and belongings to the ship, even helping to keep the worn-out crew from being washed overboard.

As soon as the wave had run his course, people sprang into action. A flurry of buckets scooped the water from the floor of the vessel to raise onto the deck and toss back into the sea. They drained as much as they could before the next wave washed over the ship. It was thankless work, one they tired of much faster than the sea.

Another wave crashed into the stern. Smaller than the last, he barely scaled the drenched sides to dribble onto the deck. The ship's stern still creaked, giving the crew pause; even the lesser waves strained the battered wood.

"When will you stop, damn it!" Enwar shouted at the fuming sea. He expected no answer.

He peered intently into the dark sky, as much as his drenched eyes could withstand, but couldn't find that faint light they had glimpsed before it was snuffed out by the oppressive clouds.

Had they all imagined it? Was their thirst for land so strong that they'd fantasised her amidst the endless sea? They did spot a school of fish before the storm hit, after a long voyage through barren waters since sailing away from their homeland shores. And they did see points of light loom larger in the night sky, lights who must have come from another land.

The thoughts of his homeland kept intruding on his mind, evoking heart-tearing pain amidst the fury of the storm. The plunging into utter darkness as the last specks of light from the land of his birth faded from view. The loss of day and night, with greater and lesser lights to separate the two, subsumed by pure blackness. No way to tell the passage of time save through the slow depletion of their stores of food. The mere thought of their circumstances made him feel ill. Made him miss their wretched home and firm land under his feet, even if that land didn't want them and had prompted their flight in the first place.

Their food supplies were running out. The ship's beams were coming undone. Lament had been an old ship upon its departure, more worthy vessels having sailed earlier on and failing to return. The crew's morale sagged with their misfortune, with the realisation that theirs was yet another failed attempt to find humanity a new home. Even a sight of land might not change that fact if it were to amount to cynical rocks standing in their way upon whom to meet the long journey's end.

A bolt of lightning streaked through the sky. The crackling light pierced the darkness ahead. The foaming sea made her ire seen in the rising swells all around the ship. Enwar froze at the sight, wishing he hadn't seen it, preferring to withstand the waves one surge at a time.

"All clear!" Okeye's voice barely rose above the noise of the storm.

Enwar looked up, unable to see the crow's nest atop the high mast beneath the black clouds and the pelting rain. With their fabric reduced to storm sails, they let the wind and the ocean currents carry them along, not knowing where to go in the strange seas so far from home. Only sporadic flashes warned them of any danger that might be lurking in the waters ahead.

Hope also ploughed through the sea in darkness, Lament's twin hull that helped steady the ship in the rocking waves. Each a ship in its own right in their home seas, but newly bonded companions into waters unknown. He looked at the broad outline connected with sturdy beams, barely visible in the darkness of the storm. It rose in unison over an ocean swell and fell together into the next trough. Its crew must be scooping the water out right now, though he couldn't see them or hear their strain.

A fresh bolt of lightning arced across the sky. "Rocks! Rocks ahead!" Okeye's voice pierced the raging storm.

Enwar peered over the bow. The momentary flash had already fizzled out, leaving the promise of danger lurking in the dark. He had to turn the ship, but not knowing the alien waters, he hesitated, trying to guess the lay of the land, praying for another flash to light their way.

A grim rock rose in their path. He smashed head-on into the soaked wood. The front beam joining the two hulls buckled with a sickening crack. Hope and Lament veered towards one another as the rear beam met the same fate.

"Turn left! Turn left!" Enwar screamed on top of his lungs. The wheel was already turning in the helmsman's hands, who knew the danger to the two hulls should they come together amidst the jutting rocks. Lament steered to the left, away from the rocks and the rocky land lying in its path, baring its side to the oncoming waves. In a prolonged flash, Enwar saw Hope veer the other way, its back to them, the current and the storm pushing it away.

A wave surged towards the darkened land, crashing into the ship that was blocking its way. Lament tilted from the force of the surge, its bowels soaking up the rampaging flood. Its companion gone, the ship swayed back and forth at the mercy of the waves, taking on more water than the exhausted crew had the strength to drain.

A flash of lightning later, the protruding rocks receded into the swells, leaving the hostile land firmly behind them. Enwar gave the command and the ship resumed its course, rounding the isle a safe distance away, the force of the storm pushing its back again.

Enwar pondered following the outline of the island in search of the severed twin hull, but one look at his own waterlogged ship convinced him of the foolhardiness of the task. Every hand – except for the captain, helmsman and lookout – worked to remove the water from the foundering ship, but could barely keep up with the waves washing over the deck. More broadside action would sink them for sure.

He saw Kalika empty a bucket by him, her weak sigh betraying her exhaustion, her unsteady feet trembling from the strain. The slender build of his childhood friend was ill-suited to the task, but no sturdier hands remained to do it. The men laboured in the bowels of the ship. He consoled her with a weak smile before resuming his duties, desperate to find a stretch of coast for them to land.

A prolonged ripple lingered through the sky. A shining, a revealing light over the approaching land.

A low coastline came into view, rising in the distance on both left and right, jutting far into the sea as if to cut off their escape should they try to run. In a moment of panic, Enwar sought to do just that before his senses returned. He took a long, probing look at the low land before the generous sky flare vanished into the clouds.

He made a decision. He had felt cheated, finally stumbling upon a land after more time at sea than they cared to recall, only to be rejected by the rocks unwelcoming of refugees from a faraway land. This beach – nestled between jutting cliffs – was the first sign of welcome they had received. As if the new land were drawing them in, acquiescing to their presence, willing to give them shelter and a place to stay.

"Head for the beach!" he shouted to Okeye, pointing at the low land who had become obscured again by the clouds and the rain. The lookout nodded, keeping an eye on the invisible target, waiting for the sky to flare up again.

"Right! Two notches!" he shouted into the storm. The helmsman corrected, turning the rudder straight towards the beach.

Enwar peered ahead, watching the friendly coast stagger closer with each revealing flash. The rest of the crew joined his vigil, making peace with the water slushing through the ship this close to the land. They'd beach the vessel in the storm to save it and themselves from being swallowed by the sea.

They couldn't see the large rock lurking beneath the waves. The ship did. The deep keel of its waterlogged hull crashed headlong into the stone. It came to a momentary halt, the beams creaking and breaking against the unyielding rock, but the wind and the swell pressed on, widening the break in the frame of the hull until the whole structure collapsed, unable to endure any more strain, leaving the scattered fragments of the ship, cargo and people to be carried by the surging swells towards the new land.

EGG

Asja bent down to pluck a short mushroom stalk with a brownish canopy from the grass. She placed it carefully inside her basket before picking another, and then another. Six caramel mushrooms later, she emptied the basket into a leather bag dangling loosely off the saddle. Then she returned to the dell graced with rotting tree trunks and moss-infested stones for another haul.

Lime mushrooms with the consistency of lump jelly. Shell mushrooms who sprouted rings like the woods from whom they grew. Rainbow mushrooms with the smoothness and shine of polished marble. Ear-like bundles of fungus who helped their tree eavesdrop on the sounds of the woods. Furry funnels who let out fumes the colour and odour of stagnant wine. All were fair game for the little girl tasked with gathering ingredients for the family meal, but with plenty of time to play with what would eventually become her food.

She stood there at the edge of the clearing, munching on her latest find – a tangy hood with pinkish fibrous flesh – when her keen eye spotted a large oval shape hiding beneath a pile of spongy leaves and moss. Intrigued, she crept closer. It resembled no mushroom she knew. She wiped off the closest leaves, revealing a smooth dome far larger than any of the food she was sent to pick. She hastened to clear the remaining foliage and stood back to marvel at the unexpected sight.

Nestled between the canopies of two majestic birch trees lay a large, oval, stone-like object. Its crusty surface formed a haphazard interlocking pattern, made all the more unusual by the sapphire light who ignited it from within. Lively sparks leapt underneath, directing the protective ridges in a slow-motion dance across the jagged surface. The girl touched them. They felt solid and smooth, more like nails than rough stone, and indifferent to her feeble efforts at prying them apart.

"Armo!" she squealed. "Have you ever seen anything so pretty?"

The mountain ram, startled by the girl's rush of exuberance, bleated his disagreement.

"We've got to show this to Ma and Pa!"

She wondered how it got there. A broken branch dangling overhead accompanied by a gaping hole in the canopy furnished a clue. She pushed on the oversized stone, expecting it not to budge, and was shocked to see it roll forward over sloping ground. It wasn't long before she had it secured on a travois tied to Armo's saddle and hauled home, the mushroom harvest forgotten in the excitement of the find.

The Mount Edars sun had risen high into the sky by the time she saw Erna picking herbs in the small garden outside their home.

"Ma! Look what I found!"

Erna looked up at the excited girl, and then at the travois poles dragging behind the ram. She hurried over and was greeted by the sight of an exotic oval stone protruding from travel cloth. She looked at Asja quizzically.

"Do you know what it is?" asked the girl.

Erna shook her head.

"I'm going to get Pa. Maybe he'll know!"

"What about the mushrooms?"

"In the bag!" yelled the girl as she disappeared inside the house.

She rushed out moments later, Tor having trouble keeping up with her.

"Have you ever seen a stone like this, Pa?" Asja pulled the cloth back to reveal it fully, her face flushed and beaming with excitement.

Tor swallowed hard, his eyes glued to the sapphire stone. He studied it closely with his eyes and hands. When he pulled back to look at the child again, his face was mired by piercing eyes and a furrowed brow.

"Where did you find it?"

"In the forest by Moss Drops."

"There aren't supposed to be any of these left. Not here," he said while his hand apprehensively caressed the rugged surface. "We were supposed to have eradicated them all."

He glanced at Asja before continuing. "I've seen an object like this once before – a ferrite egg in a mage's study. Fragments of it anyway. This one looks bigger, though; too big for a dragon. The ridges look more fragile and not at all like scales. It must be some other kind of lightning beast."

His concerned gaze fell on the child again. "Do you have any idea where it came from? Was there a lair? Giant tracks nearby?"

Asja shook her head. "It fell from the sky," she answered confidently, recalling the broken branch and the pierced canopy.

Tor squinted at her words. His hands brushed over the whole scraggy surface, coming to a halt by the far travois pole. He rolled the egg over to expose a sizeable dent in its underbelly. There were no cracks or sharp edges – it looked like the shell had recovered from the impact over time, but not enough to completely fill the hollow.

"A child of the mountain!" He recoiled from the egg.

Erna rushed to his side. She knelt to examine the egg too, but her hands moved gingerly and trembled from the effort. She had trouble getting up. Tor helped her stand again and held her in his arms until she could bring herself to speak.

"Chosen to raise a beast of lightning?" She quivered.

Tor stared at the egg with her. When he spoke, his words were carefully measured, concealing the turbulence that raged underneath.

"I don't know what Ama is trying to tell us or why she has chosen Mount Edars as her messenger, but we cannot turn our back on the sacred duty. You know that."

"First the child and now… this," Erna lamented, barely dignifying the egg with the motion of her hand. "I don't have that much strength left in me!"

"Truth be told, I don't see many years ahead of me either." Tor held her hand, trying to comfort her. "Perhaps we don't need to raise the beast. Just provide a home for the two of them to grow up together. Hopefully Asja will know what to do with the creature when she's older. We both know she's not truly a dwarf, no matter how much she may resemble one."

Erna nodded, apprehension still etched on her face.

"She's moving!" Asja watched the egg closely, oblivious to Erna and Tor's misgivings. "I can hear the shell cracking!"

Tor bent down to examine it again. "I don't see any cracks. They must be inside."

"Should we break the egg to help her come out?" the child offered eagerly, looking around for a tool she could use.

"No, Asja. We must be patient. We wouldn't want her to be born prematurely."

"Like Aunty Hilda's baby?"

"Yes, like that. She will come out when she's strong enough."

The girl sat down next to the egg, preparing for a long vigil. "I will call her

Vagokaraine," she said, "*The one who comes when she is ready.*"

VAGRAN

Vagokaraine was quickly shortened to Vagran when they discovered that the baby was a boy. Asja liked the new name just as much. It reminded her that, like her, he was an orphan who only had a home thanks to the generosity of strangers and their hospitable customs.

She wouldn't let the fledgling bird out of her sight. She followed him through the house and on his tottering explorations of the garden. He slept inside his eggshell at the foot of her bed, though it didn't last long. It kept shrinking while he slumbered before vanishing altogether. Only once did Asja keep an eye half-open to see a fragment of the shell spark and flash before being absorbed by the bird's body, a fleeting sapphire spot in his side the only evidence of the event. She didn't know what to make of it, but suspected it had something to do with his rapid growth.

When he grew too big for their modest house, he joined Armo in the adjacent barn. The ram had more spacious lodgings and didn't mind the guest, and even welcomed the warmth provided by the bird. As did Asja. She snuggled up to the thunderoc every night, pressing against the perennial warmth of his feathery chest and feeling safe in the cosy embrace of his large wings.

When a lightning bolt struck the barn and nearly set the roof ablaze, Tor insisted that the thunderoc move again, this time to an elevated part of the yard by the outside hearth. Undeterred, Asja slept there too. His growing wings proved remarkably effective at sheltering her from the rain, though not from stormy discharges who held lethal attraction to their bestial kin. More than once did she awake from deep slumber convulsing from the latest thunderbolt absorbed by the bird.

The lightning discharges seemed to be all he needed to strengthen and grow. She never saw him eat anything else. Even lengthy absence of a storm didn't seem to bother him, though his size remained stagnant during this time. Her fascination with magic led her to muse that he was able to absorb nourishment from his surroundings to sustain him during these fasts. She certainly tired in his company quickly during that time – falling asleep easily and waking with difficulty – eventually longing for a storm to come.

He spent much of his time gazing at the sky. Clouds, skylights, rainbows and rain, the pointy denizens of the celestial night, all fascinated him. Even clear skies could hold his attention for days on end. He couldn't yet fly, but Asja sensed a longing there, as if he knew that he belonged with heavenly forms rather than solid ground.

Other kids from the hills disagreed. They loved being in his company, stroking his translucent plumes that shimmered in the dark, pressing their faces against the crackling warmth of his skin, laughing at the unsteadiness of his long feet, and standing in awe of his mighty wings. They ran with him in his persistent attempts to reach for the sky, spurring him on every step of the way. And they comforted him in his frustration when his wings – impressive as they were – failed to take flight.

Her association with Vagran raised Asja's standing in the eyes of the kids. No longer was she the peculiar child who spontaneously communed with the spirits of nature in ways mysterious even to her. Now she was the self-appointed caretaker of someone imposing yet so thoroughly different that even her oddity paled in comparison. Someone who was adored by all of her friends.

Until their parents discovered just what kind of bird she harboured at her home.

As the word of Vagran's ancestry spread through the foothills, so did the dwarves' end to their children's company. They couldn't challenge Tor and Erna's sacred duty to raise a child of the mountain – whatever form he may take – but it did irreparable damage to the esteem in which they were held for having undertaken the same task many cycles earlier with what at least looked like a dwarf.

One by one, Asja's friends made themselves scarce. They avoided the bird and, as his constant companion, they avoided her too. She learned to make do with his company alone, as if his sheer size could take the place of the friends she had lost.

Only at night, in the privacy of her sleep, did another come to ease her loneliness. The land herself sprang to life in the most picturesque visions the girl had ever seen. She recognized in her the goddess Ama, known by the dwarves as the soul of their world. She was the only one Asja could confide in, the only one with whom she could share the growing pains of a foreigner struggling to fit in as a dwarf, and childhood milestones reached with an avian friend whom Peruvius Mountains had all but forgotten.

SHIPWRECKS

Enwar opened his eyes. Fine sand, graphite in colour, filled his view. A velvet crab stared at him – not two feet away – his heavy pincers resting on the ground, his violet body glistening in the sun. He scampered away when the man stirred, vanishing into the protective surf.

Pulling himself up, Enwar brushed the sand off his face. A flock of birds flew overhead, their squawking puncturing the serenity of the scene. A small wave collapsed onto the beach, racing up the slope until the foamy water touched his feet. He gazed at the ocean stretching out as far as he could see, her tranquil surface betraying the absence of wind, reflecting the brilliant colours of a dying sun.

He sat there, mesmerised by the scene, oblivious to his place in it.

A ragged plank of wood protruded from the beach at the edge of the surf. He cocked his head, perplexed by the sight. It looked so out of place, one end buried deep in the sand, the other sticking out, bare and exposed, its fibres twisted and torn. Such wood belonged with a ship, like…

Lament!

His eyes shot wide open as memories of the storm came flooding back. The enormous waves, the deafening noise, the perilous sea, the damaged ship, and the end of its long journey upon coastal rocks all came to him in a jumbled mess. Was the ship gone? What happened to the crew? Where was the cargo?

He looked around frantically. Pieces of driftwood floated on the water just beyond the surf. A punctured barrel lay in the sand not far from him, its contents already devoured by the hungry waves. Another lay scattered further down the beach, its metal rings standing exposed like hollow skeleton ribs. And… was that a human body stretched out behind it?

He ran through the surf to a pale body with dishevelled hair lying face-down in the sand, her clothes cut to expose a deep gash running across her back that must have oozed blood before the seawater washed it away. He turned her over, distraught by her lack of warmth. Kalika. His childhood friend who chose to board Lament because of him, because she trusted his seafaring expertise.

Heaving with desolation seeing her like this, he took deep breaths, head dropping to his chest. And then he stood up, leaving her to lie in the sand, gathering himself to search for others, bracing for what he might find.

His search came to an abrupt end when the fragments of a sun high up in the sky dimmed and faded from view, leaving only stars to illuminate the land. He gazed up into the sky, soaking in the unfamiliar sight. They must have been lights from another world, one he was no more familiar with than this one.

A deep voice broke the silence, a distant call that descended upon the beach. He hid behind a rock, not knowing what kind of people or beasts inhabited these lands. Then another call came, and another, edging ever closer, until he recognised the voice of Lament's lookout carrying further through the tranquil night than it ever did in the raging storm.

He responded with a yell of his own. He left the shelter of the rock, racing across the beach to the two men walking at the top. Tears fell from his eyes when he recognised Okeye and Welms – the lookout and the helmsman – on whose courage and skill he had drawn many a time. He embraced each man in turn, grateful to see them standing before him, that he was not alone in this alien land.

TEMPEST

Vagran stood solemnly at the edge of a cliff, his immense wings opening sporadically to counter the force of the wind. The foothills sprawled out beneath the precipice, their pastel contours brightening with every rise and melting into the shadow with each dip. Air currents combed through their fur – the tall, seed-bearing stalks of grass and wheat – animating them and bringing them to life until the breeze ran out of fabric, retiring from his labour by the crimson channel of River Rust.

Darkness encroached upon the land. Angry clouds arrived from the north, carrying news of Mount Zancon's eruption. The metal peak discharged with savage ferocity unmatched by others from the Ural Range. His clouds rumbled with the fury of the mountain who spawned them, threatening to vent their ire at the ground below.

The thunderoc's eyes were transfixed on the churning ashen fog filling the northern skies. They held no fear, only a sparking fascination that evoked a like response. For all the gloomy looks, it was the teal lining behind the surface froth that stoked the storm's wrath. The tempest hid it from view as well as he could, lest it warn the land dwellers of what was to come.

The simmering haze parted, giving voice to the swirling maelstrom brewing behind him. A bolt of lightning flashed through the fissure, accompanied by the tempest's thunderous applause. He traced a blistering path through the gloomy sky until he met his end at the thunderoc's wing. The bird arched to absorb the intense charge before settling back on his talons, nourished and content.

Another charged bolt crackled through the sky before being tamed by Vagran's lightning form. More followed. As if the tempest couldn't believe that his furore was being withstood, relished even, by a puny obstacle standing on the ground. The roc grew brighter with each successive strike, his pellucid feathers igniting from their power, drawing a glistening outline of a giant bird standing his ground against a vengeful storm.

Asja emerged from the shelter of the stones, her eyes transfixed on the sparkling scene. She rushed to the bird during a brief pause, but her outstretched hand failed to reach his plumes. They built up a charge directed against her, only to be met by her own rivalling flash. The blast threw her back across the ground and pushed the giant bird over the cliff edge into the expanse below.

Vagran shrieked as he plummeted through the air towards the rolling hills at the foot of the cliff. His wings flailed with fury and frenzy, desperate to avoid contact with the ground. But the ground rejected him, repelling his charged body back towards the sky. And he soared through the air higher and higher, his iridescent wings fully outstretched, steady and unmoving.

The storm beckoned.

He dived inside, cutting through the shapeshifting fog before losing himself in the lightning powerhouse hidden behind. The sky roared with distant thunder, brightening repeatedly in tune with his growl. And the storm rumbled on, passing through the Mount Edars skies without further troubling the land.

The Mount Croms skylight had neared the end of his journey before a silhouette of the giant bird appeared in the waning lustre of the southern skies. He sought to land by the hillside stones, but couldn't get close, feeling them resist him with resounding vigour. Only when his feathers changed from azure to sapphire hue – shifting the flux that coursed through their seams – was he welcomed by the vigilant stones.

The girl still lay on the ground where the exploding charge had left her. Settling on his talons, he watched over her, quiet and content in the waning day, his hunger satisfied by the retreating storm.

DIFFERENT

Asja stared at the open palm of her hand. The memory of the brilliant flash of light discharging from it still burned in her mind. But there was no singed flesh, no blisters to suggest that anything of note had passed through her skin.

What sort of magic was this? She remembered feeling it build up inside of her – as she had many times before – but never had she seen it released. It couldn't have been lightning. She was a creature of flesh and bone, not lightning moulded into an avian form like her thunderoc friend. But what else could it have been?

She knew she was different from the other dwarves. Magic came much more easily to her. But that different? To unleash uncontrollably on her unsuspecting friend? If anything, she was lucky; a dwarf in his place might not have lived.

Perhaps Obalin was right when he stopped her instruction in the art of runes. Perhaps the danger of releasing it really was too great.

She rolled over onto her side and looked at Vagran. He had grown visibly since his encounter with the tempest. His translucent feathers – playfully soft and warm to the touch – showed no signs of enduring a storm. If anything, he looked more content than she'd ever seen him, his satisfied expression standing in stark contrast to her own inner turmoil.

"Why am I different?"

She didn't expect an answer. The thunderoc could speak, though words didn't come easily. When uttered, they had a peculiar sizzling quality followed by a rumbling echo, as if a storm spoke with both lightning and thunder, each at his own pace. Asja was one of the few people who could make them out, but only if she put a lot of effort into discerning each word.

The bird only looked at her quizzically, his luminous plumes lighting the garden hearth and shimmering in the breeze unlike those of any other creature she had ever seen. They mocked her feelings of alienation from the people she lived with who looked exactly like her. But she knew that their resemblance was only skin-deep. What brewed beneath puzzled and frightened her in equal measure, as it did the few dwarves who knew of her origin.

She ran her hand across his wing as far as she could reach. It extended a great deal further, far onto the grass beyond the paved line. For a while, she had wondered how much bigger his wings would have to grow for the bird to take flight. Now she knew they were more than large enough; he'd merely lacked the skill to generate lift. In what other ways was he unlike the local birds? There was no one left on the Peruvius Range who truly knew his kind. Despite his ancestors' ties to the place, he did not belong here any more than she did.

"Would you fly away with me?" she blurted out as the thought came to her.

The sparks in his eyes arced with sudden intensity.

"Where?" the word crackled across the accompanying roar.

She shrugged. "Mount Croms to the north? Sylvan forests to the west? Goblin desert to the east? Perhaps even the Land of Frost to the south? Anywhere. Everywhere."

Her rambling did nothing to lessen the intensity of the sparks. Undeterred, she continued. "It's just… This has never really been my home. And it definitely hasn't been yours. We do what we can to blend in, and Erna and Tor do what they can to accommodate us, but it's a burden on us all. Such a burden that other dwarves have stopped even trying to bear it, and have left it to Erna and Tor to raise us on their own.

"But we're older now. Old enough to take care of ourselves. We are not tied to this place. And now that you can fly, we could leave and go anywhere we wished."

Vagran stared at her, listening intently, the charged unease subsiding with each word.

"We could look for your people. There are none left on these mountains, but they could still be living on other ranges. We could look for my people, too. I don't know who they are, but Erna told me that they'd found me beyond the western hills. At least that's where we could start."

She stopped there, not mentioning the recent shift in her nightly visions — Ama's hints that her dwarf home had served its purpose, and that her childhood was coming to an end. She didn't yet know where to go, even as she felt the growing sense that it was time to leave.

Vagran said nothing in response. His gaze veered away from her, drifting into the distance, eying the tawny clouds as they ambled through the sky. And a spark returned to them she would often see when he stared towards the horizon. A spirited spark who betrayed playfulness and excitement, and a longing quite fitting for a creature of the sky.

FAREWELL

Asja stared at the items strewn haphazardly across the floor. After moving out to the barn and then the hearth, it felt strange being in her room for any length of time. The room, too, seemed to wonder what she was doing there. The once-familiar place no longer felt like home.

She shook her head and sighed, and resumed her packing.

She picked up a pointy leaf from a dried bunch lying on the floor. It came from no more than a common weed growing on the hills before she heard the plant share his secrets with her. She still remembered her excitement at having prepared the leaves into a salve for the first time. She immediately knew that she was going to be a healer – a herbalist of great renown among the dwarves of her clan. The leaves have been a mainstay of her backpack ever since.

Some of her herbs needed thorough preparation. A wooden mortar and pestle served that purpose, as did a small cooking pot stationed next to them. She always kept a firegem handy should she need to start a fire at a moment's notice. She had less of a need for one now that Vagran was around, though his lightning outbursts were still overpowering and difficult to restrain.

She picked up the gem – a gift from her mentor mage, with bittersweet memories – and brought him up close. Golden bubbles punctuated his smooth amber surface, hinting at the warm radiance hidden within his depths. The surface bubbles of such crystals melded into scarlet, violet and indigo further inside, changing the colour of their fire as the crystal wore out and dissolved into flame.

Something she definitely did not need anymore was the woollen cover taken from merino sheep who grazed the southern slopes facing the Land of Frost, woven into a supple blanket by Erna's deft hands. As much as she loved the lush fabric, it was a heavy burden for her to carry, and Vagran supplied all the warmth she would need on their travels.

A needle and thread for mending clothes, a sharp knife, a long rope, and a spacious water bag made of lithe leaves of giant maple native to Mount Edars rounded off her travel gear. She packed them carefully inside her backpack, took one last long look at the room that had served as her childhood home, and left the house.

Erna ambushed her as she stepped outside. The old woman's grip was surprisingly tenacious for her advanced age. Asja held her in return, the reality of leaving the only home she had ever known starting to sink in.

"Are you sure you want to do this?" Erna asked after releasing the girl from her grasp.

Asja nodded, tentatively at first, her conviction growing with each movement of her head.

"It's not like you're never going to see us again. Vagran can already fly fast and far, and he's not even fully grown. We'll be back before you even notice we're gone," she reassured Erna with a strained smile.

"Think of it as an adventure," Tor reinforced what Asja had said. But his voice cracked uttering the cheerful words, and he held Asja in a long embrace even tighter than Erna's had been.

"Do you remember what to look for?" he finally asked.

"Kritall Wood. Short thin trees who entwine their trunks to make broad ones. From the air we should see a few large crowns who cover the hillside, each one made of many colours from the trees within."

"Kritall Wood is at the border between dwarf mountains and sylvan forests. I don't know why we found you there, Asja. No other people live there, I promise you," insisted Erna.

"I know, Ma. I know. But I have to see for myself."

She swung her rucksack over her shoulder and headed to Vagran. The enormous bird welcomed her with a deep bow, his chest almost touching the ground, his wings moving watchfully to steady his posture. She grabbed the outstretched feathers and hoisted herself onto his breast, before settling inside the cosy cavity in the middle of his chest that resonated with the rhythmic beating of the bird's heart.

He maintained his bow for a while longer, lowering his head in deference to Erna and Tor. Then he straightened up and extended his wings, shrouding the garden in their shadow. Their sapphire sheen darkened rapidly to grow azure hues, propelling him into the twilight sky with urgency and force, and away from the only place he has called home.

Tor held Erna in his arms as they watched their children vanish into the sky. Erna uttered a tearful prayer, entrusting them both to Ama's care.

HOPE

Enwar sat on a rocky outcrop overlooking the beach. Seawater washed up the surf to form a jagged line, channelled by mounds of sand rising and falling in a rhythmic pattern sculpted by the wind. Caverns and tunnels breathed in and out beneath him, water filling the empty spaces with each renewed surge. He could see the wave motion through a crack in the floor, a gap in the weathered rocks that betrayed their weariness. Many cycles from now, the outcrop would suffer the same fate as those further out to sea, broken and ravaged by the relentless waves until only the most stubborn fragments remained protruding from the water, the rest having been crushed and dumped over the sandy shore.

The mountain standing on the other side of the beach told a different tale. Young and vibrant, he rose proudly from the watery depths, bulge after bulge swelling into the water like ribs of stone and crystal framing the mountain range. His bulk rose in terraces overlooking the ocean, his bronze skin nourishing patches of grass, shrubs and trees. His base stood solid and defiant of the waves, with no remnants of an ancient coast jutting from the sea, the azure surface clear and inviting.

Oh, how he yearned to sail the seas again! But Lament lay broken and scattered across Scuttle Bay – as they'd named the place of their demise. With only three survivors, there'd be no making another.

A whiff of smoke entered his lungs, intruding upon the marine vista stretched out before him. Welms' hunt must have yielded success; the gull nesting grounds made for an easy target. They were fortunate to have been able to salvage some of their spears and bows from the wreckage of the ship. The weapons were put to immediate use, with their last stores of food from the journey ending up at the bottom of the bay.

Enwar took another look at the imposing range who filled his view, arriving from deep inland and stretching far out into the sea. The sight took his breath away each time he saw it; a virgin land ripe for settlement, whom they had the incredible fortune to stumble upon, the only exodus voyage he knew of that succeeded at this task. And then they crashed upon the rocks, the bulk of their supplies and crew perishing in the storm, leaving the three of them with no way to colonise the new world. His last remaining hope lay with their sister ship, that they had better fortune, that they withstood the waves and established a viable colony somewhere in this world.

The serene presence with which the mountain range towered over the land stood in stark contrast to the spewing mountains of his homeland, the cracking land who sought to drag the surface dwellers to her depths, and the swelling sea who wished to devour them both. A world in turmoil whose spirit grew angry, causing mountains to open, winds to rise and seasons to fail. A world who pitted her children against each other, until some perished and others scrambled to leave before they met the same fate.

Seeing this fertile land and her bountiful sea reminded him of the stories of old, the legends of how Rashas used to be – a nurturing land who nourished her children and within whom humanity thrived. He'd never known her like that, having been born into a world of failing harvests and withering livestock, whose numbers dwindled from constant attacks by other peoples and beasts scouring the land.

He wished he could sail back and tell his people about this place, that a new start could be made here, that any exodus ships that remained should be sent this way. He felt cheated, having drawn on all his experience and skill to sail to a new land, and when he did, having their hope of a new beginning ripped out from under them.

Movement past the last outcrop in the distant waters caught his eye. A speck emerged from the mountain's shadow to stand alone upon the placid top. It lumbered lazily across the ocean, its caramel base standing in stark contrast to its white tip.

Enwar jumped off the rocky outcrop and raced to the camp. He grabbed two sturdy chunks of wood eaten by the fire, shouted "Bring the leaves!" to his friends, and ran back to the top of the cliff, trying to preserve the glowing embers he was carrying. After the initial shock, Okeye and Welms followed him, carrying pieces of dry wood and a bag full of leaves. In no time they got a fire dancing atop the rising mound, sending a thin column of smoke into the sky past the end of the beach.

They stared together at the curious speck floating on the water. It grew as it approached, its widening base casting a shadow from the distant sun, its pearly top starting to flutter in the light breeze. Their hearts pounded from the rush of excitement. Then, seeing the rocks jutting out from the water, they moved the embers to start a new fire on top of the beach. They jumped and shouted to draw attention to themselves. The object veered to follow. They hugged and cried, and then waved and shouted some more, daring to hope again.

Enwar watched the ship as it dropped anchor in the shallow water off the low coast. The crew didn't roll up the top sail as it hung in tatters from the mast beam. The bow looked battered and bruised, with only a stump remaining of its broken bowsprit. The whole hull carried bruises from its many encounters with the raging storms, some of which it acquired after separating from Lament within sight of the coast.

The crew didn't care. They squeezed into two lifeboats for a short journey to the shore, their faces beaming, their posture jubilant. The shipwrecks welcomed their compatriots with arms open wide. The supplies they brought would ease their entry into the new world, and their numbers would make the first colony viable again.

WITCH

A campfire burned and crackled at the edge of a clearing. Her vivacious tongues pranced through the air, hinting at the outline of timeworn trees who crowded around her. Their twisted trunks haunted the glade with their presence, responding to the whistling wind with an eerie dance. *Swirling Woodlot*, Asja remembered what the forest was called, spellbound by the lurid forms that had given her this name.

Why am I here? she wondered. Kritall Wood lay far behind them. They'd scoured the forest but found no trace of people living there, only footprints and wheel tracks cutting a wild path to Mount Edars on one end and sylvan forests on the other. They followed the sylvan side until the path split, dissolving into a multitude of sporadic trails. Asja wanted to explore each one, but Vagran did not. Dense foliage suffocated him. Forest clearings were few and grew fewer still the deeper into the sylvan lands they went. They took a south-eastern path instead, heading eventually for the Land of Frost. If there were any unknown people living in these lands, this was where they'd be.

Swirling Woodlot's elder woods reached heights meagre for their age. Snow weighed heavily on their backs during the lengthy cold spells that preceded frost mountain discharges, even if their coiled branches and swivelling trunks were adept at shaking it off. And the thick bark that clothed them helped them withstand the chilling winds descending from the mountains better than their western brethren ever could.

Murky clouds who'd gathered overhead continued their journey inland. Vagran had followed them and the lightning storm they brought, eager to feed on the tempest's fury. Sporadic flashes illuminating the distant skies laid bare clues as to where he might be.

A spent skylight crumbled apart high above the eastern peak. He disintegrated into a thousand fragments, each awash with his own unrestrained light. The canopies who had hidden away from the campfire's prying flames suddenly burst into full view, rendered naked by the scorching sky.

Asja admired their spiralling shapes. A crown sprawled directly above her, her branches bent as they emerged from the trunk, giving her the appearance of a whirling dancer whose arms and posture were frozen in mid-turn. Another's limbs angled towards the ground in a stance of solemn deference. Tree trunks, sturdy and wide, were devoured by their serpentine bark that wrapped around them in a revolving pattern. Even the roots formed circular shapes on the forest floor before burying themselves deep into the soil.

Almost as abruptly as they appeared, the fiery fragments of the distant skylight dimmed from view. They left a sky faintly illuminated by dying twinkles of light. The day had breathed his last breath. The forest resumed her shadowy presence, haunting in her beauty.

Asja spied an unusual movement of leaves on the opposite end of the glade. They swooped up from the forest floor and banded together into a churning mass. It coalesced into a stable shape – a loosely humanoid one – even amidst the ceaseless motion. It reminded her of a ragtag doll with all the colours of autumn shuffling across its surface. Two eyes appeared – radiant slits of glowing amber – and a gaping hole where the mouth should have been. Whatever mysterious attraction the leaf figure may have held vanished with them.

"You are far away from home, aren't you, mage?" The mouth moved to wordy sounds of rustling leaves and whistling wind, slow and deliberate in their delivery.

Asja froze, gaping at the swirling morass of leaves and twigs, her fascination dissolving into sheer fright. Was this a demon? The sinister villain of many a dwarf tale? The makeshift creature didn't resemble one, yet its malevolent gaze chilled her to the bone.

"You do not answer?" the figure continued, creeping closer with each passing word, gathering new leaves as it went. Asja backed away from the fire, her breath stuck in her throat.

"Afraid, are you?" The leaf surface contorted into a smirk. "You better get your staff if you want to be rid of me!"

"I don't have one," Asja whispered, her voice cracking.

"A mage without a staff? Well, well, I never thought I'd see the day."

"I'm not a mage."

The smirk vanished, giving way to a furrowed brow that angled the glowing eyes further apart. "You can't fool me, dwarf! I can feel the magic seeping from you. Why are you here? This is not your land."

Asja opened her mouth to answer, but no sound came. Her heart pounded and her chest tensed up, thwarting her desire to explain herself at length. Her body trembled, ready to bolt for the treeline behind her.

"You people shouldn't leave the mountains. It's not safe!"

48

The leaves on the apparition rustled with derision. Its mouth contorted with the clamour of leaves that boomed through the glade. Asja felt it grow in vigour and presence. It grew in stature, too, as it devoured the surrounding leaves to feed its swelling frame. The eyes turned blood red, as if the fire who had raged within suddenly tasted its raw flesh. They focused squarely on Asja's quivering figure, as if delighting in her fearful stance.

The world around her started to lose shape. All sense of place left her – the humble forest clearing, the treeline defining it, the soft touch of the twilight sky. They all took on a distorted, grotesque guise.

Trees ditched their soothing leaves to reveal crooked branches with knotty sprigs flexing their twigs like knobbly, diseased hands. They moved effortlessly across the glade, as if the ground herself had conspired to release them. Even the swaying grass beneath Asja's feet lost her playfulness and lurched to face her with blades open wide.

Terror enveloped her.

The nightmare arose all around her, feeling more real than any from her reveries. At its centre stood two crimson eyes set in a swollen, sneering face. Unlike the forest scenery, they didn't move, yet held her attention while the gory shapes and ghastly forms closed in around her.

She tried to pull away, desperate to tear herself from their tightening clasp. The apparition was surprisingly adept at this battle of wills. It held her with an iron grip, weakening her ability to respond with each macabre step. She could only watch as a grisly tree crept within reach and lifted his knobbly fist to pound her into the ground.

A gigantic form materialised behind the tree, sending a thunderous tremor through the floor of the glade. His shimmering feathers sizzled menacingly with a profusion of energy their body could not contain. The open wings spanned the full length of the glade, sending lightning arcs between them who reverberated through Asja's nightmare and held her tormentors in momentary check.

The rogue eyes harrowing Asja wavered in their resolve. They greeted the lightning beast with terror of their own. Unlike the amorphous forms that crowded around Asja, they knew that this one was not an illusion. In a brisk moment of self-preservation, the animating force left the apparition; it collapsed into a silent pile of leaves and twigs on the forest floor.

With their master gone, the distorted forest forms snapped back into place.

Asja gasped, stunned by the sudden return to normality. The instant retreat of the forest dwellers left her disoriented. She dropped to her knees and watched blades of grass sway playfully in the breeze. She extended her hand to caress them, grateful for their familiar, comforting presence.

"What was that?" the words sparked from the thunderoc.

Asja looked up, realising only now what had brought her nightmare to an end. She rushed past Vagran to the abandoned pile of foliage in the middle of the clearing. It lay there inert, its surface leaves at the mercy of the wind. She could no longer feel the sinister presence that was all too real to her only moments before.

"I don't know, Vagran." She sighed, trying to reason her way through the nightmarish events that had held her in their grip. "I don't know."

AMA

Asja's gaze wandered nervously around the glade. Twisted forest forms lurked in the shadows of the dying campfire. Occasionally they moved, nudged into action by the frosty wind, triggering the memory of her tormentor and the dread of its return. She tracked each movement, fixated on what it might become, until the breeze died down and denizens of the wood fell silent and still once more. Her eyes closed with sleep.

Sudden rustling of leaves – mere steps away – pried them open. She watched in horror as the leaves rose and shuffled, swiftly coalescing into a humanoid form. With a silent gasp, she pressed deeper into Vagran's warm plumage, drawing whatever assurance she could from the latent power of the sleeping bird.

The figure stood directly ahead, upright and firm. Its limbs made of dry branches were interwoven with twigs and adorned with leaves and flower petals that had lain discarded on the forest floor. Some of the foliage that comprised its face resembled feathers whose velvety strands and vibrant colours gave the apparition an exotic presence.

But it was the eyes that held Asja in place.

The left one shone deep emerald green. She saw in it the dense forests of birch and pine enclosing the wide-open plains of western Amana and the shamrock-coloured hills who grew there.

The right eye bounded with the energy of a mountain geyser who'd been nourished with more water than he could contain, until it overflowed into myriad rivers who fed lakes and seas. The whole watery expanse bathed in the azure tones of the endless sky.

The soul of Amana dwelled in those eyes. A gentle melody accompanied their sight, as if every pebble, watery drop and blade of grass added their own unique sound, blending together in perfect harmony of a pervasive hum.

There was only one being Asja knew of who could embody the entirety of the world in whom she lived. A presence she'd felt many times in her sleep, a guardian who'd watched over her all through her childhood.

"Ama?" She trembled at the thought.

The forest figure's feathery face lit up with a tender smile. She opened her arms to welcome the fearful girl.

Her fear gone, Asja emerged from Vagran's plumage to greet the goddess with a warm embrace. She held the friend from her childhood visions until all her misgivings melted away and she felt completely safe in the goddess' presence.

"When I first saw you appear, I was scared that the apparition had returned," Asja confessed. "Was it a demon?"

Ama shook her head with a reassuring smile. "She won't bother you again tonight," the symphonic voice sounded in response, coloured by the rustling of leaves and twigs from which her form was made.

"Who was she?"

"Centane. A mur witch who sometimes travels these lands."

Asja greeted the explanation with a blank face. "A mur witch? Who are they? Local people?" her voice tapered off, her enthusiasm for finding her people quickly tempered by the horror of her earlier ordeal. The witch was not who she wanted her birth people to be.

"No. They used to live along the southern coast. Now they inhabit the islands beyond her shores."

Asja breathed a sigh of relief, grateful that she wouldn't have to tangle with the likes of Centane. As eager as she was to find the people she was born to, deep down she feared what she might uncover. She had capacities – dangerous and uncontrollable – that surpassed even those of the runemages. As terrified as she was of Centane, she had to admit that there was a certain similarity there that made her uneasy. Even though she didn't want to have anything to do with the mur, an ancestral connection wouldn't have surprised her.

"Your intuition is well developed, Asja. You should trust it more."

Asja stared at the goddess as she eased away from her. Was Ama reading her thoughts? "No…" she whispered, her eyes open wide, fearing what the goddess might say next.

"They *are* your people. You are mur by birth."

Asja gasped at the words, her head shaking with increasing fierceness. "No!"

Ama waited patiently while the girl wrestled with her heritage, pacing on the grass and staring at the ground, until she could hold the idea in her mind without the thought triggering denial.

"How? How can I be living among the dwarves then?" she asked with ferocity she never thought she'd direct at the goddess.

"The mur homeland was ravaged by humans at the time of your birth. Of those who survived, most sought refuge across the sea, on the islands of the archipelago. Your parents travelled inland. They made it as far as Kritall Wood before they died. That was where Erna and Tor found you."

"Why do I look like a dwarf then?"

"I changed your appearance. Growing up in an alien land was going to be hard enough even while looking like them. A mur, they might not have accepted at all. Like they rejected your friend."

Asja turned to look at the slumbering bird. As lonely as she'd felt growing up among the dwarves, it was nothing compared to their rejection of the young thunderoc. She was grateful to Ama for sparing her the pain. But the goddess' singular act of mercy puzzled her. Asja would hardly have been the first one to suffer hardship or die young.

"Why... Why would you do that for me?"

"I saw something in you that I hadn't seen before. And... I was hoping that, someday, you would be willing to help me in return."

Asja's jaw dropped in astonishment. The very last thing she'd expected to hear from the goddess was a plea for help. It was the antithesis of whom she knew Ama to be – a being of absolute power over the affairs of the world. What could a person of such stature possibly need from her?

"How can I be of service, Ama?"

"You are a child of mur magicians. You harbour tremendous potential, talents you know little about and are fearful of. You can begin by developing them until you can trust them and rely on them. You will need them someday. As will I."

Asja's shoulders slumped in defeat.

"I tried, Ama, I did. My father – Tor – took me to Amerot as a child, to apprentice to a mage. The mage started to teach me, but soon stopped and wouldn't carry on. I think I frightened him. After that, none of the other mages or druids would teach me either."

"Dwarf mages and elf druids know too little of their craft to be your teachers."

"Who then?" she wondered. "My birth people?" She shook her head vehemently. "I don't want to be like Centane!"

"Good. If you were to learn from them now, there is real danger that this is who you'd become. Or they would destroy you for going against them. No, Asja, I would not send you to your birth people at this time."

"Who then?"

The expression on the goddess' face shifted ever so slightly. Asja thought she spied apprehension, but quickly dismissed the idea, unable to entertain such an absurd notion.

"There is a small group of wizards who have become closely involved with the affairs of my world," she finally said. "They are even more capable than the people of your birth. You should seek them out. They may be willing to help."

"Wizards? I've never heard of such people."

"They are few, and they don't draw attention to themselves."

Asja tentatively nodded, warming to the idea.

"Where can I find them?"

"The closest place they often visit is inside Mount Ablast – a south-eastern peak from the Land of Frost. If you leave soon – with Vagran's help – you will find them there."

Asja's face brightened, beaming with hope at Ama's words. But the sparkle was short-lived. Her eyes soon sank to the floor and avoided contact, weighed down by an ancestral burden exceedingly heavy to carry. Ama reached out and held her by the shoulders, making sure she had the girl's undivided attention.

"The new mur homeland might be distant, but their magicians travel easily, and their intentions towards your adoptive people – and elves and humans, for that matter – are not good. You have seen what Centane can do. And she was only trying to frighten you.

"If you choose not to develop your skills for fear of what might happen should you misuse them, your adoptive people and many others will pay the price. Your heritage is not something you can just walk away from. Not without damning more people than you could possibly know."

With those words, she cupped Asja's face with leafy hands, gazed into her eyes with the intensity of the entire world bearing down on her, and vacated the forest figure that held the goddess' essence, leaving it to collapse in a pile of leaves on the forest floor.

VISION

A slumbering mountaintop rose from the ground, wrapped in a chilling blanket of pristine white snow. Asja marvelled at the sight, never having been to the Land of Frost, despite the mountains' frosty presence stretching to the doorstep of her home.

She stared at the summit before her, unable to divert her gaze, as if she were no more than a visitor to this strange place, a passive observer of someone else's daydream. *Ama*, she thought, reminded of the visions she'd had as a child, where the goddess had directed her to places of her choosing.

The vision took off towards the mountain peak. It rose above the icy incline, but before it could reach the summit, it burrowed into the mountainside, through the covering of snow and ice and the backing wall of crystal and stone. The disorienting journey was over in a flash, coming to rest in a hollow chamber deep inside the massif.

None of it looked familiar, made more alien by the hazy silhouettes of featureless rocks sprinkled from ceiling to floor throughout the alcove. Asja couldn't tell whether the cavity was hollowed out of crystal and rock – by people she didn't know using skills she'd never seen – or a natural feature of the mountain's core.

One sight that lacked no focus was a cloaked humanoid figure standing by the wall. Not that she could discern his exact appearance – only a bald grey head with the texture of rock, a long scarlet cloak covering the rest – but his regal posture and the prominence of a lustrous shawl against the drab backdrop of the cave made his importance palpable.

Her eyes opened in a flash. A dark sky welcomed her, framed with contorted branches and adorned with numerous twinkles of light. It took her a moment to leave the world of her reverie and acknowledge the renewed presence of the forest glade.

The sight of the red-cloaked stranger standing in a cavern inside a mountain of frost lingered in her mind. He resembled no creature she knew. No one she had seen near Mount Edars or heard about from infrequent travellers. Did Ama send her the vision? Was this where she wanted Asja to go?

She moved to get up when she noticed an unexpected weight of an object stretching across her chest. She reached to grab it. The thin shaft felt surprisingly sturdy yet light to the touch. Its smooth lilac surface twisted in places to no pattern she could discern, as if the long bar felt the need to relieve the boredom of connecting the base to the tip.

What was it? Where did it come from? She had no answers, only a further mystery to add to her vision. The stick reminded her of a mage's staff, though those were made of pliable crystal who gave them the endurance needed for the casting of runes. This one looked flimsy in comparison, as if it would break if put to the same task. Yet there was resilience to it that she felt in the steady pulsation within her hand.

She kept it, hoping that someday she may be able to unearth its secrets.

THE TREK

Wagon wheels rumbled to a halt. A little girl jumped off and ran to hug her friend. After a long embrace, she ran back to the wagon, climbed on and wiped the tears off her face. With a shudder, the wagon rumbled on. The girl sat at the back, watching the crowd of people waving farewells with heavy hands and shouting their encouragement with cracking voices, her best friend standing among them.

And then they disappeared around a bend in the road, the only home the girl had ever known fading away with them.

The wagon caravan followed the contours of the land, meandering alongside Mount Cappon at the edge of the plain. It left Hope behind, the first human settlement in the new land, a makeshift camp founded by the shipwrecks that grew into a village before blossoming into a vibrant town, nourished by the sea and safely sheltered by the mountain range. It was time to move beyond Hope and claim the endless land who called out to them.

When Timberland rose in their way, they rounded the forest, staying true to the Great Plain. A logging cabin saw them approach, the furthest outpost from the burgeoning town the humans had made. The woodcutters stopped their work to watch them pass, counting twenty heavy wagons laden with supplies and people, each pulled by a couple of oxen with their heads close to the ground, the troop flanked by hunter riders ever watchful for danger as well as a meal.

A sudden burst of light overtook them from behind as a Mount Cappon sun shot up into the sky. His blistering shine pierced the dusky land with an aqueous touch, bathing the birch forest leaves and the golden strands of the plains in azure rays drawn from the sea. They shone their light on the path inland, giving the brown land a bluish sheen, broadening the vista until it overwhelmed the eyes of the people in the front of the column with its sheer expanse.

The Great Plain opened herself up to them, her swaying grass brushing against them, her unrestrained breeze caressing their faces, her animals stepping aside to give them space, her endless sweep beckoning to them – inviting them in, urging them to lose themselves in the sea of hay. They duly obliged, moving deeper into the plain, but never losing sight of the mountain range, for they knew that, this far from the sea, it was the mountains who watered the land.

A small stream crossed their path, filling their water bags and wetting their feet. They turned and followed her meandering curves, finally finding the courage to let go of the range. Trees rose to protect the creek, a growing thicket hiding her from view, trailing her bends on her journey across the steppes, leaving nothing but the gurgling sounds to betray the presence of clear water flowing in their midst.

The caravan stopped to rest, circling their wagons around a campfire, their hunters using the last of the light to bring down a quarry for this meal and the next. The breeze subsided in the shade of the trees. The sky exploded with the azure light before falling dark, leaving the marigold hues to reassert themselves over the land, a reflection of the steppes in the heavens above.

The stream grew in size, aided by another through a breach in the bank. When she emptied her channel into a swollen river, they followed her from that point on, hopeful that her ample waters would not run dry in the mountains' time of rest, looking for an open place where the river would nourish them freely – a broad, quiet, shallow course with weak currents and schools of fish. They didn't see it that day or the next, but then a bluish line appeared in the dim light of a faraway sun, stretching well beyond the river on either side, far apart as her banks were this deep in the Great Plain.

They prodded the oxen into a hurried walk, anxious to unravel the mystery before them, their hearts beating with excitement at the thickening line filling the horizon. When the channel broadened further, they detoured with her, following the humming flow to her union with the lake – a still body of water within the heart of the plain, a sea away from the sea to ease their longing for the place of their birth.

People jumped off their wagons and headed for the lake – hunters on horseback galloping in front – until the hooves and the feet touched the grassy surf, washing over them in the quiet breeze. They stared at the wavy surface for the longest time, reliving their memories of the Coral Sea. When they turned around, the swaying meadow by the river's bank called out to them, offering space for wooden cabins and planted fields and all the fish they could catch in the stream. They could make boats to traverse the lake and explore the plains by both foot and sail.

Torrel turned his eyes away from the scene to gaze at the dense forest sprawling beyond the field and the sputter of trees reaching for the stream. His eyes caught movement on the opposite bank. A group of animals stood in the tall grass, staring at them from across the reeds. Sleek bodies with faint stripes gracing their golden hides, long teeth jutting from their jaws adorned with a thick mane, piercing eyes locked on the nomadic group, glowing amber in the olive grass.

Felines.

The dominant predators of the Great Plain.

Only once before had he encountered their kind, a single feline stealing their kill during a hunt far away from Hope. Felines didn't bother them in their town by the sea, but he feared this might change now that they encroached upon the same land. They had better circle the wagons as shelter for the night, and erect solid structures from sturdy wood if they were to stay.

The pride watching them from across the river seemed very curious about the strangers in their midst. They made him think of the stories from his childhood – the myths and legends from the land of Rashas brought over by his ancestors across the Primordial Sea. Stories of monsters roaming a dying world, beasts who hunted humans with tenacity and skill until the last of his people set sail in their ships, seeing better odds across the open sea, in search of a new land far away from home.

He reached over his shoulder and ran his fingers across the wooden bow, reassured by the firm frame stretching across his back.

They were in that world now. And they weren't going to let the felines or any other beasts drive them out of it again.

LAND OF FROST

Subdued light from a northern sun illuminated the path ahead. The Mount Edars skylight had entered the upper reaches of the sky, high enough to be seen even this far south, the most daylight the Frost Lands received short of one of their own peaks rumbling to life. But this was rare. For the most part, the local summits kept quiet and still, content to slumber beneath their cover of snow.

Like their northern cousin, the frost mountain range drew water and warmth from deep beneath the land, and released them through vents and skylights when the heat grew too onerous to bear. But the younger summits weren't yet fully grown, and lacked the stamina, skill and temperance of their older brethren. The heat was slow to build up, the skylights ejected haphazardly and far apart. The land responded by cloaking herself with snow, the last bastion of winter in a world awash with warmth.

Vagran followed the contours of the land, only rising in the presence of imposing massifs who asserted themselves over the land and blocked the thunderoc's view. He would have loved nothing more than to soar beyond the mountaintops and scout Mount Ablast from a lofty vantage point high up in the sky. But snowy winds were not uncommon, and even the most mannered of them wrapped the mountains in powdery cloaks who obscured their features from view.

The valley who sprawled out between the sparse peaks resembled the one before. Lakes, streams, boulders and trees who added character to the Peruvius Range were absent here, hidden indiscriminately beneath the snowy drape. Wherever he cast his eye, Vagran could see only a featureless white plain stretching from one horizon to the other, with nothing but mountain peaks to break the monotony of the landscape.

Another nameless mountain crest passed beneath his wings. He too lacked the distinctive ridges whom Asja remembered seeing in her vision, or perhaps even they were obscured by the pervasive snow. Frustrated by the hostility of the land, Vagran descended to the slopes, intent on scouring them for any markings he could find.

Only now did the monotony of the frost break to reveal a relief as rich in texture as any he had ever seen. Frozen fountains of sapphire ice emerged from the ground, the last remnants of illustrious geysers from the final days of the previous thaw. An icy column scaled a sheer drop where a waterfall used to stand. The oversized icicles hung on to the roof of the crystal pillar or found support in his broad base that rested on the thick ice of the receptive lake.

A silvery eagle cruised over the frozen landscape, blending perfectly into the snowy backdrop. A small herd of crystal horses stood on both banks of a meandering stream, satiating their thirst through the broken ice. Spooked by the bird, they galloped across the plain, leaving clear hoofprints in the receptive snow. It was a world alien to the thunderoc. Suspended in time, shrouded in silence and frozen in stillness. Each event preserved for posterity. Or till the next blizzard came along and wiped the slate clean.

A flock of birds rose from a wood, announcing the arrival of a snow-fuelled storm. The cover of snow lifted from the trees and saturated the air around and above them until the sight of their tortured forms could no longer pierce the veil. At the edge of the treeline, a walrus dug his powerful tusks into the flowing ice, disappearing beneath the thick cover and out of the blizzard's path. A lone wolf scampered across it instead, rushing to the relative safety of her burrowed den on the other side of the lake.

Having snuffed out the last visible vestiges of life, the wintery landscape bared her hidden face – a vast expanse of barren loneliness. Flying overhead, Vagran felt like the sole living creature in a land desolate and deadly, though no less beautiful for it.

A low mountain came into view through the blistering storm. Snow-filled air flowed like rills between the rocky ridges, replacing rivers and streams rendered still by the biting cold or trickling in silence beneath the solid ice. Folded sheets of pristine snow dominated the slopes. Vagran felt a tug on his chest feathers; it was the mountain from Asja's vision.

Light shone from her interior, released through the upper vents whom water struggled to reach. Her bulging frame left no doubt that the skylight she carried neared his birth. As did the warmth with the promise of spring, though, for now, it remained locked away beneath the mountain's crust while the winter storm raged outside.

Vagran spied a low cave opening ahead and raced the storm trying to reach her. Just spacious enough to hold his giant frame when his wings were folded by his side. He pressed against the crystal wall, closing the entrance with his exposed back and keeping his friend sheltered from the gale. And there they lay, quiet and still in the silence of the cave, entertained by the incessant sound of the wailing wind.

SKYLIGHT

Boom, boom. Boom, boom.

The beating sound of the mountain's heart echoed through the chamber. Her rhythmic motion marked the end of a cycle, and the beginning of another.

Boom, boom.

The seed had no sense of who he was. An integral part of the mountain's core, he lived in the hollow above her heart for as long as he could remember. Inconspicuous at first, he grew and prospered with each rising tide, feeding on the crystalline mass the retreating waters left behind. Now swollen to a size that could barely be contained within the chamber walls, he still saw himself as nothing more than an inseparable part of the heart's throbbing pulse.

Boom, boom…

The heart contracted, drawing out warm waters from the primordial depths. They steadily rose, engulfing her and the seed above her in their moist embrace, filling every cavity, every vein flowing through the chamber walls.

…boom!

The heart expanded, pushing the waters against the crystal rock, expelling what she could through the outbound cracks. The rest fell back into the depths to be siphoned up again, the residue that they left adding to the seed's already engorged bulk.

Boom…

The waters rose with another contraction, bearing warmth until it became oppressive. The seed sat uncomfortably in his hollow above the heart. He eyed the walls of his womb that drew closer with each passing beat.

…boom!

He pushed against the walls of rock, driven in turn by the expanding heart. They strained to contain his relentless pressure, but he'd grown too restless to be held in place. So they heaved and stretched and remained intact.

Boom… BOOM!

The heat rose to unbearable heights. The seed thought he would burst from the intensity of the squeeze. But the womb ruptured first. Her ceiling ripped open and crashed onto the mountainside.

The seed shot out with a calamitous roar, launching himself into the alien sky.

A ball of dazzling brilliance flew from the fractured mountaintop, his body forging a path of light through the darkness around him. A plume of vapour followed in his wake, rising to the clouds before abandoning the chase. Water poured from every mountain crevice, feeding streams until they overflowed and fuelling geysers until they burst.

A sweltering wave accompanied the water, unfurling a warm blanket over the snowy landscape. She warmed the icicles who littered the mountain walls. They dripped and dribbled, trickling onto ice structures frozen in mid-drop. Seeping water thinned them and weakened their clasp, forcing them to release whom they held in their grip, once again gushing freely onto the receptive land.

The wave of warmth passed through a forest of sagging trees burdened by the snow. She tempered their crust, softening its hold on the figures made of wood. The trees shook and swayed, ridding themselves of their icy load. Then they rose and stood upright, facing the dawning gleam of the rising skylight, awakened to a rare spring in the Land of Frost.

Tips of snow-covered branches melted away, shedding tears onto the ground below. Their weeping formed rivulets who followed the path of frozen mountain streams. They cut through the snow and the ice, dissolving into meandering causeways and stirring the creeks from their winter nap, until they flowed into an expansive lake, sinking beneath her slippery top.

Whole chunks of glacial ice severed from the mountain and plunged down the sheer cliffs, shattering themselves on the snow-covered slopes. There they latched onto the unsuspecting snow, gathering more as they rolled down, growing into balls of death who threatened everyone who got in their way.

The rumble alerted the subterranean denizens of the Land of Frost. As if on cue, they emerged from the maze of tunnels who criss-crossed the glacier. Furry yetis, swift-footed barbegazis, weaver spiders and snow vines, frosties and amaroks, crystallines who sparkled with countless shades of white, lampyrids whose own shine faded in the brilliant light of the new sun. They stood and watched the nascent skylight retrace the neglected path through the frosty sky, basking with abandon in his lavish glare.

The skylight cast his gaze on the rousing landscape. Steam still rose from the misty aperture who'd given him birth. Geysers large and small propelled water and vapour all around. They sprayed the silvery slopes, washing away ice and snow from the dormant land and loosening the winter's grip on the mucky soil. Rays of light shone on the mountain paths, streaked through the gaps in the crowns of trees, and dived deep into the water of glacial lakes. They illuminated a world awakening from slumber and hungry for life.

The space at the top of the world was quiet, peaceful. The skylight started to fade, his energy nearly spent, his journey almost complete. The Land of Frost was laid out before him, devouring the last rays of light he had left to give.

He had never known this harsh and unforgiving land in her usual state of fatal beauty, of lying dormant beneath her frosty shell. From the moment he'd emerged from the mountain's womb, he'd seen a world of exquisite beauty coming to life wherever he cast his gaze. The wonder of his homeland's awakening reached to the core of the skylight's being. And in his final lucid moment, he knew exactly how to respond.

He disintegrated into a million pieces, each one a miniature skylight, a seed in his own right. They lit up the sky with dazzling fervour that overshadowed the original ball of light. They parted with the last sparkle of life they still had in them so that the land of their birth may remain vibrant for a moment more. And then they fell dull, their spirit expended, plunging through the cold darkness of space over their frosty home.

MOUNT ABLAST

Asja walked out onto the stirring meadow by the entrance to the cave. A spiky cone made of snowy alabaster rolled onto her foot. She picked him up, marvelling at his sturdy yet delicate structure. Alabaster Crest, the locals called the Summit. His slopes housed countless patches of crystalline trees – a sight only seen in the Land of Frost, becoming rarer even here as wood and bark sought to assert themselves and usurp their place. But the reign of frost was not yet at an end, and the plants still suffered through the stubborn cold.

Asja breathed in the sudden season change. Gone was the snowy peak wrapped in a raging blizzard who'd fumed and rumbled with the pains of birth. In his place, in clear air, adorned with lavish columns of water and illuminated by a skylight high above, rose a beacon of life awakened from his slumber.

The side of the mountain – through which the vision took her – stood as solid and impenetrable as the rocky massif who dominated the vistas by her home.

A plume of steam shot up from the foothills as a crumbling snow ledge dissolved inside a geyser. *Was this a way in?* She quickly dismissed the idea. Even if she could find a spring peaceful enough to enter, he would lead her to a deep lake within the mountain's base whose waters poured out with each skylight's birth. No one in their right mind would have connected their chambers to that.

Her gaze shifted to the tip blown asunder by the launching of the sun. It would start healing and eventually close, but for now, it remained open, radiating every drop of heat that Mount Ablast had absorbed during his long sleep. The spacious chamber who'd housed the ball of light lay empty, exposing rare access to the mountain's inner veins.

Vagran opened his wings and rose from the foothills, carrying Asja beyond the rim of the open womb. They peered into the mountain from the edge of the mist who stood hovering over the venting peak. Darkness eyed them in return, softened by the crystal glow fuelled by the heat. The light coming from above touched and revealed only the sides of the womb at the very top.

"There!" Asja pointed to a hole nestled between two crystal veins. She tugged on Vagran's feathers until he lowered her onto the rim, the hole in the wall of the mountain womb lying directly beneath their feet.

She jumped off and opened her knapsack, pulling out a long rope made of wiry metallic fibres of a yucca plant growing by her home. She stood up, scanning for the right spot. Her eyes settled on a short but sturdy ledge jaggedly protruding from the ground. She walked across and wrapped the cord around the base.

"What are you doing?" grumbled Vagran.

"Getting ready to explore the hole. It might lead deeper into the mountain," she replied, tying a tight knot around the jutting crystal to hold the rope in place. Vagran's sparkling eyes and gaping beak made her stop. She got up and walked to her troubled friend.

"This is the mountain, Vagran. I know it! This is the summit from my vision. This is where Ama wants me to go."

A rumbling "How?" was all she got in response.

She peered over the edge of the chasm. "I'll climb down this rope." She picked up the coiling mass and flung it over the edge. The ledge didn't even notice the weight.

"With any luck, it will lead me to the chamber, or one of its connecting passages will. And if none do…" she sighed, but quickly finished before Vagran could object, "I will climb back out the same way I went in. Expect me to return before the mountain closes."

"And if you find it?" the words rumbled with surprising sluggishness, their emphasis not lost on the girl.

"Then… Then… I don't know," she finally admitted.

She stared into the yawning abyss who awaited her, a bend in her life flow, fully aware that she knew nothing about where it led. Even if Ama's vision proved true – and she couldn't conceive of doubting *her* – she had no idea what the wizards would agree to, or what they'd ask of her in return.

She cast her gaze across the chasm to the temperate lands in the north, hidden from sight by the snowy peaks of the Land of Frost. Everyone she knew and cared about lived there – except for Vagran – expecting her to return after her first foray into the wider world. As she, in her naivety, had promised to do.

"Can you wait for me until the mountain closes?" she asked her friend and got a blinked response. "And if I'm not back by then, assume that I've found what I was looking for and leave. Go home. Go look for your people. Go travel the land as we said we would. I'm sorry if I won't be there to do it with you."

She moved past the beak and pressed her body into the soft feathers of Vagran's neck, holding onto him as tightly as she could. Then she strapped the staff and the rucksack onto her back, grabbed the rope that led over the edge, and descended into the mountain.

WIZARD

Asja let go of the rope and swung into the hole. Her feet touched down on smooth stone, slippery from the moisture steaming from the womb. Her hands grabbed onto crystal shards protruding from the floor, bringing her to a momentary halt, before the knapsack slid over her head and somersaulted her onto the ground. She would have slid on had her staff not lodged between the jutting crystals and kept her in place. She lay there quietly, staring at the ceiling, her battered backpack resting uncomfortably beneath her arched back. And then she laughed.

Her laughter echoed down the passage, bouncing off the rocky walls deep within the mountain, as if Mount Ablast himself was snickering at her plan. She dislodged the staff and jumped back up, spooked by the voices in the corridor that only remotely sounded like her own.

Light streamed in from the opening, pointing at the only way out. It stayed open for now, but rumblings in the walls betrayed the healing process already underway. She bade it farewell before turning her sights to the slippery path.

Only now did she truly face it for the first time. A dark, narrow tunnel not much taller than a dwarf. She stood there, staring at the gloom, her staff hand starting to tremble, the darkness ahead keeping her in place. Until her eyes adjusted to the lack of light, and she saw the crystals who marked the way ahead. A winding, descending path stretched out beyond them, leading to the wizard chamber, she quietly hoped.

And only now did she fully process the words Ama had spoken: *They may be willing to help you.*

May be? Who were these people if Ama herself couldn't ensure their aid? And if the goddess held so little sway over them, enjoying her favour was no assurance of success. Or even safety. Asja had never seen Ama in this light, and she wasn't ready to start now.

She swallowed her unease with dark, cramped spaces, and set out deeper into the mountain. Her hand reached tentatively in the subdued light, the smoothness of the stone demanding respect. She weighed each step, placing her feet against the jutting crystals. Her staff served as a walking stick, getting caught in the crystalline clefts when they rested too far away for her feet to reach.

Her clothes grew sweaty in the oppressive heat. The warmth drawn from the depths poured out of every vent. No breeze blew to shuffle it away. In truth, a mountain never slumbered, not even a frosty one. It was a story that denizens of the Frost Lands told themselves to excuse their own lethargy during the coldest periods of the cycle of ice.

The tunnel took a downward turn. The gentle slope that led away from the mountain's crest became a steep gradient that tested her alpine skills. She turned around and faced the floor, using both hands and feet to find any leverage she could. The progress was slow, rest hard to come by.

The walls reverberated from another beat of the mountain's heart. She held onto the protrusions in the wall, not wanting to move until they'd calmed down. She heard the water slushing in the open space of the chamber, and imagined a new seed starting to form in the place of the old.

The passage led to a tunnel fork that split three ways. The crossing vein headed up, towards the mountainside. Her smooth walls had been washed by water and steam during their escape from the depths, but not enough water remained to reach these heights this long after the discharge. Asja stared at the parched waterway with renewed concern over where her own narrow tunnel might lead. But no watery hands moulded the sharp edges of the jagged crystals who assaulted her from every side.

A water bag came out to quench Asja's thirst, a long carob pod filled with crunchy seeds to satiate her hunger. She sat quietly in the dim light who saturated the tunnel, her hands and feet savouring the respite. She'd lost sense of the passage of time, locked as she was deep within the earth. She thought she had plenty of time before the mountaintop closed again, but she feared that it was her hope speaking rather than common sense.

The next junction in the path was harder to negotiate. The tunnel split into two, with both branches vying for attention. The rising one tempted her away from the wetness and the heat that oozed from the mountain. The descending one clothed herself with colourful crystals whose subtly pulsating glow rivalled the most mysterious caverns from Peruvius Mountains she had dared enter as a child.

One gem in particular piqued her interest – an opening in the wall where globules of turquoise crystal poured out through the parted stone. He looked no different from other gems gracing the passageway, but his aura did not match that of the mountain. Like an alien jewel placed there and made to blend in by the use of magic who could only be told apart by those skilled in it. To Asja, he stuck out like a sore thumb, his emanations exceeding those of the most potent runestones from Obalin's study.

Was the gem placed there to show the way through the maze of tunnels deep within the mountain? To detect any intruders who might be lurking there? To keep the passages free of water whose periodic upsurge would otherwise fill them? She set out towards him, her heart beating faster from the possibilities.

The next junction had one too, a darker azurite jewel bubbling beneath the surface of transparent stone. As did the one after. Asja could tell that a junction lay ahead from the emanations of the crystals embedded within the walls. She followed them with growing excitement, barely pausing to rest, when she sensed a pair of gems beyond the end of sight, guarding an opening where no vein crossed their path. She moved through the passage as quickly as her sore feet would carry her, stopping at the aperture between the radiant jewels to gaze into the chamber beyond.

A spacious cavern sprawled out, her sides curving and stretching as if someone had pushed the tunnel walls as far apart as they would go, creating ample space in which to dwell. Geodes of all shapes and sizes pushed through the rock to assert themselves within the space of the cave, revealing gemstones of rare beauty through the cracks in their skin, and supplying what little light the cavern was able to have.

A dark light shone from a distant corner with an otherworldly quality Asja couldn't quite place. He illuminated nothing, yet showed her the shadows of the geodes who had gathered there. *Was this a way out?* she wondered in passing.

At the other end, leaning against the wall, sat a compact figure wrapped in a flowing fabric the colour of aging garnet. His closed eyes rested above long, deep scars that lined both sides of his face. The head remained bare of cover, made of grey stone with two thick obsidian bulges protruding through the top. His gravelly hands rested on his knees, the only other parts of his body not hidden by the cloak.

The wizard from my vision! Asja's breathing quickened.

She stepped forward, eager and frightened, and made her way into the cave. The basalt floor reacted to her footsteps more excitedly than the vein, amplifying their sound until they echoed through the gloomy space.

The wizard's eyes shot open, radiating a pale bronze glow. Asja's breath caught in her throat. She watched surprise fill his face, as if he couldn't fathom what another person was doing in his cave, hidden as it was deep inside the earth. She stood motionless, locked in a stare with the mysterious stranger she knew nothing about, hoping more fervently than ever that her vision of him really did come from Ama.

The wizard's eyes widened. "A mur!?" he growled, his voice replete with scorn, loathing and grime. He rose from his spot, eyes narrowing until only wide slits of gleaming amber could be seen. The scars on his face came to life, fed by a lava furnace that ignited behind them. His hands grew sizzling red, the tips of his fingers barely restraining the heat.

Asja the child had seen angry magi drain rune stones of their essence and unleash it with no regard for the mayhem they may cause, but never had she seen a mage absorb magical power until his body glowed from its intensity and every skin pore ached for its release. She scanned the cavern in search of shelter before leaping behind the closest geode protruding from the ground.

He disintegrated a moment later as a blistering bolt of lightning shattered the rigid rock. "I'm no Rangorr!" fumed the wizard behind her, cloaking himself with crackling air and sweltering heat. Asja rose from the flakes of crumbling stone and scurried to the next protrusion deeper inside the cave. A burst of flame engulfed the dust behind her, scorching a path to the cave wall and burning an ashen stain in the unyielding ore.

The cave suddenly came alight, as if the ceiling had ruptured open, exposing her content to the skylights above. Asja glanced at the cave entrance and the open ground littered with crystal fragments that led there. The other end still lay shrouded in darkness, mineral columns protruding from the floor, hiding the mysterious dark light behind their broad forms. She couldn't see where the opening led; out of the mountain, she fervently hoped.

The crystal column collapsed over her, showering her with fractured fragments of crystal and stone ripped asunder by a thunderous crash. Overcome with panic, she bolted and ran, leaping over the smouldering rubble, dodging the pretentious geodes as she encountered them, a rumble of granite hooves following close behind. She sidestepped the unbroken rocks, the source of the dark light almost within her grasp.

A rasping beam cut through a corner of her travel bag and punctured a hole in her belly, spinning her around and shoving her back-first into a ceiling overhang. The clatter of crystal mixed with splintering bone drew a tortured scream from her lips. She slid off and fell, back-first on top of the rubble, knocking the air out of her lungs and muffling her scream. She rolled over and lay on her side, her body still, blood seeping from her open wound.

The hoofbeats neared, slowing as they approached. She strained to crawl away, but her legs would not respond. Her teeth clenched, grimacing with pain, she put all her strength into her lower arm, dragging her injured body across the warm floor, her passage marked with a trail of blood that stained the rocky ground.

The wizard came to rest.

He towered over her, standing quietly, watching her struggle. She stopped, her strength drained, and looked up at his disfigured face.

"You are no witch," the wizard spoke. "Who are you?"

Asja opened her mouth to speak, but only blood came. She coughed it out to make space for words.

"I was born... in exile... to mur outcasts... in the land of dwarves."

The wizard cocked his head, his eyes narrowing as he stared at her. "Fugitives from the war," he whispered to himself. "Why are you pretending to be a dwarf?"

"I am... not."

"You look like one."

"Ama, she... she turned me... into a dwarf... so... so that they raise me... as their own." The prolonged speech led to a fitful cough.

"Ama..." he repeated the name before interrupting himself with another thought. "Who sent you here?"

"She did... to train... as a wizard."

Warmth drained from the wizard's face. His eyes widened scanning her broken frame. Then he held his head in his hands and yelled with all his strength, "Damn fool! What have I done?"

He stormed away, clenching his fists and yelling in fury. The furnace beneath his skin erupted in an angry blaze. As his rage subsided, so did the flame, leaving a look of contrition and despair on his face. He lifted his hand, whispered "Wait here," and faded back into the darkness of the cave.

Asja slumped back and closed her eyes to rest. It took too much effort to keep her eyelids up. But an eerie feeling washed over her that pried them open again. A dark figure stood facing her where the wizard had just been. She couldn't tell whether he merely basked in the gloom of the cave or had brought with him darkness of his own. He held no definite shape, but an emptiness that felt insatiable, as if it could suck all life out of the world and be left hungering for more.

She had never seen Death, but if this was him, he looked the part.

Drained of energy, she accepted his presence, having no strength left to fight him for her life. His shadowy form enveloped her. The cave blurred before her eyes. A veil started to lift as her grip on reality slipped.

In a flash it was gone, the energetic forms of a couple of wizards materialising before her in the space of the cave.

She closed her eyes again and gave in to her fate.

FELINE

Priya tugged on a long dandelion stalk. The stem resisted her small hand with uncommon tenacity before breaking clean, making the girl stagger back with the yellow prize in her hand. She stood up and added the flower to a modest bouquet of chamomile and lavender she had picked on her morning stroll. Then she skipped through the blooming meadow to the next standalone blossom who caught her eye.

A door on a nearby log house creaked open. Voices rumbled through the morning air, the people yawning and slow from sleep. Smoke poured from the open square, carried across the stream by the playful wind. A distant sun rose through the sky, lifting the dusk with a lighter shade of tan.

The village was starting to come alive.

"Priya?" Sena's anxious voice sounded through the hamlet. "Priya!"

The girl spun around and looked towards the cabins. She smiled at her mother from far in the field and waved her bouquet of flowers high over her head. She stopped in confusion when her mother's arms started to flail and a piercing scream escaped from her lips. And then she lost sight of the village, her eyes filled with the open sky as powerful jaws pierced her chest and neck, before the feline carried her little body through the swaying blossoms, her handpicked flowers lying scattered across the ground.

Sena raced through the village, stumbling from house to house, her wretched screaming sounding ahead. She latched onto people as she encountered them, her daughter's name pouring from her lips, but try as they may, they could not get her to explain the source of her anguish.

Until the strong hands of a seasoned hunter held her in place, his eyes willing her to gather herself and speak.

"Feline... a feline... has Priya!"

Torrel swallowed hard. He stared down Sena's path, at the open field beyond the houses and the dense forest clouding the horizon. Then he turned to a hunter by his side and spat out the command.

"Eric, take the young lads and hunt the feline down."

"How many?" Eric was already putting on his boots.

"All of them."

The young hunter stopped what he was doing, his brow furrowed, his mouth hanging open.

"I will stay here with the other elders, to defend our homes if the felines attack."

Eric swallowed and nodded, grabbing a bow to strap across his back. Others dispersed to their houses, half-dressed as they were from the morning rush. They emerged moments later, spears, bows and arrows in hand, converging by the fire in the middle of the square to take pieces of dried meat to sustain them on the hunt.

Torrel grabbed Eric by his shoulder. "Stay together. We don't know if this feline came alone."

Eric nodded, a look of steely determination etched on his face. Then he turned and ran into the field, twenty young lads following close behind.

Torrel watched them blend into the grass, the villagers' stares firmly on their backs. Even Sena looked up to see them depart, her face wet from the flowing tears, her body still convulsing with the hollow sobs.

Torrel's gaze met the others' who, like him, had stayed behind, their hunting days firmly behind them. They were too old to keep up with the hunters trekking across the steppes, but their arms still had the strength to jab a spear into the feline hide. They took their weapons and headed to the outskirts, ready to defend the village, watching the riverbank and the sprawling field should more felines be lurking in the grass.

Torrel's thoughts wandered to the first time he'd faced the cats when he was still young. His hunter troop had galloped after a giant feline who'd been pestering them throughout the day. They lost him in the dense brush, only to return and find their caravan ravaged by others of his kind.

These were no dumb animals living merely for their next kill, but cunning adversaries unwilling to share the plains with the human kind. Priya was the third villager to fall to them this cycle. They came after the horses the cycle before that. The hunting suffered. Trips to the forest became rare. People started to rely on whatever food they could grow by the village and fish out of the stream.

Torrel could only hope the hunters would track down the feline, find her lair, and kill them all. To make their land safe again.

ALGALASH

Asja opened her eyes. An intense stream of light shone through the window above her bed, taking her breath away and making her wonder just how close the skylight was. She'd never seen light so bright. The beam outlined a drooping circle on the far wall, but enough light spilled over to illuminate the whole room.

She stared at the scarlet walls, not recognising them at all.

Where the hell am I?

She sat up. A stabbing pain in her side distracted her from the place. She removed the bedcover to expose sealed flesh, covering an area on the left side of her tummy that felt light and looked hollow. There was no hole, only scar tissue that rose and fell in a circular pattern. She touched it, provoking a sharp pain and a rippling change of hue.

Memories came flooding back — of an encounter with a mysterious wizard, a desperate flight, a mortal wound, and her life draining from her onto the floor of the cave. She remembered staring Death in the face, then closing her eyes to rest.

"It's healing well," a voice filled the room.

Asja spun around to look at the door, where a woman now stood.

Her emerald dress made of interwoven leaves reached all the way to the floor. Burgundy petals graced her face, wide open and fluttering.

"Welcome to our home."

She entered the room, the long-leafed dress obscuring her graceful movements, giving her walk a semblance of floating. The supple stem that emerged from her dress carried itself with nobility and grace, reminding Asja of the giant ferns by her home when they moved to the tune of the wind, though there was an eeriness to her motion that she couldn't quite place.

Asja had never seen a plant move so freely.

The plant settled down on a simple stool resting against the wall, a comfortable distance from the nervous girl.

"My name is Florella." The petals danced to the tune of her voice, lending it their smooth, velvety texture.

The name barely registered as Asja stared at the plant in her room.

"Oh", she sighed, suddenly conscious of her staring. "Um… I'm Asja."

"I treated your wound," Florella remarked, her face angling towards the girl.

Asja drew away and leaned into the wall.

Florella stopped at the edge of the bed, letting her leaves rest on the bedcover. Her head drooped. Her petals ceased their flutter.

"How are you feeling?"

"Better," Asja replied, remembering the floor of the cave, thinking that was the end.

Florella ran her leaves along the side of the bed, pressing into the fabric stretching across it. It momentarily changed colour, tracking the motion of the leaves.

Intrigued, Asja grabbed a handful of the fabric on her side. It flowed freely across her hand, softening and brightening as it moved. When she let go, it solidified to wrap her body in lush comfort, softening again when she wanted to move, but hardening beneath the pliable surface to give her solid support.

"It's made of basalt," remarked Florella.

Asja stared at the cover, wondering how hard stone could be made to forget his nature in response to mere touch.

"It's the handiwork of wizard Seolar," Florella continued. "He treasured flexibility – flowing with life in a state of peaceful acceptance, yet being prepared to turn into unyielding stone should the circumstances demand it."

Asja pressed her hand into the bedcover. It readily gave way, the way she had never seen stone do. She ran her fingers across the fabric, a squeal of delight escaping her lips. Until she saw leaves close to her hand, reminding her of the company she kept and the circumstances of her being there. She pulled back. Her smile faded.

"He really messed you up, didn't he?" Florella remarked.

"Who is he?"

As if in response, the stone wizard with deep scars across his face entered the room. *Was he just standing there, waiting for an opportunity to come in?* The look of contrition on his face certainly suggested that. It was at odds with the piercing sound of granite hooves treading on the floor, stirring the memory of their earlier encounter and the failed flight for her life.

He crouched next to Florella's short stool, his rocky limbs apparently comfortable in the cramped posture.

"I'm Shar. And you have no idea how relieved I am to see you alive."

Asja nodded. She was relieved to see his scars dull grey, with no fire sizzling behind them. The memory of his body filling up with energy to be unleashed upon her was too frightening to relive, no matter how much he may have regretted his actions now. His skin still radiated a faint glow, making her wonder whether he was always on a lookout for danger.

"Where am I?" she finally asked, eying the unfamiliar place.

"This is Algalash, our home. Algalash is a tree who grows from the centre of Amana and has an incredible view of the land," Florella explained. "I'll take you to see it when you're feeling better."

"Thank you," Asja responded politely, too apprehensive to appreciate the offer.

"Why don't you tell us more about yourself?" offered Shar. "You said that Ama has sent you to us to train as a wizard?"

Asja nodded.

"Why?"

Asja's gaze wandered around the room. "I'm not sure," she finally admitted. "She said that she needs my help, or will someday, but I don't know when or why, or what I could possibly do that she can't do herself." Frustration seeped into her voice despite her efforts to hide it.

Florella and Shar exchanged knowing glances but spoke no words, further feeding the girl's distrust.

"Is this what you want?" asked Shar.

"I would do anything to help her," Asja replied without hesitation.

"To be a wizard, I mean," said Shar.

Her confidence evaporated. Obalin's refusal to teach her came to mind. The flash that pushed Vagran off the ledge fed her doubts.

She'd been fascinated by the work of dwarf mages for as long as she could remember. They did things that no one else could, important things that made a real difference in the lives of the mountainfolk. There was no household, she was sure, without at least one item that their hands had touched, enhanced in some way through their mastery of the runes.

But it was her encounter with Centane that solidified her yearning. As much as she feared her own power, she feared the witch's more. Ama was right. The only way she could help protect her adoptive people was by developing her potential, the potential that the mages themselves had forsaken out of fear.

"Yes," she said with conviction. "I want to learn. I want to know what you know." She stopped there, unable to bring herself to say that she wanted to learn from *them*.

"Perhaps even more?" teased Florella, her petals engaging in a lively dance.

"And you want this just to help Ama?" pressed Shar. "You have no other reason?"

Asja lowered her eyes under his probing gaze. She didn't like thinking about it. It was a question she had found difficult to face, to be honest about, even to herself. But in those rare moments when she did, she let herself be excited by the power she harboured, tantalised by what wonders it might accomplish, longed to see it unleashed for all to see. And she hated herself for keeping it ashamedly hidden.

"There's this... power... inside of me. It's exhilarating! ... and dangerous. But I want to use it... I want to master it, and to wield it..." the words strained out of her, as if she had to fight herself to get them out, her face betraying her vision before she caught herself and hid it, "...so that I can help protect my people."

Shar's cold face contorted into a smirk that remained visible for a mere moment before melting back into the stone. The nod of acknowledgement that followed was much more pronounced, as was his concern for their visitor. "You are getting tired. You should rest. We'll talk again soon."

Florella agreed. "Sleep is your best friend now."

She lifted a leaf to touch Asja's hand, but stopped when she saw the girl pull back. "Perhaps next time," she flexed nervously as she got up to leave, following the stone wizard to the entrance of the room.

"Florella?" Asja called out after her. "Who is Rangorr? Shar shouted his name when he first saw me in the cave."

"Rangorr? He was our apprentice. Much like you, he came to us wanting to learn. He never finished his training. He's been captured by morlocks and is being held by them."

"Morlocks?"

"Mur magicians who rule their people. Like dwarf runemages, but more influential and far more dangerous."

Her petals flexed in dissonant motion before she turned around and walked out of the room.

Asja watched her leave. The spookily swaying stem. The gracefully flowing leaves. Suddenly, the sight of the plant body lost focus. Asja blinked and rubbed her eyes, trying to regain her vision. An inner sense rose within her to supplant her sight, feeling the plant the way her eyes could not, peering through the leaves into what dwelled beneath.

Under the surface splendour of Florella's form resided a dull pain and the accompanying grief.

EXPLORERS

Zuri moaned from exertion as she hiked up the hillside, dismayed by the mass of forest undergrowth that made a safe path difficult to find. Thorns garnished nearby trees with surprising fervour, sheltering their branches from unwanted touch, giving her no choice but to lean on her staff for protection and support.

She stood up and sighed. Elf druids hardly ever came here. She did only because a stone druid she'd met the previous day encouraged her to. A druid who'd made a deep impression on her. If he really was a druid. He said that he wasn't from around here, but Zuri had never heard of a horned stone druid living in any of the elf lands. He didn't even mention his name.

A couple more steps and she reached the top of the ridge.

The Green Lagoon spread out before her. A carpet of trees covered the land all the way to the beach. Trees of all shapes and sizes, exotic shrubs whom Zuri had never seen, as if the ridge acted like a barrier that the thorns couldn't cross.

She cast her gaze east, along the long coastline towards the city of Ucradin, where the dense elven woods gave way to a rainforest whose moisture nourished the mur people living within her span. They were a people she knew little about, save that they kept to themselves and rarely ventured beyond their coastal home.

She bounded down the slope to the sea, revelling in the freedom of merrily striding through the forest without having to watch her step. Low waves washed over the sand, cheerfully frolicking in the safety of the bay. Two wooded rocky outcrops boldly protruded into the surf, proclaiming their dominance over the sea and protecting the cove from the water's wrath.

And sure enough, there they were. Just like the stone druid said they'd be.

All the trees by the waterline arched towards the sea. The closest ones stretched out over the water as far as they could reach. The trees away from the beach bowed too, more subtly – as if some invisible force drew them to the water – and they were only able to resist the call by the strength of their roots who kept them in place.

Zuri walked up to a small solitary tree at the rocky end of the beach. His roots meandered through cracks in the stone to delve deeply into the sand. As soon as he emerged from the shelter of the stones, his trunk curved and bent ocean-way. He straightened and then dipped, as if striving to grow towards the sea rather than the sky. His bushy crown followed the trunk's lead, trying to touch the water like a parched pilgrim desperate for a drink.

She ran her fingers across the coarse bark. *It's the tree's armour*, the druid had said. It protects him from the elements, and keeps his feelings hidden from prying eyes. She continued her study of the trunk until she found a patch bare of bark. She placed her hand on the naked flesh, closed her eyes, and tried to perceive the tree's inner life.

Like the other trees before him, this one's emotions were a mystery to her. The stone druid had muttered something about her not being treelike enough to understand. But there was one sensation she did recognise – so passionate, so powerful that it flowed from the exposed wood to seep into her outstretched hand.

She overflowed with longing. She felt restless, wanting to move. Not just shuffle in place and change posture, as trees usually did, but really move – cover vast distances at great speed. There was so much pent-up energy that Zuri thought she would burst.

She jumped back. A gasp escaped her lips. She looked at the tree again – a sorry sight of a wood with a gnarled trunk and a sagging crown. Never in her wildest dreams would she have seen an explorer in him.

She looked at the water beyond the pointy crown, stepping behind him to face the same way, staring at the sea and the horizon above. And for the first time, she saw them both with the tree's eyes.

The water's hum called out to her. The breaking waves tugged at her feet. She craved the warm wetness, yearned to immerse herself in that endless expanse of rhythmic motion. To see what new marvels lay just beyond the horizon. To feel the ocean carry her to lands unknown. To overcome the obstacles and weather the storms who made every new discovery worth her while.

A creaking wood snapped her out of her daydream. Roots sunk deeply into the rocky ground. Roots who gave him life by keeping him in place.

And she understood. The crooked figure standing before her may have had the heart of an explorer, but the rest of his body was nothing more than a tree.

AMANA

Asja sat quietly on a stone bench by one of the many windows that surrounded the hall. Their enormous size consumed most of the space, giving the outside wall a honeycomb look. Still, little light entered from this part of the sky. The twilight suited her pensive mood, letting her just be with her thoughts, even in the communal space of the stately hall.

She still couldn't quite believe that Algalash was a tree. His crystal ornaments and stone walls would have felt right at home in any dwarven house. And the sheer spaciousness of his rooms was a sight to behold. He harboured many levels, she'd been told. Still nursing her injury, she was in no hurry to explore them all.

"I also like watching the sky when he's quiet and dark," Florella's voice disturbed the tranquil scene.

Asja spun around, not expecting company. After the departure of Dimotai – a visiting wizard and Shar's former mentor – she grew comfortable sitting alone in the empty hall.

"Yes. I love the patterns that the lights draw in the night sky. They are so much bigger here." Her voice hushed, full of wonder, she returned her gaze to the flickering scene.

She heard movement behind her as Florella walked to the outside door. "Come. Take a closer look."

Asja rose to follow, leaning on her staff to ease the discomfort from the wound. She walked onto a spacious terrace with a commanding view of the sky. A broad branch carried the ledge, stretching straight out into open air before beginning a modest climb, moss and ferns sprouting from the rock and giving the tree his distinctive shamrock sheen. Above them, a sea of crystalline leaves glistened in the dusk, reminding Asja of the sparkling adornments of Mount Ablast from the Land of Frost.

Asja watched Florella's petal face slowly tilt up to take in the full splendour of the night sky. She followed the cue and found herself face-to-face with throbbing forms that shone through the gaps in Algalash's leaves, complementing the sparkling crystals of his sprawling crown.

Light ridges traced spherical shapes spiralling in on themselves, their pulsating patterns causing them to ebb and flow in cyclical motion. Others puffed themselves up to enormous size, crowding out the figures in their midst before imploding and vanishing from view. Still others assembled into root-like structures, flowing from their dull sprigs into brighter joints that grew more intense with each new junction until they formed colourful lines that streaked wildly across the dark sky.

"What lights are those?" whispered Asja, never having witnessed such a vibrant exhibition from the night sky.

"They come from another world. We call her Isura."

"Another world?" A twinge of panic crept into her voice. "I thought we were still in Amana?"

"We are," the plant's petals danced in soothing motion. "Let me show you."

She walked to the edge of the terrace, away from the bulging branch who blocked the view. Asja followed, peering over the rim at the sweeping landscape. A sheer drop greeted her, ending with roots dug into Mount Midgus – the central summit of the Tetran Massif, the ancient progenitor of all of Amana. The spent mount bathed in the moisture from Sed Deep – a sea filled from the Primordial Ocean who'd found a home upon the Tetran Massif. A whisper of Thunder Falls reached into the sky, the steaming falls bounding the central range and clothing him in mist. And beyond them, a whole world sprawled out before her, stretching out as far as the eye could see.

Florella stared at Asja expectantly, as if looking for recognition in her wandering gaze. Eventually, the plant lifted one of her leaves, pointed at a distant peak, and asked, "Do you see that light rising above the open mountaintop?"

"Yes."

"That is Mount Aorai."

His identity revealed, Asja remembered the imposing crest, his renowned flat top smashed open and plastered across the mountainside. She'd only been there once before – as a child seeking apprenticeship to a willing mage – yet the distinctive presence of the Ural's highest peak had made an indelible impression on the young girl.

The skylight bathed the surrounding crests with intense radiance, blasting the Urals out of the withering shadows and rousing their residents into activities of the day. More tempered light touched the solitary figure of Mount Croms to the south. Beyond him, stirring from the darkness, lay the familiar outline of the dull grey slopes of Mount Edars.

Tears rolled down Asja's cheeks at the sight of her home. The bare summit not hardy enough to hold on to his skin, having to grow it anew after each violent burst. The clear lake by his side, an eager recipient of the mountain's gush. The rolling hills who lay at his feet and clothed themselves with the ground he had lost. And a house of stone nestled between two rusty boulders who had come to rest on a grassy knoll.

She'd seen them before from the vantage point of the sky, held up by Vagran's feathers to the tune of his heart. Now she saw them from memory rather than sight, puny as they looked from Algalash's heights. A fatalistic quality imbued her home peak that blended into the faded contours of the land. Unimportant. Indistinct. She would not return after her first foray into the wider world. She knew that now.

Forests, deserts, rivers and plains crowded out the memory of her home, vying for the attention of the rising sun. They were the lands from her childhood stories she had heard about but never seen. The dense forests who sheltered the elves past the mountains' western side. The open plains who sustained the humans living beyond them. And the menacing sands to the east who threatened to consume all who ventured therein save for the wily goblins and their desert ilk.

She cast her gaze on the flowing dunes who saturated the landscape beyond River Rust, watching them fade as they retreated from Mount Aorai's glare. But instead of being swallowed by the thickening dusk, they dimmed and brightened again, basking in the light of another sun. A sun launched by a foreign range who lit up the mountain with the colour of gold.

Asja rushed to a narrow ledge at the edge of the branch, her discomfort forgotten in the excitement of the scene. A whole new mountain range rose before her eyes, with peaks and skylights all of his own. A massif of bare sand and fiery rock – with little water to feed the parched canals – sending a blistering wind to whip up the barrens on both sides of the bluff.

Breathing heavily, her heart pounding in her chest, she continued the brisk walk along the tree's edge. Mountain ranges rose and fell, with forests and plains, jungles and swamps, deserts and lakes nestled between them, and glistening skylights of water and crystal illuminating them for her to see. By the time she returned to her starting spot, she'd counted six mountain spans, with spacious lowlands stretching between them, all flowing into the darkening ocean at the end of her view.

She no longer saw Amana as just a land, but a living creature whose six-pronged spine dug into the depths of Aia to support the lands between while they cruised leisurely across the Primordial Sea. She looked at Florella again and was stunned by the knowledge the wizards possessed by the mere virtue of where they lived.

"Where are you from?"

Florella's stem swayed in response. "I was born a generation ago in the land of mur."

"A mur?"

"No. I merely lived in their home when I was young. Just as Shar lived among the elves but is not an elf himself. And other wizards, many of whom you have yet to meet."

"Are you all from Amana?" she asked, stealing a glance at the lights above them that came from another world.

"Some of us are. We grew up here but are no longer bound to this one world. We go where the journey takes us."

"So Algalash is not really your home?"

"It is… One of many."

Asja stared at the plant whose fragmented face swayed back and forth with the elegant motion of her petals. She couldn't compare Florella and Shar to dwarf mages and their runes, so beyond the dwarves was the wizard world. For the first time since coming here, there was no doubt in her mind that she wanted to be a part of it, partake in the immense knowledge and power that it offered. And she was beginning to get an inkling of why Ama herself might value having them train a wizard who was to be in her service.

"I want you to teach me," she blurted out. "I want to be a wizard like you."

PRIMOGENUS

"This is the rift," remarked Shar, pointing to a secluded and shadowy corner of the cave.

Asja glanced at the place in passing, her mind still stuck on the broken crystal and shattered stone that littered the floor behind her. Charred walls and fractured geodes served as a reminder of her first encounter with him, as did the stained ground where she'd nearly met her end. She had agreed to learn from him now, but try as she might, she couldn't stop dwelling on what had transpired here.

"Asja?"

She snapped out of reliving her ordeal to focus on the rift ahead. A gateway to a new dimension, a self-contained space shared with no one else, where she could experiment and learn at her own pace. A plane tucked away in the southern reaches of the Land of Frost, the youngest region of Amana, the land here not yet sure who she wished to be, letting her energy feed an equally hesitant plane.

The tranquil surface made no attempt to hide the darkness that lay beyond. The rift appeared to be made *from* darkness, letting the dark reach out from the plane and touch the interior of the cave, pretending to illuminate the space with its own ghostly presence.

Asja stood facing it, her legs unwilling to move any closer. She reached out with an unsteady hand and touched the placid surface. Her fingertips felt no sensation, as if the place she was going to retreated before her, trying to make room for her by its own absence. She took a small step, then stopped and turned around, seeking reassurance from the wizard.

"I'll be right behind you." The warm words softened the cold expression of his face.

She took a deep breath and stepped into the rift.

The conduit yawned and sucked her out of the cave. Swooshing sound. Flight through the dark. A sudden stop followed by silence.

Darkness surrounded her. Nothing moved. No smell, no sound. She strained her senses to catch a glimpse of anything that would emerge from the Void. Nothing did.

She reached out to touch something. Her hand brushed only against empty space. She turned, tried again. Only then did she realise that she wasn't resting on solid ground. Her feet flailed through space with nothing to support them.

"What is this place?" her voice rose.

"Primogenus," Shar's voice came from behind her.

She turned around, unplaced by hearing the plane's name repeated again. Her eyes strained to see the wizard in the pitch black of nothingness. Even his customary faint glow was absent here.

"I can't see you."

"I know."

"Why did you bring me here?" another question ended with an uncharacteristically high pitch.

"You want to become a wizard, Asja. This is where you begin."

"You didn't say there'd be nothing here!"

He quietly chuckled. "There is something here. All around you."

"What? I can't see it."

"The darkness, Asja."

She responded with a frustrated sigh. "You are making fun of me."

"It is funny in a way, but no, that is not why I've brought you here."

"What am I supposed to do with darkness, Shar?"

"Anything you wish."

She felt Shar's probing eyes on her in the darkness ahead. It all seemed a game to him, the plane having brought out the lighter side of him she didn't often see. She turned around and faced the emptiness again, feeling his enigmatic presence and the weight of his expectations bearing down on her, but not knowing what to do.

"Darkness is potential, Asja," his voice drew closer. "Nothing exists in darkness, so anything could be. And here, in Primogenus, that potential is limitless."

"How do I tap into it?"

"You need to grow used to the company of the Void. Hear her. Let her seep into your bones. Settle into her rhythm, for the Void has a life and a voice of her own that you will have to discover on your path to wizardry."

She shook her head. "I don't hear anything, Shar."

"It is not a sound for your ears to catch. The melody is subtle, a primal resonance of the very fabric from whom the world is made. Your body will feel it when you free it from the burden that it's always carrying."

"Burden?"

"All of your thoughts. All of your senses. Why do you think we've come here, to this place of vacant solitude?"

She nodded reflexively, closed her eyes, and let her body sag in tense idleness. She could hear the racing of her heartbeat despite her efforts to subdue it. She tried to quell the fretful thoughts that raged in her mind, but they wouldn't leave her side. As she banished one, another would come. Anxious thoughts that wouldn't let her forget that she was in an unfamiliar plane whose fabric she couldn't see, in the company of a stranger who tried to kill her the last time they were here. She started to tremble.

A moment later, Shar's hands were on her shoulders. *Is he trying to calm me down?* His invisible presence only fuelled her angst. Her breathing quickened. An involuntary twitch of her shoulders shook his hands off.

"Asja…"

"Get me out of here," she asked with all the control she could muster.

"What's wrong?"

"I'm terrified!"

"There is nothing here. You said so yourself."

"I know… But the darkness… The quiet… There's nothing to hold on to… No way to tell where I am… Or what might be lurking…"

"Lurking?"

"I can't stay here, Shar! I'm sorry, I just can't."

She felt Shar's hands on her shoulders again. She instantly shoved them aside, her frenzied breathing filling the strained silence. A long moment later, light appeared behind the wizard, an outline of an opening that led into a dusky den. It traced the wizard standing between her and her escape, and an outstretched arm he'd extended to her. She grabbed onto his hand and let him pull her back into the familiar space of the mountain cave.

Florella stood in the hallway as she watched the stone wizard and his young apprentice return from their short trip to the mountain of frost. Her smile faded when Asja walked past her without so much as a glance, her eyes wet with tears. She gave Shar a probing gaze.

"How did it go?"

"It didn't," was all he had to say.

SHIP

Fire crackled beneath a copper pot. The fickle flames kept the green brew at a slow simmer. Small bubbles punctured the surface and popped with a crack, splattering the concoction across the pot walls. Leaves and bark of several different trees and shrubs crowded in the stew. Zuri stirred it carefully, keeping a close eye on the thickness of the broth.

She stood up and examined the tree again. He'd grown tremendously since she found him. The druidic enchantments she'd used on him had had a pronounced effect. His trunk, branches and roots had swollen to twice their normal girth, making the tree look oddly out of proportion. She was familiar with it; druids often used their magic on the largest forest dwellers to turn them into spacious living homes for the elf folk.

Even the tree's inner life was starting to seem sane. Not all of it – she doubted she'd ever fully grasp what it was like to be a tree – but after spending nearly a whole cycle in his company, she'd attuned herself to the finer emotions coursing through the wood.

The tree's yearning for adventure was unmistakeable. She'd spotted it early on, not needing to know anything about him to feel this desire pouring from his flesh. Now the more subtle feelings started coming to the fore. His curiosity to discover what lay beyond the water's edge. The wonder awakened whenever a bird landed on his branch or the wind rustled his leaves. The restlessness that found no release being rooted in one place. She couldn't imagine what it must have been like to harbour such fierce passions with no way to set them free.

Her body still tingled from the memory of the first time she'd conveyed her intentions through her outstretched hand – to help him become a real explorer. Not merely crawl through the lagoon over the span of a lifetime, but really travel. She wasn't certain that she could do it, but the mere possibility was enough to cause a wave of gratitude to wash over her in response, and sap to gush from every trunk pore.

She checked on the brew again. It stuck to the spoon as she swung it through the pot. It was ready. She took it off the fire and set it down by the base of the tree. Then she took out the spoon and proceeded to draw a thin wide circle around the base of the trunk where he branched out into his many roots.

As soon as the circle was complete, she moved on along the trunk to draw the next one. And then another, and another, following the curvature of the tree all the way down to the first sea-seeking branch. There, she took a different tack. She reserved the paste only for their joints. She didn't get very far before the brew ran out. She touched the side of the pot and smiled. It was still warm.

The first circle seeped into the wood, leaving a slight hollow where the bark used to be. The heat of the infusion helped it permeate the timber. It flushed moisture out in a semblance of fever, one that Zuri expected to wear off as it cooled. She didn't know whether it would work, or how long it would need to take effect. The horned stone druid didn't say.

She heard a sound at the base of the tree. She peered closer. The bark by the bottom ring stirred and creaked softly. The trunk rose a little, accompanied by a prolonged screech. The canopy leaves shook each time the branches shuddered. The trunk continued to rise, haphazardly but tenaciously, leveraging the joints formed by the hollow rings, until the whole tree stood upright in front of her, reaching his full height for the first time in his life.

She gasped. She could barely believe the effects of her own concoction. She had still half-doubted the druid's promises, but now that their result was standing before her, flexing his branches in the stillness of the day, a feeling of elation washed over her. She did it! She still had to finish infusing the rest of the branch joints, and it would probably be best if she did the same to the roots. Twigs might need some attention too, so that they could flex their leaves in the water yet form firm sails before the wind. But she did it!

Her gaze wandered across the beach and further inland. Scores of arched trees stood there, facing the sea; from little ones – like her new friend – to wooden giants who looked down on the water from a dizzying height. Trees with enormous trunks, broad branches, expansive leaves. Trees who could prowl the seas the way elf fishermen couldn't even conceive.

The sense of accomplishment spurred her imagination until it overflowed. The hollow trunk could use an opening through which to load cargo that the ship would carry, one with a door that could be securely shut to keep the water out. He needed a space where passengers would sit. Perhaps some vines who could hold them in place when a storm hit. An observation spot atop the uppermost root, or – better yet – on the highest branch just above the leaf-sails.

The possibilities seemed endless.

But first she had to keep her promise to the short, gnarled tree standing before her. She grabbed the copper pot and headed back into the forest. She needed more infusion to finish her first ship.

CHANGE OF TACK

Asja emerged from the portal. She never looked up. Eyes glued to the floor, she hurried out of the room. Shar watched her leave. Her posture was deflated, her cheeks wet with tears.

Florella appeared a moment later. She stared directly at Shar, her facial petals drooping.

"Let me guess," started Shar. "It went as well as the last time?"

Florella sighed in response. "It started off well. She was composed. I was right by her side. But the longer we stayed, the more anxious she became. I would calm her down, reassure her, but not for long. As soon as she started relaxing and taking the place in again, she would have another onset of panic. In the end, I didn't know what to do."

"You know, at first, I thought it was me. Walking through that cave to reach the planar rift must have dredged up that nasty memory. But if she's reacting the same way with you…"

Florella nodded. "I don't think it's the plane either. Primogenus might take some getting used to, but there's nothing there that could possibly hurt her. Unlike some other places she'll have to visit…" The plant shuddered.

Shar agreed. "It's a problem she'll have to overcome, or her training will go nowhere."

"You know, honestly, I've had much higher expectations of a mur's ability with magic!"

"She may be mur, but she was raised by dwarves. They clearly never showed her what she's capable of. I doubt they even knew."

Florella sighed. "I guess I'll have to draw it out of her then."

"What are you going to do?"

"The same thing Balazaar did with Erbrus."

Shar paused as he recalled the apprenticeship of the dwarf. "Leave the planes for now and focus on developing her imagination and her ability to concentrate?"

"Aha. Once she can stay in darkness by herself without falling into a panic, we can send her to Primogenus again."

Shar shook his head. "I don't think we have the time."

"What do you mean?"

"It's something I've been pondering ever since Asja came here. It was no accident that she found me inside that cave. She was sent there...."

"...by Ama?"

"That's what she said."

"I doubt she knows what really happened or why," Florella mused. "I grew up among the mur, remember? They often evoked Ama's name to explain all sorts of things they didn't understand."

"Like making them look like dwarves?"

"Hmm..." she paused, having no good explanation for the mystery. "Where are you going with this, Shar?"

"What if Ama really is guiding her? What if she changed Asja's appearance to that of a dwarf so that she could be raised by them, and has told her about the cave in the frost mountain where she could find me so that we could train her?"

"You know that Ama would never do that. She'd never send one of her children to us to train."

Shar shook his head. "Not in the past, no."

"Not then and not now. Why would she..."

"Because she's awakening!" He couldn't contain himself anymore. "Just like Lesea did two eons ago. And Atia before her."

"Those worlds awoke long before my time."

Shar nodded. "The point is that she must be trying to awaken if she is seeking our help. And she could not have sent us a better student than an exiled mur."

Florella stood quietly for a while, her pensive petals rubbing against her head.

"That is why we cannot treat her like just another apprentice," continued Shar. "There is far too much at stake. A major conflict is looming, not to mention the growing power of mur morlocks...."

"Who have Rangorr," Florella reminded him.

"Right. When the time comes, Asja will have to face them. She'll have to if she's to keep Ama's dream alive. And it's up to us to make her as ready as she can be."

"What do you have in mind, Shar?"

"I'll take her aside for a few days and prepare her for combat. Just… basics," he clarified when Florella's leaves erupted in response. "She will need the skills… in the Underworld."

UNDERWORLD

Asja stood and squinted, trying to make out the shapes ahead. Her eyes had not yet adjusted to the dense twilight of the plane. The large objects appeared close but were too indistinct to be told apart. She took another step, and then another, attempting to fathom this hauntingly familiar place. And then a gust of wind blew, the objects swayed in an eerie dance, and a gloomy memory rushed at her and held her in its grip.

It was the Iron Forest from the foothills of Mount Edars.

The wood grew at the very edge of the space she called home. A forest she had stumbled upon twice as a child, but never dared enter. What the wood was doing inside the Underworld Plane, she did not know.

She looked behind her. The faint outline of the rift could still be seen in the dying light of the plateau. It was her lifeline, an escape door from this strange, foreboding place. She had not ventured all that far from it. The steps she made took surprisingly long for their number.

She gripped her staff for reassurance. She has come to depend on it in the short time it had been with her. She'd always suspected that it could augment her skills somehow, but it was Shar who really opened her eyes to what it could do. The force that coursed through it stood ready to be unleashed on a target of her choosing. She sincerely hoped she wouldn't have to use it, and if she did, that it would be enough.

She closed her eyes and took a deep breath. Then she opened them wide, gritted her teeth, and set out into the wood.

The rocky floor gave way to a metallic one, low bushes and shrubs grew into commanding trees, the shadows of twilight melted into the darkness of the wood. Asja tripped on a root but held onto her staff to keep from falling. She would have to tread even more carefully now that she couldn't easily see the ground on whom she walked.

The hollow iron thumps of her footsteps echoed through the forest, the only sound she could hear. The forest stood dead quiet and still, except for a sporadic gust of wind who swayed the tips of the tallest trees. The metallic foliage assaulted her nostrils with their alien smell. She knew she did not belong.

Branches from the nearby trees swooped down like tentacles towards her path, jagged limbs of old iron giants, covered with lichen and half eaten by rust. Copper creepers wrapped themselves around the sturdy trunks before engulfing the branches and sprigs in their suffocating grip. Tree canopies rattled into clanging sounds whenever they rubbed against one another, spurred on by the menacing wind.

A sinister sound of scraping metal sounded from the dark. Asja stared in its direction, straining to make out the source. She thought she saw a tree crown sway but felt no breeze. Another screech, from a different side, followed by spooky calm. She stepped back, dropping her staff, the clanking sound breaking the silence as it hit the ground.

She bent down to pick it up when a pair of eyes flashed through the bushes at the periphery of her vision. She gasped, her head spun, but only blackness occupied the space. Another set of eyes, brighter this time, flared to her right. She started retreating, her feet cautiously feeling the ground, unsure of what she was seeing. If there were more noises coming from the forest, she couldn't hear them from her own heavy breathing and the pounding of her heart.

Two eyes transfixed on her in the space ahead. A deep slow growl came from the shrubs. The hair on her skin stood on end. The white of the eyes turned bloodshot red. She clutched her staff, ready to bolt. Then the growling stopped, the eyes narrowed, and Asja bolted and ran for all she was worth.

Her head pounded. Her heart throbbed from the strain. She half-leapt with each step, desperate to avoid any obstacles in her path. She glanced back to get a glimpse of the danger that followed. More eyes materialised in the space behind.

With a bound, she left the enclosed blackness of the forest. Shrieking grew behind her, like claws scraping on a metal skin. The contour of the rift came into view. The shimmering fissure shone like a beacon of hope in the glum darkness of the plane. She headed straight for it. Metal screeching gave way to scratching against stone. It drew closer. She leapt at the aperture. A shadowy form surged towards her, catching her foot, before the turbulent space of the rift swallowed her whole.

The fissure spat her out onto the barely lit floor. Shar stood there, waiting for her return. He pulled her up and embraced her with the intensity she had not seen from him before. She clung onto him in return, grateful to be seeing him again at all.

"I made it!" she exclaimed once she'd gathered herself enough to speak. "I went into the forest, and I escaped before they could catch me!"

She winced as she put weight on her left leg. She looked down at her torn boot. The heel had a gaping hole that was dripping blood. Shar took it off and briefly examined her foot. "You should see Florella about this."

Then he held her by the shoulders and stared at her with seriousness that made her uneasy. "It is good that you were able to escape, but that was not why you went there. Those... horrors... that you saw... You have to go back, and you have to face them."

RALLY THE TROOPS

Liam sat on the back of Swig, a sturdy horse and a trusted friend, the sole survivor of feline raids from the cycles past. His quick reflexes and superb speed had saved them from more than one scrape on their travels across the plains. But now Liam was content to let him amble towards the line of grey smoke rising ahead, his mind mired in the recent events.

He was there – as a member of a hunting party following a feline trail far across the plains – when the mysterious stranger approached them. They had never seen a creature like that before – tall and thin with a gaunt face, her scaled body draped in a robe, her soothing eyes the colour of deep ocean. She said that she had watched their feud for a long time, the human settlements sprouting across the plains, and the feline attacks on them growing more desperate and deadly. She said that her people might be able to help.

Her people. Mur, she called them. He had never heard of them before. They must have kept to themselves along the eastern coastline, beyond the thick jungle at the grassland's end.

He remembered Torrel's face fill with disbelief when they brought him the news, unable to imagine an end to the threat that he'd spent a lifetime fighting. Still, as the village elder, he saw potential here that he couldn't ignore. All the residents gathered to deliberate her offer. Some questioned what the stranger could do. Others doubted that felines would let them be. But so tired and weary were they of losing family and friends that they agreed to let the stranger intercede.

Runners went out to nearby hamlets. Riders on horseback went out from there. Seven elders assembled in the end, Torrel and six others to speak for the humans of the Great Plain. They headed out to Panoramic Plateau, to be there by the end of the cycle, as the oceanic stranger had asked of them. Not part of the delegation, Liam followed from afar, keeping his presence secret until the scene of their meeting.

He hid in the woods at the end of the plateau and watched the events unfold. The stranger welcomed them, as did others of her kind; all tall, scaly creatures adept at living on land, though they looked like they had come from the sea. He saw the humans welcomed, saw them exchange words – a reprieve from endless hostilities that plagued them in this land.

Until seven felines appeared on the plateau.

Their backs rose at the sight of humans, their teeth bared, their claws free. The humans crouched and gripped their spears, anticipating an attack, surprised by the ambush but intent on making them pay. But the strangers stayed true to their word and stepped in to keep the foes apart.

Animated conversation ensued, punctuated by the shouting of men and the growling of beasts. From his hiding place at the edge of the woods, Liam couldn't hear what was being said, but he could see the strangers trying to intercede between Torrel's people and the wild cats. As the day wore on, he saw the strain of toiling on the feud start to wear them down.

Would the strangers abandon their attempt?

They formed a double line between the two camps, one facing the humans and the other the beasts.

What happened next, Liam had trouble recalling, as his mind grappled with the outlandish memory.

The strangers pointed their staves at the assembled guests, drawing the human and the feline together. Bones cracked, limbs twisted, bodies contorted beyond their skill to bear, fused into a single form, part-human and part-feline, a four-legged lamia with legs and body of a cat but arms and torso of a man.

He felt ill at the sheer memory of the people he knew being warped into such freaks. The sight of their tortured faces made him tremble with disgust. He rode out of there as quickly as he could, Swig sensing his distress and galloping for all he was worth.

The magic-wielding scene stayed imprinted in his mind. He had never seen magic used before. He'd only heard of it from visitors – from dwarf and elf lands. His hunting weapons felt useless next to what he'd seen it do.

His people had grown so obsessed with countering the feline threat, and so secure in the knowledge that friendly elves dwelled in the western woods, that they'd neglected to explore what lurked in the eastern forests beyond their lands. A danger far greater than that of the cats, he now knew.

Swig picked up his pace.

The village that sent the campfire smoke came into view. Liam straightened up in the saddle, setting the terror from his memory aside. Bardown hamlet would soon be upon him. He had to spread the news as far as he could. The mur magic might be powerful, but if enough human hunters gathered with speed, they might catch them by surprise and overwhelm them with numbers.

Or so he hoped.

FACE THE HORRORS

No twilight over bare highland waited for Asja this time. The Underworld's planar rift opened directly into the wood. She gathered herself quickly, grabbed her staff and headed for the nearest tree. There she sat quietly, legs outstretched, and closed her eyes.

Her feet bathed in a subdued glow. It gradually grew dimmer until it vanished from sight. The tingling sensation remained, drawing a cautious, relieved smile. She stood up and stomped against the metal floor; it yielded no sound. She jumped, with no clatter, only heavy breathing and the pounding of her heart. She gripped her staff and headed deeper into the forest, hopeful that her stealthy movements would keep the horrors at bay.

Her eye caught an impressively large tree, his crown too high for her sight to catch the tip. Yet it was the thickness of his trunk that really set him apart. A gaping hole yawned in his side, a breach large enough for her to fit through. She couldn't see where it led, only that it burrowed into the ground a short distance away.

A hiding spot in a forest full of horrors could save her life. She could pounce upon them at a time of her choosing. She stepped forward, but froze in midstride, the darkness between the roots staring back at her. Her heart pounded. The staff trembled in her hand. Then she steadied herself, breathed in deeply, and stepped into the den.

A jagged passage received her with haphazardly shaped ridges jutting from the floor. She slipped on one, the stale dampness stealing her grip, but regained it on the thickening rust. She tackled the descent one ridge at a time, until she found herself standing at an entrance to a cave beneath the giant tree.

A spacious cavern welcomed her, except for the low ceiling, overhangs from which she had to duck to avoid. No plants she knew adorned the damp walls, though she saw morass grace the rounded corners close to the hole. She studied the niches carefully, fearful of secluded spots and whom they might hide.

She peered into the open space. None of the surface light filtered underground. Only minerals who lined the cavern walls supplied illumination of any kind. They arranged themselves into layers of varying thickness and texture – from dusky obsidian to pallid alabaster – whose meagre emanations barely let the interior be seen.

Three columns passed through the centre of the cave, resembling the tree roots who stood guard at the doorway – thick metallic vines who pierced the emptiness of the chamber and embedded themselves into the sturdy floor to anchor and nourish the tree.

Asja stepped forward to touch the closest one when she spotted movement in the dark recesses of the cave. She plastered herself against the column. Her breathing stopped. Her staff stood rigidly in her tight grip. Muffled sounds came from the dark. Shuffling steps in the metallic dirt, with no urgency that might have hinted at her having been seen.

She snuck a peek from behind the column.

A shadowy creature stood mere steps away, looking at the floor and blending into the background duskiness of the place. Its frame reached to the ceiling and only fitted thanks to a pronounced hump rising from its back. Numerous tentacle-like appendages protruded from the body, swaying in the air as it turned its head. Pus oozed from the many pores on its face and neck, and slowly dripped onto the cavern floor. The eyes oozed too – a black liquid that dribbled from equally black eyes.

Eyes that suddenly widened when they locked onto her.

It lunged forward. A loud hiss came from its mouth. Asja stepped out from behind the column, staff in hand, pointing shakily at the advancing fiend. It raised both arms with clawed fingers aimed at her throat. A bolt of purple light shot out from the staff. It struck the creature squarely in the chest. A piercing shriek echoed through the cave as the horror slumped to the ground, its lifeless body coming to rest at her trembling feet.

She stood there and stared at the still creature. Its eyes remained open but no longer fixated on her. It lay in its own secretions that flowed freely from the open chest. Its menacing arms lay limp, stretched out helplessly away from its frame. And the many appendages that covered its body rested gently on the metal floor.

LAMIA

A lamia sprinted across the field. Her muscular legs pushed against the ground, limbs stretching, hind legs ahead of the front before pressing down again and propelling the creature forward. She tired quickly, stopping to rest, changing direction and moving again, as if torn by indecision but unable to stand still.

The swift motion left the man breathless – the way galloping on a young stallion used to do – reminding him of his early days of travelling across the plains. Many cycles had passed since he'd ridden a horse at speed; he now left the hunting to young lads who had stamina for the task.

He didn't think he'd run like that again, least of all through his own efforts. It felt surreal to be given such power in his old age, to need no weapons with which to hunt, to walk the open grasslands not fearing for his life, as a supreme predator to be feared by others.

Torrel felt the feline's mind in the fibres of the lower body, directing their motion, feeling the same sensations he did, freely sharing them with her human side. He shuddered with disgust. Who knows how many humans this feline has killed? People he knew, who wanted nothing more than to live in peace in the vast freedom of the plains. And even if her jaws had not tasted human flesh, others of her kind ravaged it aplenty.

Torrel retreated to the upper torso, to the familiar arms with fingers he'd relied upon his whole life. Hands a feline had no knowledge of how to use, but wished to learn, her human-like curiosity nearly insatiable. Torrel shut these parts off to the feline mind, as if the intrusion would desecrate what was left of his humanity, the rest having been stolen by the marine conjurors with their diabolical act.

He'd seen much that unnerved him during his long life on the plains, but nothing ate away at him more than being made to live out his last days sharing a body with a creature whose very existence he had come to detest.

DEATHLESS

The planar rift led to the cavern entrance, as if it knew exactly where to deliver Asja to safety. She stepped out and promptly disappeared inside the cave. There she could prepare for exploring other parts of the Iron Forest without having to watch over her shoulder for whatever horrors might be lurking nearby.

She'd been feeling upbeat about her forays into the plane ever since the success of her last visit. It was the first time she had really put her mastery of magic to the test. The first time she had faced real danger, confronted it head on, and emerged unscathed.

Ever since her first exposure to the world of wizards, she'd been torn between a burning desire to soak in this magical world and all that it had to offer, and a fear that it had no room for her at all, that she lacked what it took to earn her place among them. Her failure in Primogenus made it clear just how deficient her mastery of magic really was. She may have been an heir to an illustrious heritage, but all she knew about her birth people was their name.

That changed the day she slew the horror in this cave.

With the horror gone, she stood quietly at the bottom of the steps, closed her eyes, and took a slow, deliberate breath. She wanted to see whether the place felt any different, and smiled at the newfound sense of safety amidst the dangers of the Underworld Plane.

She placed her staff against the nearest pillar before turning to the spot where the horror had been slain. It was bare. Even the secretions no longer stained the floor, as if it had never tasted the wasted corpse.

She bolted in panic. She groped for her staff, but only succeeded at knocking it down. The clanking sound alerted something in the deep recesses of the cave. It shuffled and hissed with increasing venom. A familiar figure entered the light of the wall. The swaying appendages, the oozing pus, the gooey liquid dripping from its eyes.

It looked bigger, though. Its shoulders broader, its hump more pronounced. And the way its clawed hands heaved at her terrified her even more.

Asja jumped back and fumbled for the staff, aiming the charge at the advancing fiend. Its claw gripped the tip of the staff before pulling back in pain, its flesh disfigured by the force of the blast. The second burst ripped its leg apart. It screamed and staggered but did not stop. Asja retreated in terror and aimed at the torso. The shot pushed the horror back but didn't bring it down. She clasped the staff with both hands, desperate to defend herself from the advancing freak. The continuous stream of light that exploded from its tip tore into the monster's flesh, ripping it as it went, until the butchered fiend finally stammered and collapsed lifelessly on top of the girl.

"Shar! Shar!" Asja screamed as she barged from the rift.

Standing right outside, as was his way, he embraced the distraught girl despite the vile secretions dripping from her clothes. Then he held her by the shoulders, ready to hear what she had to say.

"It came back!"

"What came back?"

"The horror I killed. It came back. And it was bigger than before!"

He barely blinked. "Did you kill it again?" he asked as he looked her over, her hair scruffy, her clothes drenched and reeking.

"Yes. But how could it come back?"

He let go of her and shrugged his shoulders. "It's a horror, Asja. Horrors can't be killed."

"What?" Her brow furrowed at his words.

"You can't get rid of horrors by killing them. They'll just keep coming back at you, bigger and stronger than before."

"But… How can that be?"

"Horrors don't live in the Underworld, Asja. They live inside your mind. The plane merely shows them to you, gives them a physical form that you can see. You can't kill them any more than you can kill a part of your psyche. If you want them gone, you'll have to find another way."

She just stared at him with her mouth agape.

"Why didn't you tell me this the last time I killed it? Or before I went in at all?"

"Because you didn't know what you were capable of and would have just cowered before the horrors. Like you did the first time. No, Asja, what you needed was grounding. A dependable skill that you could rely on in a crisis. Now that you have it, you can build on it, perhaps even look to deal with the horrors in a new way."

"So it wasn't about the horrors at all? It was about me?"

"It was about both of you," he reassured her. He stepped away and placed his hand across his mouth as his gaze veered to the floor, before facing her again and asking, "Tell me, this horror that you killed, what did it look like?"

She swallowed hard as she recalled the memory. "It's hard to describe. It was… sickening," she shuddered with disgust.

"Was it alone, or in the company of others?"

"I found it alone in a cave. I think it lived… lives… there."

Shar studied her intensely for a moment before his gaze wandered off into the distance. "Sounds like Pariah."

"Pariah?"

"An outcast among horrors. Even though she's a horror herself, she's not welcome among them. You know, it makes sense that it would be her. From what you've told me about your childhood, she ought to have been among the first horrors you'd find."

Asja's brow furrowed in confusion.

"Never mind," Shar cut the conversation short. "There is something I have to do. Go get some rest. I'll see you again soon."

HOME

Asja opened her eyes. They had grown accustomed to the stone walls that took on the colour of the highest skylights, just as her body had grown fond of the bed of flowing stone. It was the only reason she still chose to sleep inside from time to time, with the spacious branch stretching outside her window offering a spectacular view of the land and the sky.

She sat on the side of the bed, stretched her arms, and yawned.

"Oh, you're awake!" exclaimed Florella as she entered the room.

"I have been for a while. Just too lazy to get out of bed."

"Any plans for the day?"

"I don't know. I haven't thought about it yet." Asja got up and started putting on her day clothes. "I'll see after breakfast."

"How hungry are you?" Florella's petals engaged in a mischievous dance.

Asja looked her over. "Why?"

"Come. I have a surprise for you."

She led Asja through the hallway and into the communal hall. To Asja's surprise, several people were already gathered there. She hadn't seen them the day before. They must have all arrived while she was sleeping. She hesitated, looking to Florella for an explanation. The plant only passed the look on to Shar, who stood with the guests, waiting for Asja to come.

"Thank you for joining us, Asja. I know this is rather sudden, but you have reached an important milestone in your learning, and I wanted us to take the time to commemorate it. Nymess?" he passed the floor to the nearest visitor.

A young wizard stepped forward, not much older than Asja. Exotic bronze patterns snaked across her skin, especially pronounced on her cheeks and forehead, their quirkiness a sharp contrast to the jade eyes that held curiosity and resolve. Her olive hair nestled neatly between long pointy ears and flowed abundantly down her neck and back. Asja was struck by her elvish look despite the alien symbols covering her body.

"I've heard so much about you, Asja," Nymess began, "that I feel close to you even though we've never met. Could be because we're both young and new to the craft," she winked at the older wizards standing by her, "or perhaps because elves and dwarves don't often make the wizard ranks. I never thought I'd see a dwarf here. Only one has ever become a wizard, and with immense effort, I'm told. I'm thrilled to see you following in his footsteps. Who knows, perhaps even I will be of some assistance with your training?"

"Help that's not likely to be needed," interjected the wizard standing beside her before turning to face Asja. "I'm Deudal. I've seen you here once before, while you were still recovering, but we were never introduced."

Her white eyes and silky hair betrayed a greater age, complemented by golden horns flowing from her forehead. The smaller patterns etched in her skin looked softer than Nymess', blending into crimson towards the waist. Her deeper voice sounded more assured, befitting a wizard of some stature.

"You may be following dwarf ways, but we all know that this is not who you really are. I'm not from around here and have never met a mur, but even I have heard great things about your people. You may not have gotten to know them yet, but someday you will, and I would love to learn more about them from you and through you."

Asja bowed her head in acknowledgement. "Shar has told me about you and Nymess. I'm glad to finally meet you, Deudal."

The next guest stepped forward, the first one who held any resemblance to dwarf mages. A flowing amaranth cloak covered his entire body except for the face, its many layers hugging his figure and hiding it at the same time. Colourful gems graced his shoulders, with a more prominent one embedded on the chest. A sturdy staff rested comfortably in his hand, almost as if it were an extension of his arm.

"I'm Kei. I've not been here lately, but I'm a close friend of Shar and Florella. I can't tell you how impressed I am that you'd taken Shar on in a duel before your training had even begun."

"It wasn't much of a duel," sighed Asja, remembering her brush with death in the frost mountain cave.

"Perhaps not, but it must have taken guts to face him at all. I would never have been able to do that at your age."

"Not to mention that you've killed a horror on only your second foray into the Underworld. It had taken me six attempts back in the day. I just kept running away..." the last visitor admitted with a hearty laugh.

"It's good to see you again, Dimotai," Asja replied with a cautious smile.

Though familiar from his prior visit, she couldn't help but stare at his face. Half of it was pale and healthy, yet showing signs of incredible age. The other half seemed to suffer from an onset of decay, as if it had died despite the wizard himself being very much alive. It made Asja wonder how much use of it he still had. When he spoke and laughed, he did favour the healthy side.

He continued, "I'm sorry I've missed your training, but I know that you are in good hands with Florella and Shar. I can't wait to see you grow into the wizard that I know you will someday become."

Asja nodded and smiled. She was getting nervous with all the praise and affection that was being heaped upon her, not knowing what she had done to deserve it.

Dimotai stepped away after his welcome, giving the floor back to Shar. Asja's teacher placed his hands on her shoulders and continued, "You have left the only home you have ever known to undertake an extraordinary journey, with nothing but a mysterious vision to guide you, and your desire to be of service to your people and to Ama. That took tremendous courage. From the first time I met you, I've seen the enormous potential that you harbour inside. You have no idea how surprised and grateful I am that Ama has led you here, or for the role that she has asked us to play in your life.

"I believe I speak for us all when I say that you are one of us, Asja. You belong here. And nothing would delight us more than seeing you make this your new home."

Asja only gaped at him with mouth open wide. It was so unexpected. She looked down and stammered, trying to get the words out but not knowing what to say. It was too much to process.

Florella pressed, "So what do you say, Asja? Will you let this place be your new home? Accept us as your new family?"

Asja had never had a home where she truly belonged, accustomed to drawing comfort from Vagran's companionship. She would have done anything to be accepted into an extended family of people like herself. People who could truly understand her, support her in her growth with knowledge and skill. It never even occurred to her that somebody else would be doing the asking.

She closed her eyes and nodded.

"Then there's only one thing left to do," Florella declared as she took Asja's hand. "Come!"

She led the girl back down the passage to her room, followed by Shar and the wizards. They stopped just outside and faced the entrance.

"Your new home should know that this is your room now. You are not a guest anymore."

She held Asja's left hand. Shar took the right. The other wizards stood behind them and placed their hands on Asja's shoulders. Together, they raised Asja's hands and pointed the palms above the door. A stream of light shot out from each palm. They converged on the overhang above the door and burned Asja's name into the scarlet stone.

"There." Florella appeared satisfied with the result. "Is there anything else that we can do to make this place feel more homely?"

Asja only shook her head. Her words choked in her throat and her eyes overflowed with gratitude.

BISMIAN WOODS

Vagran laid his head on a moss-covered stone and stretched his wings across a meandering stream. The murmur of the brook lulled him to rest. The charge coursing through him slowed to match the pace. Humans paid homage to River Aug in full sweep, but he felt closer to the soul of Amana here, at the source of the great waterway, than amidst the clamour of the plains.

He watched as a leaflet dropped from the fiery crown of a white birch. It carried the fierce complexion of the canopy, its crimson centre tapering to bronze at the edges. It fluttered as it fell, carried away from the tree by a gentle breeze until it landed on the soft surface of the stream. The bottom side hugged the water, propping the dry one to look up at the woods and the sky.

Gnarled branches of an old willow tree drooped to the ground, heavy from delicate white flowers that decorated them all the way to their tips. A solitary flower let go of its stalk, and then another, and another. They touched the water around the scarlet leaf, endowing it with their snowy presence. The whole willow tree swayed in the wind, as if in approval.

An elm tree graced with oval leaves clad in sombre chartreuse tones, an elderly cedar trunk with brittle bark withering away in long amber flakes, a grove of ash trees whose canopies adorned themselves with freckled leaves that faded from rich rouge to lilac and lavender by their tips, all gave of themselves to cover the ground and the passing river. The vibrant blanket contained every colour and texture found in the forest.

The colourful canvas that stretched from one bank to the other looked no different than the chromatic cover garnered by the ground – indistinguishable from the forest the stream flowed through – as if the water and the earth had become one.

The roaming watercourse gave the woodlands life. In return, they clothed her in the florid cloak that lingered long after she'd left her childhood home.

Colourful leaves covered Vagran's body as they came to rest, the trees giving of themselves to him and the stream alike, not caring that he was merely a stranger travelling through the land, making him feel more at home here than he ever had by the mountains of the dwarves.

He didn't need the dwarves to accept him among them when the land herself claimed him as her own.

PARIAH

Asja ran her hand across the cavern wall. The stone felt smoother than she remembered. The jagged protrusions were gone, leaving tender scars in the metal skin. Rusty shades filled the gaps, causing the glowing layers of ore to shine with colours she had not seen in the cave before.

She held her staff at the ready, fully expecting Pariah to come back to life. In the Underworld, keeping her staff at the ready had become second nature. Shar's warning still echoed in her mind – killing horrors was futile; they just returned bigger and more menacing than before. But if Pariah came at her like she had before, she didn't know what else to do but defend herself in any way she could.

She left the entrance and probed deeper into the cave, staying clear of the walls in favour of darker spaces, moving as silently as her magic would let her. Pariah of old would have revealed herself by now. If she was alive again, the new one proved more elusive.

Faint shuffling came from a distant corner of the cave.

Sneaking silently from one root column to the next, Asja followed the sound. She saw the horror leaning onto a distant pillar, the pronounced hump rising from her back, the face hidden from the faint light, the swaying tentacles casting a moving shadow. Instinctively, she pulled her staff closer.

There is more to Pariah than meets the eye, Florella's words came to mind. If she were to find another way of dealing with the horror, she'd have to see what she had missed.

She eased up on the staff and forced herself to take a long, probing look at the hideous creature. She tried to imagine what Pariah's life must have been like. *An outcast among horrors*, as Shar had described her. A creature not wanted even by her own kind.

The rejection struck a personal chord within the girl, not knowing her birth people or belonging with the dwarves, the emptiness having been with her her whole life, filled only recently by the wizard kind.

A soft sobbing sound reached Asja. Pariah wept gently into the tree vein.

Something felt out of place. Pariah looked smaller, her tentacle-like appendages shorter, her hump less pronounced. The more Asja stared, the less horrific Pariah appeared. For the first time, she saw what she had imagined moments earlier – not a monster but an outcast, a creature whom no one wanted, who had no one to call her own.

As Asja studied her, Pariah began to change. The small appendages that had remained were gone. She could clearly make out dwarf-like arms, legs and torso. Lush black hair fell down Pariah's back and covered the little that remained of the hump. Or was she just bending down slightly while looking at the ground?

Asja approached cautiously. The diffuse shadow from the lighting of the wall moved gingerly across the floor. Pariah saw it and looked towards the girl, her face wet with tears, her hazel eyes glistening in the weak cavern light. Asja recognised them from a still reflection in the water of the mountain well by her old home, and with them, the little girl who was standing before her where the horror had just been.

She gasped with shock. She dropped the staff and rushed to the girl, embracing Pariah and holding her tight, fearing that she would lose her if she ever let go. Pariah didn't hug her back. Her pale body stayed cold to the touch. But Asja didn't care.

"You are home, Pariah. You are home with me."

Pariah lifted her arms and held Asja in return. She placed her head on Asja's chest. Warmth started to course through her body, bringing colour to her skin and vigour to her hold. She raised her head and looked at Asja's face. Her body started to fade, becoming translucent from the energy it harboured. Asja watched it in bewilderment, but Pariah only smiled.

"I am home."

With those words, her body grew clear. Her hands sank into Asja, followed by the rest of her. Asja jumped back. She ran her hands down her sides, awestruck by what had just happened, feeling Pariah's presence, grateful to have her back.

Feeling complete.

Then she turned around and walked away, leaving behind an empty cave that was her refuge from a time when she was without a place she could call home.

DID I MISCALCULATE?

Lyra stood on the balcony of the high temple, her unfocused eyes facing the horizon. The last sorceress she sent out had not yet returned with her report, and the earlier news about lamias didn't inspire hope.

She expected the withdrawal. Being fused with one's natural enemy was bound to be traumatic. They'd no doubt need a lengthy period of adjustment. Most of all, Lyra trusted the greatest healer – time.

It shook her to learn that a lamia had plunged down a deep gorge instead. This followed the remains of another one they'd found, killed by human hand and buried in a shallow grave. Lamias were supposed to intercede between humans and felines and bring their warring to an end, which they couldn't do if approaching their former people cost them their lives.

Did she miscalculate? Did she see something in humans that wasn't really there? They were violent, skilled hunters who'd spread their settlements across the feline plains. The only way she saw the feud ending with both species still intact was if they could be made to understand one another, and feel each other's pain as their own.

She cast her gaze at the jungle to the north. Countless trees stood between the coastal towns and the contested steppes.

When she first offered the services of her people to the warring parties, she did so as a neutral observer with no personal stake in their feud. Now she wondered whether she'd inadvertently brought that feud upon her own people.

She winced at the thought.

Perhaps she should have promoted the use of magic among the common mur instead of keeping it hidden as an arcane pursuit of the members of her order. Perhaps they should have studied magic with which to fight instead of concerning themselves with matters of the spirit.

She sighed with worry, wishing her observers would report back again. Her wandering gaze stopped at a young magician standing at the edge of the rainforest by the foot of the temple. His eyes caught hers. A warm smile spread across his face. She smiled back, momentarily unable to hang on to her thoughts of gloom.

She shook her head at the young man's spirits and her inability to deny them.

Satjan.

A new member of her order, the most talented magic-wielder of his generation. Many a seasoned sorceress had voiced her awe at the potential he possessed. She admired his skill, surprisingly well honed for a man of his age, but more than that, it was the strength of his character that truly inspired her – his ability to stand strong under immense pressure and sustain hope in the darkest hour.

She closed her eyes as they shed a tear. Their people might soon need all the resilience he can muster...

CHAOS

A spasmodic crystal rose haphazardly from the stone wall where he'd taken root, vibrant colours flowing excitedly across his fragmented face. He raised the wall with him, giving the space an oddly unbalanced feel. The light wasn't his own, but a lively display of shades and patterns reflected from a planar rift sprawling through the middle of the room.

Asja stood at the entrance to the chamber, facing the dancing gateway.

"Why am I here, Shar?"

Furrows appeared across the wizard's face, rivalling his deeply embedded scars. "Hasn't Florella explained it to you?"

"She tried, but I still don't understand. I thought I was doing well enough in Primogenus."

"Well, you can actually *be* in Primogenus now. That's a huge step. But your creations are very limited, as if made by a dwarf."

She felt the urge to point out that she was a dwarf but thought better of it. She was clearly being held to a higher standard – that of her birth people, whom she'd never met.

"Then show me how to make more advanced ones."

"I will, but exposing you to new creations will never be enough if you are struggling to conceive designs of your own. And before you can do that, you'll have to dismantle the barriers you've erected in your own mind."

"Can't we do that in Primogenus?" she pleaded, favouring the familiar plane now that she'd grown accustomed to it.

"No. Primogenus merely responds to your instructions; it doesn't challenge you with ideas of its own."

"And this plane does?"

"That's what it's for."

Her gaze returned to the chaotic motion of the rift, Shar's words giving it sinister undertones. The churning colours, smells and sounds made such an effort to distinguish themselves from the pitch blackness of Primogenus and Underworld that she became apprehensive at what might be waiting for her on the other side.

"It scares me," she admitted.

The wizard only smiled. He took a few steps towards the turbulent entrance and extended his hand. The lively shapes shone from the rift and danced playfully on the bare slate. Asja moved closer and watched the vivacious forms move haphazardly across his face. As he approached the aperture, the light covered him as if to claim him as his own.

"I can't even tell where the rift boundary is anymore," Asja's sombre tone interrupted the display, memories of the Underworld still haunting her words. "How am I supposed to get out in a hurry?"

Shar shook his head and laughed out loud. The light-heartedness of his voice relaxed her enough to move up alongside him.

"What is this plane?" she asked.

"Chaos." Shar raised his arms, looked up and cried, "Glorious chaos!"

Asja's jaw dropped, her eyes widening at the sight. Having finished his adulation, his face turned into a puzzled frown.

"Why are you still here? Off with you!"

With a practised swing of his arm, he shoved her into the rift.

The churning grabbed her. It tossed her every which way it chose. She had no sense of where she was headed. It felt as if the gateway itself didn't know. With the boundary blurred, she lost her bearings and tumbled through the last leg of the turbulent journey before being spat out of the uninviting womb.

She gathered herself quickly, picking up her staff and holding it at the ready, not knowing what kind of danger awaited her here. She'd expected the place to be unlike the other planes she had seen, but nothing could have prepared her for what transpired right before her eyes.

The very space around her looked alive. It disintegrated into myriad shapes — splotches, beads, droplets and globs, figures with an endless number of sides, contours with no beginning or end. Colourful silhouettes — from red to purple and everything in between. Dots, lines and blobs. They bobbled around, shifting, turning, coming together and breaking apart, effortlessly melding, faster and in more ways than she could fathom.

Some shattered into vivid points of light that attached themselves to distant structures. Some dissolved into a melting pot of textures and colours that immediately gave rise to a whole new set of vibrant creations. Some shapeshifted so much that she couldn't tell where one ended and another began. They frolicked all around her, as if crafting the plane itself. She closed her eyes briefly, overwhelmed by the commotion.

Their odour filled her nostrils. Every scent she knew assaulted her at once. The strongest was that of fire, of a cornucopia of materials smouldering in muted flames. The colourful display did don a crimson hue.

The noises they made were just as varied: screeching, buzzing, hissing, whining, banging and pounding, a profusion of voices of every audible pitch, talking voices without words. If there was a melody in there somewhere, it drowned in the cacophony of sound.

She couldn't tell which form made what sound or had what odour. It was all just a tangled mess of sensations she couldn't put in order no matter how hard she tried. Her head started to hurt from the immense effort. She shut off all her senses as best she could, trying to recover.

Having been scared off by her sudden arrival, unruly fragments now brushed against her on their haphazard journey. They enveloped her in their fluid embrace, scrubbed her clothes and exposed flesh, knocked her body out of their way. She activated the staff, trying to erect a barrier to keep them out. But her magic lacked conviction, producing a diffuse field that offered feeble shelter.

She peered behind her, frantically trying to locate the outline of the rift, but the space looked no different than the chaos of the plane. She turned in all directions, desperately searching for a way out, but she had lost her bearings in the tumultuous frenzy of motion and had no idea where to find it.

She screamed Shar's name. The cry dissolved into unruly chatter. A slapdash mixture brushed against her tongue, taking advantage of her open mouth. She coughed it out, feeling the urge to throw up, disgusted by the ashen taste.

Powerful arms wrapped around her and pulled her through the churning mass that had assaulted her from every side. She couldn't resist them, nor guess their intent. She felt herself sliding backwards through the turmoil, then the jumbled motion of a gateway before colliding with the hard floor of the stone room that housed the rift.

She looked up, still confused but relieved to see the familiar face of the stone wizard watching over her. The laughter in his eyes was gone but a mischievous grin still lingered, as if the plane's assault on his apprentice was nothing he didn't expect or couldn't handle.

PATTERNS

The tip of the staff came to life in a burst of fluorescent light. It assembled into a spacious bubble that formed around Asja. Barely visible at first, it steadily swelled, its membrane thickening as it fed on the energy of the staff. By the time the last rays of light departed from its tip, a formidable barrier shielded the wizard apprentice from the fickleness of the Chaos Plane.

Asja watched the swirling displays of colour that graced the surface of the orb. Unable to penetrate the translucent shell, they coalesced against it to form intricate patterns of mesmerising beauty. They made no more sense to her now than the last time she was there, but being able to observe them from the safety of her cell, without being crowded by their suffocating motion, made them all the easier to admire. She silently thanked Florella for taking the time to prepare her.

Relaxing the grip on her staff, she settled comfortably into her floating space. The protective sphere had a lot of life left in it. She felt safe within its walls, watching and admiring the flowing forms until she lost herself in them, with no sense of the passage of time.

Until the sight of Vagran's outstretched wings shook her from her reverie.

She would have recognised that wavy, symmetrical shape anywhere. It was nothing more than a loose assemblage of chips and scraps that convened in just the right place to allow the familiar form of her friend to emerge. She reached for it, but it melted away into the burbling current before she could touch the protective surface that kept it out of her arms' reach.

Did she really see that? Or were all the shards going about their usual chaotic ways, inviting her to imagine a familiar pattern where there was none? None of the other dancing contours revealed anything lucid. They streamed down their jumbled paths without crafting anything of note.

Or did they? That swirling mass of lines on the other end of her sky formed the outline of what looked suspiciously like a dwarf. Or a diminutive humanoid of some kind. A bleary creature with hazy limbs and a featureless face. It flashed before her eyes for only a moment before subsiding into the ebb and flow of the unremitting plane.

Another cryptic pattern materialised on the surface of the cell. It taunted her with its elusiveness. It flowed across the unruly backdrop and back into itself, the movement conveyed by an ever-changing sequence of colours. She had never seen anything like it, yet felt completely at ease with the mysterious motif as if she had known it since her childhood. She studied it earnestly before it could vanish, but it defied her fears by maintaining a steady presence over the mingling backdrop. She stared at it, enthralled by the motion until, for an infinitesimal moment, it encompassed her entire world.

The panorama shifted instantly.

Structures whose fickle existence frolicked with the random movements of chaos now took on more meaningful tones, even if Asja couldn't recall where she had seen them before. Slapdash motion that had prevented arrangements from asserting themselves for any length of time now took care to create a new pattern for every one it tore down.

An indigo blob became the tailfin of an overweight whale before transforming into a bare-stoned hillside that dwelled in that very same spot. Snaking lines fattened into sinuous vines wrapped around the branches of a sunny tree, swung from a braided head that materialised in the tree's place, and cut a meandering path carrying water across an open plain. Eyebrows spread their entangled branches like a forest bush, and a waterfall poured tears from a glistening eye.

Just as she thought she'd grasped the essence of a scene, it shifted ever so slightly until it could be seen in a completely new way. There was a whole world here waiting to be discovered. Or created. She couldn't tell which.

There was something different about Asja when she returned from the plane. Shar subjected her to his customary gaze. The apprehension and angst that had clouded her face on departure through the rift were nowhere to be seen, erased by sheer amazement upon her return.

AIA

Darkness. Void. A cryptic abode with no dimension and without form. A place beyond time. A world in a state of perpetual creation. The magic of raw potential.

Emotions dwelled here. The Primal Ones. In darkness, but not in silence, for they had music to give them voice.

A high-pitched quiver of anticipation. Pensiveness in her drawn-out thrum. The soothing purr of acceptance of the present state of being and the deafening roar of rage hellbent on something new. The cosmic hum of endless change. The sombre tones of apprehension of what that change might bring. And the stunning crescendo of awe at the creation they beheld.

They, and their music, propelled all change. In a place of pure potential, that change dissipated as quickly as it had come, leaving nothing behind, no trace of its becoming, as it dissolved back into nothingness, too brief to be felt, too fleeting to remember.

Aching for more, the emotions banded together, but instead of yielding a cacophony of discord from manifesting in each other's space, they interwove to fashion a fabric of reality more tangible than their own ethereal being. The fabric amplified the music that gave the Primal Ones expression. And she preserved that expression beyond the mere moment in which it arose.

A fluent fabric of lasting pose comprised of raw emotion.

The Primal Water was born.

She spilled from the Void who could not contain her essence, crafting space and time as she thirstily flowed, twisting and curling and contorting into myriad shapes, shaped by the music who coursed through her being, giving rise to an ever-changing world of fluid form.

Aia.

The universe in her totality, sustained by the vibrancy and warmth of the Primal Ones' chant.

The further from the Void the Primal Water moved, the weaker the whisper of her origin grew, and the more she yearned for a melody of her own. Sky emerged from the sweeping liquid, rising above her with his own distinctive tone. Stone congealed from her tussle with the wind, light and porous on his debut, floating effortlessly on her undulating skin.

The landmasses differentiated further still, birthing crystal and ore within their fold, and elemental beasts of every cloth and kind. Earth arose, and the needy plants rooted in her clasp. And finally, creatures of flesh and bone, the furthest removed from the Primal Ones' fibre yet most fully embodying her unsatiated dreams.

MIRRORDON

Asja stared at her own face reflected in the rift's flowing membrane, its drawn-out ripples betraying the planar wind's whispers from the other side. The scent of sea was palpable. She didn't recognise it – she'd never been to the sea before – but having water saturate her nostrils made Shar's description ring true.

She nervously tried to sustain her smile, to cast the rift in a friendlier light, daunted by the prospect of facing what lay beyond all on her own. Shar promised that Mirrordon was the friendliest plane yet, a place where she could quietly ponder the core questions facing the wizard kind. She drew comfort from his assuring words, even if some anxiety did remain.

The gateway took her to a patch of sand, fine and runny and ginger in colour, determined to stay afloat amidst a sea of blue. She spun around, expecting to see the coast rise behind her, but saw only water encroach upon the sand. Bright light illuminated the islet from high above, causing the water to darken with distance and recede into darkness at the end of her view. The sheer enormity of the sea's presence overwhelmed her. She stood rooted in place, her breathing quickened and heart pounding, waiting to see what the ocean would do.

This must be what Ayanna meant, she remembered the coastal elf's description of the sea by her home on her first visit to the Peruvius Range. Asja didn't understand it at first. To her, mountains had presence by their dominance of the landscape. But there was something awe-inspiring about the sea's ability to move with ease and assert her will upon the land. Ayanna's land was far more extensive than the patch of sand Asja stood on, but her sea also sounded more ferocious in her relentless pounding of the coast even after her fury was spent.

The water around Asja showed no such intent. Her pose was quiet and still, her breeze-induced motion barely visible to the eye. Asja stepped into the shallows, soft sand sinking beneath her feet. The water around her ankles barely moved, as if inviting her to come in and play. She stood there for a while, soaking in the expansive landscape, letting the tranquillity of the scene put her at ease.

The sea will only grow as violent as you make it, Florella's words echoed in her mind. This wasn't a true sea, she remembered, but Primal Waters gathered within the plane for visitors to shape and mould as they wished. Water undifferentiated from her relationship with the land. An elemental substance who could be mastered even by novices like her. Or so the wizards said.

Her anxiety passed, she settled down into the wet sand, letting the water gently caress her hands and legs. It reminded her of excursions to Barnden Lake in the lower reaches of Mount Edars, though the waters there surged more forcefully despite their smaller size. She closed her eyes and listened to the subtle sounds of the sea relaxing all around her.

The water's song was unmistakable. Not a common sound her ears could hear, she felt it viscerally, as if each cell in her body resonated with the tune, celebrating the emotional fabric from whom they were both made. She'd first heard her voice inside Primogenus, from a lively liquid she'd brought forth with Shar's help from the darkness of the plane. The Mirrordon's song was the same, only magnified by the sheer vastness of water present in this place.

She slid deeper into the sea, amplifying the sound, letting the melody envelop her and the water carry her, flutter her body to the tune of the song. The more she relaxed, the more harmonious her motion became until it synchronised with the water completely and the two became one.

A cone of light pressed upon her skin, the rough texture of sand scraped against her bulk. She felt vast, with only a speck of sand and a distant light to measure herself by. And she had no desire to do anything or be anywhere other than here and now, losing herself in the content tranquillity of the watery plane.

She maintained the union for a mere moment. Nor could she exert any influence over the sea's motion – she'd have to remain true to her own melody instead of letting the water overpower her with hers. But in that brief omnipresent moment, she grasped the magnitude of the power that truly accomplished wizards had at their disposal.

It exhilarated and terrified her beyond measure.

SHADOW

Three metallic trunks rose high into the air, clanking against one another in the pushy wind. Asja watched their dance, wrapping their slender stems around each other and unwinding them again to the sounds of screeching iron and scraping rust. They made her uneasy, reminding her that she would never feel at home in this wretched, foreboding place. But the outright fear was gone, replaced by apprehension of what new horrors she might stumble upon and ways she'd have to devise to bring them back home.

She felt assured by the reclaimed resilience and resourcefulness of Pariah. She respected Martyr's commitment to the wellbeing of her adoptive people, even if they were too fearful or foolish to appreciate her gifts. And she could feel the maligned wisdom of the Hag begin to take root in her, disparaged by the mage ways that distrusted what she had to say. While Asja would undoubtedly need time to fully integrate these discarded fragments of herself, and while there was no shortage of unruly horrors left roaming the plane, the influence of the few she'd managed to reclaim was already beginning to tell.

Emboldened by her success, she set her eyes upon the darkest region of the Iron Forest, a place encased in permanent shadow. She had avoided it until now, preferring not to stray too far from the forest edge lest she fall prey to a bloodthirsty horror whom she couldn't tame.

A faint glow bathed the forest from above, too subdued to have come from a Mount Edars skylight. He shone through the metallic crowns to touch the ground with diffuse rays of light, enough to grant each solitary tree his own ghostly form. A thick murky haze hugged the reticent ground, giving her life with her own haunting flow and shrouding the trees in eerie grey mist.

Asja crept in, her senses thwarted, carefully weighing each step, having no sense of the distance covered. She pushed on through the fog until she could see a sparsely filled space emerge in the distance, a region once hidden from her.

A hazy apparition rose from the shadow. Asja couldn't make out his limbs; they appeared to have been made of the gloom itself. He wore a ragged cloak, covered with alien symbols made more exotic by the missing segments swallowed by the holes. His demeanour revealed him to be more than a sorcerer, for he intimidated with his bulk, too. Hard metal and rigid stone encased his broad face, depriving it of feeling. Thick horns protruded from the sides of his head, one curling up and the other down to form a single figure of eight. And white eyes bathed in white fog pierced the shadowy veil that thrived all around him.

He wasn't alone.

Asja saw the dim outlines of other horrors milling about him, bending in deference, cowering at his feet. He towered over them, barely acknowledging their presence with an occasional glance. His touch was heavy, his step callous. And he steered their actions through their knowledge of the torment his diabolic hand could unleash, reinforced by their fear of his willingness to act.

Asja peered into his eyes from her secluded hiding spot deep inside the woods. She knew by now that, as much as she might fear them or be repulsed by them, the horrors who lurked in the Underworld Plane were nothing but discarded shards of her own fragmented mind. But there was no glimmer of recognition in this horror's eyes. They were alien to her, as if he were a hostile presence who'd forced his way into her subconscious from an outside realm.

She stayed near her hiding spot, moving to keep an eye on the tyrannical brute as he drifted through the gloom, desperate to unlock a memory of a childhood event that might have ripped him from her and locked him away in this dark and forbidding place. She remained there even after the monstrous apparition had vanished from view, swallowed by the dusk of the forest she naively thought she had come to know.

"Ah, the good old Tyrant." Shar chuckled after hearing Asja's account. "I was wondering when he was going to show up. I'm not surprised that he's been hiding in the shadow. When I think back to how long you've been shying away from your own power, that must have been the only place where he felt safe."

Felt safe? Asja winced at his choice of words. "What can I do about him?"

The slate of the wizard's face contorted into a frown. "What you've done with all the other horrors – befriend and claim them as your own. Tyrant is no different."

Asja shook her head. "No, Shar, he is different. I've watched him carefully. The way he looks… Carries himself… The way he acts… There's no part of him that I recognise. He can't be me."

"That is the nature of the shadow horrors. You've banished them so far away and so long ago that you can't even remember them anymore. No, Asja, Tyrant is no less a part of you than all the other horrors you've seen."

She retreated into her thoughts in the face of his uncompromising stance. As she watched him leave, she could hear her old doubts resurface.

Just who are these wizards? And what is their agenda with my training?

UCRADIN

A hunting bow stretched, its wiry wood straining from the draw, the string taught and ready for release. It propelled the arrow through the forest air, its feathers fluttering to keep its flight true, past the prolific palms with their drooping branches, through the leaves of shrubs standing in the way, striking its unwary target in the back.

The figure stood erect for a frozen moment, his back arched, his arms flailing about, a strained groan coming from his lips. He dropped to his knees as his strength left him, collapsing over a basket of coconut fruit he'd been gathering only moments before.

A woman screamed at the sight. Others looked up from where they stood, only to see her collapse to the ground in a flurry of projectiles frantic to end her cry.

Their cover broken, the humans emerged as one, wielding hunting weapons as they leapt from the shrubs. Turmoil ensued among the fruit pickers. They dropped their baskets and ran headlong for the safety of the town. The slow and the confused fell to axes and knives, their wasted bodies blocking the attackers' path. Others reached the edge of the woods, screaming danger at the top of their lungs. Their taller frames and longer strides let them leave their pursuers behind, reaching the line of buildings and bursting through the broad archway before the hunters could strike them down. But this entrance to the city was one of many, and it had no door to keep the intruders out.

Lyra stood on the balcony of the high temple, her attention drawn to the commotion below. Her eyes gazed at the wobbling tree crowns. Her heart pounded with the screams of her people. When a human hunter emerged to strike a hobbling mur, she responded to his cry with a cry of her own.

The hunter's eyes veered to the temple. They locked onto her with urgency and fear, warmed by a glimmer of recall that morphed into cold hate. A practised motion readied an arrow that shot towards her to pierce her chest. She fell back from the force of the impact, her back sliding down the hard temple wall, disbelief and despair still lingering on her face.

The humans poured through this entrance and others, spilling into the open spaces of the city of Ucradin, the beautiful jewel of the mur nation nestled by the Coral Sea. The natives fled before them in fear and frenzy. A few tried to resist, with no magic to aid the common folk, only the utensils used to harvest their food. But the tools of the plant-eaters could not withstand the deadly hunting arms. Their flight was cut short by arrows and bolas, their long limbs fell prey to the woodcutters' axes, their slender throats slit by the hunters' knives. Those who ran sought shelter in their homes, behind doors not built to withstand a siege. They caved to heavy blows of a hammer or an axe, and when the attackers came upon oiled torches burning in the square, to the hunger of flames too. Only the long passage to the open harbour offered any hope of escape.

A balcony door swung open. Tarja burst out of the temple. Her eyes frantically scanned the open space before settling onto a still figure resting against the wall with a bloody arrow jutting from her chest. She shrieked in horror. Her hands leapt to her face. She sprung forward, cradling Lyra's face, soiling her hands on her clothes and chest. But the high priestess failed to respond. Her eyes didn't move, only stared blankly into the open space.

Tarja collapsed onto the floor, head buried in Lyra's lap, tears streaming down her face, lost without her mentor and friend. Her despair spent, she got back up, wiping away the blood with a bloodied hand, and headed for the gaping door, concerned again for her own fate.

She ran down the broad passage. A blood-curdling scream rose from the stairway. She ran past it, not turning to see a mur body slide down the stairs with only the tip of a spear protruding from her back, scraping against the stone to slow her descent. Nor did she see the two hunters turn their gaze from their latest kill to where the stairway led, running up the stairs in search of fresh prey.

She stopped at an open doorway and turned to face her pursuers, only to see an arrow swoosh past her cheek and embed itself in the door frame. She gasped at the sound. The hunter swung his fist in rage. The two men resumed their chase, but she didn't wait for them, slipping inside the room and slamming the door shut.

The heavy wooden door would hold them for now, at least until the woodcutters' tools or the torches' flames came to wear it down.

NOT ME

Asja made herself comfortable in the open space beyond the rift. A translucent bubble heaved around her, keeping the turmoil of the plane at bay. The chaos remembered the effectiveness of her shield and didn't press. It entertained her instead with a sequence of paradoxes – sweeping changes to the entire landscape, each more audacious than the one before – completely shifting her perspective of what she was seeing, lest she forget the capricious nature of the place.

She lifted the staff and pointed at the membrane, then hesitated. Sabotaging her own protection was harder than she'd thought, even though she knew it had to be done. Chaos had to touch her to fully manifest its gift. Apparently, a show of force was all that it took to exorcise its childish nonsense and bring its more ingenious, sinister essence to the fore. Or so Shar said, seemingly in awe.

She activated the staff to weaken her shield, then nervously watched the plane respond. The cacophony of forms slowed their motion before changing direction and stopping at the membrane. They all watched a smooth orange sliver seep through the porous surface, then turn to Asja as if to gauge her response. When there was none, the sliver drifted closer, slowing as it approached, coming to touch her outstretched hand. She smiled at its coyness, confident in her ability to dislodge the intruder if the need arose. When its advances triggered no violence or revulsion on her part, it proceeded to wrap itself around her like an oversized cape plastered by the wind.

The whole vista froze in anticipation. The churning paused, shapes stood still, colours kept their place. Then, as if a switch had been flipped, it exploded in a dazzling array of yellow and orange extending all around her as far as the eye could see. She had seen Kalhar Desert sprawl out towards the horizon, but never her naked dunes consume everything before them. Only one rocky hill dared protrude from the sand, with a modest oasis finding shelter against his ample stones, providing nourishment to the tenacious plants foolish enough to make the arid landscape their home.

Scrawny creatures milled like ants about the desert wellspring. They looked short, no taller than dwarves. Their noses barely protruded from their faces, revealing their presence through twin air holes that complemented their equally sunken eyes. The other body parts more than compensated for their absence: mouths extending from one ear to the other, and the ears flapping outwards as if to fly. Even their hands and feet appeared too large for their limbs. Asja had never seen a goblin, but she recognised them from the descriptions that abounded in dwarf tales about the desert folk.

She could discern no purpose to their gathering, no productive activity that would have been pursued by the dwarves. They weren't irrigating the sand beyond the shore of the oasis, or harnessing the power of the crystals who dwelled within the rock, or extending the cave inside the mountain who served as their home. It was as if they saw no need to grow more food or improve their abode, or couldn't conceive of such things and so contented themselves with inconsequential stories and playing games.

A lone hunter armed with a bow departed from the lodge. He carried nothing more than a modest waterskin and a quiver of arrows, far less than Asja had crammed into her rucksack when she left home, even though he crossed deep canyons and sand dunes with nothing to carry him but his own two feet. Simplicity defined his actions, grit and clarity of purpose, even as the heat of the mountains drained the moisture from his body and wind whipped eager sand into his bare back. She couldn't help but snigger on a rare occasion when the arid landscape was awash with rain, seeing him stand beneath the open sky and take it all with no thought of seeking shelter from the intrepid storm.

Asja had never been to the Kalhar Desert, but what the plane showed her dovetailed neatly with the picture derived from goblin tales told by her childhood hearth — of creatures too primitive to tap the extraordinary wealth of the desert mountains, or even to make anything more of the desert herself than what they had found.

She wondered why the plane felt the need to show her this scene.

Her thought triggered a second cloth-like fragment to separate from the host and head for the breach in her protective shell. It stopped before it reached her, morphing into her cloak and staff as seen from the back, and sparking a shuffle in the forms beyond the veil.

They coagulated into a stately hall, the interior of which she'd seen as a child. She saw herself standing in the middle of the space, looking away at runemages and clan leaders assembled before her. The adoration on their faces held her spellbound as she gazed at the scene, a look she'd imagined more times than she could remember but never got to see.

How did the plane know this desire of hers? To join the runemages in their crafting of runes, to employ her talents in the service of her people, to stand before them with her gifts finely honed and have them admire her for her power and skill. She had no knowledge of the workings of the plane, but basked in the warmth of the scene nonetheless, the closest she had come to having her wish come true.

A light breeze blew from behind her, shining the day's light on the assembled dwarves, as if the wall had opened up to expose the interior of the hall to the outside world eager to come in. Goblins entered and sought to join the assembly, soiling the marble floor with their dusty feet, acting as if they had a right to be there, as if their presence ought to be a boon.

Dwarves stared at them with revulsion and menace, gripping their staves and rising from their seats, venting their distress with the pounding of fists. When Asja failed to join them, they stared at her too, their adoration giving way to disillusionment and disbelief.

She watched the plane's rendition of her as she welcomed the goblins into the hall, as the chaos encroached upon the order of the dwarves, as her body started to give off an otherworldly glow. Her figure resembled demons from the dwarf legends and myths, and grew more like them with each passing breath.

She shuddered at the sight, her breathing strained from the distress of the scene.

Had that figure truly been her, she would have sided with the dwarves against the desert raiders and ejected them from the hall without a second thought. That stranger was not her; on that, she was clear.

She closed her eyes and screamed, her staff coming to life to release a second protective bubble in the space of the plane, dislodging the chaos slivers and pushing them away. Her comfort zone shattered, her composure gone, she sought out the colourful rift and stormed from the god-forsaken plane.

She was grateful that the wizards no longer waited for her by the planar rifts. She chose not to see them in the communal hall, preferring the privacy of her own room to quell the turmoil that still raged inside.

Was this where the wizard training led? Was this whom she would turn into if she remained in this place?

She liked it better when the plane was overrun by chaos that struggled to attain utility and meaning. Establishing order to present her with actions that betrayed who she was – and confront her with whom she had no desire to be – really got under her skin.

The questions from her last visit to the Underworld Plane returned to the fore, growing as they fed on her confusion and fear.

She missed Vagran now more than ever. Tears welled up at the thought of how much she'd relied on her friend, trusting him without question. Despite being welcomed into their home, she'd never had such a bond with the wizards, and it slipped further away with each passing day.

DEMONS

Asja cautiously followed the steps, mindful of what she might encounter in these forgotten passageways. A warm glow from her staff dispelled the darkness around her, casting just enough light onto the curving walls to illuminate the stairs between them.

Shar and Florella had never told her about this place. She didn't think to explore for herself until her renewed distrust of the wizards made her wonder what secrets they might be hiding within the tall expanse of their home.

The stairs led beneath the Underworld rift – the lowest level of the Algalash tree she'd been able to find. She stepped into a dark chamber, the light from her staff illuminating the near walls.

She ran her fingers across the carnelian stone. Wavy lines snaked across the surface. She followed their contours – rising and falling and looping back on themselves – exploring the wall as she went, until her sensitive hands caressed protrusions from the stone that defied his natural curves. Her interest piqued, she brought her light to bear.

An unusual face jutted from the wall. The left half was smooth and elegant, beautiful even. The right side descended into a mire of wrinkles and creases, blemishes and blotches, with no pattern that she could see. She stared at the unusual features moulded from the stone, wondering who the person might be.

"His name was Rorzen," Shar broke the silence.

Asja gasped. He stood not two steps from her. She stepped away, wondering how he'd found her. She looked for displeasure on his face and was taken aback by wide-open eyes and a hint of a smile. She relaxed in his familiar presence, turning back to the figure on the wall.

"What is this place?"

"The Wall of Remembrance."

"Remembrance? Is this where you remember your dead?"

"This is where we commemorate their achievements. Sometimes, when life is hard, we come here to remind ourselves of what they've accomplished despite the obstacles in their path. Or because of them."

Asja looked back at the peculiar face protruding from the wall.

"Who was he?"

"A wizard of great renown, the first to unlock the secret of chaos. Before his time, chaos was seen as something to avoid, fear even. His predecessors saw no value in exposing themselves to Aia's haphazard acts. In their day, the function of a wizard was to shield their people from chaos by bringing order to what they could and keeping the rest away.

"He was the first to discover that chaos wasn't random, that there was purpose to it, hard as it was to fathom. He crafted the Chaos Plane in his efforts to study it. His explorations led him to forge a path of balance – walking on the boundary between wizardly order on one hand, and the chaos of Aia on the other. He would stand rooted in the knowledge and traditions of the wizards who came before, but allow the seemingly frivolous events of the world around him to guide him where to go next."

"What if the chaos guided him on a path that went against those traditions?" Asja asked, struggling with the dilemma in her own life.

"That was the point," emphasised Shar, then nodded. "Admittedly, he sometimes struggled to follow the guidance he received. This was an area where one of his students – Inuan – surpassed him."

Asja followed the wizard's eyes to the next face jutting from the wall. Its closed mouth and eyes conveyed serenity, as did its presence within motionless stone. Asja couldn't tell whether the person was sleeping or simply at peace.

"What did she accomplish?"

"She was the first wizard to attain the state of incandescence."

"In-can-descence?" Asja struggled with the word. She noticed now that it was engraved into the wall underneath the sculpture.

"The state of ever-present flame."

"Flame? I don't understand."

"Flame, or fire, is the beginning of change. The burning of the old to make room for the new.

"Inuan had humble origins and understood that the world of wizards was far more extraordinary than anything she would likely encounter in her homeland. She realised that she could never reach her potential as a wizard while clinging to the ways of her people. This drove her to hold those beliefs lightly so that she could release them easily when chaos nudged her to.

"In the end, she held them so lightly that they were always ready to change. Instead of a conflagration others needed, which consumed their identity and caused their world to collapse, a faint flame was all she took to dispose of them. Sometimes she went too far and struggled to act at all, but she forged a path for others to refine. She lived her final days in the state of incandescence. As a wizard, this was her crowning achievement."

Listening to Shar's soft-spoken words, Asja glanced at his stone skin that radiated a faint glow. She remembered the first time she noticed it, in her room while recovering from his attack. She'd attributed it to his wizardly prowess, as his way of always being alert to danger.

"Is this what it looks like?" she asked, pointing to his skin.

He quietly nodded.

She marvelled at the insight, realising again just how little she knew of this world and the wizards in it. Shar didn't linger, but instead moved on to the next stone face.

Asja was struck by the contrast with Inuan's calm demeanour. Wayward lines shot out from both cheeks and the forehead. At first she thought it was unruly hair, until she noticed that it also emerged from where the eyes should have been. The only part of the face she could make out clearly was the mouth, which screamed in silent agony.

"It looks like a horror!"

"A horror?" Shar chuckled. "No, that was Zimr. Zimr the Tormented, as he came to be known. You weren't far off, I suppose."

"What happened to him?"

"He grew deeply troubled in the latter years of his life, eventually succumbing to insanity. He was an accomplished wizard, make no mistake. Particularly concerned with the affairs of the mind. Some say that's what drove him to madness – he'd unearthed parts of his psyche he couldn't handle. I don't know whether there's any truth to that. I think he was just ahead of his time and didn't understand what he was dealing with to do it safely, or had the support he needed to help him recover."

"Why is he on this wall? The plaque just says *Underworld.*"

"He created the plane."

"Oh…"

"It cost him his life. He may not have known how to grapple with his own horrors, but he certainly made it easier for everyone else to contend with theirs. You know, it amazes me how someone whose own life was filled with so much anguish was still able to ease the lives of others, even complete strangers."

Asja shuddered thinking about him. If his horrors had been anything like hers, she understood how they could push his sanity to the brink. It made her even more reluctant to have anything to do with her own shadow, despite what Shar and Florella urged her to do.

"And this?" she pointed to the next face, adorned with a long bushy beard, but otherwise an ordinary-looking fellow relative to the company he kept.

"That was Erbrus — the first and only dwarf ever to have become a wizard. Many of us thought that it couldn't be done, that a dwarf's life was too short for a leap of such scale. He accomplished it through sheer perseverance. Honestly, I believe he achieved the impossible."

"Erbrus," Asja repeated the name. She'd heard it before. She probed her mind, trying to remember, when a memory suddenly grabbed her and transported her to a hearth fire at uncle Tamn's home where she had spent many evenings as a child. She closed her eyes, letting the memory fully recreate the storytelling setting from her childhood.

She recalled the deep lines of uncle Tamn's face dance in the shadows of the evening fire as he recounted the sombre details of one of the more recent dwarf tales.

In those days, Erbrus from the foothills of Mount Croms was deemed the most promising of the young dwarf mages. Despite his youth, his renown had already spread from his village and the surrounding countryside all the way to Varnam, the largest town on Mount Croms' eastern slopes. Such was the demand for his services that he spent as much time in the town as at his home, covering the winding route between them on foot.

During one of those journeys, he was walking through Gnarled Woods when the great fireball from Mount Croms passed his zenith, leaving only the distant Mount Furmis one to illuminate the forest sky. Darkness set in quickly. Demon Balazaar, who had been following the mage for some time, saw his opportunity and appeared in his path. Startled, the mage gripped his crystal staff in defence, seeing no way out without a fight.

"Easy, mage," Balazaar raised his arm in a placating gesture. "I didn't come here to fight."

"Why are you here, demon?"

"My name is Balazaar. Erbrus, I presume?"

The mage didn't answer, eying the demon intently. Balazaar continued regardless.

"I've been following your work. Very impressive... for a dwarf."

Erbrus' face remained expressionless.

"You are really talented. Your skills are already on par with those of runemages, even if they'd never admit it. And you seem to have an intense desire to help your people. You wouldn't be here on this forest path right now if you didn't."

"What do you want?" Erbrus cut him off.

Balazaar smiled. *"What if I told you that it is your self-imposed restrictions that are holding you back? That it is the old mage traditions that are preventing you from fully developing your skills? The remedies, the foresight, the sheer power of magic that you have cried out for all those times are possible, if you are willing to look in the right places."*

"How did you know..." Erbrus started to wonder before arresting this train of thought lest he expose a weakness for the demon to exploit. Balazaar only smiled gleefully.

"You are lying, demon!"

"Am I now?"

"You will say anything to get me to follow you!"

"I don't need a follower, mage. But if all those cries for help have meant anything to you, you will seek me out. Because you know that my skills greatly surpass yours, and remaining ignorant out of fear or pride is a foolish thing to do."

The demon vanished from sight, leaving Erbrus to digest the encounter in the dark solitude of the woods.

"Did he take Balazaar's advice?" Asja asked the first time she heard the story told.

"You'd think he would know better than that!" Tamn quipped. *"Unfortunately, he didn't refuse the offer. He didn't accept it either, but*

140

indecision was all the demon needed. Erbrus continued his work, but as his frustration with his own limitations grew, so did his interest in Balazaar's offer. Eventually, he couldn't take it anymore and sought the demon out. He tried to dictate the terms of their engagement in a foolish hope to protect himself from Balazaar's influence. Erbrus would decide what to learn; he could stop at any time. The demon didn't mind. He knew that, once he had the mage's interest, there was no going back."

And so it was that Erbrus apprenticed himself to Balazaar in the ways of magic. He kept it hidden from the other dwarves. They didn't know that their illustrious young mage was slowly falling under demonic influence. But the influence was changing the way he practised magic, and that he couldn't hide.

He abandoned proven mage practices one by one. He started uttering unintelligible new words and performing strange new rituals. His advice began contradicting revered dwarf traditions. His appearance started changing, too, with his skin sometimes bursting in otherworldly glow. But the most troubling were the changes to his moral stance – he had increasing difficulty distinguishing right from wrong.

Concerned and fearful, people demanded an explanation. It didn't take much for him to admit to consorting with demons. He even defended it! So corrupted was he that he encouraged others to follow. Seeing what he had become, they had no choice but to banish him. They drove him from his home and his village. He took his belongings – they didn't want them – and left the Mount Croms lands.

For a while, rumours of his return ran through the countryside. A person who knew him would hear his voice or see him appear in private. Some said that he became a demon. Others heard him beg to be allowed to return. This continued for many cycles, but the rumours eventually died out as well. He hadn't been seen or heard from ever since.

Asja snapped back to the darkened chamber where Erbrus' eyes stared back at her from his likeness on the wall. *Is this where he ended up? Is this where he mastered wizardry, with these people who are my teachers now?*

With supreme effort, she turned her head to look at Shar again. She saw him now the way she never had before. The glowing skin that would erupt in a fiery blaze. The short horns that rose from his head that she mistook for innocuous shards of rock. The affection for darkness and shying away from the light. The fondness of the Underworld – Tyrant most of all. The lauding of chaos that he felt so at home with. They all made sense now. Her teacher was not some eminent wizard whom runemages would look up to. He was a demon.

As she stared at him in terror and disbelief, his body lost focus, blurring before her eyes. An inner sense swelled within her, peering through Shar's stone skin, sensing the emptiness that dwelled beneath. The desolation and hollowness she knew would swallow her if she remained there.

"Judging by your look, you must be familiar with the legend?" His cold words fed her rising dread. "The Fall of Erbrus, I believe it is called?"

She only stared at him with an ashen look on her face.

"Except it wasn't a fall at all," he continued, "but a rise greater than any I have ever seen."

She heard him speak, but his words made no impression. "I don't believe you." She shook her head vehemently.

If she knew anything about demons, it was that she couldn't trust a word they said. The only safe way to deal with them was to avoid them. She took a step back, helping him blend into the darkness of the room.

"I expect nothing less, given your upbringing. You know, that's why we didn't tell you who we were."

"You deceived me!"

"No more than Ama did," he quipped.

Asja jolted at the remark. She didn't want to cede the demon any ground but had no ready reply. She just stood there in tense confusion.

"You clearly need time alone." He stepped back; all she could see was the faint glow of his skin. "When you want to talk to us again, you know where to find us."

With those words, he retreated to the stairway and left the room. Asja remained in the chamber alone, too shaken to move, too distraught to respond, staring at the empty space long after he was gone.

PRIMORDIAL

Vagran opened his eyes, suddenly awake. Something felt out of place. He looked around the grassy coastline in the low light of a distant sun. Solitary trees stood in their spot overlooking the cliff edge, as if nothing untoward was taking place, though he could feel the excitement coursing through the wood beneath their calm pose.

A low rumble came from the ground.

Vagran's stony ledge trembled in response. The lightning bird scrambled into the air, unaccustomed to solid stone straining beneath his weight, though no stranger to the roaring of mountains from the land of dwarves.

This stretch of coast lived far from any mountain range. She knew little of the summits' labour to give birth to their skylights. And yet, the elves' fears started to ring true, Vagran having overheard their words in the dead of night. Fears of the wildness of the land whom they wished to be docile, keeping them away from this patch of coast.

Vagran peered over the cliff edge at the flexing sea, her waves breaking against the coastal rocks, as if the ocean sensed the land's unease and responded in kind. He turned around to gaze inland. Smoke rose from a meandering fault line, clouding his view, separating this part of headland from the rest of the shore.

His eyes arced with alarm. Charge coursed through his erect plumes. As much as he relished the wildness of the land – a free spirit kindred to his own – he knew all too well how dangerous it could be to have her fervour released unchecked. Still, he chose to stay, sensing the significance of what was to emerge no matter how unfamiliar it might be, trusting his ability to take to the sky should there be a need.

A roaring crack sounded from the fault, stone tearing from stone, roots stripped of their soil.

A cloud of dust enveloped the land.

Vagran took to the open sky. The headland rose after him, free from the coastline's hold. She stood there for a drawn-out moment, tremors reverberating

143

through the earth and the trees, a satisfied groan rumbling from the ground, as if to shake off eons of sleep.

A gigantic step moved her into the sea. Water retreated before the column of rock who strode headlong with will and purpose. A rising wave surged before her, heralding her arrival to the open sea. Whirlpools and eddies swirled in her wake, filling the rift in the coastline she'd left.

The headland rose and fell as she waded in deeper, a widening chasm growing behind her, the earth straining from contact with the waves. Another step pushed her deeper still, each one taking her further from the world she knew. The angry swells rammed into the rock, coming ever closer to the grassy top.

Until the primordial came to rest by the colourful shoals of Coral Cays, seemingly content with her new home, a brand-new island settled within the reef.

Vagran watched from the sky until the dust and the waves died down, until the sea accepted the new isle as one of her own. And he settled again upon the stone ledge, quiet and content with the change of view.

DEPARTURE

A worn knapsack lay open on the floor. Asja filled it with all the utensils she'd taken from her dwarf home, except for the rope she'd used to descend into the womb of Mount Ablast. In its place she held a woven blanket – an exquisite floral creation given to her by Florella – but chose not to take it, not wishing to be in the demoness' debt, even though Vagran was no longer with her to keep her warm under the open skies.

Vagran! The memory of her childhood friend brought tears to her eyes. She wondered where he'd been all this time. Would she ever see him again? She wiped the tears and resumed packing. There was no time for reminiscing now. First she had to get out of this place. She tied the knapsack closed and swung it onto her back.

How would she leave? She lived in a stone tree who towered over Amana, high enough to see the entire land all the way to the sea. There was no passage to her home that she knew of. Demons travelled via makeshift portals, a skill she still lacked. All the rifts she knew of led onto planes, and the planes she'd been to led nowhere but back here.

She'd have to talk to the demons if she were to leave.

She closed her eyes and took a deep breath. Then, with her staff in hand, she left her room and headed down the passage.

The main hall was quiet. Asja expected to find them there. Sitting at the far end engaged in a subdued chat, they looked up when they heard her enter. She approached them, keeping some distance, determined not to linger.

"I want to leave."

Florella slowly nodded, with no hint of surprise in the sluggish movement of her facial petals. "Where will you go?"

"Home."

"Isn't this your home anymore?"

The sadness in her voice almost made Asja reconsider. She took a deep breath to regain her composure.

"No. This has never been my home. You tricked me into thinking that it was. But I know now who you are."

"You do?" asked Shar. "Who are we?"

"Demons!"

"And that means… what?"

Asja stood in silence. All she knew about demons came from dwarf legends which, apart from the ample warnings, had precious little to say about them.

Shar continued. "Where do we come from? What do we do? What do we want from people like you?"

"Whatever it is, I want no part in it!"

"Asja," Florella took over, "we didn't tell you who we are for the same reason Ama didn't. We knew that you would never agree to learn from demons, just as she did. But she also knew that learning from us was exactly what you needed to do, so she told you what you needed to know to seek us out and begin your training."

Asja shook her head vehemently. "I don't believe you. Ama would never consort with demons!"

Shar sneered in response, his head shaking as his gaze wondered around the room. "There is so much that you don't know about Ama."

"Everything we've taught you is true, Asja." Florella's leafy limbs came out from her dress in support of her words. "You must know that!"

She did. Her proficiency with magic had grown in leaps and bounds, there was no denying that. Even more, she had grown as a person, especially in the Underworld – a direction she'd never expected her training to take. She'd wept at holding her dream of mastering magic in her hands and having to turn her back on it and walk away. But she knew that demons twisted the truth ever so slightly to serve their sinister ends, and that their knowledge and guile greatly surpassed her own. She couldn't risk becoming whom they wanted her to be.

"I know I've learned a lot about magic from you. But I won't let you turn me into a monster. I would rather not be a wizard at all!"

"Monster?" Florella's head tilted back, her petals frozen in an upward stance.

"Are you talking about Tyrant?" asked Shar.

Asja nodded.

"And you think that you can just leave him behind in the Underworld?" Shar squinted at her with a sideways glance. "He's a part of you whether you are willing to accept that or not."

"Asja, we are trying to prevent you from becoming him!"

But the girl would not be swayed. Erbrus' legend reminded her of what happened to mages who made deals with demons.

"I won't become your kind of wizard. I will serve my own people, in whatever ways I can. And if I must abandon my wizard training to do that, so be it."

"And you believe your people to be virtuous?" Shar persisted. "That the mages serve them for the greater good?"

The questions washed over Asja, her mind closed to the doubt he sought to sow.

"I want to leave."

Shar and Florella exchanged glances. He slowly raised his hand. The air grew restless until a portal materialised in the space where Asja stood.

She spun around at the sound. It looked unlike any of the planar rifts she had seen. Its tranquil playfulness seemed worldly. She could smell the fresh mountain air passing through the membrane as the enticing breeze caressed her hair. She turned to Shar with a look of hope.

"It will take you home."

"Thank you," she whispered, suddenly realising just how long it had been since she'd gazed upon the house on the hilltop, her one and only home. She stepped towards the portal.

"Before you go," Shar called out. "You want honesty. I'll be honest with you. Dwarves fear us, and for good reason. If their vigilance ever wanes, we will gain a foothold among them and we will end their way of life. And not just theirs, but all of Amana's people's. That is our goal.

"You were a key part of that plan. Ama's plan. She sent you here to help us. And I still hope that someday you will."

Asja trembled at hearing his words, delivered forcefully and with conviction. As much as she professed her distrust of demons, she wasn't ready to have her worst fears confirmed. It dissolved any residual doubts she may have harboured about their intentions. There was nothing left for her here. She stepped into the portal, her face awash with tears.

HOMECOMING

Asja stepped onto the lush grass swaying in the breeze. She took off her boots to better feel the softness. The verdant weeds spread out in unruly waves that rose and fell at the wind's whim. Their rumpled posture made it look as if a herd of mountain goats had settled there for the night. She dropped her belongings and – with a squeal of delight – rolled in them too, coming to rest lying flat on her back with loose straws entangled in her hair.

A long stalk heavy with seeds leaned across her face. She reached for the kernels and held them in her hand, feeling the softness of each immature bead. An adjacent plant still flowered, her aging blossoms starting to wane. Even so, a butterfly landed on one, with delicate wings fluttering in the breeze.

Asja tracked the movement of a newly launched skylight from her vantage point in the slouching grass. Mount Edars must have discharged just before her arrival. The newborn sun still soaked the exposed mountain crest in an intense beam of light. She could barely see the peak from the blinding blanket who held the entire mountain in his embrace.

A sloping field of sleeping boulders spread out before her, sparse scraggy shrubs growing between them. She had climbed those rocks as a child, with Vagran bouncing from one to the next. The largest one rose in the middle of the field, standing broad and proud. She remembered the rush she felt the first time she had climbed to the top. And there in the distance lay the open ledge from whom the thunderoc had taken his first flight.

Past the boulders lay stone steps that climbed up the hillside. She had waddled down those stairs as a toddler and had run up them as a child. They led to the grassy hilltop with a sprawled-out stone garden, a modest barn and a humble house nestled between two rocks.

A loud bleat caught her attention. She turned to see a mountain ram running towards her. He slowed down as he approached and pressed his horned head into her outstretched hand.

"Armo!"

She hugged him, her hands reaching through his warm amber coat. She held his

148

whole neck in her grasp, something she had not been able to do before she had left home. The ram placed his head across her neck and back in what had always been their most intimate posture, his thick horns curving away from her. Then he backed up, dug up the ground with his hooves, and bleated again.

As if responding to his call, a lone figure appeared at the entrance to the house, covered with dull grey clothes and a long white beard. He didn't run but hobbled with some effort, relying on his walking stick more than his legs. She wanted to call out his name, but the words wouldn't come. She ran towards him instead, catching her father in an unrelenting embrace.

"Asja!" he exclaimed once she let him go. "I was afraid I'd never see you again!"

"I'm here, Pa. I've come back," she cried, hugging him again tightly. "Where's Ma?"

"She passed on two cycles ago." He swallowed hard as the sombre words left his mouth.

Asja stared at him before trembling in response, the jubilation of their reunion drained right out of her. He embraced her, holding her until her body calmed and tears ran dry.

"Vagran came by before that," Tor changed the subject. "He said that he'd left you in the Land of Frost."

"He did. We separated at a frost mountain near the sea. I went searching for a wizard in a place where he couldn't follow."

"Wizard?" Tor's eyes glistened at the word. He opened his mouth to ask, but it just hung ajar, adding to the expectant look on his face.

"Yes, Pa. I've found wizards in a faraway land. Powerful wizards…" her gaze drifted inwardly as she spoke, a hint of fear clouding her face, "…who taught me a great deal about magic, and what it takes to be one of them."

She lifted her staff. "And I've got this!"

He reached out to touch it, then hesitated. Only at Asja's insistence did he feel its texture with a single finger before pulling back.

"It's warm! Not like a mage's staff. What is it made of?" he asked as he gazed at the cloudlike substance that reflected the intense colours of the morning sky.

"I don't know. While we travelled through the sylvan lands, I had a vivid dream of a wizard waiting for me inside a mountain. When I woke up, the staff was lying on my chest. I don't know what it is or where it came from, but it has proven its worth many times since then. Sometimes it really feels like a part of me."

"I don't believe I've ever seen a mage, even a runemage, with a staff like this. You'll be the envy of them all," he chuckled, his eyes beaming with pride.

Asja returned a fleeting smile. She wasn't looking forward to meeting the mages.

"What's happened here since I left?"

"Nothing as exciting as in your life, I'm sure. Let me see... your uncle Tamn died... how long ago was that?"

"I know, Pa. I was still here."

"Oh, right. Well, his son Tamenor left recently. He moved to Mondan, I think. Or Mondalan. Hmm... I don't know the lands by Mount Croms very well. He lives in some town by that mountain. Their old house sits empty now. He was the last of our family who still lived here."

Asja listened to the news with a growing lump in her throat. She'd come back because she had nowhere else to go, hoping against hope to make it her home this time, to connect with her family the way she couldn't before. But now Tor was the only one left.

She studied him closely. As joyful as he was to see her again, there was frailty to him she hadn't seen before. Perhaps she was too young to pay attention to such things before she left, but it hit her with full force now. She'd always thought of him as a hardy old man, but now he just looked old. With Erna gone and his adopted daughter living her own life far away from home, she couldn't help but wonder how much reason he had to go on.

"Oh, that reminds me," he interrupted her reminiscing. "There's been word of goblin raids down by the river. They are getting more frequent all along the border. People are starting to worry about their crops... or worse. Do you think you can help them?" he asked, eying her staff again.

"Help keep the goblins out?" Asja repeated his words, her tightening grip on the staff causing it to spark. Tor's eyes widened at the sight.

"I believe so," she concluded, looking down the hillside towards the river. "But what about you? I came back for you. How will you manage by yourself?"

He shrugged his shoulders. "I've managed so far. I might not be as nimble as I once was, but I still get around. And Zelin from the valley visits me sometimes, or someone from his family does."

Asja nodded. She didn't live here anymore. Life had gone on without her.

"Do you know where Vagran might be?"

"He did return a few days ago to see if you'd come back. Other than that, I don't know. He's travelled far and wide since you two left."

Then he put his arm firmly on her shoulder, more strongly than she thought he could. "But before you wander off again, you must tell me all about the wonders you've seen on your travels. You know, I've always thought that this quiet life was not for you, that you were meant for something great in the world of magic. I'm so glad I was right." He sized her up from head to toe and smiled sincerely, his face beaming with pride.

She couldn't help but smile in return, even as she appraised her unspoken words, careful about how much to tell him.

RANGORR

Commotion at the western end of the courtyard ruptured the tranquillity of the night. A lone bolt crackled through the air. A sickening sound of charge singeing flesh. A pain-induced scream. A blood-curdling roar. Frantic steps scampering across the ground.

The clamour and discharges shook Asja from her reverie, cutting short her reminiscence about her childhood. She rose to face the town of Amerot, struggling to see the scene of the clan gathering from behind the treeline outside of the town. A blistered groan swept through the courtyard, a terminal cry from a mage she knew.

She grabbed her staff and ran.

Her path lay hidden in the trees and the brush, made harder to follow by the lack of light. She leapt through the growth with the practised movements honed in the Underworld. A wall of flame rose above the trees, scorching wood and flesh, leaving smouldering branches and cries of agony in her wake.

Asja shoved the shrubs aside and stepped into the open. A tall figure covered with flames stood directly ahead. A weak discharge from an erionite staff struck him, but his shield absorbed it with barely a flicker to its flame. An arrow followed closely behind, striking the arm placed across his body, its tip shattering on the crusty skin. They provoked another conflagration to erupt from the creature's hands, engulfing the open space and devouring the figures standing in his way.

His gaze veered to a build-up of charge at the edge of the treeline. He swung his shield of flame to meet the new threat. But this was no runic burst from a mage's staff. The bolt ripped through the fire and hurled the creature back across the ground. He staggered to his feet, bewildered and dazed, his protective arm seared and dripping blood.

Asja's staff arced and sizzled with another build-up of charge. The fiery shield brightened in response. It arched to meet the next savage bolt. It flared and gleamed, burning the missile in its midst. The shield consumed itself to keep the bolt out, but no charge touched the creature in its care.

The next circle of light started to form before Asja's own attacking charge. The fiend was faster. His magic more potent. She suddenly saw Shar's cloaked body standing in his place, ready to hurl another ball of flames. And then a figure of darkness took over her view – insatiable emptiness ready to devour her – and an overwhelming feeling of finality and death.

Sensing her doom, she broke off the engagement and ran across the courtyard to the dwarves and elves who had formed a line.

"Stand with me!" she yelled at the top of her lungs, then turned around and faced the attacker again. The muffled voices and the shuffling of feet closed behind her, giving her heart and forestalling the onset of panic that threatened to engulf her.

Only now did she take a moment to study the fiery creature standing before her. His gaunt frame stood tall and imposing over dwarves and elves alike, firmly anchored on hooves poised flexibly over cracked ground. Silver horns protruded from his head, swooping broadly to cover his shoulders and back. And myriad glowing pores covered the surface of his body, feeding the burning blaze that shielded him from attack, and fuelling the flame yearning to pour from his hands.

She trembled at the sight, recalling the first time she had met Shar. But whereas Shar had nearly killed her by mistake, this demon seemed to be here with purpose. His eyes reflected nothing but contempt for the puny creatures standing before him. She'd seen those eyes before, in the dark recesses of the Underworld Plane – she was staring at Tyrant.

The demon stepped forward. His flaming shield untested, he hurled it at the assembled troop. Asja countered with a bulwark of her own. They clashed in mid-air, fire seeking out fire, flame dousing flame, until the whole conflagration burned itself out.

The air between them clear, the demon stared at Asja, his eyes narrowing, his face contorting, his hands igniting from the intensity of the glow. The very ground beneath his hooves suddenly came alight. He thrust forward, a low growl accompanying his movements, heaving the flame forth. And when he met the protective shield, he spread out left and right, besieging the whole line.

Asja gripped her staff with both hands, pouring every ounce of verve she'd been able to gather. But her reserves were wearing thin with no waning of the assaulting blaze. She grimaced in pain as a rogue flare landed on her face. A mage to her left groaned, the smell of burning hair and skin infusing her senses.

Warriors stepped forward, their enchanted armour pressing against the inferno. Archers rose and shot their arrows, distracting the demon from his relentless charge. And mages and druids redirected their staves from the demon to Asja, feeding her what little energy each one could muster.

The protective barrier spread around the group, beating back the assault, strengthened and invigorated by their collective care. The demon's growl rose in pitch. His burning skin broke out in sweat. The trees behind him crumbled into dust to feed the hungry flames. But Asja's bubble of blistering air held them in check.

The seething barrier pulsated in triumph, its translucent flames simple and pure, the mages lacking the skill to impress themselves upon their creations. Asja tempered her own flames to help them mix, unaccustomed to pristine flares surging from her spells. She knew the wizards from the handiwork they made. Shar's essence always permeated the fireballs he let loose. She pushed the thought aside, eying the fiend who eyed her in return, anticipating his next move.

A hint of clarity appeared in his eyes. A look of hope washed over his face. He arched his back to feed on the flames the mages and druids had placed in his way. His body grew vibrant, his skin lucid. Asja cut the shield's lifeline when she saw him feast, but even in its terminal state, it held enough energy to fuel his escape. His translucent form shot up through the sky. She saw him speed north, towards Mount Aorai's dark outline. And then, like a kite caught on a string, he swung south-west, screeching as he went, before fading into the night sky over the Ural Range.

The courtyard fell still, dwarves and elves standing in tense readiness against a threat that had suddenly vanished from their midst. Non-fighters and latecomers were the first to act. They spilled into the courtyard, stumbling through the smoke, looking over the dead and the survivors alike. It took the troop a long while to recover from the ordeal. They dispersed slowly and walked gingerly, not knowing their enemy but knowing he was still at large.

Asja saw a charred indigo robe strewn across the floor. Her heart racing, she scampered to the body, his face too disfigured to make out, his hefty build draped in Obalin's cloak. She touched the erionite staff still gripped by his hand.

The mage was no match for the demon's flame.

She gazed at the smouldering bodies lying on the ground. A terrifying thought weighed on her even more. It could have been her bringing death to these people, had she not cut her training short and escaped Tyrant while she was still able.

ASHES

A flowery face swooped down until it almost touched the ground. Darkness ruled the hilltop, making the edge of the courtyard difficult to see. Undeterred, the facial petals probed the powdery ground, touching the soft surface before pulling back from the forbidding cold.

"What are you doing here?" a nervous voice pierced the silence. Asja came out from behind a tree, committed to her sentry duty while dwarves and elves mourned their dead on the other side of the town. Her staff faced the intruder, both of her hands gripping it firmly.

Florella's face ruptured into a broad smile.

"Asja! Are you well?"

"Don't change the subject. Why are you here?"

Florella glanced back at the ashen powder covering the ground. "I came to find out what happened."

Asja nodded, unsurprised. "Who was he?"

The plant looked at her uncomprehendingly.

"I know he was a demon. I saw Tyrant in his eyes," Asja pressed. "You must know him."

Florella looked back down, the petals of her face dancing in the air above the frosty ash, absorbing the residue of the attacker's presence without imprinting themselves on the soft surface.

"Rangorr," she finally answered.

Asja stared at her blankly, straining to recall the memory. "Your apprentice?"

Florella nodded.

"Why would he attack us?"

"He'd been captured by the morlocks, remember? He didn't come alone. A morlock was here, too. I sensed his presence in the trees behind you."

Asja didn't turn around to look, not wanting to risk turning her back to the demoness, even if she once used to be her teacher and friend. Still, her eyes widened at the mention of her birth people, the attack feeling closer to home than she had thought.

"Why would the morlocks attack us?"

"They've hated humans ever since the war."

"We took no part in the war."

"No, but you're friends with humans. If the morlocks move against them, will you not help?"

Asja lowered her eyes, taken aback by the demoness' probing into the politics of the clans, not wanting to give anything away. *Was it really a coincidence that had brought Florella here?*

"There's something you need to understand about your birth people," the plant continued. "Their society is not organised like yours or the elves'. There is no council of clans to iron out disagreements and map the path ahead. Morlocks make their decisions in private and carry them out by force. But their hold on power is tenuous. There are other mur magic orders – less capable but no less ambitious – whose members would muscle their way into the morlock Circle given the chance. And others, like Rangorr, who'd co-opt their purpose to their own ends. Morlocks must tread carefully to remain on top. And what safer way to do that than to send someone else to do their work for them?"

"I can't believe that Rangorr would do the morlocks' bidding. Surely he hates them?"

"He does." The petals lingered in a tentative dance. "Or at least he used to."

Florella returned her attention to the powdery ash that covered the ground. She walked back and forth, her petals fluttering in the cool night air. Suddenly, her head shot up, tracing a path north, past Mount Aorai, and on to Algalash far beyond the peak.

"He tried to escape!" she turned to Asja, her voice beaming. "Did he succeed?"

Asja stared at her former teacher searching for words, wondering how much to reveal. She wanted her to know as little as possible, but she also wanted to understand what had happened, what danger remained, and how to keep her adoptive people safe. She hated sharing information with demons, but she saw no other way of getting anything useful out of Florella.

"His body faded and he started flying towards the mountain, but then suddenly veered that way," she pointed with her hand. "Like he was being pulled or something."

Florella nodded. "I thought as much. He was on a leash."

"Leash?"

"An enchantment to tie him down should he try to run. The morlocks had sent him out on a mission, but they didn't trust him. With good reason, it seems. But why would he think he could break the leash... unless..." The demoness stared directly at the girl, her petals erect and still. "You helped him?"

Asja's jaw dropped. She recalled the demon feeding on her flame before she cut him off.

"He came here to kill us! I would never help him! None of us would!"

For all their vehemence, her words did little to soften Florella's gaze. A lengthy moment passed before the demoness looked back down at the ashen ground.

"Why did the stone turn to ash?" Asja asked.

Florella didn't look up. "Rangorr must have drained more life from the ground than she was willing to give, and she withered away in shock."

"How... How do we replenish her?"

"You can't. She'll reconstitute herself someday, when she's ready. Probably not in our lifetime." The plant picked up a leaf-full of the dust and watched it start to seep inertly back onto the floor, her leaf soon closing from the bitter cold. Then the intense glare of her facial petals returned to bear down on Asja. "Do you understand now why we wanted you to go back into the Underworld and face Tyrant?"

The question caught Asja off guard. *I'm the one who should be asking such questions, not the demoness.*

"I know what you wanted–"

"Rangorr has cracked. Morlocks got to him," Florella interrupted her, her voice rising in urgency and pitch. "They provoked him somehow to give in to Tyrant and attack your assembly. Make no mistake, all Tyrant cares about is power – wielding it against others. And if he has to destroy the world around him to do it, he will."

"That's why I left, remember?"

"That won't help you, Asja. We didn't create your Tyrant. Leaving us won't make him disappear. He's always been a part of you, and always will be, whether you like it or not."

"I will never let him control me!"

"Neither would Rangorr," Florella quipped. "And look at him now."

She turned her outstretched leaf to let the last few powdery granules seep out over the edge. The stream of dust as they fell down, the silence as they touched the ground, the lifeless pile where stone had once stood were not lost on Asja. This was no desert sand defiant in the face of the wind, or mountain gravel whose vibrancy she could feel.

She never doubted the destructive power of demons; she just didn't expect to bear the brunt of it so close to home.

"Take care of yourself, Asja," said Florella before stepping into the portal that opened behind her and closed the moment her tall, elegant frame vanished into thin air.

Asja stared at the starlit darkness where her outline had just been. She didn't trust demons; they sensed people's weaknesses and preyed upon them. Yet there was sincerity to Florella's words that kept gnawing at her. Worse, Florella's knowledge far outstripped hers. Asja couldn't argue her case against the demoness, and she was sure that Florella knew how to exploit that. That was why she had sought to avoid all further contact with her former teachers.

Rangorr's arrival undermined that plan. Powerful and capricious, he and the morlocks behind him presented a threat the likes of which dwarves had never faced. Even with her help, she wasn't sure they could withstand it. As much as she resented the idea, she saw herself being forced to lean on Shar and Florella for support.

She couldn't help but wonder whether her former teachers had a hand in Rangorr's sudden appearance in the first place...

ACCEPTANCE

The sturdy walls of Kinrum Hall had withstood the fierce arguments, shouting matches, rumbling of feet and thunderous applause of the gatherings gone by – with no lasting wear to show for their efforts – but the tense silence that descended upon them now was altogether different.

The delegations from each of the clans occupied their customary aisles, some of the seats standing alone and empty, Obalin's the most prominent among them. Gone was the quiet optimism of the earlier assembly. Orators rose in haphazard order, not competing for the right to speak, their halting words wrapped in heavy silence. The names of Ilyasah and Aorar were uttered once more, elves and dwarves acutely feeling their heroes' absence, not wanting to face the likes of demons with nothing to draw on but their own skill.

Asja sat at the back of the Peridot aisle, behind the official delegates from her clan. She soaked up each fearful word uttered by the speakers before reaching her fill, unable to take in any more gloom. She had engaged in speculation of her own, but ever since encountering Florella in the courtyard of the hall and suspecting the wizards' hand in Rangorr's attack, she couldn't discount her connection to it. And if there was one thing she wasn't prepared to share with her adoptive people, it was any involvement she may have had with the most enigmatic antagonists from the dwarven legends and myths. The Legend of Erbrus' Fall still felt as fresh in her mind as the first time she had heard it told.

"What do you think, Asja?" Galen of the Garnet clan steered the discussion to her.

She stared back and swallowed hard, her mind startled and blank. She'd been so absorbed in her own thoughts that she'd lost the thread of the assembly and had nothing ready to say.

Seeing her discomfort, Uronam, the head of the Peridot delegation, rose to interject, "I think I speak for us all when I say that we are really grateful to Asja for her help with fighting off the demon." His gaze wandered around the hall in search of support and found it in nodding heads and shouts of agreement.

"With your shield anchoring our line, we could actually fight that bastard!" spat out Tenus, a master axe thrower.

"She almost drove the demon off by herself," said the elf Evindal, his voice free from the apprehension that accompanied the voices of the mages when they talked about her skill. His fellow druids agreed.

A warm glow washed over Asja at the sounds of praise coming from the elves that the dwarves had been so slow to give. She looked at the mages. *Are they in awe, too, or am I imagining things?*

"Where did you learn to use magic like that?" asked Recha, a runemage of the highest standing among the surviving members of their order.

"From my teachers... wizards... Ama directed me to them," Asja stuttered in response, immediately regretting the mention of the goddess' name for fear of sounding boastful.

"I don't know these... wizards... you speak of," continued Recha. "Where do they live?"

"I trained with them atop the Tetran Massif."

An excited murmur spread through the hall. "The land of giants!" the delegates whispered in each other's ear.

"They've taught you well," remarked the druid Lennolene. "Could you have defeated the demon on your own?"

Asja looked down, the memory of her first encounter with Shar that nearly cost her her life pressing down on her. She breathed heavily and shook her head vehemently.

"What about your wizards? Could they do it?" asked Recha.

Her face brightened. "Oh, yes!" she blurted out, to widespread relief on dwarf and elf faces alike. Grasping the implications, she quickly added, "I mean, they don't usually get involved in the affairs of other people..."

She stopped, waiting for someone to interject and let her off the hook, but all she could see was fading hope followed by heavy silence.

"But... I could ask..."

"Will you?" pressed Recha.

The runemages' expectant eyes weighed down on her. How could she convey Shar's parting words to them? That the wizards would like nothing more than to get involved in the lives of dwarves, because they were really demons bent on manipulation and sowing discord. How could she convince Recha that she didn't really want the wizards' help in the aftermath of Rangorr's attack?

"If you could get the wizards to help protect us from the demon, we would be in your debt," added Uronam, the leader of her clan.

In my debt?

Had Obalin or any of the runemages accomplished that, he would have done no more than what was expected of him – whatever was needed to protect his people. That the dwarves had no such expectations of Asja reminded her that she didn't really belong, that they didn't count on her as one of their own. And yet, it was the first crack in the shell erected to keep her out, the first sign that she might be able to earn her place among her adoptive people. Having turned her back on Florella and Shar, she saw nowhere else to go.

We don't have to fit in, a voice whispered to her.

She spun around, confused as to its source, when she recognised the soft sound whose strength surprised her as much now as the first time she'd heard it. Pariah! The first horror she'd reclaimed, the fragment of herself whose resilience she could now draw on as her own.

She knew what Pariah said was true. She'd been cast out by Asja and her horrors alike, but endured on her own, living a life of solitude. But such a life held no appeal for the girl, especially now that the dwarves were warming to her, trying to secure her aid.

"I will ask them to help," she replied, careful not to overpromise, yet still feeling the weight of their hopes.

Recha's face brightened. The oppressive atmosphere of the assembly started to lift. The deadly danger posed by the demon no longer felt inexorable, thanks to the magical skill of one of their own, and perhaps even unexpected help from powerful beings beyond their lands.

Asja failed to share in their respite. The dread of having to face Shar again lurked beneath her cheerful face. Perhaps she should just tell the clans that she couldn't find her teachers, that they'd moved even further away or declined to help. Who would know? But that could mean fighting Rangorr without their help, and he frightened her even more.

"And if your thunderoc friend is willing to help, don't forget to travel east in search of Chromatic Hills," Recha reminded her. "If Ferev's words hold true, those crystals could well bolster our runes and help us resist demons should your teachers prove unwilling to help."

Asja's eyes gleamed at the thought. Chromatic Hills may not be in dwarven lands, but as Galen had said, goblins had no use for such things anyway. It was a small price to pay for not having to deal with Florella and Shar again.

She nodded to Recha with as much humility as she could muster.

"I will do as you ask."

KALHAR

Asja grabbed onto the translucent feathers of her thunderoc friend and pulled herself up to the middle of his chest, her favourite spot for travelling through the skies. Vagran had kept his word and returned to Mount Cougal following the assembly, as the clan delegations spilled from the hill for their journey home. Only this time he could not escape the stares of the people gathered on the hilltop. They kept their distance, fearful of the beast who'd descended upon their town. Only a handful of mages had the courage to step forward and meet the young thunderoc, the lure of Chromatic Hills urging them to make friends with the giant bird who could fly them there.

A fiery sun rose in the east, looming large over the horizon. His brilliance scorched the morning sky. Mount Uburn had erupted, starting another day over the sweeping desert. It was the cue Vagran was waiting for, tracking the fireball who served as his guide. He stretched his wings, their sapphire feathers flexing effortlessly in the distant light, and shot up into the sky.

Asja squealed from the force of the launch. She pressed her body into the cavity in his chest, supported and held safe by his translucent plumes, listening to the rhythmic pounding of the thunderoc's heart. The beat reassured her that Vagran knew what he was doing despite the tremendous speed with which Mount Cougal and the town of Amerot receded from view.

Desert dunes emerged from the darkness, their recurring shapes casting rolling shadows over the barren sand. Burning bright bronze, marred by footprints carved into the dust by the vivacious wind, their air fluttered in the heat wave unleashed by the peak. No tree or lake punctured the sprawling sand. It was a desolate landscape, one that Asja couldn't imagine harboured any life.

She had no fear of goblins, nor did she expect to see any in these sands, but she did fear the flying, flaming beasts Vagran had told her about. Scorias dwarfed his strength and pyrerocs ruled the skies, but she knew of none who could propel themselves upward the way he could. The closer to the ground he came, the faster she saw him rise.

The skylight had reached the upper regions of the desert sky by the time sturdier structures rose from the ground. Indistinguishable from the sand at their feet, their loose covering soon slipped to reveal hard rock whose presence defied the will of the wind. More followed, solitary stands of bare stone with lines carved deeply into their flesh, a precursor of what was to come. At the eastern horizon, in the dying light of the setting sun, stood the formidable frame of Kalhar's highest peak.

The skylight crumbled into myriad parts, the parting breath of the setting sun. Far below, Mount Uburn soaked up the searing light, his peak glowing gold as if on fire. And then he turned dull, the light in the sky having run his course, leaving only the faint beacons from a distant land to shine into the night.

Hidden by the night, Vagran rose from the hot sands, giving them a broader view of the mountain range. Asja's eyes strained to adjust to the sudden onset of dark, her friend taking her to a place she could no longer see – a mount visible only by the darkness he imposed upon the stars.

A faint glow to her right caught her eye. Previously overshadowed by the skylight, a small patch of hills who dwelled south of the summit now came into their own. They shone, their crystalline forms bending the light every which way, channelling the vigour the mountain had drawn from Aia's primordial depths. *Chromatic Hills*, Asja thought to herself, remembering Ferev's words that the mages had impressed upon them before the flight.

As the hills came into view, Asja kept a watchful eye for any sign of movement. Vagran touched down on bare rock close to the hills. She emerged from her travelling spot – leaving her friend to slump down for much-needed rest – and proceeded to survey the site.

Nothing moved. The hills glowed in silence, their exquisite display seemingly lost to the inhabitants of the desert.

A crystalline knoll rose from the ground directly in her path, towering over her and blocking her way. His finely chiselled features shone with violet glow, rich bronze freckles covering his face, his broad core luminous and lucid. She gazed through him and his fellow mounds, each one projecting light of slightly different hue until a kaleidoscope of borrowed colours permeated his form, a chromatic prism shining exquisitely into the desert night.

She ran her hand across his glossy face. He felt like liquid, yielding to the soft caress, leaving a hollow in her hand's wake. Startled, she pulled back. The crystal responded by filling out again, his skin smooth and unyielding, her touch forgotten but for a change of shade. She touched him again, and again, unable to fathom the flow of the crystal, mesmerised by the metamorphosis unfolding before her eyes.

She wondered how such a gem would respond to the mages' runes. And then it hit her. They lusted for the power of the crystals who lived here, undeterred by their station deep in goblin lands, and had only used the demon's attack to secure her support. That was why they'd tried to send her here as soon as they learned that she could cross the sprawling sands. Still, she couldn't imagine them having a hand in Rangorr's attack, an event they must have turned to their advantage after a hefty price.

She looked around the radiant knolls. The dwarves called them hills, but they were little more than mounds of crystal, smaller than some of the dunes she'd seen along the way. A gushing sound caught her ear. She looked at the tip of a nearby knoll to see a slow stream dripping down the side, his flowing gems the colour of young amethyst.

Mount Uburn must have fed Chromatic Hills each time he erupted, though little sustenance reached them so far from his roots. The site was precious; the only place she knew of whose crystalline structure readily responded to the whims of people, and was constantly renewed by the mountain who'd given him birth.

The sound of voices broke her train of thought. She expected to find no people here. She looked up at a nearby ridge to see two scrawny figures walking along the edge. Goblins! She grabbed her staff and pointed it at them, the tip rapidly amassing a violet glow. The goblins looked down at the unexpected sound and stopped in their tracks. One turned and ran, the other slipped and tumbled down the cliff before hitting the stone floor with a sickening crack.

Asja tracked his tumbling movements with her staff, knowing how tricky goblins could be, careful not to let him out of her sight. But the shattering sound and the cries of pain convinced her that whatever threat he may have posed has since gone. She rushed to him, her staff still raised and ready. Seeing her approach, he scrambled back until the pain in his broken leg persuaded him to stay. He lay there on his back, slightly raised against the face of the cliff, his eyes awash with terror at the sight of a dwarf mage with her staff at the ready.

His eyes widened further as a giant bird with pellucid feathers and arcing beak rose behind the dwarf. Asja quickly turned around and motioned Vagran to stop, not wanting to frighten the injured goblin even more. To her surprise, the goblin's gaze left the thunderoc as soon as the bird settled down, as if he were merely startled by the beast and had no fear of him. He continued to stare at her instead, petrified and in pain, his right leg discolouring from the break.

She stood there, staring him down, the aftermath of the goblin raid still fresh on her mind. Then she blinked and saw the charred corpses of goblins killed by her hand in the forest clearing across River Rust, corpses that had plagued her memories ever since. She pulled her staff back. This goblin had done nothing to deserve such a fate. It was she who was in the wrong here, deep inside their land without being provoked, with impure motives she could not explain.

Trembling and in turmoil, she sat down next to him, trying to regain her calm. She resented having forfeited her position, where goblins were the ones in the wrong, where she could hate them without a second thought.

She motioned towards his leg, but held back and waited, as if asking for permission. He acquiesced, letting out a deep growl when the bones snapped together, the grimace of pain gradually eased by the healing energy pouring from her staff. It had been some time since she'd practised her healing arts, not since Florella had shared her knowledge so freely. The victims of the goblin raid from the village of Darum had all been killed, and the few dwarves wounded by Rangorr had plenty of druids and other healers to nourish them back to health. She'd missed practising her craft, she realised, even if goblin bones were lighter and easier to set, and the clean break far less of a challenge than lingering wounds left behind by magic.

His injury treated, she took the time to study her patient, to see the person lying before her instead of just a goblin. His withered skin had spent many a season in the arid sands. The long scar beneath his right eye was no stranger to a cougar claw. The eyes that had held her in fear had a more enigmatic look to them now. She saw intelligence and curiosity in them, as if this creature had no relation to the savage monsters who raided the dwarf lands.

For a fleeting moment, the desert scene from the Chaos Plane played out in her mind, with the sight of the goblin hunter roaming the arid wastes. She'd dismissed it then, scornful of the desert dwellers and their way of life. Looking into this stranger's eyes, she felt less certain now, his humaneness calling out to her, pleading for her to see it. And the unthinkable thought crept up in the confusion, not yet welcome but simmering somewhere beneath – that, primitive as they may be, these people may still have something of value for her to learn.

Confused and in turmoil, she stepped away from the injured goblin, picked up a gem from a nearby knoll and headed back to her giant friend. Then they took off into the night, leaving the goblin to watch them depart from his lands as quickly as they had come.

SENTINELS

The druid Evindal stood on the riverbank, gazing upon the crimson channel of River Rust. A family of elk gathered on the other side, indifferent to his presence, drinking the fresh water in thirsty gulps. An eagle soared overhead, ever watchful for the movement of fish who did well to adorn their scales with colours as striking as the riverbed over whom they lived.

Already voluminous this high in her reach – not yet enriched by the flow drawn by the southern peaks – the water made her way down the divide between mountain foothills and desert dunes until she reached the stone ledges of Dropol Ford, strewn across her path as if in a challenge. She accepted it with glee, running buoyantly across the broad stone, bouncing vivaciously from one ledge to the next, washing over the rugged edges until they grew soft and pliable from her relentless caress. Wet and slippery, the sturdy ledges nonetheless made for easy crossing if one took but minimal care to navigate them safely.

Evindal raised his gaze to the lush forest beyond the river. Fed by the droplets from miniature waterfalls stretching across the channel, thick trees grew and flourished, holding the wind-whipped sands of the Kalhar Desert at bay. Sands too parched to sustain desert dwellers upon their dunes. But goblins were known to travel far north from their homes in the fertile desert of Kuru Kam, using the river as their nourisher and guide.

The slopes behind the elf competed with the forest in a friendly rivalry. Too high to be reached by the river's spray and lacking a wooded blanket of their own, they adorned themselves with thick tufts of grass enriched with lilac florets open in full bloom. Far beyond the sloping hills stood the enigmatic figure of Mount Reclus – the easternmost peak of the outer Ural Range. Known as Cloud Rock, his flat tip barely topped the clouds who tugged on his sides, seeking to engulf him in their soft embrace. He resisted their advances, standing like a lone island in a sea of white.

The druid stepped away from the edge of the bank and made his way to the top of the slope, settling on a spot directly overlooking the ford. He took out a seed from his travel bag, admiring the smooth caramel face, coated him with a nourishing salve, and pressed him gently into the rich earth. Then he stood back, planted his staff from an old yew tree firmly onto the ground, closed his eyes, and waited.

A tender seedling emerged from the soil, his head heavy and oversized for his stem, barely rising above the moist earth. He split open, his stem powering through the protective shell, each half receding to form its own leaf. The stem continued to rise, branching into new leaves in quick succession, forming a flat crown on top of a sturdy stalk. By the time the growth spurt had run its course, a young tree stood upon the slope, his tall trunk straight and true, his bark thin and delicate and the colour of fine clay, topped with a nascent crown of hard crust and barbs.

The elf's face broke into a smile. Much work remained to be done. Whole pots of herbal brew would be needed to coat the young tree before he could grow to his full height. A different salve would have to be mixed to let him unleash the barbs nestled in his crown at any desert dwellers who dared approach. But the new sentinel would soon be ready to stand guard at the Dropol Ford of River Rust.

The druid cast his gaze to a smaller ford further downstream. Ryunfir stood there, planting another tree, though from the distance, Evindal could only see a speck of the man. More would be planted all along the border, covering every crossing the desert folk might take, as the first line of defence against the barbarian threat.

REPORT BACK

"Back already?" shouted Recha when she saw Asja emerge from Vagran's protective plume. Despite the excitement that radiated from her face, she kept her distance from the giant bird.

Asja smiled, grateful to be friends with a creature whose sheer presence intimidated the runemages. "The hills must have been easier to see from the sky than from the ground."

Recha forgot to breathe, her mouth left to hang. "You saw them?"

Asja nodded. "We saw them shining in the night as we came close. They were quite far to the south from Mount Uburn. It must have taken Ferev many days to reach them on foot walking from the summit."

"What were they like?" Recha's breathless voice quivered with excitement.

Asja removed her backpack, took out an object wrapped in maple leaves, and gave it to the runemage. Recha took off the covers to reveal brilliant light pouring from the package.

Long fragments comprised the slender gem, their joins betrayed by a refractive line. An auburn coating hid them from sight except for slivers of light where the protective crust had parted. Tiny crystals coagulated at the cracks as if the gem couldn't wait for the nascent cloak to give way so that he could complete his birth from Aia's primordial depths into the world above.

"I found him lying on the ground by one of the hills."

"He's extraordinary!" Recha gushed.

The crystal flexed and changed colour in response to her touch, prompting the runemage to explore him again, her mouth gaping and eyes sparkling, completely absorbed in the interaction with the gem. Some time passed before she pried her gaze away from him and became aware of Asja's wringing hands and bitten lip.

"What is it, Asja?"

"Goblins were nearby."

Recha's forehead furrowed in confusion. "What do you mean?"

"They live by the hills. Two of them surprised us at night, walking and talking casually, as if they were home."

Recha took a step back, eying the girl out. "Are you suggesting that they understand the power that is locked within this crystal? That they know how to harness it?"

Asja held back, knowing what the mage wanted her to say, but haunted by the curious look in the goblin's eyes. "I don't know. I haven't seen them use or wear the gems. Perhaps they are just drawn to the beauty of the place?"

She saw the frown on Recha's face lift at her words, the mage all too eager to embrace their meaning. "That sounds about right. Goblins and their brethren are savages. Always have been, always will be. But even savages can be dazzled by the crystals' beauty, even if they lack the knowledge of the power they harbour."

She looked up at the giant bird resting on the hillside, his eyes transfixed on the new sentinel standing watch over the river ford. Then she nodded quietly, as if in conclusion.

"A few of the mages would be willing to accompany your friend on another trip. Would you mind speaking with him? We want to get enough crystals to study and use for staves and blades. Ama knows, we may need them in these perilous times!"

Asja stared at her, not believing what she was hearing. It hadn't been enough that Chromatic Hills were situated deep inside goblin lands. Now it wasn't enough that goblins actually lived there. The runemages were still going to cross the desert to take the coveted gems.

"And if the goblins attack you?" she asked.

"We can defend ourselves. Especially with your friend's help. Didn't you say that he took down a goblin raiding party virtually by himself? I doubt a goblin village would be much of a problem."

There was something about the tone in her voice that stood out to the girl. She sensed no fear in it, as if Recha knew that goblins weren't a serious threat, merely a useful one.

"Vagran and I still need to scout the goblin settlements close to the river to see if anyone other than those stone-skinned brutes is helping them."

"True," Recha agreed. "But that can wait until we return. The druids are planting sentinel trees at every river crossing along the border. Those barbarians won't surprise us again."

Recha pointed at the slope towards the river, and a magnificent tree with a smooth, tall trunk and a broad, flat crown. A couple of mages stood at the base looking up, equally impressed.

Then Recha turned her attention back to the girl. "Have you heard from your teachers yet?"

Asja's eyes opened wide at their mention. She shook her head. "They are not easy to reach." Then she smirked as a thought came to her – remembering the danger that the demon posed – and retorted with a glint in her eye, "I will need Vagran's help."

Recha stopped in her tracks. She eyed the girl out but couldn't dispatch her request as she had the others. In the end, she nodded, clutching the crystal Asja had given her, her gaze veering to Vagran, whose help they needed to acquire more.

Asja dashed back to the resting bird. She pressed herself into the soft feathers of his neck, sensing that another prolonged period of separation would soon be upon them. Instead of waiting patiently as he usually did, he unfolded his wings to envelop her, hiding her from sight.

"I need to ask you a favour," she whispered through the tears, feeling foolish for how many times she'd said that to her friend. "Could you take me back to Amerot? There's someone important I have to meet there."

THE RETURN

Asja stood on the stone floor of Kinrum Hall. Floating specks circled the mountains, projected onto the open space by the rising light of the Mount Aorai sun. Specks that would soon grow wings and start terrorising creatures big and small who dared appear on the surface of the range.

The memory of the injured goblin played on her mind. The terror in his eyes as he looked at her. The terror as he looked at Vagran, too, yet surprising indifference once the bird had settled down. As if he had no fear of the lightning beast and was merely startled by the sight. As if he feared the mage more.

Vagran did say that he had seen fiery beasts in the desert skies during his earlier travels across the endless sands. How could goblins share their mountains with the likes of rocs? Did they live underground, as dwarves once had, and only rise to the surface at night, when it was safe?

Her friend was a creature of storms who fed on lightning clouds as they rumbled through the sky. Pyrerocs subsided on open flame spewing from mountain vents. Scorias ate crystalline rock ejected in molten form. Only beasts of flesh had a reason to seek out dwarves. And yet their legends were clear that the dwarves' clash with the beasts in the War of Inheritance was a fight for their lives.

For the first time, she felt a touch of sympathy for the great mage Erbrus and his decision to consort with demons despite being fully aware of the danger they posed. She could never understand how he could choose such a course of action when all the legends warned him to stay away. But perhaps the legends had their own story to tell that deviated from the events on which they were based. The longer she dwelled on them, the more she distrusted the myths, as well as the people she'd always sought to serve.

She wasn't startled when Florella materialised by her, and she stepped willingly into the makeshift portal that led to the demons' home.

Shar stood to one side of the hall, blending into the empty place. His dull stone eyes livened at the sight of her. His body spasmed, as if wanting to embrace her while his will held it in check.

"Why are you here?" He finally asked.

Why did she come back? The turmoil in her mind raged with no resolution in sight. The only answer she had ready was the clan one.

"My people asked for your help against Rangorr."

Shar nodded, his mouth slanting. "We are keeping an eye on the morlocks, as closely as we can without being seen. Their attack was a failure. Rangorr was contained, and he tried to escape. We are not expecting them to attack again soon."

Failure? Tell that to the dozen mages, including the head runemage, whom he killed.

"And when they do?"

"We'll know about it, and we'll warn you. But we won't join the fight. Any help we provide will have to remain hidden."

Asja shook her head. "Why not just eliminate the morlocks? You can do that, can't you?"

"Not without repercussions."

The cryptic answer did nothing to dispel her mistrust. "Are you behind this?"

Shar's eyes widened at the question. They bore into her, his body perfectly still, his face giving nothing away. "If I said no, would you believe me?"

She looked down from the intensity of his gaze, backing off despite being no closer to having an answer to the burning question.

Florella's soft voice cut through the silence. "Perhaps we should ask celestials to help? They might find a way."

"You know they won't get involved."

"They might if we convince them that Ama's future is at stake. With Rangorr captive and Asja unwilling to help, they might have no other option but to act."

Florella's words sent a cold shiver down Asja's spine. "Ama's future? What are you talking about?"

"You keep asking questions you don't trust us to answer," the stone wizard shut her down again. "You came here asking for help, something you could have easily done without stepping into the portal. Why did you come?"

Asja looked down again, struggling to admit that her childhood conviction had been misplaced. "The dwarves are not whom I thought they were." Then she looked up, withstanding the intensity of his gaze for the first time, determined to find an answer to the words that have stayed with her since the last time she had stood there. "When you said that you would end their way of life, what did you mean?"

"I can't give you an answer you will accept. Or perhaps even understand. But… If you really want to know, you can discover this for yourself by resuming your training. Especially in Mirrordon. The plane has ached to have you back ever since you left."

Her breath caught in her throat at the audacity of his suggestion. "I'm not going to become your apprentice again!"

"I'm not asking you to."

She cocked her head to one side, pondering his offer. Had he urged her to return to the Underworld and face Tyrant again, she would've left them without a second thought. But Mirrordon? The most soothing and eye-opening of the planes? She could feel its pull from above the hall. And her affinity for magic and the desire to master it ached to respond in kind.

LONGING

Asja stood in the middle of a grassy field, a sea of stalks to replace the watery one from her prior visit to the Mirrordon Plane. Only, the grass was punctured by mounds of bare rock and streams and puddles who furnished variety to the verdant meadow. She closed her eyes, unafraid and at ease, letting the breeze sway her as he did the grass, losing herself in the undulating wave.

The water in this field felt different. She didn't respond to Asja's primal advances. Her tone had shifted away from Aia's cosmic thrum, coloured as she was by the earth upon whom she flowed. But Asja had spent enough time with Shar in the Primogenus Plane to hear the new melody with relative ease. Her ability to draw energy to feed her spells depended on it.

The subtle breeze who combed the grassy hair, the stoic stones who rose above the field, the earth who nourished the swaying stalks, and the stalks themselves – Asja heard and connected with each one in turn. She loved this aspect of her skill, playing with her surroundings, powering her staff and depowering it again, having nothing she had to unleash her magic on.

Only this time they pulled her in deep. She felt each stalk, each drop, each fibre of ore. They drew her into their world, impressed themselves upon her, until their longing filled her, a quivering note aching to be heard, a yearning seeking expression beneath the surface contentment of the plane.

She gasped at the sensation, overwhelmed by the flood of emotion pouring from every strand. She fought the urge to pull away, sensing the importance of the moment, feeling the unrequited desire for as long as she could. She disengaged when it overwhelmed her, trembling and in tears, sweat pouring from her every pore.

She collapsed with her staff, sitting uncomfortably in the lush grass, breathing heavily from the sudden strain. The communion with the plane still filled her mind, as if the land herself cried out to her, with yearning she didn't know how to fulfil. Asja remained focused on it, clinging on to the moment until it faded, sensing its significance to her life and practice as a mage.

She had never known the land in whom she lived to exhibit passions with intensity that could rival her own.

She picked up her staff, ready to leave, but instantly dropped it, spooked by the width of its grip. She stared at the mysterious object lying on the ground, still shining its light into the tall grass. A second strand ran the full length of the rod, thin and supple, the colour of blooming orchid. It entwined with the first, giving the staff a sturdier spine, and its tip heightened intensity and presence.

She sat there and gazed at the staff, reminded of the mystery of its company, perplexed by the nature of its being. She reached out to hold it, reassured by its firmer frame, and headed for the exit from the plane, still shaken by the events that had unfolded within it.

MAGVEN

Vesstan cast his eye across the lagoon and the many ships rooted there. Some he knew personally, others only by reputation. His gaze wandered to Fallnut, the first vessel he'd ever sailed with. The tree stood on a rocky patch of grass just beyond the surf, his short roots needing to anchor themselves in sturdy soil. Vesstan still remembered those journeys. They were brief but frequent, servicing the Coral Cays just off the coast. The small ship couldn't handle the open sea for very long, but when well nourished, would feed his fellow travellers the most nutritious nuts during the short trip.

Beechpaw stood rooted further inland, the most memorable ship Vesstan had served on. She got her name from a near-fatal encounter with coastal rocks off the Island of Yns. He was there that fateful night. They got caught in a strong current off the mountainous side of the isle. He was sure they would capsize on the rocks who stretched out far into the sea. Then he saw the ship's main iron-laced branches prowl through the water ahead. They struck twice, doing enough damage to the rocks for the trunk to pass unscathed.

And then there was Pamys. She occupied a large open area in the centre of the beach. The tree wasn't all that big, but the ship certainly was. Whoever had enchanted her had done outstanding work with the widening of the trunk. She could carry an ungodly amount of cargo for her modest height. The ship wasn't a favourite among sailors – she was in no hurry to get anywhere and was known for her leisurely journeys – but if you were prepared to spend a cycle or two drifting on sea currents, there was no better ship to do it in.

Reminiscing on his seafaring adventures brought a smile to Vesstan's face. The ships had imprinted themselves in his heart. But this time, he wasn't here for any of them. It was the enormous wood far behind the shoreline who held his attention. Magven was the largest explorer tree yet to have become a ship and was about to embark on his maiden voyage.

The sheer size of the ship was enough to inspire awe in any sailor. But more than his length or the thickness of his trunk, what impressed Vesstan was the generosity of his crown. It spread far and wide, with branches spanning an enormous length in every direction. The leaves were broad, dark green and firmly attached; holding onto them was a crucial skill for any ship wishing to harness the power of the sea. They hid equally green fruit scattered evenly throughout the crown.

Vesstan had heard of woods like these. Dwarves from the northern ranges sometimes spoke of them. The trees inhabited the Tetran Massif, a range as imposing as the woods themselves. Vesstan couldn't help but wonder how one of them could have made it all the way to the southern shores. The tree must have come from a long line of explorers – the journey must have taken generations.

"Welcome to Magven, master navigator," an elderly druid greeted him as he neared the ship. "Are you ready for the voyage?"

He stopped and looked up at the tree one more time. Magven was even more imposing standing so close and towering over him.

"More than ever."

"I'm Zuri, the master communicator. I will be your partner on this trip."

"Zuri?" He pried his eyes away from the mammoth vessel to gaze at the druid of even greater renown. "I'm sorry, I was so taken by the ship that I forgot about my fellow travellers! It truly is an honour to serve with you."

"I look forward to working with you, too. I couldn't think of anyone better to navigate Magven on his maiden voyage."

Vesstan studied the old druid carefully, the first one to have enchanted an explorer tree into a seagoing vessel nearly a lifetime ago. He wondered whether she'd had a hand in his being chosen for this mission. His navigational skills were second to none, but there were other sailors with far more experience.

"Are you ready to depart?" asked Zuri. "The cargo has been secured and everyone else is already on board."

"Yes, yes. All my business has been taken care of. I'm ready to go."

Vesstan followed the druid up the ladder and onto the deck. They occupied two of the many vacant spots and secured themselves with the ship's vines. Vesstan counted six people sharing the deck with them. It was a pitiful number for such a massive ship, but maiden voyages seldom attracted travellers.

Virgin ships were notoriously unpredictable. Before their first voyage, one never knew which instructions they would follow and which they would ignore. How they would handle themselves if they got hurt or caught in a storm. Which of the potential destinations they would reach, if any at all. Such trips were sought only by people who didn't much care where they ended up and were happy just to go along for the ride.

Zuri placed her hands onto the bare belly of the ship, slowed her breathing and closed her eyes. Vesstan loved the anticipation before the journey got underway, when the druid took a moment to feel the emotions coursing through the wood. He grabbed onto the vine when he saw Zuri's eyes open and her wrinkled hands press down hard.

Powerful roots rose from the ground. They hoisted the vessel into the air. He plummeted and rose again with each new step. His pace slowed when he reached the sand, the weight of the wood pushing the roots deeper into the ground. He slowed further when he hit the surf. The crashing waves sought to eject him from the sea, but the firmly planted roots withstood their charge. They stuck to the sand while the water washed over them and lurched forward upon her return. When the waterline rose within taste of the deck, the roots froze, the crown swayed, and the trunk crashed headlong into the turbulent water. The passengers screamed with terror and delight. Twin waves sped away on either side. The trunk remained bobbling, facing the horizon, ready to depart. Magven's maiden voyage had begun.

"Deploy the sails!" shouted Vesstan, feeling a warm southerly wind pushing against his back.

The druid adjusted the placement and pressure of her hand. The branches ahead of them moved out of each other's way. The ovate leaves stood firm and erect, catching every drop of wind with their broad blades. They strained from exertion, countering the relentless force of the waves.

"Deploy the swimmers left and right!" Vesstan instructed next. Not knowing whether the water was deep enough for a vessel of this size, he kept the bottom branches at bay.

Zuri relayed the signal. Magven lowered his crown into the sea. The branches flailed through the water, churning until she spattered foamy white. Then the leaves stiffened, the limbs locked, and the main branches moved back and forth in harmonious motion. Each one pushed against the water with leaves and limbs spread out to the full, then returned and plunged again for another lap. Each collision with the sea tilted the ship to that side. The passengers tilted with him, holding on to the vines for all they were worth.

Without waiting for an instruction, Magven stretched out his bottom branches too. The longest ones scraped the seabed at first, but quickly corrected to push against it instead. This gave the ship an added burst of speed, helping him slice through the tenacious waves, driving a churning maelstrom beneath his bow and leaving a simmering fissure in his wake.

Vesstan placed his hand next to the druid's. He had no magical training, but even he could feel Magven's exertions reverberate through the wood. The whole trunk flexed and heaved with each swimming swipe. Upper branches creaked from the strain, struggling to contain the full force of the wind. The sea erupted in frenzy on each side of the ship, bubbling from abrasive contact with his abundant foliage. Only the roots were resting idly, content to stay out of the ship's way.

"Magven is taking strain," Vesstan warned. "Angle the leaves not to carry the full brunt of the water or the wind."

"The ship is fine," Zuri disagreed.

"We are clear of the shore. We don't need to push him to the limit anymore."

"He is pushing himself to the limit," Zuri insisted. "Magven has been waiting for this his whole life. He wants to see what he's capable of. We should let him."

"And if he breaks?"

"Trees can mend quickly, especially with my help. I will watch him."

Vesstan weighed the druid's words briefly before nodding in agreement.

"At least turn two notches to the right. Straight at that skylight. Our first destination lies in that direction."

"The Coral Cays? That's where we are taking this ship?"

"It's the closest port. If something happens to him, help will be nearby."

"Very well. But let me know should you reconsider," Zuri advised him with a grin before imparting the instruction.

Having been idle until now, all the segments of the giant root dipped into the water. The ship suddenly veered to the right, then straightened again once they re-emerged.

The skylight was not even halfway through the sky when a Coral Cay port appeared on the horizon. Vesstan placed his hand next to Zuri's again, a look of consternation spread across his face. But there was no hint that the sails might be buckling, or the swimming branches tiring from the effort. He looked at the druid for confirmation.

"I know this journey used to take you several days in Fallnut," Zuri sought to explain, "and I know that you have never taken a ship like this on his maiden voyage–"

"No one has."

"Right." Zuri smiled. "What I'm trying to say is that, even though Magven doesn't yet know how best to sail or swim, or where his limits lie, he should be allowed to discover them for himself. We don't really know what he's capable of either."

"As long as his actions don't put us in danger."

"I will see to that."

"All right then. Turn left. We'll sail around the island. Turn… Turn… There! That should keep us clear of the reef."

Vesstan watched the familiar island go by. The port nestled in a beautifully sheltered bay, coral emerging beyond the submerged land, reaching far beyond the thick jungle canopy who covered the surface of the isle, a protocell who kept her own water away from the sea, secluded and coloured by the bioluminescent reef.

The coral arms forced Magven to round the isle at a wide berth. He watched her reach out to others of her kind, a close-knit knot of isles and reefs who welcomed seafarers to the archipelago's western shores.

"Looks like someone is finally getting tired. Or wants a more even tan," Zuri speculated. "Magven wants to pivot."

"What? When?"

"Now."

Vesstan nodded with urgency. "I'll warn the passengers."

With the preparations made, Zuri relayed her agreement. The ship's enormous branches started pushing sideways, enough to effect a leisurely turn of the trunk. The people rushed across the deck opposite the movement of the ship, holding on to the vines lest they slip on the wet deck. The swivel continued until the last dry patch of wood was swallowed by the sea. The ship then resumed swimming, this time in breaststroke style.

"Good timing. I was just getting thirsty." Zuri grinned, drenched from the sea-soaked branches who now soared above them.

"Care to get us lunch while you're at it?" Vesstan asked.

Zuri thought for a moment, shrugged her shoulders, and brought down a damp branch laden with fruit. Vesstan picked a few and passed them on to the passengers while keeping two for Zuri and himself. The rich texture was surprisingly filling, with superb flavour to match.

"With this fruit, we don't even need the food stores," he said.

"He is one amazing ship," Zuri agreed.

"Once we pass Kryhm Atoll, we'll have to make another four-notch turn. I don't know whether the Srish skylight will be up to guide us. We might have to turn first and correct later."

"Assuming that storm doesn't throw us off track."

Vesstan looked to his left, at the darkening skies hanging over the sea. A flash of lightning betrayed the heavy storm clouds coming their way. A gust of wind blew across the deck, unsettling the sails and tilting the ship.

Vesstan felt a moment of panic. He breathed deeply, remembering that there was no need to rush to the nearest port. He was not in Fallnut anymore. Magven was far more capable of weathering a storm. But Vesstan's apprehension didn't pass unnoticed.

"Let me try to talk some sense into Magven," the druid offered. "A storm like that should not be taken lightly, even by someone of his size."

Two gusts later the edge sails came down; Magven lowered them into the sea. There they helped resist the onslaught of swells and keep the ship steady on course. The passengers opted to wait out the storm in the cargo hold, except for one daredevil who chose to bear the brunt of the raging sea. He joined Vesstan and Zuri on the open deck, carefully tending to the youthful explorer.

A large wave slammed into their side. The ship listed precipitously before dropping back into the trough. On Zuri's advice, Magven extended his branches sideways as far as they would go. They followed the vacillation of the sea, helping to break the waves before they reached the trunk. The upper branches stayed half-raised, using the power of the wind to cut through the storm. Usually still, the roots steered furiously, trying to keep them on course.

By the time the clouds parted enough to reveal the bare sky, the skylight over Rimm was nearing the journey's end. Magven turned and steered towards the most remote island of the archipelago. Vesstan gazed at the passing sky over the distant water, rapidly darkening now that the skylight had disintegrated and nearly vanished from view. The explorer in him couldn't help but wonder what lay in the alluring darkness of the open sea beyond the furthest isle, with no mountains with skylights to show them the way. Humans had come from there, he remembered. He could scarcely believe that they were courageous enough – or desperate enough – to attempt the journey, in ships far smaller and shoddier than his own. He wondered sometimes what that would be like – to undertake a long journey where all you could see was a dark sea under the night sky. He shuddered at the thought.

The ship approached the tail of the island where the Vanishing Bay was slowly crumbling into the sea. Vines and weeds bobbed on the waves as soil and stone disappeared beneath them, leaving behind a muddy trail to remember them by.

The tiny remote island had slipped off Amana's floating shell and was tearing herself apart in her desperate efforts to reach the land again, and rejoin her on the endless journey across the Primordial Sea.

Light petered out of the remaining pieces of the dying sun, snuffing out the last of the radiance from beyond the clouds. From his vantage point on the highest branch, Vesstan could still see dense water thick with silt surrounding the ship. He navigated around the isle to the welcoming port on the other side of Rimm.

It was time for rest and replenishment. Magven walked to a grassy spot away from the beach and buried his roots into the nourishing soil. The passengers disembarked, with the cargo following shortly. Vesstan pressed his body against the damp wood at the base of the tree in a customary gesture of gratitude for a journey well taken. Zuri soon joined him, her weaker hands and feet taking longer to scale the tall ladder from the deck to the ground. Then they left the explorer tree to regain his strength, soak in the hospitality of a brand new world, and imagine the countless journeys that still lay ahead.

LEAP

Asja ran through the shadowy forest. The clatter of metallic footsteps echoed through the trees. Bloodshot eyes followed her, with new ones popping up left and right. She turned her back to them as she raced, desperate to get away, no longer concerned about the noise she made.

A giant pair of eyes terrorised her. Softer, the colour of dusty charcoal, they lacked the savage bloodthirstiness of their scarlet followers, directing them instead to hunt her down. She scrambled to get away, leaping over roots and ducking under branches she could barely see, but the cackling eyes stayed with her, glued to her as she ran, looming larger each time she glanced back at them.

Exhausted and desperate, she turned around and stood her ground, drawing every ounce of energy from the forbidding forest and unleashing it on her pursuer, screaming at the top of her lungs from the immense strain. But the creature absorbed it, growing stronger from her exertions, mocking the futility of her efforts to escape or kill him.

"Asja! Asja!" A persistent voice broke through her nightmare.

She opened her eyes to Florella's face, the still petals stiff with concern, the leafy limbs holding her by the shoulders. She grabbed onto the plant in a tight embrace until her breathing slowed and her distress died down. Only then did she feel Florella's petals caress her face. She let go, uneasy to have the demoness so close. Florella backed off, retreating to a safe distance, but not leaving the girl alone.

"Was it Tyrant again?"

Asja nodded. "How did you know?"

Florella pointed behind the girl.

Asja turned around to look at the broad branch of the Algalash tree on whom she had slept, preferring to stay out of her room and the bed of flowing stone that had sheltered her on her prior stay. The myriad specks of light illuminated the night sky with their faint glow, teasing out the ample branches and the foliage who covered them.

The lush plants who grew by Asja's new bedside were reduced to ash.

She stared at the chilling space, dumbfounded by the sight. Then she slowly turned back towards her mentor, unable to look directly at her face.

"I'm sorry!" she uttered, breathing heavily.

Florella waited for the girl to gather herself before motioning with her outstretched leaves. "Come with me. There's something you need to see."

They made their way from the branch to Asja's old room, through the passage and the hall, and onto a lower branch on the other side of the tree. A patch of earth nestled in the hollow where Florella liked to rest. Asja had been there before and couldn't help but admire stunning orchids who grew in this place, especially now that her own garden lay in ruin.

Florella pointed behind them, urging Asja to follow. She did, moving past the orchids to equally stunning lilies, and other denizens of the rainforest from Florella's youth. And then she saw a gap in the foliage, a cool space where nothing resided but powdery ash.

She stared at her teacher, not knowing what to say.

"Many cycles ago, when I was a young acolyte, I too drained the flowers of life, far beyond what they were willing, or even able, to give. They had opened up to me; I knew them more intimately than I'd known anyone else. They trusted me to nourish and guide them, and I betrayed their trust.

"Before I realised what had happened, they had crumbled into dust. And that's how the garden stayed – a blanket of powdery ash from which nothing grew. It was only recently that the rim started to renew into earth from whom these flowers emerged," she concluded, caressing a young lily with her supple leaves.

"That is a long time to look at a dead garden. Why didn't you replace it with fresh earth?"

Florella shook her head. "I'd rather keep the ash. It reminds me of the danger of what we do."

The sombre look on Florella's face caught Asja off-guard. It connected with her, prompting her to worry about her teacher's wellbeing, surprising herself by how much she cared.

"What happened to you?" she asked, remembering the first time she had seen Florella, and the pain and grief she sensed beneath the leaves. She patiently waited while the plant settled, and listened thirstily when the words came out, trembling and broken at first, speaking of her childhood in the dense rainforests from the land of mur.

The sprout opened her leaves for the very first time. Her tender stem barely held her weight, leaning on shallow roots who struggled to support her. A gentle breeze wiped a water droplet from her shoot, dropping her onto a dry twig that lay alongside her. Her senses clear, she gazed at the newfound world, trying to take it all in, all at once.

She felt drizzle on her face when the trees above her couldn't restrain the rain, soaked in the sun when the mountain from across the sea launched him into the sky, gently swayed in the breeze tempered by swaying grass, watched butterflies grace blooming flowers with their busy feet, and bobbed to the sounds of the forest humming all around her.

Until she closed her leaves to sleep.

When she opened them again, solid walls of brooding stone had replaced the protective woods. A high ceiling of hard crystal stood between her and the sky lights. And her soft loam of nurturing earth found herself bound by marble slabs, left consigned to a remote corner of an empty room.

A tear rolled down her leaf, and then another, falling back into the soil from whom they'd come. She felt no wind, no murmur of the woods, no siblings nearby with their comforting presence. Even a distant skylight struggled to make himself seen, sneaking into the room through a crack in the wall, leaving her to adjust to her newfound home in the heavy dusk of loneliness.

A woman walked into the room. She poured water at the plant's base, crooning as she worked, and then settled into a nearby chair. The plant drank thirstily, until the water brought on a memory of rain-doused trees who used to shelter her, and the abiding grief of their absence. She lived on in her corner but didn't flourish. The woman continued tending to her needs with water and fresh earth. But tall as she had grown, buds would not form nor flowers come.

Until she felt the knobbly hands wash down her leaves with a moist sponge, leaving them glistening and wet as if showered by rain. Hands hardened by the labour of tending to the plants. The care in their touch stayed with her, and she responded with cautious affection of her own.

She grew buds, small and tentative at first, unsure of their welcome. The hands caressed them, surprisingly gently for their worn skin. The buds began to rouse, revealing soft petals of lavender and wine. Seeing them, the woman's face broadened into a warm smile. The buds opened further, spreading into flowery blossoms as the plant bloomed for the first time in her life.

The woman showed her off to visitors who nodded with approval, and the plant added new flowers to her shoot, with oversized petals to drown out her solitude. Children ran in and marvelled at her bulging flowers and scent that filled the room. She etched lines of ginger and rust into their burgundy hue, each a pain of separation from the kinfolk she had known, a memory of grief for what she had lost. With each new visit she grew further still, dwarfing her forest siblings with her towering frame, forming patterns unseen on flowers of her kind.

A commotion erupted outside the house. Screams of terror and clanking of weapons. The woman barricaded the door, but it caved to the blow of an axe. A spear found her from across the room, piercing her chest and tossing her into the wall. Strange people walked in, but they didn't dwell, yanking the spear out and rejoining the turmoil in the street.

The plant reached out with her lower leaves, lifting and caressing the lifeless hand, her stem rocking in fitful motion, teardrops collecting on the petal edge. Her vibrant flowers stained with fresh pain. Her floral fragrance masking the stench of death.

The woman's people eventually came to collect her remains, with slumped shoulders and faces raked with grief. The plant's leaves waved their last goodbye, her petals fluttering in the stale air, her old life leaving her this time. She watched the woman being carried away, the only one whose wellbeing she had learned to care about other than her own.

The gift of caring stayed with her in the quiet, empty house. It burned in her as she rose to leave, tearing her roots, leaving them in place, the discarded grounding of a being who had outgrown them.

Asja stared at the plant standing before her. A demoness, as she'd thought of her ever since her departure, a label that no longer seemed to fit. The vision of her exterior melted away once more, revealing the pain buried underneath. But alongside the anguish lay a dreamy aura the girl had not yet seen, the essence of her being, a presence who felt more like Florella than the standing plant did.

She moulded the pain into exquisite creations that touched the core of those who saw them, moving them to marvel at the beauty on display, not knowing the hardship from which they had sprung. She lived for those moments that gave meaning to her pain, coming to appreciate them with the passage of time, leaving the poverty of her heritage as a plant little more than a distant memory.

COLOURING

Asja sat on top of a rock, her staff resting comfortably across her lap. Its luminous tip that had shone upon the Mirrordon landscape now lay dim, letting the grassy plain recede beyond the end of her vision. She kept her eyes closed in any event, soaking in what she had seen, seeking to perceive it with her deeper senses that pierced the outer form into the essence of being.

The longing washed over her, forceful and unquenched, but more primal than Florella's dream. A proto-dream who stemmed directly from Aia's cosmic wish. Like Primal Water before them, fragments of the landscape sought to create a melody of their own yet found familiarity and comfort in their collective song. They were destined to differentiate themselves from it over the span of time, once their longing grew to unbearable heights.

Touched by their desire, Asja dipped her finger in a nearby puddle and placed a drop of water onto a blade of grass. Isolated and alone, the droplet hung onto the tip for the longest time, straining to hear the melody of the pool from whom she was torn. And then she slid down the steep surface, leaving pieces of herself behind as she went, splitting into flying tears upon her collision with the stalk, her exhilaration lost to the thirst of the ground.

Asja took another drop and exposed her to the grass, but instead of leaving her to fend for herself in an alien world, she held her safely in the palm of her hand before plunging her back into the receptive pool. Her experience coloured the droplets all around her, rippling as it went, broadening the water's hum as she shared the adventure none of them have had.

A jolt coursed through the girl, a surge of energy coming from the puddle. She felt the water's exuberance, enriched by the unique experience of a single drop, a new insight into a more expansive way to be.

Encouraged by the prospect, Asja turned her attention to a nearby stream – a modest flow of calm water running over smooth ground. She raised a rock through the stream's bed, placing an obstacle in the water's path. The myriad droplets strained to avoid him, flowing left and right around the stubborn stone, but for a few daredevils who used the stream's power to propel them against the hard surface and into the air above, before plunging back into the flowing mass further downstream.

The murmur of the stream shifted in response, each courageous droplet adding her own unique tone, until the whole stream exploded in a symphony of sound far removed from the water's primordial hum, continuously fed by new droplets rising from the stone, their longing quenched but for a moment in time.

Asja and her staff tried to soak it up, but it quickly overcame their ability to contain and burst through the tip in an outpouring of light, illuminating the meadow until she couldn't make out the rocks rising from the grass, and the stream became nothing more than a meandering line.

Jumping with excitement, Asja slipped and fell off the rock, grazing her knee as she hit the ground. The sharp pain coloured the water's tone as it coursed through her, distorting its harmony and turning the staff's light into searing heat that scorched the grassy plain right before her eyes. Distraught by the sight, by the lives and dreams of countless stalks cut short with her mishap, she disconnected from the stream, letting her blistering staff fall silent and still.

She stomped and cursed, dismayed by her failure. By the breach of trust that the grass, water and stone had placed in her. She breathed in deeply, trying to regain her poise. This was what the Mirrordon Plane had been created for, she remembered. Its world was resilient to magicians' mistakes and would recover and be ready for her next attempt.

Still, she couldn't help but acknowledge how much more there was to her training than learning to draw and unleash the energy she found. If she were to serve as a practitioner of magic, she'd have to condition herself to use that power as intended no matter her lot, or the hardships she'd undoubtedly suffer along the way would turn her into the kind of wizard she'd once left her teachers for fear of becoming.

A WORLD WITH NO NAME

"Good news," Shar greeted Asja as she entered the hall. "Empyrean has agreed to help us. Help us free Rangorr," he added when he saw the blank look on her face.

"Em-py-ree-aan?" she yawned, still waking up from her outdoor sleep.

"He is... a celestial." Shar shrugged his shoulders, as if he just gave up on trying to describe a creature for whom Asja had no frame of reference. "Florella and I made Ama's case to him, and he agreed to help."

"Just Empyrean?" Asja wondered, lacking Shar's enthusiasm for having Rangorr freed after having to fight him for her life, and imagining how dangerous it would be to face the morlocks in order to free him.

"One celestial is enough."

He gazed at her for a long while, a cryptic expression covering his face. Then he spoke. "There is something you need to see."

He got up and headed for the doorway.

"But I haven't eaten yet!" she protested.

"It won't take long."

Asja hurried behind, following him out of the hall and up the gentle stairway towards Shar's section of the tree. An innocuous-looking portal dwelled in a far corner of the room. He stopped and extended his hand, asking her to go through first. She hesitated, not knowing where it led, until reassured by a comforting glance. She walked through a still membrane lit by subdued light, offering no hint of activity or danger waiting on the other side.

She didn't recognise the smooth amber walls she found there, or the thick bronze veins running through them, even if the pattern they formed looked oddly familiar. She followed one as it curved and looped, coming to an end only to repeat itself on a smaller scale, a pattern within a pattern recurring until it grew too small for her eyes to discern. She placed her hand on the malleable surface, sensing the land's need to create herself anew, even if each new creation looked suspiciously like the ones before.

She gave Shar a questioning look.

"This is Isura." Seeing her struggle to recall the name, he added, "The land whose lights you see in the night sky."

Her eyes shot wide open with surprise. She wasn't on Amana anymore? She was on a whole new world? She stood back and stared at the wall again, now recognising the pattern she'd seen in the starry sky time after time.

Her jaw dropped as the implications hit her. This was how easily demons travelled between worlds? All they had to do was step into the right portal? She knew that they weren't bound to Amana, but the full force of what that meant didn't strike her until now. She was dealing with beings to whom Amana was just another world, and Ama one goddess among many.

But before she could dwell on it, Shar walked on to the next portal and extended his hand, inviting her in. The neighbouring world she'd love to learn about was just a stopover on today's tour.

The next world bore no resemblance to anything she'd seen. The viscous fluid obscured her sight. She struggled to follow Shar, moving her limbs with effort, not used to having to fight her surroundings for every step she made. She was relieved to see the outline of the next portal, and eagerly stepped through its faint frame.

She gasped when she emerged on the other side.

She floated in space with no surface to set her feet upon or a solid object to hold onto. A thought of Primogenus flashed through her mind. Only this was no meagre plane made to aid her training, but vast open space within Aia's cosmic span.

Asja gazed at the sky, following the curves of the Primordial Ocean, the dark surface rising and falling and looping in on itself as Primal Waters meandered through empty space. Clusters of lights shone through the dark, illuminating the waters beyond their land – each a world of her own, swimming across the surface of the Primordial Ocean at a cosmic pace.

Asja remembered the first time she'd seen all of Amana from Algalash's heights, illuminated by skylights launched by the mountains, hemmed in by water on every side. Is this what her land looked like from the vantage of space?

She looked down to see a world shrouded in mist, with no light of her own, barely discernible from the Primal Waters upon whom she rested. Until a rumble from the ground disturbed the tranquillity of the scene, and an explosion ruptured the surface of the land to propel a luminous ball of light into the night sky.

The skylight burst through the clouds as he rose, illuminating the land stretching all around him, revealing her spine – two spiralling ranges who circled three times around the central peak before subsiding into the ocean at the furthest tip of their reach.

Asja breathed heavily, her heart racing at the sight, her hunger lost in the grandeur of the scene.

She whispered, "Who is this world?"

Shar smiled and said, "She's still being born. She has no name."

Only now, as the skylight peered higher into the sky, did Asja see that no land connected the sprawling mountain ranges. They rose from the water, the outline of a realm who was yet to be. No spheres of light outlined their contours, their peaks too immature to pull off such a feat. Only the central mount – the heart of the new land – could trawl the watery depths for crust and light and heat.

"Can you see the elementals?" asked Shar, pointing at the clouds.

Asja looked closely at the water on the outskirts of the land. Amidst the churning of fog in the blowing wind, she sensed a presence, a will to separate from the liquid mass, to sound a note higher than the deep bellowing of the sea.

The mountains, too, stood tall and erect, more so than she would have expected from a world so young. Their essence lacked the freedom of movement possessed by the wind, rooted in place from which to nourish the land, but she saw them harden as if to make a stand, and bulge and posture towards that end.

And resisting them both with all of her might was a spirit of water, an aching presence who rose with the clouds and washed over the land, seeking to drag them both back into her depths. But they prevailed, rising even higher than the water could reach and, having heard their own unique tone, eager to hear more.

Asja had never known creatures such as these, faint yet pervasive, fluid of form, their mastery of their element seemingly complete. They reminded her of Vagran, with the command of lightning as his natural trait. But even he had to mould a hard outer shell to keep the charge from pouring out of him and taking his life along with it.

"I wasn't there to see it, but I'm told that Amana came into being the same way," Shar said.

Asja gazed at the stone wizard, suddenly curious about his age. The scarred face, the crusty voice, the way he spoke and carried himself all hinted at an ancient being, far older than anyone else she knew. He may not have been present at Amana's birth, but it wouldn't have surprised her had he come along soon after.

She had branded him a demon, and still stood by her reasons for it. But she was beginning to see just how much more there was to him. She leaned onto his side, grateful for the gift he had given her today, knowing that it was beyond anything her adoptive people, and perhaps even her birth people, could yet conceive.

It was elementals who were helping craft the world beneath, but if their actions were meant as a hint of what celestials could achieve, there was indeed no need to ask for more than one.

Without the pull of a mature land to hold him back, the skylight reached high into the space above and disintegrated before his time. He crumbled into countless parts, each a fragment from the depths of the sea, a sliver of Aia who had longed to emerge from her moist womb and into a life of his own. They gazed in wonder through the breadth of space, their stare for the first time unstifled and sweeping, burning through their own light in the thrill of the scene. And then they fell back towards the land, luminous drops of water and earth leaving trails of light in their wake, eager to establish themselves in their new home.

Shar took in a deep breath, as if to absorb the spaciousness of the place. Then he looked at the girl leaning on him, his face breaking into a mischievous grin.

"I think it's time you learnt how to travel."

TIME

Arezan stood on a hill overlooking a mountain range. His webbed hand rested on his forehead to block out the sun the closest peak had just hurled into the sky. He opened his backpack to take out a multicoloured gem and proceeded to encode the skylight cycle into the lattice frame.

He silently thanked Hloim – the mage he'd encountered in the land of dwarves whose insight into crystals had left him with this gift alongside the knowledge of how to use it. He thought back to how welcoming the mage was of a sorcerer from foreign lands, a trait he was warned not to expect among the dwarves. He smiled to himself, thinking he'd left the mage with a gift of his own, remembering how thirstily the lad had soaked up all the mur lore. Then he put away the gem and stood on a ledge to take a probing gaze at the foreign landscape.

The wetlands spreading before him all the way to the range should have felt close to home, his own people having come from the sea. Yet they felt alien, the foliage of thick-rooted trees colouring the water a sickly shade of green, swarms of insects roaming the marshlands and pestering creatures big and small, the earth herself mixing with the water to form suffocating sludge. They reminded him that he didn't belong here any more than in the desert sands he had just crossed on his journey east.

A myth of his people kept playing on his mind – that there was a time, not long after they'd first emerged from the ocean, when the land felt pristine and the mountains short and young, that only one summit had the power to release seeds and light into the skies above, a central mount who fed and illuminated the entire world. There was but one cycle for all the inhabitants of Amana.

What that must have been like, to have but a single measure of time! A common understanding, something to share no matter where you lived. Excitement welled up in the astrologer just thinking about the prospect.

Now everywhere he went, people had a different relationship with the mountains and the sky, acquired different hues from the land in whom they dwelled, tended different plants from the seeds the summits scattered across the ground. Only their language has remained as one, though with sounds and words that gave it a local feel. And all because the land grew mountain ranges tall enough, and deep enough, for them to unleash skylights of their own.

As if Ama wanted her people to be different.

OBALIN

Asja gazed nervously around a small room. The Chaos Plane had recreated the place well, no doubt dredging it up from her childhood memories. Stone shelves coaxed out of the back wall took up most of the space, their weight-bearing backs carrying crystals large and small, comprising every shape, colour and texture the little girl could conceive.

An object in the corner of the table caught her eye. A most elaborate crystalline structure, one she didn't recognise at the time. Now she knew it as a periapt, a medium that elder yetis used to capture their memories once they sensed their end was near. She wondered what Obalin intended to do with it, being in his prime and, as she now knew, going on to see many more journeys of the Mount Aorai suns.

The runemage himself sat behind the table, eying her. She remembered his stare as she stood at the entrance to his study, wishing to master his rune-making skills, unsure of what he might say or do. Only she was older now, and less in awe of the mage's skills.

She let the scene unfold, watching the world of her childhood through adolescent eyes, wondering what the plane was trying to tell her, fearful she wouldn't understand or approve of its message.

Obalin's facial expressions commanded her attention. They told her so much more about the man now than they did when she was a child, caught up as she was in trying to learn and make a good impression. Curiosity and annoyance that a girl from a distant, little-known village would seek to learn the runes. Relief at her modest ability to put different kinds of crystals and gems to memory. Fascination at her knack for intuiting the properties of the crystals and how they might be used. And absolute dread at seeing her draw power from layered tourmaline without the aid of instruction or a staff, as if the stone had sought her out and wanted her to tap into the tremendous power locked within his core.

The mage knocked the crystal off the table and into a corner of the room. His brash movements and muttering under the breath left no doubt that it was not an accident. As did the icy stare that followed, leaving an indelible scar on the little girl.

Now she faced it again, lacking fear of the mage, peering deep into his eyes in search of what the plane wanted her to see. Obalin feared her. She remembered that. Her immense talent coupled with mysterious origins were what drove him to end her apprenticeship and urge the other mages to do the same – an act that filled her with self-doubt and left her an outsider yearning for their approval.

But there was more to his fear than she had known then. With the plane's help, she spied angst of what was to become of the mage ways if she were to join their ranks. What would become of their traditions, of their ways of serving their people. He didn't have answers to any of these questions, but the mere thought led him to shut her out.

Even more, a hint of jealousy sparkled in his eyes. Envy from a mage whose bright star was still on the rise, who hoped to head the runemage order in the cycles to come, when faced with an acolyte whose natural talent far outstripped his own, and whose actions he could not predict, let alone control.

Asja knew the look well. She'd seen it in the eyes of every mage at the gathering of clans. Even after Rangorr's attack, when the druids grew welcoming of her after seeing her skill on display, the mages' stance had remained the same. Was she fooling herself that there was a place for her among them, that she could earn their respect and trust with her own deeds? Did they merely turn to her in their hour of need, and would turn away the moment that need was met?

It led to unpleasant speculation, a heretical thought she hadn't considered before – whom did the mages really serve? *Ordinary mountainfolk* was the reflexive answer, but seeing them put their own ambition and prestige ahead of that service made her wonder how much of the sacrificial spirit from the days of old was still alive in the mages of today, and how much had devolved into a naked quest for power.

She felt like a fool for leaving the wizards and cutting her training short for fear of turning into a tyrannical, power-hungry demon, when the mages she sought to join were on that very same path.

She left the scene and exited the plane, her composure shaken and her thoughts scattered, still determined to use her talent and skill in the service of her people, but increasingly distrustful of those who led them.

AMBUSH

The mighty Ural peaks passed by Asja in a blur. She homed in on the towering central figure of the range, and then on the flat Mount Cougal top. The portal spewed her out on the outskirts of Amerot before dissolving into thin air.

She hovered over the ground following the journey's end, sensing the grass beneath her and the trees all around, and then let go of her misty form to coalesce into that of the dwarf. She breathed heavily, her heart racing from the stress of the foray, her first away from the safety of the planes.

She remained still, her gaze wandering around, straining to make out any movement in the night. The town was awake, illumination furnished by many crystalline gems placed strategically atop buildings that lined the streets, but none of the people she saw in the distance paid any attention to her corner of the wood.

She stood up and breathed a sigh of relief. Her sudden appearance on the outskirts of the town had passed unnoticed.

Excitement welled up inside her. Dependent for so long on Vagran to take her places, she could now reach them on her own, in less time and with minimal effort. It wasn't quite so simple, she realised. Familiar places were easy to find, but exploration was a frustrating undertaking with the limited vision afforded by the portals as they tore through wide open spaces at breakneck speed.

She thought back to the gateway Shar had conjured in the space of the hall for her return to her dwarven home. She lacked the skill to craft such a doorway, hers needing the traveller to do half the work by fading into mist whom the portal could absorb. She wondered again whether the mist could coagulate into flesh that was not a dwarf, but her hazy form had a memory of her origin she dared not erase.

She left the wood and headed into the town, standing tall and walking measuredly but with purpose, not wanting to raise suspicion. A few nods of the head to passers-by later, she reached the study of the runemage Recha – a tall, slender structure forged from the rising hillside. She knocked on the stone door, and when she heard an answering voice, opened it and entered.

Recha stood behind a table of crystalline bismuth, his crisp lines winding onto themselves, changing colour as they receded from the centre, their number revealing the age of the rock in whom they were born. Moruk, her close associate and a respected runemage in his own right, stood by her. They both looked at Asja with expressions of guarded welcome, the many gems strewn across the surface hinting that she'd interrupted them in their work.

"I come from my wizard teachers," the girl began, skipping formalities, as was her way. "They've agreed to help us."

"Excellent!" said Recha before her gaze started to wander and a touch of nervousness crept into her voice. "Are they here?"

"No, I came alone. They sent me to prepare for the next attack."

"Another attack?" Moruk jumped. "When? Where?"

"At Sentinel Grove. They asked for mages and druids to gather there – like we did here – to entice the demon to come."

Recha's brow furrowed at the words. "Why?"

"They've been spying on the demon ever since the attack, and they've discovered that he'd waited for the gathering of the clans, knowing that he'd find all the mages assembled here. His goal was to kill as many of us as quickly as he could."

"So… If we were to gather again, this demon… would attack?" asked Moruk.

Asja nodded. "That's the plan."

"Are there other demons to aid him," asked Recha, "or is this one acting alone?"

Asja bit her tongue. The question implied ties to the morlocks, though Recha knew too little to ask about them. Asja wrestled with the answer, not wanting to bring her birth people into this. She doubted that the runemages had the means to uncover her mur origins, but she didn't want to risk them lumping her with their enemies.

"They didn't see him associate with any other demons," she replied.

"Still, now he knows about you," Moruk pointed out. "If he attacks again, he'll be more careful… and deadly."

"That's why we must lure him to Sentinel Grove. This will give us an advantage we didn't have here."

"But here, we barely managed to contain him!" Moruk protested. "And only after he slaughtered everyone who got in his way before we formed a defensive line."

"Imagine if he'd attacked you first," cautioned Recha. "That could well have been the end of us all."

The thought troubled Asja, too. She was supposed to put her trust in Empyrean – a celestial being whom she knew nothing about. She knew since her journey to the nameless world that immensely powerful beings other than Ama did exist, but they clearly had their own agenda, having done nothing to interfere with the mur machinations so far. And if she lacked faith, she couldn't expect to convince the runemages, whose trust in her was shaky from the start.

In the end, she resorted to the only course of action she could think of that would make the mages buy into the plan.

"My teachers will be nearby, ready to help if we need them," she said with as much conviction as she could muster.

Moruk and Recha looked at her thoughtfully before exchanging glances. "We will call an urgent council to discuss your proposal. If the other runemages agree, we will ask the druids to meet us at Sentinel Grove."

Recha's words trailed off into uncomfortable silence. Asja kept waiting, not quite believing that this was the end of the matter, until Moruk's words made that clear. "Thank you so much for your help, Asja. I don't know what we would have done without your teachers."

And finally, the girl understood. She nodded with a weak smile, turned around and walked out the door.

Yes, they appreciate my help, she thought angrily, *but not enough to include me in the council. They feel indebted to me, but not enough to offer anything of substance in return.* Confusion and ire raged in her as she walked down the semi-lit street.

Why did their approval still mean so much to her? Why did she lie to convince them to pursue this plan instead of risking their rejection by telling them the truth? She hated that, no matter how much she learned, how much her magic skills overshadowed theirs, they remained her superiors.

She trod the meandering streets until she reached Kinrum Hall – its doors wide open with no sounds of assembly – and quietly slipped inside. The floor was dark, the hall empty. No light shone through the crystal ceiling, no figures scaled the Peruvius mountainside. She didn't need to see them to remember the solitary heroes risking their lives to rid the mountains of the flying beasts.

Oh, how she had wanted to be them! She had stood there as a child, watching the animated display on the floor of the hall, fancying herself a hero of the people, only wielding a runemage's staff instead of an axe. She never liked the general rising of the dwarves that followed, finding it too complicated as a child, with no lone warrior to emulate, no role model to look up to.

She snorted derisively at the thought that the runemage order claimed continuity with the mages from that time. The ulterior motives behind their service made them unworthy in her eyes. And if her heroes of old had fallen from grace, perhaps ordinary folk deserved a second look. They did win the struggle that the heroes had started. Perhaps they had a larger role to play in the struggle ahead. She didn't know what it was, or how to bring it about, but the thought stayed with her as she left the hall, crossed over the crumbled courtyard, and headed back into the wood.

The first marker on the way to Sentinel Grove lay due west. She leaned on her staff and closed her eyes, recalling the whole itinerary, preparing to portal to a place she had never seen.

SENTINEL GROVE

The motion had stopped, Asja's inner sight having spotted the final marker on her journey – a new skill she had honed in her portal training. She stood in the tall grass, the swaying tips tickling her ankles beneath the robe. Swooshing of leaves high above her caused her to look up.

Mighty sentinels rose on either side, towering over other trees in the forest and the grove. Their crowns rustled menacingly, branches rubbing against branches and leaves against leaves, signalling the presence of an intruder in their midst.

Asja stood still, not wanting to provoke them, not knowing what would trigger a defensive response. She thought she was safe as a dwarf, a friend of the elves and their druids, doubting that sentinels could sense the mur essence beneath her dwarf look. Still, she stayed in her spot, not running away nor rushing in, not brandishing her staff but ready to raise a shield should canopy thorns begin to fly. The sentinel crowns rustled some more, until the absence of danger prompted the stalwart trunks to resume their rigid posture, giving her their permission to enter the grove.

She set forth, bewitched by the ground on whom she walked, admiring the emerald glow of the grass growing in the grove. Druidic enchantments permeated the place, energising her staff with no effort on her part. She understood now why Empyrean had chosen this place to face Rangorr again. Drawing power was so easy that mages and druids could put up a fight here. Druids must have appreciated this, too, making steady efforts to regenerate their charms despite only rarely travelling to the place.

The trees in the grove looked nothing like the towering sentinels guarding the perimeter. Their slender trunks with smooth bark grew to a modest height, needing only smallish roots to hold them in place. But their number far exceeded their size. Their roots entwined, permeating the moist earth, nourishing their trunk and all the ones nearby. The stems sprouted branches who went every which way, mingling to form a single canopy who dressed herself with leaves and kept out light, wind and rain, crafting a secluded space for druids to stay.

"Who are you?" a shaky voice came from inside the canopy.

Asja stopped, her staff at the ready, soaking in the sounds coming from the dark. She strained her eyes, but couldn't see any forest creatures or more exotic beings dwelling inside.

"I'm Asja," she said. "I come from Amerot."

A small figure holding a crystalline staff came into the light. His silky robe hinted at a mage from the west, where Peruvius Mountains met elven forests along a bulging line, making the fruits of forest craft easy for dwarves to obtain. A dense beard covered a face with few lines of worry and age, the teal hue revealing lineage from the Topaz clan. His warm eyes and friendly demeanour pointed to the west too, surrounded by the mountainfolk and their elven friends, far from the dangers posed by the desert.

"Are you a mage?" he asked, eyeing her staff.

"I'm a wizard apprentice."

"Wizard? Hmm… I've never heard of them."

"They are masters of magic who live on the Tetran Massif."

"The land of giants!" His face brightened at the words. "My name is Hloim. I'm a mage… hoping to become a runemage someday," he admitted with a grin.

"What are you doing here? I thought this was a druid shrine."

"It used to be, generations ago, before elves and dwarves came to an understanding. See these?" He tapped on a giant statue covered with vines, making a loud ringing sound. "That was our ancestors' addition to this place."

Only now did Asja realise that more than trees lined the sylvan grove. Crystalline statues stood at the edge of the thicket, covered with creepers and leaves, their organic footprint smudging the crystals from whom they were made, until they could barely be spotted amidst the plants growing from them. Common quartz, Asja recognised the soiled crystals, unsurprised that more precious stones weren't used to sculpt statues of this size.

"How did they get here?" she wondered.

"Smaller geodes were transported on wagons, and then assembled and moulded into statues here. At least that's what the runemages told me." He shrugged. "Apparently, you could see the fault lines when they were first made, but they've since fused together so well that they look like they've come from the same slab."

"Why would mages erect crystal statues at a druid site?"

"Back in those days, mages and druids worked closely together. They chose this place – the easternmost of the druid forest shrines – to gather within for its location. It took as long for the druids by the western sea to travel here as it did the mages from the foothills of Mount Granat. But with this being a forest site, mages were at a disadvantage – they drew their power from mountains rather than woods. So they did the next best thing – they transported the most potent fragments of the summits and had them erected here. Ingenious!

"Did you know that, back then, both mages and druids had permanent presence here? There were always some mages who wanted to learn the druid ways, and druids the reverse. That's why the sentinels were planted – so that the magicians could tinker with their craft and not worry about a forest feline looking for a meal. It didn't last, though. I guess the druids went home and had no mountains nearby to fuel their spells, and mages could only find forests, low and meagre at that, on the lower foothills of the Peruvius Range.

"Damn it, I'm babbling again! Enough of that! What brings you here?"

Asja only smiled at the wealth of information pouring from the mage. "I've come to scout the place. There's a good chance that mages and druids will use it to set a trap for a demon. I've never been to Sentinel Grove. I wanted to see what we'll have to work with."

Hloim stared at her, his mouth open wide.

"Haven't you heard that a demon attacked Amerot during the gathering of the clans?"

He shook his head. "When?"

"Three Aorai cycles ago."

"I've been travelling longer than that. I had no idea," he lamented, his cheerful demeanour gone. "What happened?"

"A demon came out of nowhere. He appeared on the outskirts of the town and started killing people in the courtyard of Kinrum Hall. We scrambled a defence and contained him, but then he just vanished."

"He's still alive?"

"Gone for now."

Hloim shuddered, as if a mere thought of demons made his skin crawl. Then he cocked his head, giving Asja a probing gaze. "You were there, weren't you?"

She nodded.

"You know, I've always thought of demons as these mysterious fiends who seek to lead us astray. I've never heard of them actually killing people!"

"This one did." She grimaced, thinking of the mages they'd lost in the attack, especially Obalin.

"So the runemages sent *you* here – a magic wielder from the land of giants?" his words trailed off in wonder, as if her mention of conjurors he'd never heard of gave her an exotic quality he needed time to digest.

Asja sighed. "I wish they did. I came here on my own. There's a reason that Sentinel Grove was chosen, and I wanted to know why." She looked Hloim straight in the eye and smiled. "Your knowledge of history has really helped me."

He grinned, as if trying to be of as much help as he could. "If you ask me, the single most important reason for both mages and druids to make a stand here is that this is the one place where both can truly fight. Druids have the enchantments that have saturated the earth and infused the plants growing from her, and mages have the crystal statues with the energy those contain."

"I'm sure the sentinel trees standing watch would come in handy, too," Asja added.

"Oh, yes. I just wish these crystalline warriors could do the same. Look at them! Standing tall as a tree, all armed and armoured, but none can even move!"

Asja looked at the statue closest to her. A huge dwarf warrior adorned with sturdy armour made of rutilated quartz, the golden threads woven into the emblem of the Citrine Clan. His right arm raised high, holding a heavy hammer as if to strike, his expressive eyes fixated on a target not two steps away, his bearded face lined with exertion that never saw release.

She closed her eyes to better feel the quartz, his sizeable energy pent up and ready for discharge. But instead of channelling it to her staff as she normally would, she kept it within the crystal, redirected and repurposed, softening the rigid joints until they could flow. The hammer came down in response, the back bending, the posture shifting, until it struck the ground directly below, ending its motion with a loud thud.

Hloim's hair stood on end. His breath caught in his throat. He looked ready to bolt should the giant statue come to life again. When it didn't, he turned to Asja, seeking an explanation for what he'd just witnessed.

She only winked and smiled in response.

"How... How did you do that?"

"It's a skill I learned in my wizard training."

"Can you teach me?"

The question caught her off guard. It didn't occur to her that he would ask because she didn't think that he could master it. Only one dwarf ever did, and it took him a lifetime to do it.

She studied him closely, his mature look, the hopeful expression on his face, the excitement in his voice. She sensed no reservations that all the mages in Amerot had, no trepidation of what might happen if they departed from established mage ways, no angst at being upstaged by another more skilled at his craft. Just a pure desire to learn and grow.

She thought back to the time she had spent listening to the primordial hum inside the Primogenus Plane, feeling the motion of Primal Waters inside the Mirrordon Plane, seeking to sense and influence Aia and be influenced by her in return. It was a major investment of time and effort, even for a mur.

"It takes many cycles to learn this skill, and you may have to learn others first," she added, remembering her time in the Underworld.

"Right. It always does," he replied, seemingly exasperated, though she sensed an undercurrent of defiance, of relishing a challenge to rise to and overcome. "Can you at least show me how you did it?"

"For you to appreciate that, you'd have to be able to draw power from the crystals and use it in ways you haven't before."

He responded by gripping his staff firmly and feeding it until its tip shone with the golden light from the statue's stone.

She shook her head. "Stop draining the crystals of their force. Redirect it into their joints, use it to soften them so they can move." Seeing his blank look, she quickly added, "I'll guide you."

She melded with the crystal once more, traversing the familiar pathways, searching for the presence of a mage within their fold. When she found him, she hovered around his haze, thwarting his attempts to drain more energy out of the stone. And when he drifted, confused as to which way to go, she nudged him into the crystalline lattice, softening the rigid frame as they went, until the forearm started to rise, taking the hammer along with it.

Hloim gasped at the sight, as if frozen by his own spell, staring at the hammer that had barely left the ground. His hand eventually moved, reaching tentatively to touch the giant warrior as if to convince himself that he was still real. And then he turned to Asja, tears running down his face, spellbound and overwhelmed by what he'd just done.

She stared back at him – at the hazy form of a dwarf – as her inner sense glimpsed the essence lurking underneath. A thirst for knowledge, a drive to learn that would stand no barrier imposed by the mages, a desire to tread into worlds unknown and reinvent himself each step of the way, a longing that lived for the thrill of discovery and drew meaning from each new find.

She basked in the ecstasy of a dream fulfilled, feeling it as her own, blown away by the grandeur of an ordinary deed she had long ceased to see. They remained standing in the grass, neither speaking nor moving, locked in each other's gaze.

When Hloim's eyes finally did move, their attention was drawn to the object in her hand.

"What happened to your staff?"

She looked at the staff she held, suddenly aware of its broader spine. A third strand had appeared and woven its delicate frame around the other two, its smooth texture the colour of fine amethyst. She knew nothing about the mysterious tool that her life and practice had come to depend on, save that it was connected to her somehow, filling out from profound experiences she's had, reassuring her in its own cryptic way that she was on the right path, hinting that someday she would come to understand the forces that were at work in her life and the end to which they toiled.

ERBRUS

Asja raised her hand to trace the contours of a wrinkled, bearded face etched into the stone wall – a dwarf who took a forbidden path that led him away from his people and caused him to be forever lost to them. She stared into his eyes, trying to discern the person behind them, wishing she had met him.

"Did you know him?" she asked Shar.

"He was Balazaar's apprentice, not mine, but I knew him well."

"What was he like?"

Shar stepped away, pacing back and forth, as his unfocused gaze dropped to the floor.

"He was moderately talented, though exceptionally so for a dwarf. He knew little of the ways of magic and even less of himself, and much of what he thought he knew, he had to unlearn. He failed more times than I can remember." The stone wizard chuckled at the thought. "We were amazed at his resolve.

"I asked him about that once. Why was he so determined to become a wizard? What kept him going? He said he wanted to be an example to his people. He wanted to show them what they could do. So impressed was he by what he learned here that he burned with the desire to share it with them."

"Did he?" she whispered, remembering the tragic end to the legend of his fall.

Shar shook his head. "He tried, many times. He visited mages, people he knew. They rejected him, either fleeing or trying to fight. They feared the knowledge he possessed and where he had learned it. Later, he approached others too, ordinary folk who didn't know him. They welcomed him when they saw what he could do, loved to have him among them, but they admired him with such fervour that he ended up being the one to flee!"

Asja's brow furrowed in confusion.

"He wanted his people to be like him," clarified Shar, "not worship him."

"What did he do after the dwarves rejected him?"

"He was old by the time he stopped trying, and broken in spirit. Before the end, he did what the rest of us do – he travelled to other worlds where he could be of service."

Asja breathed in deeply, trying to imagine what his life must have been like, having succeeded at achieving significant magical mastery, far beyond anything dwarves had ever done, only to have it thrown back in his face by the very people he sought to help. She was unnerved by how closely Erbrus' life resembled her own.

"You have an advantage over Erbrus," Shar interrupted her train of thought, suspiciously aware of what it might be. "You have a gift he did not have."

Her mind promptly drifted to her mur origins, whose proficiency with magic greatly surpassed that of dwarves. Wizards often reminded her of it.

"You can see dreams," Shar concluded.

Dreams? She stared at the wizard without seeing him, lost in thought. Is that what her vision of Hloim's thirst for knowledge was? His dream? What does that even mean? And how did Shar know about her encounter with the wandering dwarf mage?

"Florella told me," explained Shar. "You saw her dream, didn't you?"

Florella's dream? She recalled Florella's story of her childhood, of a plant who suffered great loss and heartache, but used it to surpass her natural limitations and blossom all the more beautifully for it. And she remembered Florella's essence who appeared in her vision, a dreamy aura who drew meaning from the magnificent floral creations rooted in the pain.

She nodded, understanding what he meant, not needing him to explain.

"That is an incredible gift," whispered Shar, his voice cracking.

She gazed into his eyes, more expressive than she'd ever seen them, realising that this was a gift he did not have, appreciating how truly rare it must have been.

She followed the thrust of his words, thinking back to the dwarf mage at Sentinel Grove and his dream she saw, his sense of elation at having moved the statue through his own efforts, not caring who she was or where she'd learned her craft. His dream who moved him more profoundly than her example ever could.

And an idea took root in her mind.

Did other dwarves have dreams of their own? Dreams they knew little of, dreams they wished to fulfil but didn't know how? Dreams she could see and help them with if she developed her gift?

She looked at her teacher with sudden clarity.

"I'm ready."

MOULTING

Asja gazed at the gateway to Purgatory, a swirling rift whose frame dissolved into thick bronze mist, or was perhaps made from it. The spinning mass acquired shades of yellow and gold as it melted into the light, coiling towards the centre of the surface, shimmering with heat from the blazing plane. She understood now why Shar called it the Plane of Fire. She couldn't imagine anyone entering and emerging unscathed.

A vivacious flare escaped from the plane and wrapped herself around the smoke-filled frame, her many tongues licking the sweaty air of the small room. Asja gasped at the sight. The fire looked more real than she'd expected her to be.

Shar placed his hands on her shoulders and turned her to face him. No smile graced his face. No humorous quip came to lighten the mood. She saw only pain in his eyes, as if he knew what awaited her in there and winced at the memory.

"Do you remember how to face the Watcher?" he asked.

"The only way to fail is to hold back," she recited automatically.

He sighed with relief. "You are as ready as you'll ever be." His words were adorned with a hint of a smile.

"One last thing," he added, provoking a nervous look. "I need your staff."

"My staff?" She pulled it closer and gripped it tighter. "Why?"

"The Watcher is the essence of the plane itself. You can't kill him without destroying the plane. You also can't shield yourself from him unless you hold back. And I don't want you distracted in there by such futile thoughts, so…"

He held out his hand. She hesitated for only a moment before placing her staff in it, and her trust in him. Holding it firmly, he backed away, leaving her to face the ravenous appetite of the Plane of Fire all on her own.

Scarlet steam belched from the ground, to crackling sounds and the smell of ash. Menacing clouds gathered overhead, fed by the rising mist, churning erratically before her eyes, teasing water from them with their seething fumes. She couldn't see the sky above her or the distant ground; smoke obscured them both.

She set forth boldly, stepping over rough ground she struggled to see, not knowing where she was headed. *The Watcher would come without warning*, Florella had told her. She remembered her first foray into the Underworld. Running for the exit would be easy, the first thought on her mind. The only way she knew she'd stay was if the whereabouts of the rift were hidden from her. So she pressed on, her eyes closed to lose her trail, her steps concealed by the pervasive fog, the last semblance of the flaming frame melting behind her into the smouldering haze.

A mountain of smoke erupted in her path. She opened her eyes to see it come to life in a crackling ball of fire who burned away the mist, leaving a tentacled beholder hovering in its place. The flames rose once more, then subsided to reveal a giant eye staring at her, his crimson pupil a narrow vertical slit enveloped with subdued flames readying for another gush. Numerous tiny eyes barely protruded from the beholder's sides, as if anticipating their chance to join the reaching appendages in their eerie dance.

She stepped back at the monstrous sight but stumbled on the uneven ground. The Watcher pounced upon her mishap, his many limbs pressing on her, his enormous eye staring her down, omnipresent and all-seeing. She quivered in the presence of a monster as menacing as the worst horrors lurking in the Underworld.

She fought to squirm away but lacked the strength to shift the beholder's bulk. She reached for her staff, forgetting that it wasn't there. Without her weapon, she felt helpless, never having mastered the art of using magic unaided, never having thought she would need to. In desperation, she screamed Shar's name, and when she didn't hear his hoofbeats through the searing noise, she called on Ama instead.

A small eye at the end of an appendage leapt at the thought behind her plea. It isolated the thought and revealed it for others to heed. The tentacles swarmed around it, each following a different link, teasing out a separate idea, an experience, a fantasy that may have fallen stagnant from lack of recall. And before she knew it, her relationship with the goddess was laid bare for the giant eye to see.

The Watcher gazed over the display, as if sizing it up, before returning his attention to the root thought. There he stood still, the flames of the iris rising once more, gathering into a concerted mass and shooting out as a unified beam, striking her plea for Ama's help and setting it ablaze.

Aghast at the sight, Asja scrambled to put out the flames. She sought to quench their thirst with her own dwarf form, a gift Ama had given her at the time of her birth. But her near death by Shar's hand frustrated her efforts, as did her duels with horrors where Ama was nowhere to be found. And she watched as the flames devoured her cry for help, distraught in the knowledge that she couldn't depend on the goddess for aid.

As the conflagration ravaged the root of the structure, the fire spread onto the ones it touched. Gone was her sense that Ama presided over the affairs of the world, the wizards' independence thwarting her efforts to protect it. Perished the conviction that Ama worked for the benefit of her people; sending her to be trained by demons undermined the foundation upon which it lay. Even Ama's benevolent nature couldn't withstand the flames' lust, no matter how fervently she wished it to be true. The Watcher knew no compassion for how much of herself she'd invested in those thoughts, only the cold hand of logic and the relentless pursuit of truth. His fire consumed the entire structure, devouring the goddess she'd worshipped as a child, leaving behind nothing but a smouldering husk, a mysterious stranger she knew next-to-nothing about. And she wailed in anguish at losing the bedrock from her childhood, the person she once thought she could rely on and trust without question.

A probing tentacle spotted a sizzling end of Ama's link to mages and clan leaders, following it to unearth her relations with her adoptive people. Terrified at the prospect of losing that too, she fought to obscure her thoughts from the prying eyes, shifting from one to the next as quickly as she could, desperate to leave them with nothing to latch onto. Her frustrating efforts soon bore fruit. The Watcher's limbs flailed back and forth, unable to hold onto her thoughts for any length of time.

Until she remembered the words the wizards had pressed upon her while preparing her for a visit to the plane: *The only way to fail is to hold back.*

She'd thought they meant for her to be tenacious, to fight the Watcher with all the strength she had. The true meaning of the phrase struck her only now. She couldn't withhold anything from the beholder's sight, or the very purpose of seeking his presence would've been thwarted. The realisation was enough to disrupt her defences, giving him the opening he needed to infiltrate them again. She watched helplessly as he submerged her adoptive people in his insatiable blaze, torching her youthful loyalty to them the way he had the goddess.

The intentions of dwarf leaders, the promises they'd made, the very words they'd spoken tumbled into the flames. She remembered their disapproval for having a thunderoc as a friend. She recalled the distrust of the mages for her wishing to join them, their unwillingness to instruct her in the art of runes, their decision to shun her once they sensed that her potential greatly exceeded their own.

But before the whole structure could be unmoored from its underpinnings and consumed by the flame, Martyr rose up – a horror she'd reclaimed from the depths of the Underworld – and sprung to its defence. Martyr fought the fire with a single memory – that of a wandering mage skilled at his craft, the teaching of whom had touched Asja deeper than any magical display she had ever seen. Seeing her success, Martyr added another memory – that of a frightened goblin injured in a desperate flight from a dwarf mage, but grateful for the healing magic that mage was willing to give.

As Asja's relationship with mages and clan leaders perished in the flames, Martyr helped a new one rise to take its place. Her troubled affair with dwarf leaders yielded ground to relations with the common folk – people who didn't see her mastery of magic as a threat, but were grateful to have her by their side. Even more, if the second memory held any sway, not only dwarves might someday be welcoming of her skill.

Could her influence really spread beyond the dwarven lands? An enterprising eye sought to know. She was an outsider after all, never fully accepted by the mountainfolk despite having been remade to resemble them. Did she even belong with her adoptive people? The Watcher's giant eye put her place in the world to a test.

Liquid flame poured onto her sense of home. It caught and grew, but burn as it may, it could not dissolve the tenacious fibres that held it in place. Pariah wouldn't let it. The first horror to be reclaimed and no stranger to living in exile, she hung onto those strands with a survivor's will. Her tenacity helped them strengthen and grow beyond the foothills of the range, hinting that Asja's role might not be contained to the affairs of the dwarves, nor the benefit of her skills withheld from other lands.

Unaccustomed to having his flame strengthen the structure he sought to burn, the Watcher shifted focus to what her role might be. Hag strove to furnish an answer, but, as the most recent horror to have been reclaimed by the girl, had none to give. She knew that her mur heritage was to be built upon and put to use, but not to what end. The traditional runemage roles that Hag scrambled to provide promptly perished in the Watcher's flame.

One by one, Asja's remaining thoughts came under fierce scrutiny of the giant eye. One by one, they burned and withered whenever her defence of them proved less than true. By the time the beholder was done, he'd purged much of her convictions from her mind, leaving them lying in heaps of ash on Purgatory's floor.

His work done, he released her from his hold and rose above, then sped away into the obscuring smoke in search of fresh fuel for his fire. She struggled to get up, distressed to gaze at her own cinders, distraught at how thoroughly overcome she'd been by the beholder's gaze, at how much of her lay consumed on the floor of the plane. She understood now why the doorway to Purgatory resided in the most remote chamber of the Algalash tree, and why Florella and Shar had waited so long before letting her venture here. Had she come unwitting and unprepared, not enough of her would have survived the ordeal for her to live.

And yet, what remained felt lighter, as if a heavy burden accumulated throughout her lifetime had finally been lifted. And stronger, feeling that she could actually depend on the remnants of the structure that had withstood the Watcher's gaze. She felt able and free to choose her own path instead of having it chosen for her by the people accustomed to the role. She didn't know exactly what that path might be, but for the first time, she knew that it was up to her — and her alone — to lay it out.

ARCHON

A solid dome of deep indigo clouds stretched through the sky, their surface smooth and polished as if by a potter's hand. Their crown broke with the circular motion, churning and swirling every which way, fed by the smaller cells who sought to descend into the crowded bulge.

A bolt of lightning streaked through the sky, his flashy outline stamped upon the brooding backdrop, his movement accompanied by a heavenly chorus, not having a clear destination in mind, just arcing through the sky to herald the arrival of the storm.

Vagran hovered high above the ground, beyond Mount Aorai's flat tip, letting the air currents carry his outstretched wings, waiting for the storm to come to him. He loved this moment, when the tempest was close and ready to unleash, but had to make an effort to reach out and touch him. He didn't wait long. The next flash of lightning eagerly obliged, striking the lightning bird from across the sky.

He revelled in the ecstasy of wave after wave of charge washing over his body, his feathers standing erect, glistening in the glow of the maelstrom's assault. Until a lone discharge struck the mountain below. And then another. And another. Dividing the storm's attention between the summit and the bird.

Vagran peered at the flat mountaintop, unaccustomed to sharing a storm's fury. A lone speck stood on top of the mount, still sparkling from the storm's caress. Vagran angled his wings to come closer to the peak, seeing the speck grow into the form of a dwarf, his body covered with glistening jewels no doubt taken from the mountain's depths.

Or were they the crystal plunder from Chromatic Hills, fashioned into runic armour to test against a storm? He expected the armour to take longer to make from the little he knew of the casting of runes. Yet there the dwarf stood, withstanding the heaven's fury, the way Vagran thought that a mage could not.

He moved closer, until he could see the dwarf's face angled back at him, his attention clearly drawn to the bird in the sky. For a moment their eyes met, each one locked in the other's stare, momentarily oblivious to the raging storm, their bodies resonating in unison with the charge the tempest was so gracious to provide.

And then the dwarf vanished in a sheet of rain as the pent-up dome unleashed upon the land.

A DEMON'S BARGAIN

"How could you promise our help?" Florella stood in the communal hall, staring down at Asja from her full height. "You know we won't get involved."

"This is Empyrean's plan, not ours," Shar reinforced her words.

Asja lowered her eyes, only briefly glancing up at her wizard teachers, feeling the full brunt of their displeasure. She knew this moment would come ever since her encounter with the runemages at Recha's study in Amerot.

"Will he stand against the morlocks too?" the girl asked.

"If the morlocks come with Rangorr?" Shar sought to clarify, getting a nod in response. "I don't know. But he will free Rangorr. That was his promise to us."

Asja shook her head. "That wouldn't have convinced Recha." She kept quiet about not having told Recha about the morlocks' involvement in the first place.

"Asja, your task was to convey Empyrean's offer of help to the runemages," Florella reminded her. "Not to promise whatever you had to promise to get them to accept it."

Asja's breathing quickened. Her gaze wandered around the room, her eyes unfocused, searching for a counter. "I'm sorry I promised your help to my people," she began, "but I can't do this without you. We can't. We barely contained Rangorr the last time he attacked, and now we know he's not acting alone."

Asja looked at each wizard in turn, her eyes filled with pleading, desperate to make them understand. "I don't doubt the celestial's power. Not after seeing what elementals can do. So why doesn't he use it? You could take on the morlocks yourselves, especially if the other wizards helped you. Ama could do it effortlessly. But none of you want to get involved.

"I'm not like you. I can't just stand aside and let this happen. I can't be neutral when my people are going to be killed."

"We are not asking you to stay out of it," Florella corrected her. "We are asking you to help in a way only you can."

Asja looked at the plant blankly before spreading her arms, not understanding, exasperated.

"Why do you think we've invested all this time in training you?" interjected Shar. "Helped you reclaim your horrors? Sent you to moult? It was all to prepare you for using your gift!"

Asja's gaze wandered as she tried to make sense of his words. "Seeing dreams?"

"That's what it looks like to me," he said.

"Why would you care about my gift more than anyone else's?"

"Because your gift could be the key to ending your people's way of life and awakening Ama!" he replied with passion he seldom displayed. "But I can't tell you how to use it. Only you can discover that."

Asja only stared at him, not understanding his words but swayed by the fervour with which they were said. She recalled her last visit to the Wall of Remembrance and the idea that germinated there, that she might be able to sway dwarf runemages by empowering their dreams. Could she do the same with the morlocks? Did they have dreams too, dreams who would respond to her aid and turn them from their warpath against elves and dwarves?

But then she recalled her encounter with the witch Centane amidst the crooked limbs of Swirling Woodlot. The witch who revelled in the power she had over the girl and fed on her fear.

"The morlocks worship power," Shar's voice broke her train of thought, with insight into her mind she had come to expect. "They might have suppressed their dreams to do that. Or perverted them. I can't really tell. But you can."

"You want me to go to the morlocks?" asked Asja, her words slow and deliberate, her voice rising with shock.

"No!" Florella stared at Shar. "Look what happened to Rangorr. And he used to be one of them."

Asja's eyes shot wide open with surprise. Rangorr used to be a morlock? A morlock who trained with the wizards and went against the Circle?

Nodding thoughtfully, Shar said, "Not until you are ready."

Asja breathed a sigh of relief, not wanting to go against her teachers but having no intention of putting herself in harm's way as Rangorr had done. Her thoughts wandered back to Hloim – a young mage whose dream she saw and helped fulfil, at least the one time she was with him. A dream so hungry for knowledge that he was willing to obtain it from any source he could.

She recalled Sentinel Grove — a sacred druid site, influenced by their magic the way all runemages were to some degree. Druids, who appreciated her skill when runemages feared it, and welcomed her help when runemages avoided it. And an idea took root in her mind, a way for her to save her people even with the runemages standing in her way.

"You used to live with the elves, right?"

The deep scars on Shar's face briefly came to life as the lava furnace ignited behind them before his face returned to its customary stoic stone. "A long time ago."

"And you've been helping them ever since? To learn new skills and expand on their knowledge of magic?"

"To change their ways, yes. Not all that successfully. Why do you ask?"

"Runemages have blocked me at every turn, only accepting my help when they had no other choice. But druids are different. After we fought off Rangorr, they wanted my help. They didn't fear me the way mages did. They weren't envious of me. If we can convince them to follow the celestial's plan, we won't have to convince the runemages. Druids can convince them instead."

"And you want me to come with you because of my history with them?"

Asja nodded tentatively, daring to believe that her teacher was convinced.

"Few of the living druids know of me, and those who do are not my friends."

"I can vouch for you!" she said without blinking. "We can visit those who were at the clan gathering first. If they know they can count on us to help, they will agree to Empyrean's plan. I'm sure of it!"

"They won't welcome me!" his gruff words rumbled through the hall.

She retreated a step, taken aback by the force of his reply, but too committed to her plan to back out now. She gazed at his stone eyes, locked in a stare she dared not break lest she unwittingly signal her surrender, her eyes pleading for him to relent. He stared back at her, standing silently for the longest time, before his gaze dropped to the floor and his shoulders slumped. She waited for what seemed like an eternity, not wanting to disturb him, her excitement waning with each passing breath.

"I will come with you," he finally said, his eyes back on her. "But there is one place in the sylvan lands I must visit first."

Asja's face ruptured into a smile. She watched him turn and leave the communal hall, her body tingling with excitement and relief, for the first time daring to believe that they'd be able to counter the morlock threat. Florella watched him too, but her stem convulsed instead, and her flowers secreted a poignant shade of red.

STONE DRUID

A dry branch cracked on the ground. Lotur looked up, spying footsteps in the forest brush. They grew louder, as if their maker made no attempt to conceal them. The shrubs parted to reveal an elf boy running through the woods. He entered the glade and stopped in front of the hunter, clearly wanting to say something but unable to get the words out.

"The stone druid… is here," he finally spoke, out of breath.

"Stone druid?" Lotur squinted at hearing the news.

The boy nodded wildly. "I saw him… standing… by the stone mound… in the Watery Quag."

"What did he look like?"

"Grey… made of stone." The boy clenched his hands and placed them on his head, index fingers pointing up. "He had horns… dark horns."

"That's it!" Lotur slammed his fist into the palm of his hand. He looked around the glade as if searching for something. Then he turned back to the boy, placed a heavy hand on his shoulder and bent down to look him in the eye. "He's no druid."

The boy looked at him with big eyes and swallowed hard. Then he turned around and vanished into the forest, in the direction of his home, opposite from where he'd come.

Lotur nodded to himself, watching the boy go. Then he hunkered down, pondering, as he rummaged through his travel gear. *Druids don't have horns. They aren't made of stone. They don't stalk people in the night or make them disappear. Demons do that.*

He thought of Nymess, a troubled young woman who'd lost her way, an outcast among elves whom he loved nonetheless. It was his love for her that nurtured his hope that she'd come back to them someday, that she'd see the value of her life and not seek to end it. He'd never forget the way she looked at him that last time, her face beaming with hope before she vanished before his eyes. Only then did he see the stone demon sharing that space, before he, too, melted into the night.

Why did the boy even go to the bog? Doesn't he know that the place is cursed? People have ventured there and not come back. The youngsters just can't help themselves, flirting with danger for kicks and giggles. Still, he was grateful that the boy did, or he wouldn't have known about the demon's return.

He pulled out a long arrow with a thick shaft and a crystalline tip. He pressed his thumb against the pointy gem, reassured by his pulsating vigour, grateful to the mage for having enchanted him. The last time he'd come up against the stone demon, the light wooden arrows for hunting forest animals had shattered against his body. He was a young hunter then; he didn't know who he was facing.

He did now. He looked up to see his friend enter the glade carrying a hare. A small meal that would have to wait. They had a bigger and far more dangerous prey to catch.

AWAKENING

Shar stood in the open space, his hoof-like feet mildly sunk into the muddy earth. A claystone mound rose from the floor, reddish grey and striking against the forest scene, touched by the foliage growing at the edge of the woods.

You haven't changed much, the wizard looked him over, accustomed to the mound's curvaceous form. He reached out to touch the perennial rock, running his fingers across the rugged skin. The stone felt warm and welcoming of his touch, as if the ancient slab still recalled his presence after the two had gone their separate ways.

His gaze fell on a tree beyond the forest line, settled over a rubble of stones at the edge of the mound. A gnarly forest dweller who'd sought to live beyond the comfort of the woods, laying a claim to a corner of the knoll upon whom other trees dared not intrude. But now the roots were as stiff as the stone beneath them, with no life left in the ancient trunk, a dry husk attesting to the passage of time.

Shar remembered a time, long ago as if in another life, when the tree was vibrant and young, seeking to thrive beyond the safety of the forest, with tenacious roots who instilled terror in the hard rock.

A mound of claystone rose from the field, resting upon a base of solid granite, his modest height affording a good view of the open plain. He'd stood there for as long as he could recall, warmed by the shy rays of the distant suns, washed by the rain they had brought into the sky, caressed by the blades of grass swaying in the wind, content to remain in his spot and simply be, each day and night blending into the next.

An encroaching forest started to bother him, sprawling across the plain and crowding the northern view. He rose higher, but new trees came faster than he could move. They settled next to him, overwhelming the grass who retreated before them, leaving a muddy patch at the base of the rock.

The trees shied away from the swampy ground, their roots preferring more supportive soil, forming a forest line that avoided the bog. The mound breathed a sigh of relief, grateful for the silver lining amidst his misfortune, soaking in what remained of the open view.

Until an oak seed sprouted in an earthy hollow on top of a humble boulder at the edge of the mound.

The young tree stretched his serrated leaves, his roots spreading through the patch of dirt. And when they'd scraped the bottom of the earth, they dug deeper, into the stone, seeking anchor and nourishment from the hostile rock. But the boulder clenched his body to deny it, waiting for the brash sapling to wither away and die in the exposed, unwelcoming place.

Foiled by the mound, the tree cast his roots as wide as he could, spreading until they touched the watery ground, enveloping the rock in their firm embrace; an embrace that grew tighter with each passing day.

The boulder struggled in the tree's grip, straining to move, labouring to breathe. He clamped down, trying to resist the roots' choking hold, trusting his rough skin to withstand the wooden limbs. But the tree nourished his roots more than the boulder his skin, healing their wear against the hardened stone. And they steadily ate into the boulder's frame, cutting and crushing it with their embrace, working tirelessly to grind it down.

Seeing a struggle he could not win, the boulder grew bulges to push the roots aside, creating a gap through which he could flee. He poured through the hole as quickly as he could, growing two arms to push himself out, mimicking the fluid motion of his foe. But the tree didn't leave his escape uncontested. The roots crept closer, cramping the breach, cutting lines in the supple stone, drawing a pained groan from the escaping rock.

Finally, the roots clamped the hole shut, splitting the boulder in two, crushing the remaining rock under the tree's weight with no hope of flight.

The boulder lifted himself off the muddy field, turning to stare at the tenacious tree. He'd only ever seen his nemesis from beneath his boot, looking up at the towering trunk with dense bark and a high crown. Now he stood face to face as an equal, free from the roots' grip. The change of posture dispelled his fear of the tree. He reached back and touched the parts of him who fell in the escape, but the roots crowded around the small pile, claiming the leftover stones as their own.

He moved on to the mound of claystone in whose shadow he had lived his life. He invited the knoll to leave this place where he no longer wished to stay.

But the mound resisted the offer, never having been challenged by the place of his birth, not having mastered the skill of travelling across the land. The boulder pressed his face against the familiar stone, humming a quiet farewell. They were no longer one and the same, even if the same rock filled their bronze frame.

As he turned to leave, a puddle of water appeared in his way, offering him a view of whom he had become. He stood and stared, charmed by his reflection in the still surface, stunned to see a lithe body where a boulder had once been, parallel lines etched deeply into his gaunt face, fresh wounds on a slender frame toned through his desperate efforts to escape.

And he trudged through the swampy ground, leaving the tree and the mound behind, a creature of stone in the sylvan land.

Shar reached out and held in his hands a brittle root of the dead tree, roots who had tried to take his life but gave it to him instead. He thanked them for triggering his birth, and for the life he's been able to live.

"Let's sleep here tonight," he said to the dwarf girl, his companion on this journey. "We can travel to the elves tomorrow."

They settled in beyond the forest line in the feeble light of a sylvan day, illuminated by a distant sun high in the sky over the western range.

AN OLD GRUDGE

A warm breeze whispered through the trees. The branches remained unmoved; only the flutter of their leaves betrayed the presence of the wind. He brought word of warmth descending from his summit, a blanket of heat drawn from Aia's depths to cover the foothills and rejuvenate the land.

Asja opened her eyes. The day looked no brighter than when she'd closed them to sleep, only the shade having changed from lime to violet hue. A new skylight must have taken to the skies while she slept, to replace the northern one who had run his course.

Growing accustomed to perpetual twilight was the hardest part of journeying through sylvan lands. She missed the clear contrast between day and night brought on by the closeness of Peruvius peaks. No mountain ranges ran through these forests. No lonely summits rose from the woods. The only light came from distant peaks who punctured the horizon with their rising suns. A luminous day was a sight to behold, brought on by rare alignment of the skylight cycles.

She looked over at Shar's sleeping place. He lay there quietly, looking back at her. It was the first time she had slept in the wizard's company, having long occupied her own side of the Algalash tree. As if on cue, he rose from the floor, standing tall and broad, stretching his limbs from stillness and sleep, a pleasant rumble coming from his throat.

Her eye caught a subtle movement of shrubs at the edge of the woods. A glittering gem protruded through the leaves directly behind Shar. Another appeared in the broader bush on the other side of the tree. They hung in the air, as if sizing up their target, before being let loose across the open field.

Shar groaned as twin arrows dug into his back, slicing through the stone and piercing his chest. He looked down at their protruding tips, their crystalline edges the work of a dwarf mage, liquid fire from his heart dripping from their heads. He gazed at the girl, a look of grim finality etched on his face. And then he collapsed back onto his resting place, his body hitting the ground with a lifeless thud.

Asja jumped and screamed, a high-pitched shriek of distress and disbelief. She leapt to his bed, her hands holding the wizard's head, unable to process the surreal scene. She looked up at the woods to see new arrowheads emerge from the leaves. Instinctively, she reached out to summon the staff by her bed, catching it as it flew in a practised motion, pointing it at the tree and unleashing hell.

A blistering inferno poured from the tip, stripping the trees of their bark and the shrubs of their leaves, revealing the two elf hunters who hid in their midst before ravaging their skin as it knocked them down. The staff continued to spew until scorched trees and charred flesh were all that remained of this part of the woods, fuelled by the soggy ground beyond the forest line before she crumbled into powdery ash.

Asja dropped her staff and turned back to her teacher and friend. His eyes stared into the fullness of the sky. The lava oozing from his wounds solidified on his chest. She ran her fingers across the lines of his face, hollow scars that had shone with burning light the first time she had seen them. And then she buried her face in his, her long hair covering them both, her body convulsing with bitter sobs until she could barely whisper through the pouring tears.

"I'm... so... lost."

CHILD OF THE MOUNTAIN

The fire dipped as Moruk fed her another branch, her many tongues sampling the new meal before jumping to devour it and cook his meal in return. He turned the spit, the fish staring at his hand as it grasped the wood, the head still attached though the innards were gone, their place taken by the stick to hold the fish to the flames.

He loved the smoked aroma of fresh trout; the townsfolk having been generous enough to furnish him with a few. He gazed at the houses of Amerot from beyond the courtyard, glad to be out of his study and beneath the open sky, even if only for a late morning meal.

If runemages and druids accept Asja's offer, they'll be on their way to Sentinel Grove, with more mornings like this to look forward to.

He looked at Recha sitting across the campfire, enjoying the quiet interlude, lost in her own thoughts. He liked these times together the most, when she didn't have to be the head runemage, or grapple with the fickle politics of the clans, but could let it all go and enjoy the more esoteric questions, the reason both of them were drawn to become mages in the first place.

"Where do you think children of the mountain come from?" he asked out of the blue.

He chuckled as her head pulled back, startled by the question. She shrugged her shoulders. "From the mountains, I guess. Hmm… From Ama, you could say."

He shook his head, having a hard time with the notion that a living dwarf could emerge from a ball of light shot out by a mountain, though seeds were known to rain from the sky and take root within fertile land.

"Where do you think Caleb came from?" She turned the tables on him.

He thought of Caleb – the first child of the mountain spoken of in the legends. When dwarves first reached the foothills of Mount Edars, they found a dwarf child already living there. Where did he come from? No one knew. So a story spread that he came from a mountain seed who'd been given life by the goddess herself.

His gaze veered to Mount Aorai's open top. The skylight had long since come apart high above the land, leaving the torn womb to heal in the others' light. He remembered asking himself the same question when he was a child, not knowing how a creature of flesh and blood could emerge from a place of crystal and stone.

"The legends say that the archon Aorar was made of crystal and stone, and that Metallus' skin had turned to iron from prolonged use of runes," Recha went on, following his wayward look. Then she added, "Would one of us have befriended a roc?"

He looked back, dismayed by the folly. Caleb, too, had befriended a young ferrite living on the peak, a dragon of lightning with scales made of iron. Moruk shuddered at the thought of what it had taken to bring the ferrite down, hacking through the scales to be walloped by the charge. Dwarves had lost so many warriors that day. And the beast wasn't even fully grown.

The Elegy of Caleb mourned their deaths at length, the first cautionary tale to be captured in a myth that challenged how dwarves felt about children of the mountains. He couldn't help but recite the sombre words, thinking what it would take to stand up to Vagran should he turn on them.

"I'm not so sure that was a good idea…" he let out.

She returned an understanding smile. He was one of the few mages who never warmed to Vagran, even as the bird hauled in exotic crystals from the goblin lands.

"…but he has been useful, I'll give you that."

IN AN EMPTY HOME

Asja sat on a rocky ledge on top of a cliff, her eyes staring blankly into open space. Mount Edars' foothills sprawled out in the distance, descending until they reached the end of the Peruvius Range. Frost mountains took up their mantle past the valley to the south, their white peaks rising into the sky beyond the horizon. A chill was in the air, the Edars peak not having discharged recently enough to dispel it.

The little house on top of the hill stood empty, the boulders who graced it feeling desolate and alone. Tor had passed away since Asja's last visit, a brief appearance before the gathering of the clans. She found his grave next to Erna's in the field past the stable, a simple mound of stones embellished with a well-used horn, his favourite tool for greeting the open vista beyond the hillside ledge.

She couldn't bear to go inside the house, preferring to sleep by the outside hearth, the place she used to share with Vagran. The place of laughter and exuberance from her childhood now felt completely desolate and empty. Even the neighbours had stopped coming to visit now that Tor was gone.

Her eyes stared at the horizon, but all her mind saw was the look on Florella's face when she pushed Shar's limp body through the makeshift portal. She couldn't remember what she expected the plant to do. She must have hoped against hope that there was a spark of life left in that stone that the healer would reignite. When she could not, Asja ran away, not able to face her teacher again, not after Shar died accompanying her on a journey he warned her not to make.

Why did he come with her? All through her training, they'd instilled in her the understanding that they didn't get publicly involved in the affairs of Amana's people. It was desperation that fuelled her plea. Still, she didn't expect him to relent, his change of mind taking her by surprise. Now she regretted ever having asked him to come.

Why did the elves kill him? What did he do to them to make them react this way? The druids she'd met at the clan gathering were warm and friendly people, open to her involvement and welcoming of her gifts. Were other elves really that different? She had to admit to herself that she'd met too few to know.

Then she remembered the Legend of Erbrus' Fall. He'd done nothing but try to help his people, yet they banished him from their midst, willing to fight him if he dared to stay. Did Shar try to help the elves beyond their ability to receive? He never talked about his brushes with them in any depth, as if this were a part of his past he didn't want to revisit. One thing she knew for sure – the goodwill she once harboured towards the elves had died with him.

She gazed into the distance, trying to picture the coastline who hugged the land beyond the elven forests and the frost range. Her birth people dwelled on the eastern islands. She'd never seen them. She didn't know the lay of the land, where they might be found. She'd never even been to the seas who harboured the isles of the archipelago. Any exploring she could do with her new portalling skills was bound to be exhausting.

Only you can free the morlocks' dreams, Shar's words echoed in her mind. She shuddered at the thought but stayed with it even amidst the fright. Her Dream Seer skills lacked refinement, only beginning to be harnessed with intent, far too unsure of themselves to grapple with the morlocks. But, perhaps, the dreams of ordinary mur were not beyond her ken? She'd let her fear of Rangorr and Centane keep her from getting to know them. Perhaps her idea of helping ordinary dwarves rather than the mages applied to her birth people as well?

A sudden gust of wind enveloped her from behind. She spun around just in time to see a giant bird land on the boulders beyond the ledge, his pellucid feathers fully erect, sparkling in the light of the distant suns. Then his enormous wings folded closed, and his neck stretched out towards his childhood friend.

"Vagran!" she ran towards him, embracing him with delight, burying her face in the soft plumage of his neck. "I've so missed you!" Then she stepped back, wondering, "Weren't you supposed to be carrying the crystals from Chromatic Hills?"

The giant eyes blinked in response, but sudden arcing served a stark contrast to the excitement they displayed when he first learned that runemages were asking for his help.

"They look at me... as a beast of burden."

Asja winced at the crackling words and only held him tighter. She'd long realised that the runemage order was not a place to make friends, but it still hurt to see their calculating ways perturb her friend as well.

"I saw a crystal mage... wield a storm on Mount Aorai," the thunderoc sizzled on, his eyes gazing into the distance, his feathers fluttering from the memory.

Asja stared at the giant bird, taken aback by the wonder in his eyes. The mage must have really shown some skill to impress a beast who was lightning himself, no doubt aided by the gems they'd taken from the goblin lands. Perhaps the dwarves weren't as helpless against the morlock threat as she'd made them out to be. Perhaps she really could turn her attention to her birth people, as Shar had implored her to do.

She banished the thought and hugged Vagran tighter, not wanting to leave his side, not ready to put her gift to the test in an alien land just yet. She stayed in the reassuring presence of her friend for the longest time, a comfort she had sorely lacked of late.

AORAR

Silence descended upon Kinrum Hall. The clan aisles stood empty except for the front rows occupied by the runemages. Their subdued talk of Asja's offer had drawn to an abrupt halt when a druid appeared in their midst, his hair and clothes scruffy, his face sombre as if made of stone. Invited or not, he looked keen to speak, and mages always wished to hear the news brought to them by the forest folk.

"What brings you back to us, Evindal?" Recha ceded the floor.

The druid drew a deep breath to gather himself, still tired and ragged from the long trip. "Ryunfir and I were travelling to the Cedar people in the north when we came across a burned-down forest by the Watery Quag. We thought it odd that a wood sheltered by a bog would be so vulnerable to fire, so we made a detour to investigate. We found two elf bodies lying in the ash, ravaged by the flame, with no faces left on them. I thought it peculiar that the fire would overcome them so suddenly that they couldn't escape. Then we found out why. A section of the bog had lost her muddy form and was now covered with fine white powder, cold to the touch. The same dry dust that now lingers at the end of this courtyard."

Recha's eyes narrowed as she processed the druid's words. "Another demon attack?"

Evindal nodded solemnly.

A ghostly murmur spread through the hall. Evindal's words gave their caucus new urgency and depth.

"Do you know who the elves were?" asked the runemage Moruk.

Evindal shook his head. "We didn't stay to talk to the locals. As soon as we understood what had happened, Ryunfir went to alert the druids while I rushed here."

"When did the attack happen?" Moruk probed.

"Warmth still lingered in the burned tree stumps, so it couldn't have been long before we found them. This Aorai cycle, I'd say."

Moruk only nodded, joining the other dwarves in their rumination.

"Asja did say that the demon would attack again," Brana broke the silence, a recent addition to the runemage order, surprisingly outspoken for his young age.

"She also said that her teachers would warn us before the attack came," quipped Recha. "I guess they are not as capable as we've made them out to be."

"Or their motives aren't as pure," suggested Moruk.

"Are you having second thoughts about their offer?" Brana tackled their misgivings head on.

"What offer?" Evindal chimed in.

Recha sighed at having to explain again before catching herself in front of their druid guest. "Asja came to me during the last Aorai cycle. She wanted us to gather at Sentinel Grove, both mages and druids, and set up an ambush there. Her teachers believed that the demon would get wind of the gathering and use the opportunity to attack. She said that they would be there to help us."

"It would be our chance to eliminate–" started Brana.

"You weren't there during the last attack!" Moruk cut him off.

"Sentinel Grove…" Evindal pondered the place, ignoring the bickering of the dwarves. "I've been there once. It would give us an advantage. Definitely better than facing the demon here…" his words tapered off as he realised that something was amiss. "You haven't decided yet?"

Recha shook her head. "We don't know anything about Asja's teachers save what we hear from her and can glean from her skills–"

"Which are most impressive," the druid interjected, his tone leaving no doubt as to the high regard in which he held them.

Recha nodded lightly before continuing. "We don't know what their motivations for getting involved are. They never have before."

"Remember that Asja is not a normal dwarf," Moruk pointed out. "She's a child of the mountain."

"That doesn't make her untrustworthy!" Brana blurted out.

"No, but it does mean that she serves Ama first and foremost, and Ama's ways aren't easy to fathom."

The head runemage's words came with the finality that left the hall in silence. All sat quietly, thoughtful expressions taking hold of their faces. All save Evindal.

"Druids should hear of this offer, no matter your decision," he said.

Moruk's face contorted at the words. "You would face the demon without us?"

"We already are," he lamented.

Before anyone could respond, a scratching at the entrance to the hall distracted them from the conundrum. A heavy wooden door creaked as it opened. A lone dwarf stood in the doorway, his body glistening in the light of the day. With heavy footsteps he entered the hall, his stone feet resounding against the floor, a battle axe strapped to his side. A woollen coat clothed his body, covering his torso where the dense stone of his legs grew into the delicate crystal of his arms and face, which retained enough light from the skylights abroad to pierce the twilight of the great hall before Mount Aorai's own sun could take to the skies.

The runemages stared from their aisles, watching the stranger approach, their hands resting uneasily on their staves. And when he stopped in the middle of the hall and gazed at the assembly, they only stared at him some more as if mesmerised by his radiant eyes and the reflective lines of his face.

"Who are you?" Recha's voice broke the silence, the trembling tone a mere shadow of the confidence she'd projected only moments before.

"Aorar," a deep voice rumbled through the hall.

No one dared speak. They sat frozen in their seats, lacking any comprehension of where he'd come from or who he might be. Only Brana's face brightened at the sight, his eyes gaping at the floor rather than their guest, at the centre of the hall where dwarven history came to life each time a Mount Aorai sun rose through the sky.

"Aorar from the legends?" his whispering voice pierced the silence. "Who once led our people against the flying beasts?"

The crystalline dwarf slowly nodded. He gripped his axe and brought it to his chest — the metal sparking from contact with his hand — before putting it back with a self-satisfied grin.

A rising murmur spread through the hall, lifting shoulders and brightening faces as the mages found their voices at their sudden change of fortune. None dared ask where Aorar had been all this time or why he failed to aid them in their earlier scuffles with the goblins and the demon.

"Ho... How?" Recha came closest to voicing their confusion.

"New enemies have risen against us. I'm here to fight them!"

Evindal seized his chance. "Indeed, they have. A demon is killing our people, both dwarves and elves. We are planning an ambush in the forests to the west, at an ancient druid shrine whose enchantments will aid our magic."

Aorar's face came alive at the elf's words. He slammed his fist into the palm of his hand, embers and sparks flying from the contact.

"When do we leave?"

SANCTUM REEF

Mistral ruffled the crowns of jungle trees facing towards the ocean. They flexed their branches with the flow of the air, bowing inland, away from the sea, careful not to antagonise the wind. They bowed the other way just as soon as he left them, bracing themselves for the next blow in the well-rehearsed dance of the coastal woods.

A swooshing breeze entered the island from the inland side. He pushed the foliage aside on his way to the deepest section of the forest. There, with a flash, he dissolved into nothingness, with only a thick mist remaining in his place, coagulating into a woman of short stature who promptly hid in the thickest shrubs, falling completely silent and still.

Asja slowed her breathing and quieted her heartbeat, her eyes racing from left to right, scanning the jungle for any sign of movement. Careful not to give her presence away, she crouched in the tall grass, fearful of who might have seen her come. When she heard voices coming from the sea, she hid further still, lying in a cramped posture with her face pressing on the ground, waiting for them to fade away.

When they didn't, she listened closely, straining to learn what she could about her unsuspecting hosts from their sounds alone. There was laughter, splashing in the waves, playful shouts and retorts through the shallows by the surf. They weren't coming closer. She breathed a sigh of relief.

Her senses alerted her to the faint company of enchantments. She looked in their direction and saw a speck of land rising from the sea – the island of Uqatera, the home of the morlocks, ever watchful for intruders who may encroach upon their shores. She shuddered at the prospect, having no desire to come any closer than she already was.

She'd expected to be alone, thinking the isle too small for the mur to settle here. She'd planned to study them from a neighbouring atoll – a safe distance away – should they spot her and threaten her escape. Watching them from the treeline was too close for comfort, but she crept forward anyway, her curiosity about her birth people trumping her urge of safety.

Four slender figures stood in the swaying surf, their feet planted firmly on the slippery rock. Barely any clothing clung onto their bodies, and what little there was dripped from having tangled with the waves. They looked like no creatures she had ever seen. Dwarves would no doubt find them ugly – tall and thin, bordering on frail, their teal scales covering their bodies as if they'd come from the sea before settling on land. That bag looked much too heavy for them to pull through the crashing waves. But pull it they did, adding the colourful fruit as they picked it from the coral vines when the water withdrew enough for them to reach it.

Water droplets glistened on them like pearls, shining in the bioluminescence of the coral reef. There was a surreal quality to the scene, as if these people knew nothing of the morlocks or their affairs with a demon and the dwarves, but were content to live a simple life amidst the bounty of the sea.

When a skylight rose from a nearby isle, his beaming rays dispersed the bashful dusk. Her people stood exposed upon the coral reef, the sea's radiance overpowered by the sky, the manifold colours washed out in the intensity of the sun. She could see their bodies on full display, standing and watching the rising ball of light, the glistening drops of water lending a crystalline feel, their graceful movements resisting the sway of the sea. Their beauty struck her, their tall frames, sinewy limbs, elegant proportions.

She felt something stir inside of her that she couldn't explain. She'd never felt it in the company of dwarves. They were familiar and comfortable, cute and charming, but never attractive in this sort of way.

Her breathing quickened. Her heart started pounding. Waves of warmth rushed to her face. She tried to calm herself, needing her wits about her should danger arise, but her body reacted of its own accord as long as her eyes remained glued to the scene.

Flustered, she snuck back into the shade of trees as quickly as she felt safe. She thought of portalling home there and then, to leave her learning for another day. In the end, she chose to walk away and explore the other side of the isle, far from the people in whose presence her body reacted so wildly.

A floating log off the coast of the neighbouring atoll caught her eye. A curious sight: a tree of that size stranded in the narrow space between the two isles. When his branches moved, she recognised him as a ship, a spacious trunk who could sail the seas and carry passengers and cargo. She's heard the legends of Zuri and Vesstan from the travelling elves, how they'd crafted such vessels and taken them to sea, but had never seen the fruits of their labour. This one may have been abandoned; he did tread deep within the tide.

Wanting to examine the ship more closely, her gaze fell on a makeshift bridge connecting the two isles. A curious contraption, unlike the bridges she'd seen stretch over rivers and streams who were carefully woven from the roots of living trees, this one was no more than two tree trunks felled together – though their roots still held them in place – one of whom didn't even reach the other side. The mur who made it must have been novices, with much still to learn about their craft.

BRIDGE

Piercing rays from a brilliant sun shone through the canopy of a giant tree as an aqueous skylight ascended through the sky. Few rays touched the ground to fire up the restless leaves before they were overcome by shadow again or swept up by the playful wind.

Magven had taken root on the eastern slopes of Wintry Rise. The gentle hill oversaw the coast of the Aguan Isle from the mur side of the archipelago, renowned for her lush forests washed by numerous waterfalls and streams scattered through the land. They made a picturesque landscape, majestic enough to pull the seasoned explorer away from his beloved sea.

Magven watched the waves sparkle with borrowed light from watery suns before slamming against the rocks with force and foam and fury. The scent of the sea still tantalised his leaves, reminding him of the adventures that beckoned just beyond the horizon. But the urge to travel was not as strong. He'd delayed his departure time and time again.

Even though he settled on the slopes overlooking the sea, he rivalled the tallest trees growing on the hilltop. He'd almost forgotten what the western side of the island looked like; many night skies had come and gone since he'd last sailed those waters. He strained to rise further above the ground in hope of seeing the land lying in the shadow of the hillborne trees.

And then a gust of wind humbled the branches of the concealing canopies.

And he saw her.

An amber freckle in an emerald sea who covered the seaward slopes of the neighbouring isle.

Deep marigold hues burnished the air around her. Some fell to the floor to paint the ground on whom she stood. Her body's movements mimicked the motion of the wind, slow and graceful and lavish in falling leaves.

The gust passed. The tree trunks straightened, their crowns filled, and the fiery marigold tree from across the sea vanished from sight.

Magven stirred. He tugged on his roots, but they were slow to respond. Too many cycles had passed since they frolicked with abandon in the ocean swells. His trunk and branches too had grown rigid from disuse. Forgotten by the druids, he tugged on them nonetheless, tracing a tortured path across Wintry Rise.

His limbs ached from pushing against the muddy soil and sharp stone and the roots of jungle dwellers too slow to step aside. He watched the trail left in his wake; there was none. Too many skylights marked his journey towards the western shore.

The golden crown adorned with clusters of flowers both scarlet and bronze beckoned to him from across the water. The sight of her carried him through bruising squalls and bitter rain. He didn't see the dense boscage who grew on her isle and faded behind her into mossy mist. It was but a backdrop to her fiery complexion, making her stand out above the water's edge, silent and still as if in waiting. He called her Tirzah; he didn't know her name.

Dogged roots pierced the sodden ground and tasted the bittersweet water of the western sea. He had reached the shore. There was nowhere further to go.

He watched Tirzah from across the chasm. She gazed at him in return. Her branch laden with flowers and leaves reached across the water. One by one, scarlet petals fluttered and fell to the murky tide who swelled between them only to be carried away by the merciless sea.

Tears welled up in his leaves. They bubbled to the tips, a thousand glistening drops arrayed on leaf edge who plummeted as dew to the lowly ground and watered the grass stalks with their unquenched longing. He stared at the petals fading into the waves, quiet, broken.

Emboldened by his stillness, the jungle reclaimed the ground on whom he stood. Vines the size of small trees slithered up his trunk. Velvety moss settled on his branches, thick and heavy from the splattering surf. Birds made nests in his ample crown and welcomed the shrieky chirping of their young.

A chick plunged through the air beneath the nest, landing on the soft blanket of petals and stalks. Another followed in her path, but frantically flapped her short wings to travel past smaller trees to the sandy shore. An older bird jumped last, his sturdier wings carrying him over the water until Magven saw him land on the opposite isle.

Again he stirred. His trunk swayed in the absence of wind, leaning tentatively across the divide. The shadow he cast came and went before Tirzah responded in kind. As if on cue, their trunks creaked and descended through the air, falling in unison towards one another. Their tips touched, palms of leaves brushed against each other, and the uppermost branches clasped together in a snug embrace.

Magven's bark ripped open from the strain. Protracted rifts ran the full length of the trunk, tearing through layers of crust to expose the aging wood. The vines he carried stretched further along his stem to bolster their embrace. They cut through his skin from the weight they held, but were too thin to withstand the immensity of his bulk. A branch buckled. The bond started slipping. And he cursed the wooden hands who were too old and brittle to hold her in their grip.

Feeling her slide from his grasp, he stretched his roots deep into the ground. Past the sea and the stone and the roots of jungle trees who shared the same land. He dug into the bedrock upon whom the isle slept and thrust against it with inexorable force. The isle moved. The shore advanced into the surging waves, squeezing the water up the seaborne cliffs.

The trunks advanced headlong past each other. Magven's crown reached the opposing shore upon whose cliffs he could rest his head. And he wrapped his many arms around Tirzah's shorter stem, gentle and firm in his embrace, resolute never to let her slip from his grasp again.

AN INVITATION

Asja emerged from her house carrying a coil of rope. She hadn't thought of the house as hers since the first time she'd left with Vagran all those cycles ago. She didn't expect to find herself living in it again, even briefly, or rummaging through its supplies for another journey. But she'd left her rope on Mount Ablast and never replaced it, and she felt uneasy going on a lengthy trip without being able to draw on its aid.

She gazed south, towards the sea and the isles of the archipelago, seeing them through the memory of her daily portals to the lands of her people. Those visits were now at an end, interrupted by Dimotai's invitation to visit him at his home.

Dimotai. The elder wizard whom she'd met during her stay in the Algalash tree, held in high regard by both Florella and Shar. She'd dared not approach him following Shar's death. Merely seeing him in a vision led to anxiety and fear. But so filled was his demeanour with concern for her wellbeing, and so heartfelt his invitation for her to come by, that she couldn't help but accept his offer.

"Where are you going?" the voice of a sleepy bird crackled behind her.

She stopped packing, not having realised that Vagran was awake.

"A wizard has invited me to his home in the Dead Mountain. I'm getting ready for the journey."

"Dead Mountain?" The sleepy feathers ruffled on his forehead.

"Apparently, it's a solitary peak deep in the goblin lands, on the eastern side of the Pyrenees. I'd never heard of him either, but that's where Dimotai lives, and that's where I need to go."

A touch of concern crept into her voice. She'd never seen that part of the world. She wasn't looking forward to exploring vast tracts of open desert in search of a mountain using nothing more than tunnel vision afforded by a portal. As rapid as such travel was, searching for an unfamiliar destination was not.

"I want to take you," the thunderoc offered, rising to his feet by the abandoned hearth and shaking his wings to loosen them from sleep.

The offer caught her by surprise. Vagran knew she could travel easily now, much faster than he could fly, even if exploring new lands was an intricate undertaking. Was he trying to help her, or just looking for company?

She recalled their first journey together, the exhilaration of taking to the skies on the wings of a young roc. She remembered the majesty of the Urals laid out before her as he carried her to the town of Amerot. She reminisced on how safe she felt looking down on Chromatic Hills, knowing that she could rely on such a powerful beast for protection and escape.

Did she have the time to accept his offer? She didn't know. If the mages did decide to gather at Sentinel Grove, she'd want to be there with them. She might not have viewed them as allies as she once had, but with Shar no longer there, she wasn't going to let them face the demon all on their own. She just hoped she could count on the celestial's help as much as they could count on hers.

KURU KAM

On the second discharge of the Mount Aorai sun, Asja repeated to herself, making sure she remembered, *the runemages from Amerot will depart for Sentinel Grove*. The journey wasn't long – half an Aorai cycle, if that – though it took much longer to invite the druids living beyond the Great Plain, far away from their easternmost sacred site. She'd have to return soon after the second skylight vanished from the sky if she were to keep her promise of standing with them should the demon come.

She struggled to suppress a smile. They accepted her offer! She didn't think they would, especially after her meeting with Recha and Moruk ended on a sour note. But they did, and they were in high spirits about it. Even as she left the Amerot mages to their preparations, she could sense no despair or gloom saturate the ancient town as it had done in the aftermath of the last attack.

She took a deep breath of the warm mountain air. Rolling hills of verdant green passed underneath. She soaked up as much view as she could from the safety of the hollow beneath Vagran's heart, with erect feathers of his chest plumage keeping her from plummeting down.

An elven sentinel sprung up before them – a solitary tree with a tall trunk and a sparse crown rich in thorns rather than leaves. He stood watch over a shallow crossing where rusty water flowed at leisure. A handful of gazelles feasted on the grass on both sides of the ford, oblivious to the feud that raged between the peoples who lived beyond the banks.

The crimson channel of River Rust stretched out into the distance, snaking between the Edars foothills and the Kalhar dunes, too spacious to be hidden by the trees growing on her banks. The giant bird veered to match her flow, following the broadening river on her journey south, to the end of the vista overseen by Peruvius Range. When she encountered the white mountains to her right, she changed course, striking out into open desert, not wanting to hug a frosty mountain range, but receiving water from him nonetheless.

The ample course entered the goblin lands, welcomed only by dry air and coarse sand. Even as Vagran descended from the mountain height, Asja could spot no movement across the bare dunes, as if desert dwellers preferred the shade of trees who sheltered the nourishing waters in the hostile land – a patch of forest who didn't know where her limits lay but followed the rusty channel wherever she went.

Until the sprawling sands reached the edge of a stone terrace – a solid barrier of pumice-like rock who resisted the onslaught of the desert by rising above her, the bedrock of Amana born of Primal Waters in tussle with the wind. Unwilling to let himself be covered and forgotten, the pumice rose with the land to keep out the encroaching sand.

The river carved a path through the rising rock, eating away at his porous flesh, freeing countless bubbles trapped inside his core. Stubborn chunks of rock who resisted, she flowed around, washing away the softer tissue that connected them to the terrace, isolating them from the plate from whom they grew, leaving them standing proud and alone, remnants of where the whole bedrock once stood.

The river cut down, too, deepening her channel in the impure rock, broadening her reach with each puff of air she released from his grip, carving tiny veins in the soft stone. The single broad canal scattered into myriad follicles, each carrying water through her own abode on the desert plateau.

Moss emerged from the weathered surface kept supple and moist by the flowing streams. Grass took root in the porous rock, her roots feeding on the fluids trapped within his crust. Shrubs emerged from the thirsty grass, their leaves the colour of olive and sage. Trees rose far above the stone, anchored safely enough to withstand the wind.

The plants sprung up all across the terrace, wherever the scattered river was able to reach. Their colour betrayed the thirst with which they often lived, shifting from bronze to green with the vacillation of the streams. The supple leaves of agaves and aloes, the spacious cones of prickly cacti, yuccas who grew to the height of trees, all stored within their flesh what the moody waters sometimes failed to give.

Asja sighted movement in the sparse foliage, people going about their tasks until they spotted a shadow moving across the land, and stopped to gaze at the sky above. Goblins. The people of the desert, whose presence she had to get used to where she was going. Only this was no desert like Kalhar to the north, whose dunes shifted with each blow of the wind. Kuru Kam lived rooted in a rock, nourished by many plants and a river passing through on her way to the sea.

She saw the endless waters in the dying light of the day, filling the southern horizon in the river's way. The watercourse spread out to enter them, the desert streams scattering into myriad brooks, each looking to end her journey in her own place. They fell over the edge, seeping down the cliff face to return to the ocean from whom they'd been siphoned by the mountain roots.

Vagran turned to hug the coastline, following her east, keeping low to see her contours now that the skylight had vanished from the sky. His tired wings thanked him for it, holding still, angled to propel him onward without having to flap.

Asja closed her eyes, lulled to sleep by the rhythmic sound of the vexing water dancing with the shoreline, and the length of the journey to the desert range along the southern end of the vast land. When she opened them again, a massif of bare rock stretched out before her, his contours bathing in the light of a distant sun, partly hidden by the clouds slithering down the cliff.

"Are these the Pyrenees?" she shouted into the wind.

"Yes," Vagran's voice sounded in response.

She gazed at the sprawling massif, the muscular ridges made of solid stone, the roots who dug beneath the dry sands to anchor the summit and draw water from the depths. But they dug too deep, feeding springs too warm to be held by the land. They took to the sky instead, turning to clouds and drifting in the wind, giving the sands only a short reprieve, soon leaving the desert thirsting for more.

A sizzling sound pierced the cloudy mist. Vagran turned his head to the sight of a blazing fireball hurtling towards him. His body tensed. His feathers stood erect from a rush of charge. His wings angled to propel them upwards, shifting his frame out of the way. The flame passed beneath him, catching only his tail, scorching his feathers but not his skin.

A winged figure emerged from the clouds following on the fire's trail, rushing towards them with built-up speed, his body ablaze with the molten stone, a beacon of light in a sea of haze.

"Scoria!" the roc screeched, his voice rising in pitch. His eyes arced. His beak parted to release the pent-up charge.

The lightning bolt shot through the sky, striking the advancing dragon. Flashes of light rippled across his scales. His flaming wings suspended their motion, a momentary spasm before he resumed his pursuit.

His back arched as he drew in a gust of air to fuel the furnace inside. His magmatic body glowed from the heat. Light escaped through the gaps in the scales, revealing the passage of flame through his throat and head. His back recoiled, coughing out a molten shot, a piece of himself gushing with the flame.

Vagran's eyes widened at the sight. He steered to avoid the incoming missile, his dodge more sluggish than the one before, lacking the charge he'd already released. His body rose, his feathers locked into a protective shield, withstanding the collision with the blistering fireball, absorbing the molten stone that clung to them tightly, lessening the heat that seeped to his skin. Still, the bird groaned in pain, momentarily distracted from his escape.

He looked at the clouds around him. A grey haze leisurely floating on the wind, not trying to churn, completely lacking the will for a storm. The thunderoc needed them charged, angry, seething with fury, if he were to replenish the charge that he had lost.

Asja did not. She steered the wind to squeeze the enclosing cloud until she shed rain. Her staff drew on the sudden exuberance of the sky until it sparked, struggling to restrain the energy it gained.

"Hit him again!" she screamed to her friend.

Vagran turned and faced the dragon. His back arched, the charge building up, readying for release. A flash of lightning escaped from his beak, bolstered by another rising from his chest.

A composite bolt seared through the sky. A sizzling discharge struck the pursuing beast. His body seized, his groan drowned out by the thundering crash. He floated there – flaming, his eyes closed, his wings limp, a motionless mass in the open sky – before plummeting through the cloud towards the distant ground. They watched him fall, dropping beneath the haze and within sight of the land, before his powerful wings stretched open again, taking him away from the thundering bird who'd dared encroach upon his domain.

Asja couldn't see the thunderoc's face, but she felt the arcing in his body ease, and the feathers of his chest lose their electric glow to resume their carefree flutter in the wind. She pressed her face into his soft down, suddenly aware that her skills complemented his, grateful that he'd come with her on this journey, even if it took longer and made them a target of the flying beasts living in this land.

Vagran resumed his eastward course, using the charge he had left to keep them airborne, his body exhausted and sore, his wings lacking the strength to soar above the cloud. When he spotted a lonely hill through the obscuring mist, he veered towards him, touching down on the flat top and folding his wings to rest.

Asja climbed out of the bird's plumage to see his eyes close and sleep take hold. She pressed her face against him, grateful for his companionship and care. And then she took her staff and kept watch over her friend, peering as far as she could through the crawling cloud, not knowing what to expect in this alien land.

OGRE

Asja looked at the scorch marks on her friend's belly. She touched the singed feathers that wriggled away from her hand. Thinking them more sensitive than she'd realised, she softened her touch even more, carefully running her fingertips across their pellucid shapes, only to see them back away even further, and Vagran's body with them.

"That tickles!" the thunderoc sputtered, half-asleep.

"Sorry!" she replied, more aware of his gentle side now that she'd aided him in a fight, instead of merely sheltered by him as she used to be.

He stretched his legs, and then his wings – their tips spanning the full width of the plateau – opening them in all their splendour, their translucent feathers flexing with newfound charge. She gazed at them, mesmerised by their dance, reminded anew of her fortune to be friends with a creature of such rare beauty.

"You can really sleep!"

"Hard to recharge here."

He settled on his feet, staring blankly into open space, not yet fully present.

Unable to restrain herself, she pointed behind him and whispered, "Look!"

Shaken from his stupor, he spun around, his gaze eying the sands stretching beyond the hill, until they settled on a solitary mountaintop rising towards the horizon. The lonely summit had no range to feed him stone, yet reached for the sky nonetheless, his pointy tip growing steeper the higher he rose. Now he lay silent, no skylight having left him in living memory, his pale face drained of the colour of the desert around him.

"Is that…"

"Yes!" her excitement overflowed.

The Dead Mountain. Mount Urus. Dimotai's home.

"How…" his voice trailed off.

"The clouds hid him from view. I saw him when they lifted," she explained as she walked up to his side. "We landed here, within sight of the summit, and didn't even know it!"

He glanced her way, the sparkle in his feathers mirroring her excitement. She returned his gaze, then pressed her body into his lush plumage reinvigorated by the slumber.

"Thank you for bringing me here."

"Can I take you to the mountain?"

She stepped away, gazing into the distance, at the slender peak who awaited her.

"No," she shook her head. "I need to be alone."

She sighed, remembering her past encounters with Dimotai, a good friend of Shar and Florella who took a liking to her as well, and whom she looked up to in return. Now that she was here, within reach of his home, she was less sure that she was ready to face him again, in the aftermath of Shar's death that she had unwittingly caused.

She looked up at her friend, a knot of worry forming in her stomach, her mind already imagining the encounter. Vagran blinked. He spread his wings, his eyes arced, and he took to the skies with a sudden rush of charge. She raised her hand goodbye and continued to wave until his giant frame was no more than a speck in the sky, soaring high, his best defence against the dragons living in these parts.

She tied her staff to the trusty rucksack on her back and walked to the northern end of the plateau, to where a rugged path meandered along the hillside. As she scaled the gentle slope, an aroma caught her attention, a faint scent she didn't expect to find. She hurried her descent, touching the flat ground with a soft thud. A crack in the rock wall invited her in. She peered inside the dimly lit cave, and seeing no one, walked into the sunken space and the pool of water who dwelled in there.

Water. She didn't expect to find any here. Her water bag was still half-full, having conserved its load during the long flight. But the surface of the pool looked cool and inviting, as if her precious value shone through the liquid.

Asja leaned over the edge of the pool and broke the surface to retrieve a leaky handful. She brought it up to her mouth and drank slowly, savouring every drop. She reached again, feeling the water's story, impressed by her enduring presence beneath the arid sands long after the Dead Mountain had stopped drawing more.

A stone pillar detached from the nearby wall. She saw him move out of the corner of her eye. She reached for her staff, but strong arms grabbed her by the sides before she could pull it out, lifting her high into the air and placing her atop broad shoulders with rough skin made of flesh and stone.

An ogre! She gasped, disoriented by her new location, and grabbed his head trying to arrest her slip.

"Hold on!" the ogre grunted as he walked to the entrance of the cave and set off into the open desert, towards the slender summit made of pale stone.

OKALL

The ogre's strong legs carried them at a steady pace. He traversed dunes, walking up and down as if crossing waves, losing sight of the mountain and regaining it again. She held onto his head each time his posture shifted, like a child struggling to stay atop a busy adult.

Thoughts of struggle had long since left her. The ogre made no attempt to harm her, no move to threaten her life. She wondered whether he even knew who she was, with no dwarf having travelled beyond the Pyrenees. Still, she kept her staff on her back within easy reach, and herself in touch with the desert sand, not knowing why the ogre was walking to the mountain or what awaited him there.

A gathering of rocks rose in the distance, their domed heads like mushrooms dotting the landscape. Their creamy hues barely stood out from the fiery dunes in the dying throes of a faraway sun, but their solid forms did command attention, a rugged oasis amongst the shifting sands. Holes in their sides appeared as they neared, large enough for people to fit through them.

Asja gulped. A settlement stretched out before her. She didn't expect to find one here so long after the mountain had ceased to breathe. But enough water must have remained in the channels beneath the sands to sustain them to this day.

The ogre's pace quickened at the sight of the people. They saw him approach as he climbed to the top of a dune. Excited shouts followed, with more people spilling into the open space. By the time he descended to the solid ground outside the caves, it seemed as if the whole village had assembled there, dozens of goblins and a handful of ogres curious to see whom their friend has carried to them.

"Dwarf," he said as he put Asja down, pointing at his load as he mingled with them. And then he turned around and joined them in staring at their visitor, looking pleased with himself.

Asja stared back, reminding herself that these were not the goblins from River Rust, that they had no reason to attack a dwarf on sight. Still, her hands trembled as she gripped the leather straps running across her chest, ready to reach for her staff at a moment's notice, determined not to be surprised again, her senses well attuned to the hum of the sand.

A goblin woman emerged from the crowd. She walked slowly, as if measuring her steps. She stopped a comfortable distance away from Asja, outside of where the dwarf might have felt the urge to act.

"You parched?"

She extended her arms and offered a water bag.

The gesture stunned Asja. She studied the woman closely, looking beyond the pointy ears and the sunken nose, now seeing a person in place of a goblin. She couldn't judge her age, but the wrinkles in her skin did speak of the passage of time, even if pronounced by the harshness of the desert life. The markings on her clothes and the dignity of her posture suggested some standing among her people.

Asja stepped forward and took the water bag, afraid that she'd be offending her host if she declined. She drank slowly, quenching the thirst that had grown over the long walk, with her eyes fixed on the woman and the crowd, careful not to let her guard down.

Her thirst quenched, she returned the water bag with a grateful smile. "Thank you."

The goblin smiled in return. "I am Garia, shaman to this people."

"I'm Asja, a mage among mine." She felt no need to delve into the complexity of her relationship with dwarves and their runemages.

"I can see." A touch of wonder lit up her eyes, spying the tip of the staff protruding from Asja's back. She quickly arrested her stare to step aside, extending her arm and bowing her head. "Please, join us. Share meal. Rest from journey."

Asja looked at the shaman, seeing nothing but sincerity in her invitation, as if her people took great pride in their treatment of guests. There couldn't have been many travellers coming here anymore.

"Thank you."

As she stepped forward, the crowd dissolved back into the caves, leaving her standing alone with the shaman. Garia led the way, walking as slowly as before, heading for the entrance.

The cave failed to capture Asja's imagination, bare rusty rock inside and out. She expected as much from a goblin tribe. But Garia didn't stop there, walking straight through to the other side. Asja followed her into the light and another spacious clearing filled by the same crowd.

Walls of rock shaped like a crescent stood tall all around her, leaving the far end open and exposed to the desert winds. Trees rose beyond the people, rooted in the desert soil, short and scrawny by her standards, but seeing any trees at all was more than she'd hoped to find.

Four goblins emerged from a side entrance and walked to the middle of the space. Each one carried a sizeable basket filled with food that they placed on the ground before walking away. Garia thanked them and sat down by the baskets, motioning for Asja to do the same. When she did, several others stepped forward, forming the inner circle that surrounded the food, Asja given some space not to be crowded by her hosts. Others sat further back, in a semi-circle enclosing them, leaving the visitor's back turned to the caves with no people behind her.

Asja took off her rucksack and the staff attached to it. The long, dainty object with an entwined body caught everyone's eye, but they held back, not saying a word, letting their eyes do the talking. She sat down on the dusty floor with her belongings kept close and looked at the food laid out before her. She recognised dried meat in one basket, some kind of roots in another, but the rest looked strange, especially the spiky, hairy balls in the basket closest to Garia. She gulped when the shaman reached for them and took one out.

"You lucky to come when cactus fruit ripe," she said.

She skilfully removed the spiky shell to expose a layer of cactus hair. Deftly peeling it off left her with a moist, pale, yellow fruit that looked nothing like the contents of the bowl. The fruit promptly disappeared inside her mouth, to closed eyes and a sigh of delight.

Convinced by the display, Asja cautiously took one out, cleaned it, and placed it in her mouth. The soft texture melted away, releasing the supple juices of the desert fruit, more than she thought the food growing here could have. It brought a smile to her face. As if on cue, others reached for the food, enjoying it as much.

"Thanks to Rago and hunters we have meat." Garia pointed at another basket.

Rago leaned forward at the mention of his name. "Not easy," he shook his head. "Animals go when mountain die. Others burrow deep in ground. Hard to find."

"I didn't expect to find anyone here," admitted Asja. "How can you live without water?"

"Water here." Garia tapped the ground with her hand. "Level rise when Pyrenees erupt. Clouds bring more," she raised her hand to the sky. Then she started shaking her head. "Not enough. Some day, water run out and we have to move."

"It's remarkable that you haven't had to move yet," remarked Asja, genuinely impressed.

After the members of the inner circle had their pick of food, they passed the baskets to those behind them. With the sharing of food, the atmosphere of the whole gathering relaxed. Some children took the opportunity to leave their place and run across the courtyard. One boy stopped by Asja's staff, eyeing it with great interest. He reached out to touch it, but drew back at Garia's stern word. Asja only smiled and reached for the staff, placing her hand on its long spine, inviting the boy to do the same. He glanced at Garia, who held back, before touching it again. When nothing happened, he withdrew his hand, only to return it at Asja's urging.

A faint glow enveloped the staff. A subtle pulsation traversed its spine. "Whoa!" the boy exclaimed, his eyes wide open with wonder. He held it as the glow grew and the pulsation surged, but pulled back when the tip started to spark. Asja laughed and released the staff, letting the sparking subside.

"He very curious," Garia apologised for the boy's intrusion, unable to hide her own astonishment at the display she'd just seen.

The boy's interest reminded Asja of her own curiosity as a child about the mages' crystals and the runes they used. "He will learn much."

"Dwarfs have most beautiful staffs," Rago's admiration mirrored the boy's. "Never see crystal like this."

"I don't think it's made of crystal," mused Asja.

"Dwarf staffs made of crystal, no?"

Asja sat up, Rago's apparent familiarity with the ways of the mountainfolk catching her by surprise.

"How do you know about dwarves?"

Rago started to stammer, prompting Garia to interject. "Carar, great shaman before me, have vision. He see mountains after Pyrenees, far, far away in another land. He see people live there. People like you." She gestured at Asja.

"He show us how to gather water like your people," she continued, pointing at the stone shaped into a gutter-like structure that ran the full length of the cave rooftops and drained into holes in the ground. "He show us how to grow food like your people." She stood up with her arms outstretched, pointing out the dense line of cacti growing at the far opening and protecting less-sturdy plants from the desert winds. "He show us how to draw light from crystal like your people." Her gaze wandered to beautiful gems embedded in the rock around the courtyard, shining with tender glow in the light of the day. "He teach us many things from his sight."

Neither new nor expertly made, the goblin handiwork still went beyond what Asja thought they could achieve. She couldn't help but wonder whether dwarves would learn as readily from a culture so alien to their own, and advance in ways they had not valued before.

"When he tell us his vision, we, us all, want to meet dwarf," Rago added.

The way they looked at her made Asja uncomfortable. Genuine admiration filled their eyes, a sense of gratitude that felt out of place. Her people had done nothing to help the goblins. Quite the opposite. Looking into the eyes of the people seated beside her, she glimpsed the effect that the ongoing skirmishes across River Rust had on the goblins living there. Their hatred of the mountainfolk was not shared by their distant brethren.

"This staff wasn't made by dwarves. I've had a vision, too. I saw the face of the wizard who was to be my teacher. When I woke up, this staff was lying on me. I don't know where it came from. I've never seen another like it."

The goblins in the inner circle nodded, apparently comfortable with the mystery of its origin.

"Do you come to teach us?" asked Garia. "Much from Carar vision we not understand."

Asja's breath caught in her throat. The possibility hadn't even crossed her mind. Not long ago, she was still concerned about her safety visiting a goblin village.

She shook her head. "I'm still an apprentice myself. I'm here at the invitation of a wizard. I wasn't expecting to find anyone nearby."

"Wizard?" Garia's face lit up.

Garia knew of the wizards? How did these primitive people learn about the wizards?

"He told me to meet him inside the mountain." Asja looked at Mount Urus, the wayward glance helping to conceal her surprise. Not knowing how much goblins knew, she wouldn't share that Dimotai actually lived there, but it did remind her that she had no idea how to reach him. "Do you know how to get inside, now that the peak no longer opens by himself?"

The goblins shook their heads in unison, except for Garia.

"Shaman Cave," she said.

Both the goblins and Asja turned to her expectantly. Garia's gaze wandered from one to the next, making Asja realise that, like the dwarf runemages, goblin shamans kept secrets about their craft, even from their own people. To her surprise, Garia continued.

"When I learn to be shaman, Carar send me to cave in Mount Urus, to be away from people. Cave inside mountain, deep inside, behind cave of Ursul people."

"Ursul people?" Asja's eyes widened. "Is this another tribe living nearby?"

Garia shook her head. "Ursul people gone. Go when mountain die." Then she continued, "Tunnel go from cave of Ursul people to Shaman Cave. Maybe tunnel go deeper into mountain?"

"You are not sure?"

"Shaman Cave dark. Small tunnel dark. No light."

Asja thought she saw a look of discomfort cloud the shaman's face. She only nodded, grateful for the information she received, sketchy as it was.

"When must you go?" asked Rago.

"As soon as I can," Asja replied with urgency in her voice.

Silence set in following her reply. She could see the disappointment on their faces and felt a pang of regret for wanting to leave so quickly, but she did need to see Dimotai, and the dwarf plan was already in motion.

"Then you must rest," Garia stated as she got up, looking westward at a burning sun. "Uluru light high in sky. Best leave when sky light gone."

Asja expressed her gratitude for the hospitality of the tribe before following the shaman back into the caves.

The amber rock looked less bare than before, the shallow lines sculpted by the wind adding character to the dry stone. The beds of packed sand she walked past looked comfortable, even if the leather holding them was torn in places, the animals it came from having long since departed from this desert.

The section of the complex Garia led her to looked like a room, hiding from other chambers behind a natural wall, with a low entrance the only way in. A high hole in the outside wall let in the light. Her bed stretched out in the far corner, in better condition than the others she had seen. A full water bag stood ready to quench her thirst, the only other item in the barren room.

Asja put her staff and backpack down and stood pensively by the empty bed.

"You carry all world on shoulders," Garia pointed out.

Asja turned around and sighed deeply, realising what her worrying must have looked like to the shaman. "No, these problems are my own."

"Wizard you look for, he can help, no?"

"I believe so," Asja remarked, the tone of her voice not reflecting the words' conviction. "I hope so."

Garia nodded and was about to leave when she stopped and looked at the girl again. "We all wish you stay." Her voice broke with sadness, as if an opportunity of a lifetime had come by unexpectedly and then slipped away.

Asja watched her leave. The thought of their need weighed heavily on her as she lay down to sleep. Though committed to finding Dimotai and continuing her training, she felt a tug to stay in this alien land and help these people realise their dreams.

DAY OF DARKNESS

Arezan stood by a large crystalline structure sprawled out in the middle of the cave. His legs pressed against the enclosing rock, as if the crystal were shy and didn't want to make his presence known. Now exposed, he kept quiet and still, letting the mur astrologer do his work.

Arezan leaned over the glittering face of the geode with a pointy gem in his hand and gazed at the ridges subtly raised from the flat surface. He placed his hand over a single peak, releasing glimmers of light from the jewel he held, watching them vanish into the crystal lattice.

He stepped back and wiped the oil secreted from his forehead. It was tiring work, demanding prolonged stillness. He breathed deeply and walked out of the cave, seeking to break the monotony of the task.

The Everglades greeted him every time he looked outside. A mixture of water and land unlike any he recalled from his distant home, yet so pervasive here as if there were no other way for the land to be – like a shallow sea, sheltered from the wind by close-knit trees, watered tirelessly by the many peaks who dwelled within Serpentine Span.

Serpentine Span.

A twin mountain range who crisscrossed and twisted across the land like a pair of smitten snakes. Summits rose like scales from their crested backs, rising even higher where the two met. He'd never gotten used to this strange place, having crossed Peruvius Mountains and the Pyrenees on his eastward journey to come to this land.

The aquatic creatures who lived here thrived in their swamp. Crocodiles and tortoises, frogs and snakes, lizards and fish, all found home in the stagnant liquid. Colourful flowers of immense beauty floated on the drab water, waterlogged trees supported each other searching for footing in the slimy mud, dense reeds stalked out the shallower basins, looking like moss growing on bark from the vantage point high above.

If there were people living here, they did a stellar job of hiding from his sight.

261

His body and mind rested, he returned to the crystalline table and the many peaks rising from it. A fortunate discovery, that – learning the secrets of crystals from a dwarven mage during a chance encounter on the Peruvius Range. He'd augmented them further since, surpassing Hloim in the insights he imparted, until they could hold the knowledge of the cycles he had gathered travelling through the land.

He reached out with his gem to release more flickers of light into the southern peaks of Serpentine Span, imprinting into the open geode the skylight cycle of each summit. And then he stepped back and let out a deep sigh as the broadest grin spread across his face.

His work was done.

He breathed in deeply, savouring the moment, basking in the knowledge that the cycle of every peak found in Amana had been encoded into the lattice frame. The culmination of the work of mur astrologers from ages past, who'd set out across the land to preserve the cycles of the mountains they found. He was not among them, having been born to the last generation dedicated to the task. Now he stood alone, in an alien land, as their work had come to its end.

The stream of light pouring in suddenly brightened, washing out the faint crystal glow, before vanishing as quickly as it had come, leaving the cave basking in the subdued radiance of the distant suns.

Perfect timing, Arezan thought, smiling at the dying skylight's honouring of the moment. He held his gem over the open geode, above Amana's central peak, discharging a lively spark into the crystalline structure, bringing it to life.

A minor mound on the Pyrenees spine flashed with caramel light. It remained ablaze for a while longer, signifying the length of time its skylight would continue blazing through the sky as it rose ever higher, before disintegrating into myriad pieces and fading back into the night.

Two more peaks flashed one after the other, on the opposite ends of the spacious table, their glow fading steadily until they blended back into their mountain range. A third flashed moments later, close to the middle of the structure, on the central range of the Tetran Massif who brought together the six spinal ridges of Amana's land.

The display continued in the darkened place, some peak flashing in a corner of the geode, some summit radiating a discharging glow, the ingenious spectacle laying Amana's diurnal cycle bare for him to savour in all its intricacy.

And then it stopped, the glow having drained from all of the ridges running across the table, until the whole structure lay dull before him, blending into the duskiness of the swampland's night.

Arezan peered at the structure, surprised to see the display end so soon. Indeed, the crystal mounts came to life once more, shining their light after a brief pause, continuing the display for a while longer, before the energy of the spark was spent and the table fell dark again, this time for good. But his mind stayed stuck on the brief interlude, not expecting the hundreds of peaks who dotted the land all to be quiet at the same time. And yet, there would be a time in the not-too-distant future when no light would come from any part of the sky, when all the peaks would fall silent in unison and darkness would reign supreme over the land.

Eerie ambience descended upon the cave. A sudden shiver washed over him. A sense of foreboding he couldn't explain. Perhaps he was just caught by surprise, he tried to convince himself, even as a feeling gnawed at him that there would be more to this portent than a brief absence of light.

SHAMAN'S CAVE

Asja stepped forth onto the loose ground. Her foot sank, pushing the sand off the ridge and down the broad slope on either side. She glanced at the line of footprints trailing behind her, following the dune crests snaking across the desert. With its slender tip, the staff sank far too easily to be of any use and could do nothing more than bide its time strapped to Asja's back.

With skylights nowhere in sight, Isura's lights illuminated the land. Asja thanked them for their shy company, not wanting to be seen, not feeling ready to face the wizard in the mountain following Shar's death. Like a brooding presence, the tall silhouette of his home blocked out the lights from the sky ahead.

She gazed back towards the rocky caves hiding in the distance behind the rising dunes. She'd worried about running into goblins when she first set out, knowing that this was their land, hoping that the lack of water would have forced them to move. Now she felt torn having to leave, having received a welcome warmer than any that her adoptive people had been willing to give.

She thought she knew what goblins were like. She'd seen the carnage left by them, killed enough of them in the last counterraid. Primitive savages, like feral beasts who couldn't learn and whom you couldn't trust. But this tribe did learn. And there was an innocence to them she hadn't seen among the dwarves, like little children before they learned to lie. The antithesis of runemages and their scheming ways. Perhaps there were too few of them and their desert lives too harsh to afford them the luxury of intrigue, but it was one luxury she did not miss.

Solid rock emerged from the dunes, eroded by sand blown by the wind. A silhouette of a tree passed by in the distance, with no leaves to adorn his crown, a dried-out husk hollowed by the heat. A spacious pool sprawled out beside her, the tiles of her floor dried out and cracked, thirsting for the water whom they used to hold. Skeletal remains of a desert lizard lay in the dust beside her path. A landscape who'd died along with the mountain, revived in a haunting spectacle by the light of the stars.

A gentle hum arose. Asja looked around but saw no source to the sound. The rock and the sand lay in perfect stillness, joined by only a shadow of the faded life. She looked up, at the distant lights from another world, and heard them blink. She stopped. The faint echo of the stars held her in place. How could any sound come from so far away? She closed her eyes to better hear them, resuming a slow walk with her eyes shut, hearing the stone on whom she treaded, and the whisper of the beings who passed away without the water, as if their death were merely a transition, and they were alive in a way she could feel but not grasp.

A narrow canyon rose before her, snaking loosely towards the mount, the deathbed of a river who once had the power to cut through the stone and mould him to her whim. She entered the winding passage, walking on the loose sand in near darkness, the high walls letting in only a sliver of the lights.

A brilliant light exploded behind her, a new sun borne of the Pyrenees. His rays streamed past the layered walls, bathing their faces in a radiant glow, the lines drawn by water and wind sculpting the colours in which they were seen, as if a fire had been lit in the stone, each line sounding a note to match the hue. A festival of colour with no people to give it. A living presence in a world she once thought was dead.

She emerged from the canyon as if in a trance, looking at the mountain with newly forged eyes. She searched for an opening, a cave in the foothills, hoping that Mount Urus had conspired to bring her here, and was as welcoming of her as Dimotai seemed to be. She spied a hole in a distant bulge, a dark spot hiding from the light on a bright stone face. She set out towards it, climbing the gentle slope, her staff finally finding some use aiding her walk across the rising land. A gust blew as she approached, scattering sand across the face of the cave. Taking it as a sign, she gripped her staff and entered.

A spacious interior welcomed her, brightly lit where the rays could reach, a floor well-trodden by bare feet, desert animals painted on the walls, depicting life as it used to be. A feeling of loneliness washed over her, a craving for company, as if the cavern had been forced into solitude after a lifetime of camaraderie.

She spied an opening in the far wall, a gap much too low for her to walk through. Wasting no time, she took off her backpack, held it in one hand and the staff in the other, got down on her hands and knees, and crawled into the wide tunnel whose ceiling hovered close to her head.

The light from the cave soon deserted her, leaving her hands to feel their way ahead. She heard no sound save for her own slithering across the sand. She brought her staff to life, only to be blinded by the intense glow in the cramped space. Subduing her staff, she tried to spy the passage forward. Her impatience started to rise. She grew tired of dragging herself across the dusty floor.

The beam of light illuminating the tunnel diffused as the walls spread further apart. A distant barrier came into view, the light hitting the sombre stone face.

Seeing the end approach, she redoubled her efforts, a surge of excitement fuelling her movements, until she felt the ceiling rise above her head, releasing her to the freedom of the inner cave.

She stood up and dusted herself off. The muted light from her staff brightened the cavern – a humble hollow with a low ceiling, a far cry from where she had come. She extinguished her staff for a moment, to be greeted by perfect darkness even after her eyes had time to adjust. This felt more how she had imagined Shaman's Cave to be, reminding her of her first visit to the Primogenus Plane, except that she no longer feared the dark, having learned to welcome it and see herself in it.

She sat quietly in the darkness of the cave. It occurred to her that Garia might have never seen the interior, unless she brought a light crystal with her before she became a shaman. Asja soaked in the perfect solitude of the place, stillness undisturbed by events beyond the mountain walls, letting it wash away her stress the way Mirrordon Plane once did.

Rested and at peace, she stirred her staff awake, looking for a way out of the cave save the one she had used to enter. A small opening caught her attention, only slightly above the ground. She shone a beam of light directly through the gap but saw no end to the narrow shaft. She continued her search and found two others, even more cramped than the first had been. Disheartened, she returned to the first one and put her arm through the crack, wondering how she would fit through such a tight hole. She recalled Garia's face as she spoke of a tunnel, and the look of unease that accompanied her words. No wonder, if this were the size of the gap she had tried to crawl through. But she did say that the passage might lead deeper into the mountain, reason enough for Asja to follow.

The thought of portalling through the tunnel crossed her mind. She quickly dismissed it, understanding the danger of such an endeavour. Used to the freedom of wide-open spaces, a portal would be impossible to control within the confines of a shaft. She wondered about making the passage in her misty form instead, but winced at the thought, having made no attempt to master the skill, always content for the portal membrane to suck her in and send her on her way.

She studied the opening again – a long, last look while she still held the light in her hand. Then she took off her backpack and tied it around her ankle, and tied her staff to the other end of her bag. Her belongings secure, she got down onto the floor of the cave and, in the dying light of her fading staff, crawled head-first into the tight hole.

She felt like a worm, wriggling through the snug space with her arms tucked by her side. The freshness of the experience soon wore off, replaced by the cramped reality of the place. Solid stone pressed down on her head. Hard walls rubbed against her shoulders. She looked to her side, her ear touching the floor, but saw nothing, the light of the staff dragging behind her long gone.

She tried to lighten her mood, thinking how lucky she was that her slender frame could fit inside this gap. Some dwarves she knew would have got stuck by now, assuming they even made their way in. But the humour didn't stay; the oppressive rock who coiled around her squeezed it right out.

Sheer dread washed over her. She stopped moving and breathed in deeply, fighting back the onset of panic. The odour of dry stone filled her nostrils. The rock became her whole world, crowding her from all sides, not letting her move anywhere but forward. Her arms pressed against the tunnel walls as she tried to reach for her staff. Stuck in place, she drew on the energy of the rock without its aid. The charge took longer, long enough for her to grasp the futility of the effort. Any discharge here could bury her under an avalanche of stone.

The realisation of her powerlessness suddenly struck her. No matter how explosive a bolt or scorching a blaze she could unleash, she couldn't force her way out of the mountain's embrace.

Was this how Shar felt? Was his decision to travel to the elf lands borne of his frustration with my unwillingness to listen?

A wizard as old as the forests themselves, he must have known that he was flirting with danger before he was killed by the vengeful elves. Her predicament could have been avoided with a better developed ability to portal, but his was in her hands rather than his own.

She realised that it was her clinging to the goodness she saw in dwarves and elves that drove Shar to do what he did, as if it were some special quality that her people possessed rather than comfort that stemmed from her connection with them. She started to cry, realising that, had she listened to what he was telling her, he would still be alive.

The mountain held her as her body convulsed. The suffocating clasp suddenly brought comfort. At least for a moment, before her nose filled with snot and she struggled to breathe. She lay there, her mouth wide open, feeling humbled by the stone and her own lack of judgement. By the time she continued to move, her impatience had left her. She moved one contortion at a time, with no thought of where she was going or whom she sought to meet, one moment blurring into the next inside the dark bowels of the dead mountain, with no skylights to trace the passage of time.

A faint scent of water reminded her of her goal. She wondered whether it was the tears lingering on her face. But the scent didn't wane, only strengthened as she continued to plod. The passage soon widened, her movements sped up in response, until she landed head-first in still water, her hands coming out to cushion her fall.

She knelt in the channel and untied her rucksack before it followed her in and wet her belongings. And then she sat at the end of the tunnel, with her feet in ankle-deep water, munching on dried meat and drinking with abandon, knowing that she could refill her water bag to her heart's content.

Distant light caught her attention, barely rising above the darkness of the cave. She followed the waterway towards the only thing she could see, the water swooshing around her, marking her steps. She refrained from powering her staff again, reluctant to intrude upon the tranquillity of the place. The ceiling gradually materialised above her, the pale sapphire hue borrowed from the lights. The walls of rock emerged soon after, giving shape to the canal she was in, a large tunnel coursing through the mount.

She stopped to admire the spacious waterway. This must have been a river while the summit had the strength to draw fresh water and push her out with force. Now she remained parched and empty, a channel holding on to the little liquid she had left at the bottom of her shaft.

The lights grew more numerous as Asja continued to walk, dangling from the ceiling in crystalline strands, their shine reflected in the still water ahead. When the channel rose and left the water behind, they bathed the smooth stone instead, giving form to the mountain vein, helping her come to life. The mountain might be dead, but there were still creatures here who called him their home. Asja felt welcomed by them, guided on her journey to the heart of the summit, as if they knew the wizard and approved of her visit.

The channel broadened deeper inside the mountain. Pools of water formed within the vein, pillars of rock rising to hold up the ceiling, crystalline overhangs gracing it with their presence, shining with a kaleidoscope of colours from the ocean of lampyrids living on their surface.

The vein widened further still, opening completely to an underground lake who covered the floor of a colossal cave. An enormous structure rose from the stone, a body of rock supporting a broad chamber, weathered by the flow of water from the cycles past. The chamber stood still – the heart of the mountain who had ceased her beat. Above her, in the spacious hollow looking at the ceiling, lay a ball of sediment who fed on retreating waters, a nascent seed who never left his womb, the mountain having died before he could be born.

Asja gasped at the sight. She'd seen it before from the other side, having climbed into the open womb of a mountain of frost. Only then, she lacked the light to see the interior in full, and knew far too little to value what she did see. She sat down to take in the wonder of the place. She closed her eyes and reached out to the wizard within the seed, hopeful that he would answer and show her a way in.

NECROMANCER

Asja heard the pressing of feet on the stone floor. She opened her eyes to see a cloaked figure standing before her, strange markings gracing his hands and neck, and a lopsided face, half of which seemed to have withered away.

"Dimotai?" she whispered.

A broad smile spread across his face, struggling through the decay but no less sincere for it. He opened his arms to welcome her. She hesitated for a moment, peering deeply into his black eyes, daring to believe that he accepted her despite what happened to Shar. She got up and rushed to embrace him. He crouched to receive her, still taller than the young dwarf.

She clung to him, grateful for his invitation. Her body convulsed with sobs, wishing that she could hold Shar again as well, having to make peace with his death one more time. Dimotai held her in his arms, giving her as much time as she needed, only letting go when she was ready to part.

"You would have come to me even if Shar were still alive," his soothing voice fluttered in the air.

She winced at his words, suspecting he'd known, glad she didn't have to be the one to tell him.

"Why do you say that?"

"Because there are important things for you to learn," he said, half-pointing at his welted face, "that I'm better equipped to teach than either Florella or Shar. I trust that's why you're here?"

She stood silent for a moment, wondering why she'd heeded his call. And then she nodded, aware of her lack, wanting to resume her training, thankful that the wizard would have her.

"Then come!" he urged gleefully, wrapping his arm around her before they both vanished from the still chamber of the mountain's heart.

A dusky interior welcomed her. Earthen walls crowded around her and moved away again in haphazard fashion, faintly lit by the earth herself packed tightly within the seed's bulk. She had no idea how she got there. She had not seen Dimotai's technique. Her eyes lit up with excitement, but dulled again quickly, sensing that there was far more at stake here than the mere mastering of a new way to travel.

She adjusted her posture to match the floor of the chamber, the smooth, uneven surface offering no aid. The features of the place reminded her of goblin caves, only these seemed even less interested in sheltering their occupants, as if the whole place were altogether indifferent to their presence.

Dimotai leaned against the dimly lit wall. "As the waters drained and the air dried, cracks started to appear." He smiled as his fingers ran across the dry surface. "There's something... poetic... about living inside a skylight-to-be who had the potential to enrich the land with his light and his life."

"What do you do here?" she asked.

His hand came up over his mouth as he glanced at the floor. The left side of his face winced before his gaze rose to match hers.

"After Rashas died, I came to Amana. I was shattered then. If you can imagine your whole world crumbling to dust, that was how I felt. A new desire arose in me then – to understand these worlds we live in and the life they harbour. I was desperate to avoid the repeat of Rashas, and I couldn't think of any other way."

Asja's brow furrowed with confusion.

A mischievous smirk lit up his face. "Let me show you..."

He spun around and headed for the exit. She quickly followed.

FALKRA

A wall of clouds appeared on the horizon. Vagran welcomed their sight, having had his fill of coasting through clear hot skies over the Kalhar Desert. Distant rumbling barely reached his ears. A flash of lightning lit up the clouds. The misty veil snuffed out another. They grew weaker as the cyclone moved south, the final throes of a dying storm.

He gazed with longing as the tempest blew himself out before he could reach the summits, leaving a solid rainbow to emerge through the brightening sky. A column of colour born of the moist air left in the wake of the raging storm. Her base throbbed and fluttered in a way he'd never seen, having witnessed many rainbows on his long flights through the rainy skies.

He descended from the heights to see a flock of birds mingle at the base, their looks transforming as they passed through the colours, their velvety forms standing out against the auburn backdrop of the Peruvius Range. They rose in unison through the arc of the rainbow, a single murmuration made of countless birds, breathing, flexing, shrinking and expanding, thinning as it went two ways at once before winding back through the receding clouds who had turned snowy white.

Vagran watched the silent display unfold before his eyes, the birds' eyes closed, their wings responsive, feeling the flock and their place in it in a way he didn't grasp, responding to the shifting movements with the speed he couldn't match.

He spotted a golden mass at the bottom of the flock whose hue asserted itself upon the droplets of the arc. He moved closer for a better look, intrigued by what kind of birds could shine so brightly and fly together so tightly that they gave the guise of a single form.

And then the giant bird flexed her enormous wings, and his breath caught at the fiery sight.

A pyreroc!

He thought of flight but held back. The blazing bird made no attempt to hunt him down, nor moved to protect her piece of the sky. She remained at the base of the rainbow, her fiery feathers swaying in the breeze, the countless droplets colouring her flame. Seduced by the display, he descended further still, the pulsating murmuration giving him space, inviting him deeper into its fold.

And the snowy white birds swarmed around them, an anchor to the flock within the rainbow's shape.

When she moved away from the swirling birds, he followed her into the mountains, surprised to see her head for Mount Ire rather than the Pyrenees, where pyrerocs were known to live.

UNDEAD

The lower chamber opened to a shadowy passage. Dimotai forged ahead, the dull sounds of his footsteps gently rumbling through the motley floor. Asja followed closely. The surface beneath her feet felt smooth and slippery, as if polished into ice by the water's flowing hand, the legacy of a stream who'd lived here long ago. When she closed her eyes, she could still hear the rhythmic current pouring down the vein to the drawn-out beat of the mountain's heart.

The tunnel end opened to a column of light coming from the walls in the centre of the seed. They revealed a spiralling staircase that coiled around the well as high as the eye could see. Dimotai followed the winding steps before departing down an unassuming passage who soon grew spacious compartments within her jagged walls.

He stopped by a curiously shaped pile of stones.

"This was where I started," he said. "If I may, let me introduce you to Rumbul."

At his command, the mass of stones started moving, wriggling and whirling into a more elegant shape. It grew four legs and a torso. The legs pushed against the floor to let it stand. It took a step towards Asja, and then another, the ground trembling from the weight of the rock, before coming to a halt in the empty space in front of her.

She recoiled from fright. "What is this... thing?"

"A golem, Asja. A stone golem. It was my very first creation. It took me nearly twenty cycles to perfect its motion. Stones can be very... uncooperative. But now it can walk, run, climb and jump. It can even be taken on a journey if you watch it closely."

"Is it alive?" Asja eyed its still, formidable frame.

Dimotai shook his head. "No. At least no more than the rocks themselves are. I animated it with enchantments. It responds to commands if you know how to give them. But that's all. It has no wants or needs, and nothing it seeks to do or become."

Asja extended her hand and touched the golem. Its leg felt hard and coarse. Basalt, she guessed. A common rock in the Kalhar desert, she didn't know how easy it was to find here. She ran her hand across the thigh and onto what she thought of as the chest. The golem remained motionless, as if it hadn't even felt her touch.

"Rumbul cannot respond to your touch any more than the mountain or the cavern can," Dimotai explained. "It's just rock that moves at my command."

"Why did you make it?"

Dimotai shrugged his shoulders. "I wanted to start at the beginning, understand what makes Amana's creatures tick. I decided to use something common but hardy; something that couldn't be damaged easily, yet could be replaced easily if it were. Rocks were an obvious choice.

"When you spend so much time getting your creation to move properly, you learn to appreciate just how sophisticated creatures like you and me are. You also realise that, no matter how much you arrange stones into the shape of a beast, nor how much time you spend getting it to move like one, it's still only a poor imitation."

The wizard's words made Asja think of Vagran. As a child, she'd often wondered how a creature made of lightning could be alive. How did he maintain his bodily shape? What made him different from an ordinary storm? Her curiosity was piqued all over again.

Dimotai raised his hand; the golem retraced its steps back to its resting place. Another necromancer creation was waiting further down the passage. Asja noticed it as soon as they turned the corner. Its ribbed features reminded her of her recent journey from the Okall Caves, where she saw well-preserved skeletal remains of desert creatures big and small.

"Is this a skeleton you animated?" she guessed.

Dimotai smiled. "Yes. This was my second project. The chamois skeleton was perfectly preserved – fully assembled and undamaged – before I started working with it. A rare find."

"Is it more capable than the golem?"

"No, not really. It is more elegant, and it was much easier to make. I knew what I was doing by then, and the joints were a boon, but the end result was practically the same – a lifeless assemblage of bones made to move by the force of magic.

"The next creation, however, is far more interesting."

He waited for them at the next level of the spiralling staircase. A dull grey glow betrayed his presence. He stood upright, his body dead still. Even so, he was a fearsome sight.

Two powerful legs supported a stocky frame. Muscles rippled beneath the dull red skin, part flesh and part stone, covered by a thick mane of blackish grey hair stretching the full length of the torso. The face had none. A bone fragment took its place, passing through the nose, with two more piercing an ear. Deeply set eye sockets withdrew from the face, protected by thick eyebrows and a jutting forehead. Three canines protruded from the lower jaw, parting the lips to reveal a jagged assemblage of teeth threatening to add their grip to any bite the creature would take.

Asja had never seen a red ogre before. Bigger, stockier and strikingly wilder than his Okall cousins. No dwarf legend spoke of these brutes, their race too remote from her home range to carve a name for themselves in the dwarf tales.

She noticed severe scarring on his right cheek. Something must have taken a heavy swipe that dug out the eye and cut parallel lines into the skull, down the neck, and across the shoulder and back. It left no doubt as to the cause of death. The bloodshot wound blended well with the ogre's naturally red skin. It showed signs of patching, though Asja couldn't tell whether this was the work of Dimotai or the desert folk.

"I named him Tuilk," Dimotai introduced the ogre. "I came across him at the sands of Galwe. Those lines you see cut into his face are cougar claw marks. He was dead when I found him."

"What happened to him?"

"Sometimes ogres and cougars go for the same prey, and it ends badly for one of them. It was a fresh kill for the cat, one that I put to good use."

Asja looked at him quizzically.

"He was dead, but his body could still be salvaged. I immediately set to work. The enchantments restored the blood flow and preserved other essential bodily functions. I patched up the wound as best I could, until the body was in working order again. It was my finest work up until then, not least of all because much of it wasn't mine."

Dimotai raised his hand to lift the enchantments holding the ogre in place. Tuilk took a deep breath and opened his eye. Asja bolted, then stood waiting to see what the ogre would do. When nothing happened, she cautiously returned to her earlier spot, looking the brute directly in the eye.

The emptiness that stared back at her sent shivers down her spine. The blood-red eye that met her gaze felt much the same as the gaping hole on the other side of his face. It held no glimmer of recognition. No consciousness grasped her presence.

"It's empty!" She continued to stare with her jaw hanging open.

"Yes. The body is alive, but the eye... There's nothing there."

"I don't understand."

"Neither did I. You can imagine my surprise when I looked into the eye to discover that the ogre was no more. I had restored every vital system of his to full use. His eye – it works. When he moves, he can see obstacles and avoid them. He can hear you, and he can feel your touch. He can hear me talking about him right now."

Dimotai looked at Tuilk as he said that. The ogre returned his gaze. They stared at each other for some time before the ogre looked away as if nothing had happened. Asja took a step closer and lifted her arm. Tuilk looked at her raised hand but did not respond to the touch.

"I can't believe it!" Asja was thrilled to be standing in the company of such a wild and imposing creature without having to fear for her life. "What is he now if not an ogre?"

"A zombie."

"A zombie?"

"A creature not unlike the skeleton and the golem. His body is fully capable, but that's the only difference. By restoring it, I was hoping to capture the elusive volition that makes the creature who he is in life. I didn't."

He reflected on his failure just long enough to see Asja's cheerless reaction.

"But not for long!" He raised his finger as his exuberance returned, a lopsided smile spreading across his face. "I realised my mistake soon after."

He bolted and hurried down the passage. Asja trailed his strides up the stairs to the next level of the seed. She found him standing beside a short, scrawny, goblin-like creature, but hideously deformed, with little resemblance to the dwellers of Okall.

"Who's that?"

"She was a goblin who'd also met her end in the desert sands. I restored her as I did the ogre, but with one crucial difference – the magic that animates her body no longer sustains it. She has to feed if she is to live. I didn't know what effect that would have, if any at all. I had a hunch that it was important, though perhaps not in a good way."

"Well, she didn't die," remarked Asja.

The wizard laughed. "No, quite the opposite. I first noticed that something was

276

afoot when I saw her devour a fish she'd caught in the underground lake. This convinced me that she wasn't just going to wither away and die. She sensed what her body needed and went after it.

"I took her into the desert. I wanted to see how she would fare. Not very well, it turned out. Her hunger must have been ravenous. She dug into everything that crossed her path – corpses, insects, even a desert pangolin who was bemused to see her attack him before getting peeved and bashing her skull in."

"Is that why her head is deformed?"

"Yes."

"And she survived?"

"No, of course not. I had to revive her again."

"Without mending her injuries?"

"Ah!" Dimotai raised his hand dismissively. "She doesn't need to look pretty. Besides, I soon learned what I could from her. She didn't become a zombie; she turned into a ghoul. It was an improvement; she acted of her own volition. But it was such a base motivation that it led to a very violent – and very short – life. It had little in common with how goblins lived. It was not what I was looking for.

"I had to get a new creature to continue the experiment."

Asja followed his gaze to a dark opening in the stone wall. It housed an ordinary-looking desert wolf. He came at Dimotai's command, and he sat down by the necromancer's feet. She had seen many wolves on the mountain and on her travels. Nothing about this one hinted at his undead nature.

The wizard continued. "The ghoul taught me that, whatever it is that is absent from the revived creature, it helps sustain her. Take that away, and the creature can think of nothing else but her bare need to feed. She becomes a slave to her hunger. She lives every waking moment trying to satisfy it.

"So I tailored my spells to provide the sustenance like I did with the zombie, just not all the time. These new enchantments absorbed nourishment from the light. As long as the wolf was out in the open desert with the skylights burning bright, he didn't need anything more. Inside was fine too, if the fire was strong enough. But in the darkness, he needed to feed."

"So he was a zombie during the day?"

"No! He was not!" Dimotai's hand swung through the air. "I was most amazed to see that. I must have tapped into some capacity of the body to act for reasons other than dire need that remained dormant in the ogre. The wolf – the lycan, as I call him – fed when he had to, but he did things at other times too. Silly things.

Walking down the passage and back again. Spinning on the ground chasing his own tail. Stupid things I've seen wolves do in the desert."

"And at night? Was he a ghoul?"

Dimotai nodded apprehensively. "At night, he transformed into a monster more bloodthirsty than any I had ever seen. I had previously let him out into the open desert to see whether he would fare better than the ghoul. He did. He soon became the terror of the coastal caves. The villages were terrified of the beast who stalked them at night, but mysteriously vanished during the day. Once I realised what was going on, I brought him back here."

Asja looked at the wolf again. She knew wolves as skilled hunters, especially in packs. She also knew them as warm, affectionate and deeply loyal companions. She just couldn't imagine the ordinary-looking desert wolf who was sitting in front of her as a slaughterous fiend.

The wizard continued. "Curbing their sustenance was an important step. It brought out their ability to act of their own accord. What I needed now was something to dampen or broaden that ability, something that would deliver them from being a slave to their urge to eat. I had no idea what that might be or how to produce the effect. In the end, I found it by accident."

He extended his left arm. Something moved in the dark recesses of the cave, flapped its wings, and landed firmly on the outstretched arm. Then it folded its wings and remained still.

"I befriended Misa a long time ago, while she was still roaming the Dead Mountain caves searching for food," he explained, looking tenderly at the bat. "I was by her side when she died of old age. I moved quickly, determined to keep her body working, propping it up with enchantments before any decay could set in. I think I managed to salvage all of it.

"The result? She acts in death much like she did in life. She is still a sly and cunning hunter. Unlike the lycan and the ghoul, she has patience and restraint; she pounces when the time is right, not when the urge to feed overcomes her. She has lived in the desert caves since that time without causing mayhem. And she still remembers me and comes to me when I call.

"She is the closest I have come to overcoming death."

"It sounds like you've succeeded, Dimotai," Asja responded with genuine awe, enthralled by the bat.

"I thought so, too. I've watched her closely for many cycles. I've never seen anything that she was lacking that other bats had. I don't fully understand it, but there must be something about the body, some way that it's able to keep its urges in check that dissipates soon after death, but can be maintained with necromantic enchantments if one applies them in time.

"Still, I couldn't shake the feeling that there was more to life than this. From all the time I've spent watching bats, I've come to know them well. Their lives went from mysterious to clever to predictable. I knew what they were going to do, when and why. Even when their actions brought them grief, they dutifully repeated them time after time. They seemed powerless to change. They reminded me of Tuilk, actually – zombies that appear to move of their own accord, but are really going through well-trodden motions. The volition that I was after in my undead creations, I was no longer sure really existed in the living ones.

"I switched to studying goblins soon after. I've seen them shape their world to suit their needs. I've even seen them develop new traditions when times demanded it. If bats didn't have what I was looking for, I thought, goblins surely would. Their customs were far richer, their interests more diverse.

"That made it all the more distressing to discover that their lives were almost as habitual, almost as set in their ways as those of bats. I was ready to give up."

"What kept you going?" Asja asked, realising that they wouldn't be having this conversation had he done so.

"I witnessed the death of a shaman."

"Huh?"

"Not just any shaman. Carar the Visionary. That's what people called him for the visions he's had of the dwarf way of life, and the insights he's gleaned from them. I wasn't a particularly close friend, but close enough to be present at his deathbed.

"As he breathed his last breath, a flash of light filled the cave. I couldn't see, but I felt it… pass through me…" he paused, closing his eyes and moving his hands all over his body, before continuing with a smile. "When I could see again, I looked into his eyes, but my friend was no more, as if an empty husk of his body remained after he had left. It looked no different than the corpses of other goblins I'd animated before. I didn't know what that light was, but I sensed that it was the missing ingredient I'd been searching for."

Asja felt his excitement rise in her as well. "But you know now what it was, right?"

Dimotai chuckled, gently nodding. "I discovered a lot about it… with the help of celestials."

"Celestials?" Asja remembered Shar's promise of Empyrean's aid, and the elemental display at the newly born land that was meant to imprint upon her the scale of their power.

Seeing the glimmer of recognition in her eyes, the necromancer continued. "They came to me after Carar's death. They seemed to know what I had seen. They explained what the apparition was, but they didn't just tell me; they showed me. It was thanks to them that I discovered the secret that I'd been searching for all this time, the reason that I'd come to Mount Urus in the first place.

"But why am I rambling about this? You should go see for yourself. It's far more extraordinary than any story that I could tell."

He moved his arm to release the bat. Then he set out further down the passage and up the spiral staircase, towards a distant cave who shone the distinctive pattern of an otherworldly rift onto the passage wall.

FIRMAMENT

Asja stepped into the rift. She felt no movement, no rush of air or flurry of sound that a gateway would make by moving her at breakneck pace through the cosmic span. The outline of the rift remained where she'd left it. She wondered what kind of opening this was, and whether there really was a plane waiting for her on the other side.

The opaque gateway walls started to change, vibrating with light and darkening again, flickering with innumerable colours from Amana and beyond, increasing in fervour until their newfound form asserted itself with a resounding bang over the gleaming interior of the mountain cave.

Asja forced her eyes shut, unable to withstand the sudden onslaught of light. She covered her ears, too, lest they drive her senseless from the cacophony of sound. She let go of her staff but didn't hear the clank as it hit the ground. Standing there, feet apart, ears and eyes shut, she tried to shut out the presence of the otherworldly place she suddenly found herself in.

Her eyelids lifted a sliver, staring down at the floor, attempting to ease her into the newfound scene. The cacophony subsided, relegated to background clamour as her muffled ears grew acquainted with the sounds. Piece by piece, she allowed her surroundings in, careful not to let them flood in and overwhelm her.

The company of a gurgling brook was the first she sensed in her midst. Before she saw or heard the stream, she felt the water's flowing emotion resonate through the crowded scene. The meandering channel pulsed with a harmonious quiver – her form fuzzy, fluent and ever-changing – to which Asja's eyes needed time to adjust. When they did, she spied a fish swimming in the water, his delicate fins fluttering against the current, his golden scales glittering with light borrowed from beyond the waterline. A tuft of grass clung onto a dirt patch, stoically resisting the watery caress. A gang of boulders reduced the width of the course, their bulk resting on the rocky bed, their faces washed smooth and sparkling in the sun.

Memories of the Mirrordon Plane awoke in her, whose interior she'd perceived through its hum and longing. She had no sense of where the stream was. She felt the flowing form drawn to her, as if the brook were pulled out of her world to

281

answer the girl's unconscious call. Asja reached out to touch her, having no sense of the distance between them, and pulled back startled when she felt her hand immersed in the cool wetness of the watercourse.

As she drew away from the scene of the stream, she sensed its form fade to make room for the grassy face of a knobbly hill rising through the water. Rugged roots of slender trees intruded upon the scene, mingling without disturbing the watery flow, as if it made sense to have the two dwell in the same space.

As she looked out, more fragments of Amana's landscape joined the scene, rising through it or entering from the sides. There was no pattern to the fragmented landscape, no place she could recall who would arrange them in such a manner. The more she looked, the more she saw through the erratic mural, pieces of vistas alien to her eyes crowding behind the adjoining scene until she couldn't tell where one ended and another began. Even distances she struggled to judge, tricked she was sure by the fluid-like substance who comprised this place, letting her see through the bubbling structure yet reacting like water to the pressing of her feet. She picked up her staff and watched the ground ripple in response before coming to rest and sharing her vista once more.

The same pattern replayed all around her – endless fragments of scenes mixed and scattered throughout her view, overlaying one another, blending together until she couldn't imagine anyone telling them apart. A thought of the Chaos Plane came to mind; only this was no playpen uniquely responsive to her needs and whims, but a cosmic locale of staggering complexity and scale, as if the whole of Amana had come together in this one place and filled the horizon everywhere she looked.

A deafening noise thundered through the sky. Asja staggered to the ground in fright. Her eyes shot up, frantically scanning the heavens for a sign of danger. She gasped when she saw a large opaque structure with a luminous heart come loose against the backdrop of more distant light. He flexed one fin, and then another. His tail propelled him forward with a powerful downward thrust, his body gliding effortlessly through the glittering sky.

The texture of his skin stood out from the dreamy nature of the plane. Colourful patterns filled the periphery. Lacking light of their own, they shone nonetheless, outlined and revealed by the adjacent glow that clearly sheltered a furnace of some kind. The gaseous veil did not extend to the heart of the body, allowing numerous circles of light to fuse and shine with all their might. He reminded Asja of a large fish whom she'd seen pass by the coral isles, but made of smouldering clouds lit up by lakes and rivers of light.

She stood there with her mouth agape and eyes transfixed on the moving mass. Her initial fear gave way to wonder at the first sight of a celestial being.

"Magnificent, isn't he?"

Asja turned in the direction of the voice. A wolf-like creature gazed at her with curiosity and tenderness.

"Who is that?"

"An astral. We call him Beluga. He comes here sometimes," explained the wolf.

"Astral?"

"A harbourer of stars. A universe unto himself."

The explanation did little to ease Asja's bewilderment.

"I'm Tenaya, by the way. Who might you be?"

"I'm Asja," she replied as she took her first keen gaze at the wolf-like creature.

She wasn't really a wolf, more a hybrid being of some kind. The paws, ears and long snout were unmistakably wolfish, even if the jaw did move in ways odd for their kind. The turquoise mane fitted in as well, though it seemed to shine with more than the light reflected from the ground. And were those wings attached to her back? Asja couldn't be sure. Their outline stayed close to the body, but their translucent interior shimmered and sparkled with the muted brilliance of the landscape behind her.

"Visitors of your kind are very rare, Asja. How did you come here?"

"Dimotai sent me."

"Dimotai?"

"Yes. I entered through the rift by his home."

"I see. Well, then your company is no accident." Her face contorted into a peculiar smile.

"He told me about a form of life that goes beyond his experiments. He said that I could find it here."

Tenaya cracked a wide grin. "Was he showing off his experiments again?"

"Yes, he was."

"He's very proud of them. What did you think of them, Asja?"

"They are amazing! I've never seen a wizard craft creatures like that. I didn't know it could be done. But... they didn't turn out quite the way he'd hoped. He wanted to make them fully alive and... they weren't."

"Like that ogre who was mauled in the desert? A scary sight, that."

"Yes. Dimotai patched him up, though. He completely restored his body. But the ogre didn't go back to who he used to be. He became... a zombie."

"Of course he didn't. He lacked the key ingredient."

Asja's eyes open wide. "What's that?" She held her breath at the hint of an answer.

"His essence, of course. Speaking of which, I don't recognise yours. Where are you from?"

It took Asja a moment to gather herself after Tenaya's dodge. "Uhm... I was raised by Erna and Tor, dwarves who lived by Mount Edars, in the southern part of the Peruvius Range. My birth parents were mur, but I'd never met them. They died when I was born."

Tenaya stared at her closely, her gaze deepening with each word she spoke. Asja could see a reflection of the plane in the wolf's eyes as the petite celestial probed the depths of her soul. And then she saw a reflection of herself. Not the familiar outline she'd seen displayed in still water, but a deeper awareness she'd felt but never seen.

The wolf backed away from the intense stare, her wings moving to steady her posture. Her mouth opened broadly in a self-satisfied grin.

"I thought there was something familiar about you! Most unusual!"

"What?"

"Come see."

The wings fluttered again, moving through the air faster than eyes could follow. They stirred a hum within the nearby space that enveloped them both. The landscape resonated in response, melting away from their field of view, making room for a whole new setting to arise in its place.

Asja gasped at the completely new vista she suddenly found herself in. Did they just move, or did the plane move around them?

"Where are we?" she whispered.

"Is there nothing here that you recognise?"

Asja looked around, studying the features of the landscape, trying to relate them to the sights of the world she had seen on her travels. When that failed, she revived special places from her most treasured memories, places who held wealth of meaning for her, but she couldn't find any in the haphazard landscape.

Frustrated, she went back to her first reaction to the nature of this place and how much it reminded her of the Mirrordon Plane. She closed her eyes to better feel the emotions who dwelled here. They lacked any ties to her life save for one strand whose essence she could feel in every scene laid out before her, as if someone had been to all of these places and left a piece of herself in them; a strand Asja could feel coursing through her own flesh.

She stared at the wolf, her breathing quickened, hoping for an answer.

"She was your mother."

My mother? Tears dropped from her eyes. *Is this how one feels their mother?*

She looked at the landscape again. She saw it differently now, changed as it was by her mother's presence. Her hand trembling, she reached out to touch, to feel her mother's essence in each rock, stream and tree, as if she could get to know her by the impression she had made on the world in whom she'd lived.

Tenaya looked away to a vista close by that promptly rearranged under her gaze.

"Your father's essence is over here."

Asja followed the wolf's eyes to discern another strand running through the place, no less familiar than the first, mingled together within her own being. As if her parents gave of themselves to shape her, but in the process gave birth to someone new.

Emptiness overcame her.

The hollowness of having her parents ripped from her life before she could meet them, a hole no one she had met had been able to fill. To her astonishment, the plane echoed her feeling of loss, adding her own emptiness to that of the girl, amplifying her longing a thousandfold, as if every strand of the Celestial Plane met her loss with a desolation of their own.

"Who is this place?" she asked, overcome with dread, not expecting to find such anguish here.

"The people of Peruvius Mountains call her Firmament. The Heavens, as they say. A place free from the hardships of life." A wry smile spread across Tenaya's face. "To your birth people, she is Paradise. A place of unspoilt beauty. The world in her pristine form, before she could be tainted by the disorderliness of life."

"Paradise?" Asja repeated with a puzzled frown. "But she feels so... so... empty."

"Filled with yearning?"

"Yes."

"That is her nature. She's a dream nursery. This is where Amana's dreams are born. This is where they are nurtured and helped to recover when their efforts to become real fail, as they often do. All of Amana's dreams… except you."

A NEW DREAM

"Did you find her?" a deep voice sounded from the room.

Tarja pried her attention away from the door to focus on her partner's unanswered question. The mention of Lyra reminded her of why she had left him in the first place. Shouts of anger, screams of terror, and bloodthirsty hunters moving swiftly through the blood-soaked streets.

"They killed her!" she cried, overcome with convulsion and sobs, the image of her dead friend lying against the temple wall burned into her mind.

Eilon breathed deeply, trying to regain his composure, a dip in the portal membrane betraying his struggle. He didn't shift his gaze towards his partner, but she came to him, looking down at him with glistening eyes. They remained in silence, a drawn-out moment of tortured acceptance, a pained recognition that their friend and mentor would not be coming with them.

A bang on the door shook them from their stupor. The hinges clanked against the stone wall but remained in place.

"We have to go!" Eilon sounded the warning.

Tarja nodded, slowly, still in a daze. She looked at the wooden door holding the human hunters back. No way to run out of the temple. No way to save their people whom Lyra's actions had doomed to this fate.

"I need you here, Tarja."

She shook her head and stepped forward to sit in the open space between her seated partner and the swirling portal. The churning slowly subsided, revealing the faint frame where the otherworldly reality intruded upon the room, and the shimmering membrane that led out of it.

Eilon's body started to fade, losing presence within the temple space. His vaporous aura passed through Tarja on his way to the membrane, and then merged with the aimless portal to guide it out of this place.

He burst out of the temple and the city of Ucradin, leaving the terror and the destruction firmly behind him. Flying over the Niverlin Rainforest who'd nourished the mur since long before his time, he sped over the sprawling savannah whom the forest became here, with her large herds of zebra and bison grazing peacefully upon the pasture. He crossed over rivers and streams crisscrossing the land in a network of waterways – a gift from the mountains who watched over the plains. He passed by hills and bogs, canyons and caves, all nestled within the forests and the plains, all home to human and elf kind.

He didn't see these wonders of Amana with his mur eyes, more felt them as he moved through them as a part of the land he traversed so freely. A fragment of Tarja came along with him, to guide her the same way or pull him back to the fleeting safety of their temple room should his journey end in peril. But now her presence was wearing thin, stretched as it was across the vastness of the land. He slowed over a forest whose thin tree limbs banded together to form colourful canopies arrayed in lockstep. And beyond her lay the imposing summit set upon a mountain range made of crystal and stone.

He descended into the forest and ended his journey there, unable to sense danger in the moment of his arrival. His body condensed from the travelling vapours at the base of a tree. And then he hid among the raised roots, not knowing who might have been there to witness his trespass.

Tarja gasped as the sharp edge of an axe tore through the wood. Another swing smashed against the door, sending splinters flying and gouging a jagged hole in the battered frame. An eye peered into the room, a dark gaze filled with hatred for her and her kind. She looked away, thinking of the patch of forest where Eilon lay in wait, dissolving her body into a vaporous mass who could make the journey through the makeshift gateway. Another blow dislodged a gnarled piece of wood. A hand entered through it, searching for a latch, unable to find it.

Her body rose as mist, draining slowly into the entrance behind her, her frightened impatience impeding the flow. The hand retreated to let an arrowhead in. Let loose through the cleaved hole, it flew through the misty mur before striking the far wall and landing with a clank. Moments later, the last of Tarja's body poured into the portal, which promptly closed and vanished from view.

Eilon held his partner's misty form, watching her coalesce in his open arms. The haze came together but would not turn to flesh. Only then did he see the gaping hole in the swirling fog, a chaotic void that would not fill, that could not materialise except into a wound, a grievous gash that Tarja could not survive. She chose not to end her life there, but maintain her shadowy existence for a while longer, feel her partner's presence as much as she could. She reached out and touched his face with a hand of mist, embraced him all over with a touch he barely felt.

Contorted lines rose on Eilon's face. A tortured cry escaped from his lips. He reached out to hold her, his outstretched fingers moving through the mist, but her loose form passed through his hands, leaving them grasping, desolate and bare. He let go of his flesh in response, turning back into vapour to match hers. And they mingled together next to the plaited tree, fused into a single shadowy form, until that too began to disperse, scattered through the forest in the light breeze.

Only their dreams remained, robbed of any means with which to act in this world. His − a dream of serving as a protector and a shield, in whom others could find shelter and strength. Hers − a dream of forming a bridge to those unlike her, of coming to know herself through their alien eyes. Neither came to be, co-opted as they were by Lyra's vision and then rejected by the warring peoples from Amana's plains.

They mingled, too, trying to fill each other's emptiness, but had nothing to give save the taste of their unbecoming. Unfulfilled, they left the forest and the land to return to the dreamworld from whom they had sprung. But they didn't leave whole; a small piece remained, a new dream within the land born of their shared longing.

Unaccustomed to having her dreams give birth to dreams of their own, Ama came to see her with her own eyes. A dream conceived in the emptiness of another, who burned with the desire for having it filled. A dream with no new experience to offer or seek, only the passion for bringing to fruition the experiences of others. The goddess looked with puzzlement at the dream's lack of ambition. And she gasped with awe at the promise it held.

Moved by resplendent hope, Ama sought to hold onto the dream, give her a reason to stay within her world. She gathered the misty remains floating through the woods for the naked dream to clothe herself with, who turned back to mur flesh in answer to her plea, crafting a body that could recall the memories of her people, hone and leverage all that they had achieved. But the squeal of a wagon wheel put pause to Ama's plans, and she altered the newborn's look to resemble those travelling through the wood.

The baby cried. The wheels came to a halt. An elderly dwarf couple climbed off the wagon and took the crying orphan child in their arms. They looked for the parents but saw no sign of other dwarves being near.

A child of the mountain, Ama whispered through the canopy leaves. *A child of the mountain*, the forest repeated from one tree to the next, until the murmuring echo saturated the Kritall Wood. The dwarves looked up at the swaying branches and rustling leaves. They looked through the gaps in the foliage, at the mountain summit to the north-east, still smoking and rumbling from a recent discharge. And then they looked at each other, their faces ashen and mouths agape, as if they understood the sacred obligation that they held in their charge.

They climbed back onto the wagon, the orphan girl still with them, before resuming their lumbering journey along the forest path, to the rising mountain beyond the Kritall Wood – Mount Edars, their home.

DEATH

Her parents' untimely deaths weighed heavily on Asja's mind as the otherworldly vista flickered all around her. The countless fragments of the Firmament Plane who filled her view lost coherence, fading and brightening again, threatening to leave her only to reassert themselves, the farewell of a place she'd previously encountered only in myth. And then they died down behind the gateway walls until she stepped back through the dimensional rift and into the dull interior of the mountain cave.

Something felt out of place. The skylight cavern had lost her glow, despite the rift itself still shining with celestial grace. She looked away at the cave walls, only to see their gleam drain before her eyes. Something stood in the far recesses of the cave, sucking up every drop of light who passed through the rift. A shadowy figure she'd seen twice before, who'd come to announce her imminent death at Shar's and Rangorr's hand.

She frantically peered into the darkness of the cave, searching for any sign of danger. She saw none, no subtle movement or a pattern out of place, no hidden intruder to threaten her life. Still, she kept her staff at the ready, trying to quieten her breathing in the stale air, distracted by her heart pounding in the silence of the cave.

A shadow moved across the wall. She spun around to see the darkness advance towards her. She still saw no threat, even as Death crept closer. Frightened and confused, she stepped back and leaned into a hollow in the wall, trying to make herself as inconspicuous as she could. No one approached for Death to warn her about. No one save Death himself.

Her eyes blurred as her vision opened, seeing beneath the surface of the ghastly creature and into his soul – a cauldron of death and dissolution of every kind. A hunger for destruction that far surpassed anything she had seen in Rangorr or Centane. As if he lived to make everything else die. And she saw no one to end here but herself.

Panicked, she sprang into action. Her staff sparked in response. A sizzling charge shot out from its tip to strike the approaching shade. No bang accompanied the flash. The shadow devoured the crackling bolt to no effect that

Asja could see. She unleashed a firestorm in response, sweat dripping from her skin in the heat of the blaze, drawing on every morsel of energy she could squeeze from the stone. Death absorbed it all, slowed by neither the charge nor the flame, still creeping towards her through the darkness of the cave.

She pressed her body against the hollow in the wall, wishing she could vanish into the rock. By the time she thought to run, Death was upon her, stopping a mere arm's length away. She stared at the empty face, outlined against the air by the complete lack of motion or light, sucking in her breath as it left her mouth. She stood still, unable to move or speak, the imagined image of her parents' last moments playing on her mind.

"You still fear me, despite the gift I've given you," a slow, deep, hollow sound echoed through the cave.

She swallowed hard, struggling to breathe. "What gift?"

No answer came. Only a memory of her first encounter with her teacher Shar, her bleeding on the ground with a broken back, forced to confront her mortality for the first time. And then a glimpse of Florella's dream when she woke up, the first time she had looked into the essence of another being.

It had never occurred to her that her brush with Death might have been instrumental in unlocking her gift, whose true potential she was only beginning to grasp.

She remembered her moulting in the Purgatory Plane, seeing her own torched fragments lying on the floor. She didn't see Death then, but understood now that he was indeed there, burning away her old self so that a new her could emerge.

She thought of the choices she'd taken, the decisions she'd enacted that would have made her dead to her people had they been revealed to their full extent. She flirted with Death then, consciously or not, recognising at some level that she'd rather take this risk than make safe choices that betrayed who she was.

With every change she'd made, no matter how small, she realised Death was there to take away whom she used to be.

She peered deeper into the essence of his being, forcing herself to look through the absent contours of his face and empty space where eyes should have been. She felt his thirst for death again but stayed with it even as it made the hair on her body stand on end. She saw an insatiable craving to consume and devour; not wanton destruction to spread misery and pain, but simply to end what had come to its conclusion to make room for what wished to be.

She saw him as the agent of change, and a natural ally of chaos and demons who found so much solace in its disorderly dance.

Death's link to demons reminded her of why she found their teaching so hard to stomach, and why she'd run away from them once before. She didn't want the old to disappear every time she chose something new. She didn't want her parents to leave, even if their death had given life to her. There was a finality to Death that she truly feared, like a loss that could never be replaced, the loss of her parents a wound that had never healed.

She gazed at the emptiness of the figure before her. She expected no help from him, doubting he even knew how to ease the dread that his own work wrought. She gasped when she saw him try, darkness moving forward in the shape of a limb, reaching out to her forehead and dissolving from sight, leaving a decaying mark where his finger had just touched.

A desert scene unfolded in his place. She came face-to-face with the roaming goblin from the Chaos Plane. She remembered his stoic endurance of the rain, and of the desert wind who blew coarse sand against his back. Only his facial features didn't match her memory of them. His serene expression said little of the harshness of the place, as if he accepted what the desert had given him and felt no need to change it, as if he were an integral part of the landscape she found so hostile, with no more reason to complain than the air or the sand themselves.

But the goblins of Okall did change it! her memory cried out, reminding her of their growing of food and rainwater reserves. And yet, their mindset felt no different than that of the goblin from her vision, as if they'd learned to change their world without absorbing the angst of imagining that change fail. As if they sought the wonder of creating something new without losing the acceptance of what already was.

Lost for words, she stared at the goblin's interaction with his world, no longer able to dismiss it as too primitive to be worthwhile or warrant a second glance.

She recalled beyond the Death-induced scene to other imagery she'd endured in the Chaos Plane, confronting her with creations far removed from what she was able to conceive, as if chaos knew who she was and purposefully placed the opposite in her way, as if to challenge her present way of being so that she may grow into something more.

As she stood alone in the quiet cave pulsating with Heavenly glow, she understood that her time with chaos was not yet at an end, and would not be until she learned to heed its work wherever she encountered it, and value its creations beyond the confines of the plane.

CARAR'S DREAM

Carar looked up as the people who'd gathered at the foot of his bed shuffled out of the way. An elderly man had entered the room. He walked surprisingly freely for his apparent age, his walking stick giving little aid, as if it weren't really made for that purpose. He stopped when he reached the head of the bed – a base of porous stone lined with worn furs, holding in its care the dying shaman.

Carar's face lit up with a smile. He'd called for the wizard, wanting to see him one last time. Dimotai's face may have lacked the goblin features of the Okall tribe, and its decaying side may have frightened children and adults alike, but Carar relied on the man's council later in life, once he'd been set on his path by a woman equally arcane.

He still remembered the first time he saw her, beauty and elegance in a dusty corner of a cave, her face a thousand petals dancing in unison as she spoke, a vibrant plant who towered over him in a desert where plants barely grew.

She showed him the home of the mountainfolk, their love of crystals and the magic these harboured, unlocked with runes placed with knowledge and skill. He marvelled at the world they chose to create, sturdy houses of stone filled with light and warmth, fields brimming with food planted by their hands, structures that brought water to wherever they lived, tools of crystal used for shaping stools and crafting clothes and making utensils beyond his skill to grasp.

He saw in them a people unwilling to settle for what was given freely by the land, but exert their will upon her, make their desires firmly known. As much as he loved the goblin way of life, he saw that it could be so much more, that they didn't have to submit themselves to the whims of the sands, to endure hunger and thirst when water failed to pour from the mountains, to suffer encroaching cold when the summits fell quiet and still.

His heart bled when he saw the dwarves treat his brethren from across the Pyrenees with the same callousness as they had the land. Still, he refused to abandon the vision he had seen, a dream of all that his people could be. When Kuru Kam tribes refused his call and hardened their resolve against the dwarven ways, he sought to pursue them here, far away from the conflict at the border of their lands.

He guided his people towards the world he saw, his resolve tested each time they stumbled, his patience tried with each thoughtless rebuff. He wished he had dwarves near to show him what they knew, the wizards unwilling to give him the answers he sought to make his learning painless and quick.

His heart pounded at the first rune he found, seeing it clearly in the crystalline mind. His memory burned from the first flame he coaxed out of a gem brimming with latent heat. It was all it took to sustain him on his journey, to commit his life to it amidst the hardship, to withstand all the failures that would come his way.

One by one his people retraced his path, learning the way he did, adopting what he'd found, shifting the landscape of the goblin ways. He encouraged them every step of the way, but fought fiercely to protect the goblin soul – their communion with the land and the creatures she sustained.

He could feel the dream within him fill out, his shadowy silhouette take physical form, his quiet hum flourish into a melodic song. His people remarked on it, feeling the intensity of his presence, moved by the dream made flesh.

He closed his eyes as they filled with tears, grateful for the gift he had received from Ama, a world in whom to become who he'd dreamed to be. And he breathed his last breath on a bed of soft furs, furnished by the many people whose lives were changed by his.

The dream burst out from the slumbering flesh, a body too frail to aid him any longer, having given its all in the service of its dream. He scattered in the open space of the mournful room, filling the air and the stone and the people standing there with the ecstasy of his release, leaving a part of himself with each being he had touched, a memory of the experience of his own becoming.

He sped through the desert and the sky, beyond the confines of his goblin home, unimpeded by any obstacle presented by the land. He spread through the wide reaches of Amana, moving through the world at the speed of thought, leaving behind him a change of hue, a shift in the tone of the world he knew.

Other dreams welcomed him, weary of the struggle to make themselves seen, to break through the lives of emptiness and routine. They soaked in his company and the promise he embodied, sharing in his success, hoping to make it their own. He lifted them up with his very presence, letting them savour what they may someday be. And then he returned to his place in the Heavens, dreaming a grander dream than he had before.

Dimotai stood by the bed, his eyes closed, his mouth agape, infused with Carar's realised dream, hugging his chest to keep him in, stretching the moment of release for as long as he could. He opened his eyes once the event had passed, no longer seeing his friend lying on the bed, instead holding on to a part of him, and the memory of the life that the man had lived.

LIMBO

Asja stood as if frozen on the frosty ground, her eyes focused intently on the path ahead. Her initial memory was of the Land of Frost and the snowy summits who dwelled there, though Dimotai had told her that even the Peruvius Range who kept dwarves warm by drawing heat from Aia's sweltering depths used to be cold and snowbound in his youth.

A wall of stone rose to her left, with no protrusions for her hands to grab. An endless chasm gaped to the right, just beyond the narrow ledge she was meant to cross. She shouldn't look down, she knew, but couldn't help but steal a glance at the abyss waiting to swallow her should she lose her footing and slip from her path.

She leaned forward and set off, stepping ahead with purpose unwarranted by the icy ground. Her foot slipped. She caught herself mid-fall and continued undeterred. She slipped again, falling flat on the frozen stone. She got up quickly and resumed her hike, reaching a bend in the path and a change in slope. As she felt her foot slide, she grabbed onto a crystal jutting from the wall, but couldn't hang onto the smooth surface or arrest her fall. She let out a scream as she slid over the edge, the narrow ledge receding from her view, before she shifted her eyes to gaze at the chasm, the distant ground hurtling at lethal speed.

A solid thud announced her impact with the ground.

She rolled over, her breathing heavy, her heart pounding from the rush of the fall. And then she burst out laughing, amused at her own chagrin at having slipped from the ledge and fallen yet again.

She flexed her limbs, feeling no pain from the sudden contact with the ground, clothed as she was with an illusory form furnished by the rift that was well suited to the dangers lurking in this plane.

She'd tried walking slowly and carefully, watching her every step, but couldn't avoid a misstep somewhere along the way and the long fall that followed. She'd tried crawling along the ground, her clothes less slippery than the boots she wore, but the cold soon numbed her flesh, stifling her movement until the most innocuous slip sent her tumbling over the edge. It was as Dimotai had said – the plane knew her limits and pushed just beyond them, nurturing her hope that she'd reach the other side only to snuff it out in an instant that felt all too avoidable had she only been more careful and tried harder.

She grinned at the ingeniousness of it all. A failure carried no cost but her own reaction. The first time she fell, she shouted and cursed, livid with herself for a clumsy move that would have cost her her life anywhere else. A dozen falls later and she shrugged it off, focusing on what to change for the next attempt, no longer getting in her own way.

She took her hat off to the wizard who had crafted this plane, relishing the chance to learn from her mistakes without the price these carried in the world outside.

For now, she's had her fill of the doomed adventure. She turned around and headed for the rift, thinking of coming back one more time before her time with Dimotai had to come to an end, and her commitment to the runemages take centre stage.

As she approached the churning breach, a thought popped into her mind, an idea so bold she nearly dismissed it on sight. She took her staff that was resting by the rift and pointed it at the snowy peak. And then she closed her eyes and stood there in silence, letting her staff take in the little heat that the mountain was able to give.

She felt the distant beat of the mountain's heart, waters rising and falling in rhythmic motion, the oppressive heat trapped within the walls. The breath barely moved the hardened crust, held in place by the relentless cold. The summit felt as solid and real as any mount from beyond the plane.

She merged her mind with the crystal she'd come to love, searching for openings through which the heat could escape, sealing them with a minor flexing of the walls. The heat rose with each sealed gap until the mountain shared nothing with the world beyond.

The cold intensified around the summit. The pressure grew beyond what the womb could bear. An undersized skylight took to the sky, forcing the mountaintop to burst open and the heat to pour through the gaping hole.

Asja watched the escaping heat from the premature birth melt the snow and the ice strangling the peak. They washed down the mountainside, the challenge of the slippery pass washing away with them.

As the mountain's dream came to life in the sun ascending through the warming sky, she couldn't help but wonder how many of the obstacles she faced in her life stemmed from unfulfilled dreams she had encountered along the way.

TURTLE RUN

Tall, scaled figures stood alongside the trees over a bare cliff overlooking the beach. Cool sands stretched on both sides of the bulge, hugging the sea as she enveloped the isle, giving the forest a reprieve from the badgering of the waves. The bulge spread well beyond the sands, coming to a rounded tip deep within the swells, rising to a crusted rock from whom to stare them down. The Salient, as he was known, had withstood the ocean's fury when the rest of the isle's face had crumbled into sand. The most ambitious of the waves still relished the thought of testing their mettle against the defiant rock.

Colourful lights shone from the water beyond the shallow surf, a coral reef making her presence known in the darkness of the sea, giving the lagoon and her mur town their name – Bioluminescent Bay. Radiant jellies frolicked in the water of the atoll, taking on the colour of the phytoplankton upon whom they fed. Some lost their anchor to be swept up by the encroaching waves and washed onto the beach, sharing the luminescent splendour of the sea with the sleepy land.

A hidden vent let off steam deep within the isle. Restless leaves rustled in the wind stuttering from the gaps in the summit walls. Another tremor rippled through the ground. And then the flesh of the mountain peak ripped apart to eject an aqueous light into the night sky.

The rising sun blanketed the beach with his light, drowning out her colourful hues with his own glare. His fervour waned as he rose, spreading the ocean colours instead of washing them out, until the whole beach and the surf beyond sparkled with the coral's motley shine.

A warm wind whistled through the forest, a herald of the warmth draining from the peak. He stirred the people from the shelter of the trees to settle at the bare edge all along the cliff. There they waited, their slings at the ready, heaps of pebbles resting by their feet wanting to be hurled towards the awakening beach.

As if on cue, the sand stirred within, collapsing in on herself, revealing nests of turtle hatchlings all along the shore. One by one, they emerged from the safety of her fold to make a reckless dash towards the enticing surf, until their tiny bodies covered the island beach, their fins swimming through the sand, stumbling and rolling, their balance challenged by the sparse rocks standing in their way.

Attracted by the motion, seagulls descended upon the shore, squawking excitedly at the sight of food. But the vigilant people stirred into action, their slings hurling stone after stone, whizzing through the air gunning for the birds. Most whizzed past their target to be swallowed by the surf, but a broken wing here, a fractured skull there, and the seagulls soon lost their hunger for the young meat. Only the boldest among them dared run the gauntlet of stones to emerge with a hapless turtle in their clenched beak.

Satjan sat in the lush crown of a fig tree at the outer tip of the bay, watching the seasonal spectacle unfold yet again. It brought on the memories from his youth, of the mur survivors taking to the sea to escape the destruction of their homeland. Watching his people's animated motion, he knew they remembered it too, the exodus scars fuelling their care for the hapless hatchlings.

There was innocence to their actions, a naïve drive to protect the weak from those who sought to harm them, stemming from their own unmet desire to be shielded from harm by human hand. That charge once rested with Lyra and her order. Now it fell on him and the morlocks of the Circle.

He resented his mentor for neglecting her duties and bringing their people to the edge of ruin. For dabbling with spirit magic instead of spells that would aid them in combat. For thinking well of the plains people despite their endless warring. For crafting magic to overcome their savagery instead of sheltering her own people from it. And for meddling in their lives with no way to withstand their response.

He did everything he could to succeed where she had failed: to preserve the ways of his people, let them create a new home for themselves on these coral isles, and not worry about those who wished them death from across the sea.

He wondered sometimes what it would be like to live among people who weren't so fragile, who could face the reasons for their exodus and thrive nonetheless, who were strong enough to stand on their own instead of needing him to stand up for them. His heart leapt at the dream of a powerful mur nation whose members had his resilience and grit. But he saw no need for himself in such a world, and he banished the thought as quickly as it had come.

AN EMPTY NEST

Asja woke up with a start. The nightmare involving Vagran held her in its grip. Its nonsensical twists continued playing on her mind, their vivid forms urging her to weave them into a coherent story. She tried and failed to bring order to the jumbled mess, in the end certain of only one thing – Vagran's urgent need of her.

She looked around the barely lit room that had served as her home – an empty space within a mountain seed who never became the light of day. She touched her forehead at the spot of decay that Death had left there, the only evidence of her stay. She understood now the role that Death played in her life, the way he aided her maturation and growth, no longer seeing him as someone to avoid. It made her feel closer to Dimotai, who must have faced Death many a time during his long life, each encounter adding its mark to the decaying scar on his face.

She gathered her belongings and swung her rucksack over her back. She would miss this simple place and the otherworldly powers dwelling at its doorstep. Nowhere had she felt the presence of dreams more lucidly than here. Nowhere had she felt a stronger urge to weave their desires into her daily life.

Her host was surprisingly understanding of her need to leave, seeing it with a timeless quality afforded by his age, hoping to see her again when the time was right, once she'd taken care of her folk and friends. She hoped so too, feeling her stay cut short and her learning unfinished.

A nascent portal stared her in the face. She dissolved and entered its aimless depths with no sense of where she was headed, letting her bond with her childhood friend be her only guide. She sped across the deserts and their fiery peaks, drawing ever closer to the Peruvius Range. The northward flow of her journey unnerved her, watching the cloud-covered Mount Reclus peak pass by. The tip of Mount Ire rose in the distance, the Fuming Mount as he was known, a flaming summit whose magmatic skylights rivalled the brightness of any sun unleashed by the Pyrenees.

A familiar mass of charge stood atop a lesser peak on the mount's northern side. She ended her journey at the foot of the crest, hiding behind a rock as soon as her solid body took form, not knowing who might be lurking here beside her thunderoc friend. She peeked from behind the stone to see Vagran standing pensively in the open space, his wings folded tighter than she'd ever seen them. He pressed his face into the rocky ground, his soft feathers rubbing against the stone.

She breathed a sigh of relief, seeing her friend alone and free from danger. She jumped out from her hiding place and ran to the bird, who just stood there, oblivious to her presence.

Bewildered, she scanned the place. The markings on the ground caught her eye, lines clawed haphazardly into the rocky floor, and a pyreroc feather pressed into the stone. Her movement slowed, not recognising the giant plume that had left its mark, her friend's down lacking the fiery hue.

"Vagran?" she called out, not wanting to risk being trampled by the distracted bird.

Vagran's head turned her way. Surprise flashed across his face, but his body failed to react. His downturned eyes looked blurry and sullen, as if bathed in liquid that held back the charge.

"Who is she?" asked Asja.

He looked down once more before sparking a single name.

"Falkra."

Asja followed his gaze to the patterns on the ground. Only now did she see a large footprint overlapping the feather, pressed into the congealing stone. Her mind imagined a sequence of events, a bleak picture she sought to confirm before assuming the worst.

"What happened?"

Vagran swallowed. His head lifted, his stare aimed at the horizon.

"We are hunted up north."

Asja followed his gaze.

The land of giants lay before her – giant mountains, giant trees, giant people. This was where the oldest dwarf legends said the dwarves had emerged. She couldn't imagine it being true. Dwarves steered clear of the place, venturing no further than the southern foothills of Mount Granat, except for occasional foolhardy youth who roamed the dense forests to the north in search of adventure. Dwarves had dealings with giants in the past, even if such encounters weren't widely known.

One thing was clear – even though no clashes had occurred between the two peoples, dwarves did not seek the company of the oversized and reclusive people of the north.

She'd seen the rusty glow of the Mount Aorai sun before she set out to find her friend. The fiery light from the Fuming Mount now illuminated the Peruvius skies. The dwarf mages were well on their way to Sentinel Grove. Any expedition to the north risked not reaching the shrine in time and leaving mages and druids to fend for themselves should the demon come. But Vagran's distress threw her in turmoil, one she had to heed no matter the risk.

"If you want to go after them, I'll go with you," the words left her mouth before she thought them through.

Vagran blinked in response, a rush of charge betraying his surprise. Then the charge arced through his eyes, and his wings flew open for the journey north.

GIANTS

Thick mist covered the ground. A sporadic patch of green broke through the haze, the pines barely visible in the alien night. The brooding form of the Granite Mountain overshadowed their presence, a lopsided mount rising through the darkness, his top crawling with woods, his sides scarred by the wind. The first of the Peruvius Range, Mount Granat's age reflected in his attitude rather than the wear of his peak, like a cynical man with bad posture who still packed a punch.

Asja had never been to the northern end of the Peruvius Range, having only seen it from the Algalash tree. He felt more imposing up close, dominating the landscape with his bulk, hinting at the hefty stature of the creatures who dwelled at his feet.

She strained her eyes peering through the haze. She'd never met Falkra or any of her kind. The scuffle with a scoria was the closest she'd come, a pyreroc sharing a lava dragon's love of flame, though the roc enjoyed greater lightness of being, lacking the molten stone's substance and weight. Such a creature ought to be easy to spot, Asja thought, if she were indeed to be found in the forests of the north. If only the ground would release her cloudy sheath and let them look unimpeded. Gazing at dense woods in the dark of night was challenging enough.

Vagran unexpectedly veered to the left. Her eyes followed his lead to sight a fire flickering through the mist. She stared at the flame, but saw no giant beast materialise in her dance, as if no more than an ordinary campfire burned in the clearing. She did see two humanoid shapes standing nearby, their giant frames silhouetted against the blaze.

The thunderoc's feathers suddenly stood erect. Asja looked beyond the flame, scouring the forest and the mist for what her friend might have seen. A second, more subdued fire appeared in the dark. It moved through the clearing in fits and starts, as if pulled against its will. She gasped when she saw the fire form the outline of a beast. Only this one felt darker and heavier than she imagined a pyreroc to be, weighed down by molten stone rather than fluttering with the freedom of the naked flame.

Where did the giants find a scoria? She couldn't imagine them crossing the Kalhar

Desert to reach the peaks of the Pyrenees, where lava dragons were known to live. Then she remembered Falkra's nest on Mount Ire, on an inaccessible summit within remote dwarf lands. Did the scoria live here too? Or amongst the northern peaks, beyond dwarven reach? If the beasts sought to resettle their former home, their efforts weren't going well.

Vagran's body tensed following the sight. He dropped closer to the trees, his wings charged and steady, barely open to slow their flight. His head swerved left and right, scanning the night landscape beneath them. Asja gazed more intently with him. Giants with a scoria in their hands might have pyrerocs, too.

The thunderoc angled his wings, steering away from the forest clearing illuminated by the fire. He stuck to the tips of tall trees, where his broad form did not hide Isura's lights, nor his wings flutter to expose him with their breeze.

Asja felt a rush of charge course through his body as they approached the northern foothills of the Granite Mountain and a light who shone from within their cave. She gazed in that direction, but failed to make out the form, unprepared for her friend's sudden burst of speed. Her body tingled at the thought that Falkra might be in there, but felt her presence more from the pounding of Vagran's heart than anything her eyes could discern.

His colossal body hugged the rocky slopes, navigating their contours with practised skill. He sped past the hardy woods growing on slanted land, their tips gently swaying in the bird's wake, before setting his talons down on the cave's hill and lowering his head to keep to the ground. Asja emerged moments later and walked to the edge of the cliff to survey the forest below.

She spotted movement in the woods; more people of the north lurked here than she could see. No structures she recognised stood amongst the trees. The cave and the woods with a single campfire felt more like makeshift lodgings than a settled outpost, as if this were nothing more than a hunting party moving through the land.

Shouts from the clearing drew her attention, loud enough to be heard over the dense woods. The giants had dragged the scoria to the campfire, the four of them having a mighty time moving the molten bulk across the grassy ground, leaving only scorched earth trailing behind them. The dragon struggled to resist, his mouth chained shut, his wings clamped to his body, the chains sprinkled with molten stone from contact with torn scales. Strong arms wrapped in fur tugged on them until the beast landed on top of the fire burning in the clearing.

Asja watched the proceedings with a puzzled frown. The campfire would not hurt the dragon; if anything, she would serve as sustenance to the beast. Could the giants really be so ignorant?

The six giants encircled the scoria, keeping their distance from the lively flame.

They drew long spears and pointed them at their captive. Their sturdy grip on the shafts surprised her, until she saw the crystalline points rumble to life. They sizzled and pulsed, unleashing bolts of lightning to strike the beast and mingle with the flame.

The scoria groaned in response, unable to open his mouth to let out a cry. The lightning permeated the blaze, charging the nourishing heat, eating away at the protective scales that bathed in the flame, until the molten stone poured through the pores and the spears hungrily absorbed the escaping flares. Asja watched in horror as his raw limbs pressed into the chains, his guttural sounds haunting the woods, his body dissipating before her eyes, leaving only a puddle of lava to feed the fire who had taken his life.

They are arming themselves with the fire from the beast! It dawned on Asja as she watched the scene. *Don't they know how to release her from gems, or unleash magic of their own?*

A claw scraped against the stone behind her. She turned to see Vagran quivering at the sight. His wings stretched open and pushed against the ground. He reached forward, his head menacingly close.

"Free Falkra. I will distract them."

She gulped and nodded, spellbound by the anger seething in his eyes. He turned to leave when he veered back, the feathers of his face glowing from the charge.

"See you at Sentinel Grove."

He spread his wings and sped away, hugging the mountain slope on his way to the sky.

Her breath caught at the sight and the parting promise he made. She hadn't presumed to ask for his help, or even what help he could give should they fight the demon in the cramped space of the grove. She shook her head, putting the thoughts aside. His offer of aid would be of no use if they didn't get there in time.

She hurried down the winding hillside, her staff and rucksack strapped to her back. She traversed it as quickly as she dared, holding onto rocks to steady herself in the dark.

She hid behind a shrub when she reached level ground. Looking between the trees of the thinning woods, she struggled to see the giants in the clearing, only heard their jubilant cries. Their celebration muffled the sound of her footsteps as she snuck to the entrance of the cave, behind a giant watching the commotion too closely to notice her creep behind his back.

A luminous body welcomed her, lying on the floor in the middle of the cave.

Thick chains held her in place, secured by metal latches bolted to the stone. Glowing eyes stared ahead, diffused and unfocused, as if resigned to their fate. They followed the dwarf as she entered the cave without showing surprise or prompting the body to move.

"Can you fly?" whispered Asja.

The eyes widened at the question, then narrowed to focus on the stranger before them.

"I'm here with Vagran," the girl quickly added, realising that Falkra likely knew nothing about her.

Falkra's eyes flamed at the mention of his name. She turned her head, but the beak barely rose before the chains tightened to keep it in place. They made sure that the pyreroc could not unleash her flame, merely secrete it like sweat through her seething down.

Asja walked to the nearest latch to grab hold of the chain. She tugged on a link with hands wrapped in cloth, but couldn't move it, the chain too taut to be deterred from its task. Falkra pressed against the floor, giving her bind what leeway she could. Asja pulled again, struggling with the weight, moving the link along the latch before sighing in frustration as it slid back to its starting place when she stopped to catch her breath. She set her feet against the latch and tried again, dislodging the link in a concerted tug. She breathed out and wiped the sweat from her brow, brought on by exertion as well as the heat.

Falkra didn't move. She must have understood the perils of making a noise before she could shake off all of her restraints. Asja rushed to the latch on the other side of the cave that held the second chain pressed against the beak. A sharp sizzling sound stopped her in her tracks. She spun around, peering through the cave opening into the night sky.

A flash of lightning pierced the mist, turning the night into day, betraying the silhouette of a thundering bird hovering above. The bolt sought out a giant standing by the campfire, slamming into his flesh and hurling him into the flame. His companions jumped to rescue him from the blaze, his spasming body powerless to act.

A second bolt sizzled through the sky. The lightning struck the assembled group, the charge passing through each body in turn, knocking them to the ground, their locked joints freezing their cries, the veins of angry pink popping beneath their skin. They lay there in a frozen moment, their limbs twitching from the overload.

The giant by the cave grabbed a crystalline shield and, with a roaring challenge to the thundering bird, ran down the scorched path to his fallen friends. Shouts from others echoed through the woods. Their footsteps converged on the exposed dell.

Seeing her chance, Asja grabbed onto the chain and dislodged it with a laboured tug. The metal clanked against the stone surface as the pyreroc's head rose free. The bird lay flat once more for Asja to free her wing. Her back arched in response, held down by the remaining shackles, but her legs and wings pressed forward instead, wiggling the flaming bird free from their hold.

She stood up in the cramped space of the cave, her wings open and pushing into the stone, her feathers of dancing flame pulsating with furore, the purest embodiment of fire Asja had ever seen. The girl watched the pyreroc with a touch of envy, reminded of how effortlessly command of the elements came to the beasts.

Another lightning bolt streaked through the sky. Asja returned to the mouth of the cave to see the giants who'd reached the campfire raise their shields in defence. The bolt struck the protective ore and vanished into its frame. The giant crouching behind it remained unscathed.

Another grabbed a spear lying on the ground and directed it at the roc above. A bolt of his own sped towards the bird, accompanied by the scoria's newly consumed flame. Vagran absorbed the incoming charge with natural ease, but shrieked in pain from the blended blaze. He plunged towards the ground before steadying his flight, speeding away from the giants at treetop height, his punctured belly arcing from oozing charge.

"I need your fire," Asja shouted to Falkra, taking her staff into her hands, not knowing how to unleash fire and lightning in tandem, and having no time to experiment now.

The pyreroc obliged, parting her beak to spew an inferno through the mouth of the cave. Lightning pulses sizzled from Asja's staff, enriched by the flame as they left the cave, shooting along the path to the open dell. They struck the giants in the side and back, bringing them down beneath their raised shields still standing guard against the menace above.

Asja leaned on her staff from the exertion, needing momentary rest.

"Go!" she yelled at the bird, urging her on with the motion of her hand. Falkra stepped out and took to the sky, her outstretched wings burning with untamed flame.

Asja watched the clearing, breathing heavily from her efforts, gathering her strength for a renewed assault should their enemies recover to contest Falkra's escape. But their twitching bodies rolled across the ground to put out the fires who fed upon their flesh.

As a portal membrane formed within the cave, Asja cast one last look at her new friend. Her fiery form pierced the night, her broad wings lost to the licking flames rising hungrily through the dark sky, as if the air were too heavy to hold them to the ground.

A moment of envy accompanied the sight. The girl understood why the giants coveted Falkra's traits. She too wished she could be like her friends, soaring with no need of effort or skill, just closing her eyes and letting her nature do what it did best.

AMALGAM

Boreas grazed the slopes of the Tetran Massif, descending from their heights with reckless abandon. He spread out across the plains, blowing through the wide-open spaces, lifting the clouds and the desert sands, touching the blades of grass and the crowns of trees, creating waves on still water and nudging the streams on their passage to the sea.

Lightness of being was all he'd ever had, stretching over the land and the ocean beyond. His body knew no limit, no cloud to contain him, no summit he couldn't get around. Amana's wonders laid themselves bare for him to see and marvel at on his endless journey.

He saw a blanket of snow he'd sculpted collapse into an avalanche of death and mused at what it took to cover a patch of land in a suffocating grip. He nudged a river's flow into a boulder's path and wondered what it would be like to stand unmoving while others cut their teeth on his rigid skin. He carried delicate seeds in his hand and thought whether he, too, could reproduce the way they did, and have offspring who were accomplished winds of their own. He wished to wilt in the shadows and bloom in the sun and experience all the adventures he sampled on his passage through the land.

A thought occurred to him; an idea so bold that it brought his blowing to a sudden stop. He was a wind after all, spread-out and vast when he wished to be, sampling everything he touched with his many limbs.

He whisked blades of grass from Amana's plains, droplets of water from her lakes and streams, fertile earth mixed with desert sands, even licking flames from the fiery peaks, and countless other fragments he'd courted on his travels as he mingled with the land. He blended them all with his airy form, shaping a body to match his ambition – the first being of flesh to set foot upon Amana.

He breathed a deep breath, reminding himself of who he used to be, anticipating the many experiences he knew his body could impart. He set out across the land, but tired quickly, having covered but a moment's passage from his earlier life as a wind. He tried to flow, but his efforts yielded only sweat. He flexed his limbs, but flames would not come.

Not only could he not unleash the elements within, he had to take in more merely to survive. Aghast, he tried and tried again, labouring to coax out the effects he sought but unable to engender anything of note, never having had to toil for it before.

A gentle breeze caressed his face. His eyes overflowed at the simple gesture, one he hadn't taken notice of before. And he wept for what he had lost, his heart aching at his windswept life, grasping its wonder for the very first time. He gained none of the skills for which he had yearned, only lost the expansiveness of being he once used to have.

He continued to labour as one cycle blended into the next. The adventures he sought slipped from his grasp, the decay brought on by age thwarting what little skill he'd been able to master. Until the wear proved too much for the body to withstand, and he welcomed the release that he found in Death.

But his dream lived on.

The essence of his longing acquired a life of his own.

His primal yearning sparked a following of dreams who shunned their thoughtless lives to get to know themselves by denying themselves first. They left the Paradise of ignorant bliss to seek the Heaven of knowing themselves fully, and they went through Hell in their efforts to reach it.

EMPYREAN

The presence of dwarves mixed with crystals, trees and earth flashed before Asja as she sped through the Sentinel Grove, unable to restrain the portal's flow. No sense of elves. No sign of the demon. She swung around in a wide arc and brought the portal to an abrupt stop. A gateway materialised in the open space between the sentinels and the grove. Her misty form emerged through the membrane before the gateway vanished from sight.

The mages turned at the swooshing sound to stare at the smog who appeared in their midst. They gasped when the mist assumed dwarven form, a figure they remembered from the gathering of the clans.

"Asja?" whispered Recha, her eyes still bulging and jaw trembling from the sight.

Asja looked around before letting herself relax, comfortable that her senses had proven true and no danger awaited her here.

"It's just me." She raised her hand to reassure the runemages. Then she turned to Recha. "Where are the druids?"

"Tyriell and Brielle are here." Recha pointed at the two elven figures freshly emerged from the grove. "Others are on their way."

Asja winced, not having sensed the elves on her approach. She nodded and set out towards the perimeter, seeking the company of the trees whose protection they may soon need. She turned around when she heard a familiar voice call out her name. Hloim ran towards her, his radiant face beaming with excitement. He flung his arms around her in a tight embrace. She responded in kind, warmed by the affection shown by a mage, remembering the moment they shared the last time she was here.

"Thank you for coming," he said, his voice filled with gratitude, as if he'd craved her company ever since that time.

"It's good to see you, too."

"Have you heard from the wizards?"

Her brow lifted with surprise at his mention of them. She must have made more of an impression than she'd realised for him to remember her teachers.

"They say that the demon has learned of our gathering. Whether he'll take the bait... We can only hope," she concluded with a buoyant tone, firmer than it had reason to be, seeking to convince herself of the truth of her own words.

Her hand trembled at the memory of her encounter with Rangorr and her looming death in their duel before seeking shelter in the dwarven line. If she did have to face him again, she prayed that it would be with Empyrean by her side. She'd nearly forgotten that the celestial's mission was to release the demon from the morlocks' hold, a goal sought by Florella and Shar. She shook her head, not wanting to revisit the wizards' concerns. She just wanted Rangorr gone, and herself and her people to live.

The lines on Hloim's face mirrored Asja's concern before a hopeful glint entered his eye. "There's someone you must meet."

He turned back to the grove, but stopped when a dwarf made of crystal and stone approached them from the shadows. Asja stared at his hard features and radiant eyes that reflected the daylight coming from the sky. He held no staff, making her wonder whether he was really a warrior rather than a mage.

"This is Aorar – a warrior and a mage," Hloim echoed her thoughts, introducing the dwarf before he himself could. Then he turned to the girl. "This is Asja—"

"I've heard a lot about you," Aorar's voice rumbled through the clearing before Hloim could say more.

The remark caught Asja by surprise. "Oh? I've never heard of you," she replied, not knowing how to be honest without sounding impolite.

"You will." Aorar grinned and walked away.

She watched him go, baffled by the encounter. The energy that exuded from him took her breath away, matched only by his self-confidence. How has she not heard of such a potent mage? And a warrior to boot? She looked to Hloim for an explanation.

"It's the archon. From the legends..."

She gasped as she made the connection, recalling the display from Kinrum Hall, feeling sheepish for taking so long, having seen that tale unfold thrice before. What magic was at work here that a dwarf from a time long gone could come back to life? A thousand questions hit her at once, but they'd have to wait for a more opportune time.

As she watched him mingle with the dwarves, her eyes blurred, a vision bubbling up beneath his hard exterior. A relentless pursuit of the collective hopes of all the dwarf people. The desire to live free from foreign threat and lay claim to what they needed to thrive. No room for the claims of others. No place for doubt that had recently come upon her. She shuddered at his single-mindedness, even as his strength took her breath away.

"Asja!"

She dispelled the vision at the sound of her name.

"Will you join us?" asked Recha. "We are going into the grove for quiet contemplation, to prepare ourselves for the demon, should he come."

She shook her head, rattled by the encounter, wanting to keep her distance from the elves following Shar's death, and from the runemages until they welcomed her among them. She remained in the clearing as the mages and the druids headed for the treeline. A crystalline statue caught her eye, a giant warrior adorned with leaves and vines, wielding a hammer as if he'd just struck a blow. It brought a smile to her face, taking her mind off the rift with her people, remembering the effect his change of posture had had on Hloim. A rare mage, who welcomed the opportunity to learn from others not of his kind.

The thought led to another – would his thirst for knowledge and discovery have an interest in the knowledge that the dwarves had lost? Would he be willing to go to the goblins of Okall and relearn their love of the land while sharing his mastery of crystals in return?

She ran and caught him on his way to the grove. "I have an offer for you, a chance to both learn and teach in another land. Can you remind me to tell you about it once the danger of the demon has passed?"

His face brightened at the words and the mention of another land. "Where? Who? What do they need from me?"

"There's someone who wishes to learn about the power of crystals, but they have much knowledge of their own to share."

His eyes widened. "Like Arezan! The astrologer I met when I was young…" his words tapered off as he turned back to the grove, an even broader smile stretching across his face.

Asja's breath caught in her throat. She'd heard of mur astrologers and their study of the skies. She wondered what Hloim would say if he knew that the mur were behind the demon threat, whether his memory of Arezan would be tainted by that. She banished the thought for another time, struggling to focus on the task at hand.

Her gaze fell back on the statue, his mighty weapon and fine armour shaped from the sturdy crystalline frame. If only he could move like Rumbul, he'd be a challenge for Rangorr to overcome. But it had taken Dimotai many cycles to perfect the golem's motion, and he was the undisputed master of his craft. There'd be no sense in her even starting in the little time they had left.

Still, her mind entered the quartz once again, eager to traverse his delicate pathways, remind herself of the depths of power harboured by the crystal. Her journey came to an abrupt halt just beneath the surface. Confused, she continued to probe, stumbling in the dark, unable to find a way in, as if the lattice she knew so well had grown shy and unwilling to let her in.

She shook her head and cursed under her breath, unable to believe that the skill she'd practised countless times before could prove so troublesome now. *What's going on? Has the quartz changed since the last time I was here? Have my doubts and misgivings somehow sapped my skill?* She looked at the statue again and could swear that those still, expressionless eyes stared back at her.

Flustered, she walked away, towards the perimeter she had sought earlier. She saw movement beyond the sparse treeline and froze in place, straining to make out the figures treading through the shrubs, her staff charged and ready. She relaxed when she saw a druid come into the open, followed by two others, carrying gnarly staves and leather backpacks.

"Evindal." She recognised the leader of the group.

He smiled and waved to her, his demeanour as warm and friendly as it had ever been. She wished hers could mirror the elf's, but Shar's death at elf hands had put a damper on her relations with them, no matter how much she may have liked Evindal and the druids, and valued the support they'd given her beyond that of the dwarves.

She directed them to a bushy area within the sentinel line where four mountain rams grazed on the lush grass surrounding their wagon, to unburden themselves and rest from their journey before joining the others in the quiet grove. And then she sat on the forest floor and leaned her back against a sentinel tree, his smooth bark close to the roots free from the barbs who adorned his crown.

Her thoughts wondered to her thundering friend, the wound he'd sustained in the scuffle with the giants and his escape before they could unleash another strike. She'd have to find him after this fight was done, should he need her help to recover and heal.

The thought of Falkra brought a smile to her face, even as it reminded her of how their lives had drifted apart. She'd often wondered how Vagran had spent his time away from her, where he'd been, whom he'd met. He'd never mentioned having a companion besides her. Still, she was glad that he'd found someone to share his life with who could understand him better than any dwarf, especially in a land where the giant beasts of old were all but gone.

She closed her eyes to rest in the shade of sentinel trees.

When she opened them again, the rouge Mount Romlan sun had vanished from the sky. Darkness had taken hold of the woods, tree canopies hiding the night lights from the ground, with only a faint glow radiating from her, betraying the energy contained in the charms.

Asja turned to the sounds of rustling leaves to see figures moving through the bushes, making no attempt to conceal their approach. Their banter betrayed druids from the coastal tribes. Lennolene and six others emerged from the foliage, the last of the delegation of the forest dwellers to meet at the shrine.

More than the sound of footsteps came from the woods. The trees behind the elves started to shimmer, as if obscured by a membrane fluttering with motion. The swooshing portal sounds permeated the space. Mist emerged from them, barely visible in the glow of the ground.

Three tall, scaly figures materialised from the fog. A fiery one appeared beside them, a demon she'd seen before, unmistakably clear in his own light.

The druids turned at the sound, their banter coming to an end.

Their staves barely lit up from the energy of the place when a raging inferno engulfed them all, the ravaging blaze drawing and muffling their cries. Asja gaped at the scene in disbelief, her mouth still open from her tries to warn them, though no sound came beyond helpless whimper.

The druids collapsed, overcome by the blaze. The shrubs ignited from the heat of the flame. The attackers rushed past the burning corpses to head for the sentinels and the grove beyond. Their gaze veered to a figure standing by a tree, her magical form a beacon of light even on enchanted ground.

Asja bolted and ran for the safety of the grove.

They ran after her, the flaming demon leading the charge. A deluge of barbs brought them to a halt, unleashed by the canopies blanketing the sky. They drew blood before fiery shields rose to keep the thorns at bay.

"They're heerreeee!" Asja found her voice.

The first mages already stood in the open, their eyes drawn to the burning shrubs. Others emerged from the darkness in response to the screams, their bodies wearing their ancestors' armour – enchanted to withstand the fury of the beasts they'd taken up arms against in the Inheritance War.

Asja breathed a sigh of relief when she saw Aorar stand beside them, wielding an axe rather than a staff, though still arcing from the energy of the quartz. She stopped next to a crystal statue and turned to face the attackers, rattled by the look of surprise and fear in the eyes of her friends. *They were taking no chances*, the thought played on her mind, overwhelmed by the number of morlocks accompanying the demon. Terror welled up at their renewed advance, released from the barrage of the sentinel trees, the thorns of their crowns spent to the last.

The quartz beside her creaked with motion. The giant warrior rose to full height, finally standing up having dealt that blow. He moved forward, the ground trembling from the weight of his steps. He came to a halt in the open space between the treelines of the sentinels and the grove.

Asja gasped at seeing the crystal do by himself what she hadn't had time to make him do. Her ire rose even amidst the wonder, wishing she had seen what dwelled within the quartz instead of being shut out the last time she'd tried. Her longing intensified with the luminous glow as the crystal came alive with an inner light. And then the giant statue shattered in a blast, scattering quartz fragments all across the grass.

A being of light stood in his place, his enormous wings flowing through the air, his body pulsating, dimming and brightening, as if deciding whether to stay or fade. The sight brought on a memory of the Firmament Plane, of Tenaya and the landscape unconstrained by this world. Only Empyrean loomed larger than the tenderer of dreams, his form far grander, his presence more imposing. If the crystalline warrior had failed to deter the morlocks, the towering celestial surely would.

The morlocks stopped at the sight as if rooted in place, gazing at the being who stood in their way. Rangorr did too, his eyes widening at the otherworldly view. He lowered his head and resumed his charge, running with the frenzy Asja had never seen, the being of light squarely in his sights.

The forest shook from the fiery hooves pounding against the ground.

Empyrean faced the charging demon, his posture hunched, his wings open wide, as if readying for impact. Asja watched in horror as Rangorr ran through the sentinel line, the celestial wielding no weapon with which to restrain him, having built up no charge ready for release. But his wings closed in a flash, capturing Rangorr with their translucent glimmer.

And the angel embraced the demon, obscuring him from view with his pulsating form.

Rangorr's body glowed with swelling light before the radiance coalesced into a chain that broke and fell onto the ground. A cacophonic resonance sounded from him next, before it too shattered from the embrace. The blazing shield was the last to go, the celestial drinking the flame until none remained. Then he opened his wings, revealing the fireless demon free from the morlocks' binds.

"Go home!" he whispered, his symphonic voice rousing a wind to carry it through the grove.

Rangorr stared into Empyrean's eyes. The look of hope overwhelmed the contorted features of his face. And then he vanished from the celestial's embrace, two teary drops moistening the ground in his place.

Empyrean gazed at the people around him, momentarily distracted from their deathly feud. He made no move nor uttered another word before fading from their sight, only shattered quartz able to attest to him having been there at all.

Asja stared at the empty space, unable to process that the celestial was gone while the morlocks still loomed large. Two of them recovered before she did, their staves bursting with ire at their main weapon having been taken from them by a meddling creature from beyond this world. Asja and Aorar raised theirs in response, the staff and the axe spewing a protective barrier between them and the mur.

A bolt of lightning slammed into the shield. The bubble shifted to meet the charge, burning it up, consumed in return. A thin membrane remained in its place to guard against another strike, fed by the staves of druids and mages who drew their power from the forest and the quartz, amplified by the enchantments cast upon the land.

The second bolt failed to make an impression, dissipating from sight before Aorar's axe. Two more struck in tandem and vanished without a trace as the assembled conjurors stood in unison, nourishing a shield that sheltered them all. Asja breathed a sigh of relief as powerful spells from the two morlocks failed to make an impression.

The wall held. The grove had done her job.

The third morlock stayed out of the fight, mysteriously settled behind the first two, standing perfectly still. Asja saw the focused look and recalled Rangorr feeding on her shield the first time she'd fought him outside Kinrum Hall. She moulded the flames coming from the mages, enriching their pristine nature, endowing them with her own essence to prevent their loss.

Shivers washed down her spine at the sight of the morlock's eyes locking onto her, as if he'd kill her with his bare look. She stared right back, not backing down in the battle of wills, before turning away, seeking a change in the forest who fed their spells, a way to break the stalemate and unleash hell back at the trio without weakening her shield and being hit in return.

She felt a tingling sensation as her life force drained from her leg. She screamed in pain when the cold engulfed the inside of her thigh. Her bone crumbled. The morlock's staff suddenly came to life, as if he'd used her as a source of power rather than the land. She leaned on her staff as she forced him out. The shield wobbled in response. The morlock seized his chance to weave magnetic resonance through the weakened wall and fling the armoured mages back into the grove.

Asja's protective shell collapsed. Aorar flung his across, exposing the druids at his end of the line. A blistering inferno engulfed them moments later, the two morlocks spewing flames together. Seeing them fall, Aorar hurled his axe with all his might, dampening the morlocks' flame as it passed them by to embed itself in the neck of the third. He staggered back from the force of the blow, blood spewing from his cleaved flesh, his bloodied hands clasping the moist handle. His gurgling cut short, he collapsed and fell, the staff by his feet left humming alone.

The pair stared at their fallen comrade as if unable to take in the sight. Then they turned back to the mages and druids no longer sheltered by the protective shield. A furious bolt struck Moruk's staff, shattering the crystal and the master alike. Brielle fell next, leaving Evindal the last druid standing at the grove. Mages found their feet and responded in kind, their many flames singeing the morlocks' scales.

A morlock's staff sizzled from the blaze when his attention fled to the whistling treeline. He turned to face a giant form blocking out the stars. He shrieked at an arcing chasm coming to devour him. Vagran caught him with the tip of his beak and sliced through the neck and legs with one clean bite.

The last morlock swung his staff at the giant bird and unleashed the inferno intended for the dwarves. The flames engulfed the feathers and the skin and the gaping wound still raw and oozing from the clash to the north. The beast wobbled, his wings lost their charge, and he fell crashing down into the trees below.

Asja rose at the sound of her lightning friend tormented by the flame. She stared at his majestic wings collapsing and his enormous body plummeting to the ground, and she shook her head and cried in disbelief at the sound of trees breaking and loose feathers and leaves mingling in the air.

She rushed forward, but her leg gave in, bringing her face-down into the luminous grass. She leaned on her staff and scrambled back up, paying no heed to the last morlock, to Aorar closing in on him with an unsheathed knife, or the many discharges that ravaged his body from mages and the druid alike. She hobbled to the woods as quickly as she could, her fallen friend the only thing on her mind.

The roc lay sprawled out on the ground, his body leaning on one side, pinning a bent wing mangled in the fall. A tree trunk pressed down on his head and back, pulled by the branches flattened by the roc. Lightning seeped from the hole in his belly and the many wounds on his back and wings. His body convulsed with the last of the charge as his lifeblood drained out of him.

Asja hobbled to embrace the depleted body of her childhood friend. She tried to lift his outstretched wing and snuggle closer to his soft down, but it just lay there oblivious to her tugging, its weight more than his spent body could bear. She crawled her way to her favourite spot – the soft hollow of his chest that had kept her warm and safe on countless journeys through Amana's skies. She pressed her face into his giant feathers, looking for the rhythmic beating of his powerful heart, a melody she had fallen asleep to more than any other. But the once-vibrant feathers drooped limply across her face, and his mighty heart fell cold, silent and still.

ZEPHYR

A cool night reigned over the forests of Bon. Ever since the last remnants of the Mount Granat sun had been swallowed up by the hungry sky, the warmth of the mountain started to fade from the trees and the earth. Elves who filled the glade watched the tiny sparkles reassert themselves over the night, but glanced expectantly at the slumbering Bristland Peaks hidden in the thick darkness to the west.

An olive skylight shone through the treetops, followed by faint rumblings of an awakening range. An emerald sun rose to his left, piercing the night with his distant light. The twin peaks of Chinnan and Rozaril had discharged in close succession. A warm wind was sure to follow.

The elves scrambled to the grove in the middle of the glade, who housed the oldest and most majestic of trees, looking for comfortable roots on whom to lie, their faces flushed with nervous excitement, their nostrils filled with the coarse smell of earthy loam and impending rain.

The distant rumbling rose in intensity and pitch.

And the music started.

It began with the flutter of leaves. The discarded foliage from the colourful ground stirred in response. Bushes and shrubs joined in the play until the forest filled with shuffling and murmur brought on by the wind. The elves rested in their own silence, quivering in anticipation of what was to come.

Sagging willow branches swayed in the wind to the soft chiming notes of their lilac blooms. The velvety tone of the dangling flowers rang through the woods, their silky shells clattering against one another, countless tiny bells frolicking in the cacophony of their motion, striving to make up for their diminutive size with the vibrancy of their flow, competing to outdo each other with their dance and song. The music permeated the grove, resonating through the air, gaining a life of her own.

Voices rose to complement the rustling and the chimes, whispering in the waters who seeped down the cliff and speaking through the rumble of the rapids they fed. The eastbound streams rose, fed by the swelling tide, fusing the voices into a pervasive hum, a thundering roar that announced the presence of the forest nourished by the two mountain ranges she was nestled between.

Tree vines joined the symphony of the woods, exposing their fibres to the gathering gust, their confidence rooted in the tenacity of their twine. Their taught strings quivered in the wind, each delicately weaving his own distinctive tune, a life story that rippled through the music of the wood. The strings came together in a harmonious flow, an ode to the forest from each strand, leaf and stone.

A hollow branch let the breeze fill her only to expel him with the sound of a flute. Crisp notes rose from the aged wood and filled the forest air, catching their breath and exhaling again, their naked form naive and unadorned. They spoke of a life vibrant and unpretending, fully satiated with the beauty of the grove.

And then a flower fell, a cord snapped, a weathered branch cracked from the strain, their demise announced with a giant mushroom's gong. Their music stopped, their broken bodies mute and still.

But the symphony went on.

New branches and trees took the place of the old, breathing their own notes into their joint creation that continued to amaze the elves who lived there as long as Zephyr continued to swoop through the forests of Bon.

RUINS

Asja sat on a rock overlooking the beach and watched the calm, soothing motion of the sea. The surface of the water glistened in the sun as he touched the horizon, rippling gently in the evening breeze. The ripples grew as they neared the shore, forming low waves who washed softly over the beach and left bountiful foam in their wake. They swept the surf along and took the froth to the furthest extent of their reach, before spreading it across the sand when they retreated back into the sea.

A surreal quality permeated the scene that did little to quell Asja's distress. These waters, she was told, provided refuge to her people from death by human hands, but all she could see was her own loss imposed upon the scene.

Each wave who broke on the sand made her think of Vagran's fatal crash. Each disorderly retreat into the sea reminded her of being left alone. It wasn't his absence but the finality of it that made it so difficult to bear. Wherever she was on her journey, no matter how long she'd been away, she had been comfortable in the knowledge that she could reach him whenever she needed him, or he needed her. Now that comfort was gone.

She saw an albatross in the distance, keeping close to the water, flying away from the land, his wings fully outstretched and riding the breeze. She closed her eyes and watched him grow into the silhouette of a roc. She remembered the newly born bird stumbling around their house, and a young adolescent stretching his wings in their yard. An unlikely friend who didn't have much to say but never left her guessing how he felt, who never lost his wildness even though it had no place in the dwarf way of life, whose enormous size and power she'd come to depend on, as if the world around him posed no threat, especially when she was by his side.

She cursed the morlocks for severing the last link to her dwarf past. Their rise among her birth people had marked the loss of her link to them, too.

She hobbled across to the other end of the ledge. Her leg could still bear no weight – the bone having crumbled into powder, she was sure. She let her anger keep the despair in check, leaning on her staff and staring at the shore.

Outlines of buildings littered the land. Buildings with derelict walls reclaimed by the jungle, the forgotten ruins of a once-great people.

She left what once was the docks to walk along the main street into the city. Tall grass and young trees mingled with the stone to obscure the path for her to follow. She brought her hand to the overgrown ground to feel the exuberant cries of children racing through the street, and the strain of food gatherers as they hauled their catch from the jungle and the sea. She stepped into a building through a broken door, hacked open with the blade of an axe. She spotted a patch of earth in a corner of the room, home to plants who thrived on the moisture brought in by the wind. She rested her hands on the moist walls, only to feel them cry out with the blood of people whom they used to hold.

She'd never known her people in this setting. She felt cheated, incomplete, the people she'd watched live across the isles a remnant of the culture that had built this city, a mere shadow of their accomplished past. They'd never recaptured the spirit who crafted this world, living day to day with no future in sight.

She hobbled back to the shore, where Aorar and Ilyasah waited for her to return.

Ilyasah, a legendary elf archon of tremendous skill and speed, who appeared in their midst following the druids' demise, when his people saw the full power of the morlock order and cried out for revenge. A cry that grew louder in her each time she took Evindal to another tribe to deliver to them the wasted body of their druid. Even as she fought to stay numb to their wails, the memory of Shar's death still harrowing and raw.

Like Aorar before him, no one could explain where Ilyasah had come from, having been absent from elf lives for many generations. But she did feel the intensity of their cries spread through the land, the same fervour she now felt coursing through the archon.

She shook her head, not caring who he was, only for his resolve to strike the morlocks down.

She saw no way forward but to cut out the cancer from the mur soul.

"Are you ready?" Aorar's voice rumbled through the dusk.

Asja nodded, looking at the dwarf and the elf in turn before turning her attention to the sea and the morlock island hidden in the night.

"How many are there?" asked Ilyasah.

"Nine," said Asja. "There were twelve before the attack."

"Assuming they didn't replenish their number," cautioned the elf.

"This is the time of their turtle run festivals. They'll be distracted with that for now," she reasoned, then shook her head. "Doesn't matter. I have two legendary warriors with me, and surprise on our side."

She embraced her companions, wincing at the memory of her childhood friend. No affection warmed this group, only a craving to end the morlock threat, a drive that Ilyasah and Aorar lived for.

Still, Aorar offered a word of caution. "Didn't you say that their island is enchanted? That there's no way to approach them without being seen?"

A satisfied smirk spread across Asja's face. "I have a plan."

UQATERA

Water splashed across a stone ledge as a waterlogged trunk broke the placid surface. The ship came to rest against the slippery rock, his sparse branches flexing to keep him in place. His belly flung open, a section lifting to release three figures huddled in his hold. Two grabbed onto the bark to pull themselves out, then pulled the third one up by her arms. She turned around and extended her hand to touch the wood in a gesture of affection before the ship closed behind them and receded back into the depths.

Asja bid Fallnut farewell as he settled in the water to await their return. Abandoned by the elves in his old age, his trunk set too deep beneath the waves, his limbs too brittle to battle the rough seas, he'd spent his days languishing by the mur islands before she found him off the coast of Aguan. Now he'd brought them inside Uqatera, the morlock island stronghold, swimming beneath the waterline and the enchantments hugging it, even if the journey did take long and his lodgings lacked the dryness of the younger ships.

Asja looked around to get a sense of the cave, welcoming the faint bioluminescent glow after the journey in the bowels of the ship. She squinted when a bright light arose within the cavern and turned to see a firegem shining from Aorar's axe. He lifted it to better illuminate the cave, and then, aware of his short stature, gave it to Ilyasah to do the same.

A marine cavern greeted them, with smooth walls polished by seawater, seeped in moisture and covered with moss. The ledge extended a while further, running along the side of the cliff, until it rounded a corner into a hidden crevice, coming to an end in a wall of rock.

Ilyasah followed the turn with the axe held high, illuminating the moist ceiling of the cave. Lines appeared in the stone at the end of the ledge, straight cuts where the roof sagged towards the floor. The elf archon strained to reach the lines, but they remained just out of his grasp.

"A mur could reach them," remarked Aorar.

Asja agreed. She stared at the ceiling, realising that the morlocks had knowledge of the cave.

"Can you sense their presence?" whispered Ilyasah.

She closed her eyes for a moment before shaking her head. Emboldened by their absence, she raised her staff to move the slab of stone from its ceiling spot, lifting it across the floor of the room before laying it down out of their sight. And then they stood still, letting silence descend upon the cave, lulled into safety by the lack of sound coming from the hole.

Ilyasah returned Aorar's axe, removing his bow and arrows too, and placed his hands and feet onto protrusions from the wall to help him climb through the ceiling hole. Asja followed, needing help to rise from above and below. Aorar came last, the elf pulling him through the high trapdoor. When they found themselves inside the new room, Aorar ignited the axe once more, shining its light into their new abode.

A storage room greeted them, filled with sheets of cloth and damaged stools. Wooden boxes lay discarded along the walls, mixed with chandeliers, cooking pots, tufts of fabric and glass art. Thick ropes and rusty chains kept them company. A broken barrel with the lid half gone, a stone slab shaped like an altar, colourful pieces of a fractured mural. All covered by dust and plants able to thrive in the murky interior of the place.

A pile of rocks took up space by the entrance to the room. Their colour and texture didn't match the wall; they must have been brought in from somewhere else. They reminded Asja of Dimotai's first creation, only these were far cruder than the wizard's meticulous craft. She touched one with her hand. Her gesture provoked no response, the stone seemingly oblivious to the intruders walking by.

The storage room led to a dimly lit passage, the only light coming through a small window placed high up on the far end. Aorar extinguished his axe. They waited for their eyes to adjust. Asja used the time to weave the magic she had mastered for the horrors, muffling the sound they made when in contact with the stone.

She placed her hand on the passage wall. The hard surface felt warm to the touch, as if sustained by more than coral life and waves of heat coming from distant peaks. The rock showed no sign of having been cut or beaten into place. No sharp edges got in their way, the ceiling, walls and floor all seamlessly flowing into one another.

A second passage snuck up on them a few steps on. Asja peered ahead, spying a pile of rocks resting in a crevice, and an opening in the wall a short distance further. Had this been any other place, she'd have assumed them the handiwork of the island herself. Here, she suspected the use of magic in the shaping of her interior to the morlocks' ends.

The whole place felt like a forgotten corner of their island home, where one could easily get lost amongst the tunnels and crevices and obscure items discarded along the way. Asja wondered whether the morlocks had made themselves an escape route should they face an attack, where they could slip away quietly through the opening in the floor and the cavern who led to the open sea.

A dull sound of footsteps rose from distant stone.

The three intruders froze.

The steps came closer, reverberating down the passage. Asja quietened her breathing and tried to blend into the rock. Ilyasah slowly reached for an arrow, the deliberate motion making no sound. The closest to the fork in the passage, Aorar held his axe ready. The steps stopped, followed by opening and closing of a door.

The archons and Asja waited a while longer before letting themselves relax. No more sounds came from the passage, as if the walker had come alone and was cocooned in his room. They exchanged knowing glances before proceeding as one, walking stealthily and briskly into the adjoining passage, looking for a door in the dim light of the tunnel. When they saw one, they quietly encircled it, Aorar standing to the right and Ilyasah to the left, with Asja facing it straight on.

Her heart started pounding. The staff felt sweaty in her hand. She gripped it harder, depending on its power as well as its support. She knew what morlocks could do. This was the first time she intentionally sought them out and willingly put herself in the harm's way. She knew she risked her life, even with the two archons standing by her side. But she didn't care.

She nodded to Ilyasah to let her in.

The elf gripped the handle and swung open the door.

Asja leaned on her staff and leapt inside, taking in the contents of the room as quickly as she could. A cloaked figure stood in the far corner, looking at the items on the shelf by the wall. He turned around at the sound, his eyes widening with surprise, his throat constricting and choking. He covered it with his hand but couldn't disrupt Asja's spell. His other hand reached for a staff leaning against the table. It flew into his hand, followed by an axe that cut into his chest. He stood there a moment longer, gaping at his assailants with terror in his eyes, before all feeling left them and his body collapsed onto the floor. Ilyasah came in last, his arrow resting in his hand unused.

The morlock never made a sound.

Asja stared at each archon in turn. Pent up tension released with a deep breath. A subtle nod of thanks for their support. A hint of a smile at the job well done. They left the room and returned to the passage – leaving the dead morlock lying on the floor – and quietly closed the door behind them.

The next door came upon them quickly. They swarmed it as they did the first, careful not to make their presence known. Ilyasah opened the door for Asja to burst in, only to find it empty, the table and the shelves collecting dust, as if their caretaker hadn't been there for some time. A chain attached to the far wall looked oddly out of place. *Was this Rangorr's room?* Asja wondered in passing.

A turn in the passage led to more doors left and right. Asja stormed the first to find herself face-to-face with two morlocks sitting across the table. She focused her staff on the throat of one, leaving the other to holler in alarm. A swing of an axe cut his cries short before Ilyasah closed the door and dispatched the silent mur with an arrow to his face.

The intruders stood silently for a brief time, relaxing from the sudden flare of action, as if oblivious to the yells that had sounded moments before.

"Pellu?" an anxious call came from the passage.

Asja exchanged glances with the archons, their looks far less reassuring than before.

"Pellu?" a woman's voice came through the door, with the sound of footsteps approaching in a hurry.

Aorar yanked the axe out and took up station in a corner, his back pressing into the wall by the door. Ilyasah moved to the other side, a hunting knife unsheathed in his hand. Asja hid behind the table atop the slain morlocks, their bodies and blood obscured by the stone frame.

The door opened. A cloaked figure rushed in. Ilyasah reached for the door handle as Aorar swung his axe into her back. A pained cry escaped her lips moments before the door closed shut.

"Deja?" a deeper voice echoed down the passage.

Ilyasah sheathed the knife and grabbed his bow and arrow again. Their presence revealed, he burst out of the room, took a quick aim at a figure standing in the shadows, and let go. A throaty groan sounded from the mur as the arrow pierced his body and lodged in the wall.

Not taking pause, Ilyasah pushed on, readying his bow again as he ran. Aorar yanked his axe out and followed, struggling to keep up with the sleek elf. Asja hobbled far behind.

Ilyasah reached a stone pillar, the frame of a wide gap in the wall that lacked a door of the earlier rooms. He gazed briefly past the pillar into the space beyond before retreating with haste. A bolt of lightning followed his face, sizzling through the air and striking the tunnel wall. He peeked again, provoking a second discharge that illuminated the chamber and left charred marks on the brown stone.

Aorar broke cover and ran headlong for the second pillar. Lightning followed, cutting a line in the rock behind him. Ilyasah emerged into the sudden light and shot an arrow aimed at its source. The arrow shaft glanced against the staff and struck the morlock in the holding arm. He pulled back with a loud groan, letting go of his staff in pain.

A shimmering bubble enveloped the wounded mur, growing to encompass another standing behind him. Ilyasah drew an arrow and let loose, only to see it bounce off the shield and break against the ceiling above. He drew another, holding it at the ready, staring at the barrier that had suddenly appeared between him and his prey.

The morlocks started to retreat, walking backwards away from the attack. Aorar broke cover again, his axe in hand, dripping blood. The protective sphere dissipated for a moment, letting through a blast from the wounded mur. It lacked his earlier force, but still brought the dwarf down, his body covered with dust, the stone of his leg fractured and loose.

Ilyasah shot the arrow at the weakened sphere, but could not reach it before its strength returned. He drew and shot another, giving Aorar time to scuttle away. They stood behind the pillars and watched the morlocks retreat, unable to find a way to overcome their defences.

A blistering bolt of lightning struck the stone frame above the retreating duo, bringing down rocks on top of their shield. Caught off guard, the morlock strained under their weight, feeding energy to the shield over their heads. The rocks bounced off and fell on the floor, as did the mur, the elf's arrow protruding from his chest having forced its way through the weakened ward.

Asja breathed a sigh of relief. She faced the remaining mur, her staff staring down a bloodied, empty hand. He pushed a stone off his leg to make a shuffling retreat into the passage behind the hall. Too injured to run, he turned instead to a rock-filled crevice, releasing a discharge into the reclusive abode until it started to glow with otherworldly light, stopped only by another shot from Ilyasah's bow.

The hallways stirred. The walls screeched, the energy from the blast rippling through them. Ilyasah ran past the fallen mur and into the passage beyond. A pile of rocks rose to block his path, risen from their crevice by the morlock's spell. Stone ground against stone until they floated freely in the murky tunnel, suspended by the force coming from the wall. Beyond them, a lone figure stood in the hallway, his blood-red eyes transfixed on the elf.

"Satjan!" Ilyasah spat out, grinding his teeth at the head morlock.

The elf readied an arrow as he forged ahead, but the stones interfered, moving to block his way. He stepped aside, drew and let go, only to see the stones match his movements, one taking the force of the shot, split in two by the crystalline tip. Deflected by the rock, the arrow glanced against the stone wall, sliding past the morlock's head and the gasp of surprise that followed. The mur turned and vanished through a hidden gap, leaving Ilyasah's ire to well up between empty walls.

Asja stared at the dancing rocks, mesmerised by the handiwork of the mur, taken aback by how different it was from Dimotai's. The rocks made no attempt to form a coherent shape, satisfied to shuffle about in a disjointed mass. As the elf moved, so did they, sensing his presence, matching it step for step. When he stepped forward, they crowded to keep him out. When he tried to muscle his way through, they slammed into his body until he pulled back in pain.

Aorar stepped up, leaning unsteadily on his healthy leg, and swung his axe at the nearest stone. Split in two, the pieces floated with the morlock's force, each half still blocking his way.

"They are trying to delay us!" Aorar yelled.

Asja caught up to the wounded dwarf, moving beside him to take on the rocks. None shifted to block her way. Perplexed, she stepped into their line, but failed to elicit a response. They ignored her as if she weren't there, vigilant as ever to block the archons' way.

"They know you are a mur!" Aorar blurted out.

"Go after him!" Ilyasah cried out to Asja. "Stop Satjan!"

She leaned onto her staff and hobbled on, down the tunnel after the morlock, past the rocks keeping her friends at bay. When she reached the opening in the wall, she peered briefly through, and then slipped out of the archons' sight. It erupted in flames moments later, the blaze pouring out into the hallway, the flares licking the walls and igniting the passage beyond.

"Noo!!!" screamed Aorar, swinging wildly to whack a stone with the blunt side of his axe, sending him flying far down the passage. The rock landed and rolled across the floor, and then stood still, free from the morlock's animating force. The dwarf struck again, and again, thinning out the barrier in their way, until Ilyasah slipped through in rapid pursuit.

A scorched room greeted him, wood burning against the walls, charred stone smouldering with heat. He placed his arm to shield his face, but pressed on, walking until he saw Asja's figure standing beyond the flame, facing away from him, at an opening in the wall. A body lay on the ground behind her, a cloaked corpse horribly disfigured.

"You got him!" he blurted out, looking at the twisted contours of the head morlock's face.

She turned around, the grimace on her face betraying her pain.

"Centane got away."

RASHAS

Shar stood on rocky ground in the centre of a clearing. His breath still caught in his throat at the thought of it, standing atop Mount Midgus – Amana's central peak – Tetran Massif's heights having been beyond his reach not so long ago, before he became a wizard and learned to travel as they did.

Mist gushed through the open space, fuelled by Thunder Falls and driven by the wind. He couldn't see the falls, only the waters of Sed Deep who fed them – the inland sea surrounding Mount Midgus and hoisted upon the range – in fortuitous moments when the gust blew hard enough to part the clouding mist and reveal the sea beyond the island's shore. The sound of the falls filled the moist air, a background roar without shift or end. Columns of light descended through the gaps, striking the ground and the water around him, illuminated by the brightest suns in all of Amana. Shar gazed at the spectacle unfolding around him with a pang of regret that this secluded place stood unseen by ordinary people living in this land.

A slender figure wearing a dusky cloak emerged from the fog. The right side of his face lacked expression, seemingly frozen in a grip of decay. A sombre look graced the left, though it couldn't suppress a hint of joy at the sight of his friend.

A warm smile filled Shar's face. "Dimotai!" He embraced his former teacher and held him tight. "It's been too long."

Dimotai nodded, the sight of his protégé lighting his mood, but unable to lift the forlorn look that held him in its grip.

"What happened?" asked Shar, realising that this was not a mere reunion to catch up on their friendship.

Dimotai struggled for words, swallowing hard trying to regain them. "Rashas is gone," he finally said, his voice trembling amidst the clamour of the falls.

"Gone?"

"Sunk back into the Primordial Sea."

Shar recoiled at the news. His stone features contorted in disbelief. He'd been to the world more than once, and his friend and mentor had made a home there. They both loved the dramatic nature of the place, high-rise mountain peaks who shot out luminous skylights higher than anywhere else, rivers who washed over the land with urgency and force, canyons who carried breathtaking scars from the wind's fury, grasses and trees who clothed the land with tenacity and vigour lest she be reclaimed by the rapacious waves. A world hungry for life, eager to make something of herself. And now she was no more, swallowed up and gone as if she'd never been.

"How... How did this happen?"

"Rashas was desperate to awaken, but her people would not. In the end, she lost hope and let herself go, crumbling before their eyes and taking them with her into the ocean depths."

Shar's thoughts immediately ventured to Amana's newest dwellers. Two ships had sailed across the Primordial Ocean and made their landfall at the foothills of Mount Cappon. They seemed to have ended their journey there, having established an outpost by their landing site. He'd thought of them as intrepid explorers from a distant land rather than desperate survivors from a dying world. They struck him as primitive – people preoccupied with little more than their own survival. He understood now why they would be that way, given what they must have endured where they had been. Still, the thought of having them here triggered his concern.

"Do you expect the human presence here to be a hindrance or a boon?"

Dimotai pondered the question for a moment before offering a reply. "There are too few of them here to sway the course either way. But one thing is clear – they did not help Rashas ascend, nor did they even grasp what their world really wanted from them."

Shar stood in the misty clearing pondering Dimotai's answer long after the wizard had gone. By the time he departed himself, he looked like the weight of Amana had taken residence upon his shoulders.

The two wizards left behind a clearing far more attentive than it had seemed. Ama herself had listened to every word they'd said. She'd long known of the existence of others – beings from other worlds, who moved between them at will and held no allegiance to the place of their birth. She'd seen their lifestyle as a betrayal of their homeland and was dismayed to discover that some of her own children had joined their ranks.

News of Rashas' demise shook her to the core. She shuddered with an earthquake that rocked the summits and the sea. A world not unlike herself was lost to Primal Waters. After all the time and effort she must have spent rising from the ocean, growing and nurturing a land fit for her children to live, and blossoming with countless creatures of every kind, she couldn't imagine what it must have taken for Rashas to give up on her dream and take her own life. She feared being left to the same fate and would take steps to a different end.

These wizards... they'd seen and learned much on their travels. Perhaps their wayward lifestyle wasn't a vice, as she had thought. Perhaps she could even gain from their attention and counsel.

AN APPRENTICE RECLAIMED

Asja stood on a high terrace of the Algalash tree, where a broad branch clothed with crystalline leaves rose to the sky. No skylight hovered over the horizon, leaving Isura's lights to shine undisturbed.

The splendour of the scene was lost on her. Her birth people still preoccupied her thoughts. She thought they'd be better off with the morlocks dead and gone, with nothing to do with the cancer but cut it out. Now they were left with no one to lead them, with nothing but uncertainty to take the morlocks' place.

If she were honest with herself, she'd really wanted revenge, hoping to reach closure over the death of her friend. But the hole he'd left in her life still loomed as large, and Centane would no doubt want revenge of her own.

Worse, dwarves and elves used the end of the morlock threat to resume their hostilities with the desert folk. Even as she lingered there, word was going out to mobilise the warriors for a struggle not unlike the war against the beasts. She would have supported this effort not so long ago, and had called for it at the gathering of the clans. Now she had to find a way to bring it to an end.

She turned around and pressed her fingers on the familiar wall. The carnelian stone felt warm to the touch, his reddish sheen barely visible in the subdued light of the stars. She walked into the room she once called home. The basalt bed that had wrapped itself around her every time she'd come to sleep still lay in the same corner of the room. The room itself looked undisturbed, as if no one had taken her place since she'd left the wizards following Shar's death.

Her eyes teared up from the onslaught of memories. She didn't think she'd see the place again. But she couldn't turn down Florella's plea to return, if only for a short visit, to receive the good news the wizard had to share.

She left her room and walked down the short passage to the open hall. Florella stood there, facing away from her. At the sound of footsteps, she turned around, her face graced by the most exuberant petal dance Asja had ever seen. The plant bent down to embrace the girl with a sea of leaves. Asja hugged her back, her body aching for her teacher's presence. They stood in each other's embrace for the longest time, until the wizard apprentice once again felt fully at home.

Florella let go of the girl and moved aside, revealing the company of a visitor Asja had not seen – a tall, slender figure with a scaled body the colour of shallow sea. Her eyes opened wide. *A mur? Here?* He stepped forward, looking straight at her.

"Thank you, Asja." He bowed gently as he spoke. "Thank you for not giving up on me."

Her brow furrowed at his words. What did he have to thank her for? She looked into his eyes but saw neither the malice of morlocks nor the innocence of their people. A blend of the two gazed back at her, as if he'd chosen not to partake in the tyranny he knew all too well.

She looked at his slender body and, in a flash of recall, saw the gaunt frame of a demon standing tall and fiery in the courtyard of Kinrum Hall. She looked at his arm, the scales thickening from the elbow to the wrist, and saw them morph into crusty skin on an arm placed defensively to keep arrows at bay. An arm that still bore a scar from her lightning bolt.

A gasp escaped her lips. She glanced at Florella, unable to accept the connection that her mind had made.

"It's Rangorr," Florella said, her head nodding to a petal dance.

Asja turned back, peering with her inner sense through the turquoise scales into the essence beneath – a dream who burned with the desire to share what he knew with his people at large, who'd become one of the morlocks so that he could learn something worthy of being shared, and who'd apprenticed himself to the wizards when his affair with the morlocks ended in dismay.

Her breath taken away by the splendour of his dream, she bowed in return despite her short stature, grateful to finally see something good come of her actions that day.

He waited for her to look up again before his voice pierced the room. "How much longer will you let your Tyrant run amok?"

Her eyes opened wide. She swallowed hard, unable to respond. His eyes peered into her, burning with the clarity she hadn't seen before, pregnant with the knowledge of having been in his own Tyrant's grip, as if he saw himself in her, who he used to be. She looked away, unable to withstand his stare.

A shadowy rift called out to her. The sound of a plane whose denizens had tasted acceptance and would no longer be dismissed. She had resisted the call, preoccupied with the looming conflict on the eastern border – now that the morlocks no longer posed a threat.

But Rangorr's piercing gaze would not be denied. Dwarves and goblins would have to wait. She took her staff and headed to the Underworld. Much unfinished work awaited her there.

WORLD TREE

Ama opened her hand. A single seed graced her palm, a flat speck of indistinct shape, caramel in colour and hard to the touch. She took a deep breath of the misty air and blew gently at the dormant seed. A warm smile spread across her face as she felt him awaken and begin to stir. And then she tilted her hand and let him drop to the ground, on top of a fertile mound of soft, receptive earth.

A tiny seedling sprouted from the seed, held by roots dug firmly into the loam. He rose through the soil and the grass, looking over the patch of land from whom he had sprung. A solitary tree on top of Mount Midgus, the progenitor mountain of all of Amana.

When his roots spread deep and wide, he rose further still, safe and stable, piercing the rolling mist. Thick bark clothed his trunk, adding to the weight of the branches above. Broad leaves sprouted from the wood, adding little to the pressing mass, save when the wind passed through them with purpose, swaying the whole tree with his forceful breath.

Tenacious roots dug through the summit cap, breaking into the chamber to the mountain's heart. Many cycles had passed since a Mount Midgus sun had seen the lights of the night sky. Spewing furiously to form the land around him, the ancient massif had since fallen still, leaving the important work of nourishing the land to the younger mounts who could endure the strain.

The deep roots tapped into the ore in the mountain's core. Stone and crystal flowed through their veins. The trunk hardened into carnelian stone, more adept at holding up a tree of a mountain's height.

And the tree rose further still, his branches punching through the gathering clouds, secluded from the land by the Thunder Falls' rain, yet holding all of the land within sight of his tip.

Ama gazed at the gargantuan trunk standing before her, mammoth branches reaching through the sky, an elongated canopy blocking out the suns. Crystalline leaves sparkling in colourful rays of light. Roots spread through the ancient mountain to hold the tree in place.

She stepped back to the edge of the isle in the centre of Sed Deep to take a more expansive look at her newest child. And when that wasn't enough, she withdrew further still, over the choppy water of the inland sea, until her eyes could take in the world tree in his full size.

Algalash stood atop the flat summit of Mount Midgus, the heart of Amana, the central spot from whom the whole world was made. A worthy home for any wizard who may choose to stay.

URC

The bustle of the war camp surrounded Asja's tent. Dwarf and elf warriors had answered the call and gathered on the slopes of Delden Ford, in the southern reaches of the dwarven lands. Mages and clan leaders welcomed them, with fresh warriors trickling in each day.

Asja could still hear their jubilant cry roar through the camp when they saw her arrive. The hero of the morlock raid, the one who had ended that threat and paid a heavy price, back with them to support their war against the desert folk. And only war was on their minds.

She shook her head to dispel the thought, not willing to give in to her fears of the dwarf war machine swelling and raging unchecked. Her thirst for revenge had run its course. She had kept her change of heart from the dwarves, waiting for an opportune time, when she could use her newfound sway to steer them to a different end.

Could she steer the goblins away from the war as well?

She turned to the side of her tent that faced River Rust, and goblins and ogres who lined the other bank. Then she sat down quietly and waited for the night to take hold of the camp.

A shifting portal burst out of the tent. It sped down the sloping hillside to reach the river and the eastern bank. It rose from there, over the trees and the sparse dells filled with goblin bodies sleeping in the open, and bands of people sitting around the fires. It moved past the sentries at the edge of the camp, people carrying leftovers from the evening meal, brutes of flesh and stone tending to their clubs, tents adorned with hunting weapons worthy of a chief. When it reached a spacious tent at the end of a clearing, it circled over as if watching the place but too excited to stand still. Then it dove through the walls of animal hide and disappeared into the darkness inside.

Asja's staff came to life in the interior of the tent, illuminating the dirt floor with thin furs lying to one side, and a goblin standing beside them with a sharpened bone in his hand and a look of terror on his face.

A face with a long scar beneath the right eye. "It's you!"

"Dwarf mage!" whispered the goblin, equally stunned.

"I saw you by Chromatic Hills. What are you doing here?"

He stared at her blankly, as if perplexed by having to explain his presence to an intruder in his tent.

"I bring word of dwarf raid. Your people come, take crystal from us."

Asja's brow furrowed at his words. The mages' craving for crystals had the effect she feared. Reaching an agreement with the goblins will be harder now.

The goblin cast his dagger aside and pulled his shoulders back, dignity and pride radiating from his posture. "I'm Urc, hunter from Hatar tribe of Mount Uburn."

Asja's face flushed red, embarrassed that she had to be reminded of the courtesy of introduction by a desert savage. "I'm Asja, a mur conjuror whom Ama remade to look like a dwarf."

She could see from his popping eyes that her words had the desired effect, putting her unwitting host on the back foot and distracting from her poor manners. It took him a moment to gather himself and resume the conversation.

"I know mur people. Very strong. They help us against dwarfs."

It was her turn to be surprised. "The morlocks?"

Urc nodded with a confident grin on his face.

"They're not here yet, are they?"

He just stood still, a stoic expression covering his face.

"They're not here because they're dead! We attacked their island stronghold and killed them all! They won't be coming to your aid." She shook her head as she spoke, her words coming out slowly to highlight his predicament. She chose not to mention that one morlock had escaped lest she give Urc hope.

He remained silent at her words. She wondered if he believed her, and then whether deception was even a part of their culture, something they were capable of.

"There others," he finally replied. "Strong fighters who join us. You see if you cross river." His sudden look of renewed confidence seemed strained.

"Ogres? I've dealt with them before," came the sneering reply.

"Not this ogre…" Urc's words tapered off, oozing awe.

Asja's eyes narrowed at his tone. It was only one ogre, and the way Urc spoke of him made her think of… Aorar? Did ogres have a champion of their own who came to aid them in their time of need? What about goblins? If there was more than one hero among the desert dwellers, another one must have been a goblin.

Who were these beings of power who materialised on the eve of war? She put the question aside, thinking to ask Florella or Ama at a more opportune time.

"Powerful warriors have rallied to us, too. A dwarf with the strength of ten men, who can wield magic more skilfully than any mage. An elf who can move with the swiftness of a hare, and whose aim—"

"Why you come here?" demanded Urc, his voice rising in frustration.

"To warn you. You cannot stand against us. Leave this place, or you will see Death."

"And go where?"

The simple question stopped her cold. There was no place where goblins could go and be safe from dwarf meddling so long as they had something with them that the dwarves desired. She knew this. So did he.

"You bring death to us," he continued, shaking his head. "Here. Mountains. No matter."

"As have you. You've raided our lands and killed our people."

"Assai tribe who live here speak of raid where thunder bird attack them from sky, and dwarf mage attack them with fire..." He spoke with great flair, stopping only when he saw an ashen expression rise on Asja's face. "You do that... You and giant bird I see."

She ground her teeth in anger at his lopsided description of their counterraid. "Those raiders had crossed the river and razed our villages, killing everyone they could find. They got what they deserved!" Her heart pounded from the memory of that day.

She studied Urc's face, but saw no pleasure at the dwarves' loss, despite the animosity he held towards them, as if he partook in the conflict purely from concern for his people, a concern seemingly at odds with his crude look and simple speech. His genuine care touched her in a way the runemages' sophistication never did.

"If we withdraw from the river and pledge never to attack your people again," she offered, "will you do the same?"

"I no trust dwarf words," Urc spat out.

"They don't trust yours either, but we've got to start somewhere."

He sighed, staring at the floor, deep in thought. Then he looked her straight in the eye. "I talk to Assai people."

She nodded in gratitude, realising that this was as much of a concession as she could hope to get. "I will talk to mine."

She gripped her staff, preparing to leave, when it occurred to her that she had never enquired about the aftermath of their last encounter.

"How is your leg?"

A look of surprise flashed across his face. His features seemed to soften in response. "It heal good. Thank you."

She nodded with a warm smile before conjuring another portal and vanishing from his tent.

A NEW BEGINNING

Asja sat on a wooden stool, her shoulders rising erratically, her arms crossed on the table, her head buried in them. She couldn't get Urc's words out of her mind. She'd hoped to convince him to leave and avoid the bloodshed. She thought that if goblins knew just how hopeless their cause was, they'd see reason and withdraw from the river lands and return to their homes deep in Kuru Kam. Brokering an agreement between the two peoples was an altogether different proposition, one that needed concessions to be made by them both, something she had no confidence in being able to exact.

She sighed, wondering how to bring the matter before runemages and clan leaders without them dismissing her out of hand.

The hair on her neck suddenly stood on end. A familiar swooshing sound passed through the wall. The tent shook and heaved from the chaotic swirl. The air in the distant corner started to churn, like a shimmering mirage born of heat. It settled on a spot, a makeshift portal taking form, spewing moist air heavy with the smell of the sea, and a vaporous form who saturated the place.

Asja bolted, reaching for her staff, leaning on it to steady herself as the first mur she'd ever met materialised before her. She pointed the tip at the witch, drawing power from the hillside until it sported a violet glow. Centane readied hers in response. The two magicians stood face to face, their staves glowing in the gloomy air, their eyes locked in a mutual stare, each ready to unleash upon the other, neither willing to make the first move.

The crimson glow vanished from the witch's eyes. The pent-up charge of her staff died down. She opened her arms wide, no longer able to respond should the dwarf choose to strike. When Asja failed to act, she cast her staff aside, standing empty-handed before the rogue mage who still threatened to take her life.

Asja gasped at the gesture. The sole survivor from her raid stood before her again, this time unwilling to escape. The thought of killing her on the spot played on her mind, ending the morlock threat once and for all. And yet, she couldn't bring herself to do it, disarmed by Centane's unexpected act. She followed the witch's example, releasing the energy from her body and her staff in response.

"Why did you spare me?" the witch's words pierced the silence.

Asja anticipated the question. Even in her petrified state, the witch must have known that something was amiss, that her escape stemmed from Asja's unwillingness to act. Asja cast her mind to their last encounter, to Centane's flight through a makeshift portal, to her watching the witch leave, unable to bring herself to cut off her escape, and her prior face-off with the leader of the Circle that had disarmed her and shattered her resolve.

The fleeing morlock vanished in the distance, slipping away through a slit in the wall. Unhindered by the rocks, Asja followed in pursuit, hobbling through the narrow passage, fearing her prey's escape with each strained step. When she reached the same gap, she slipped through as well, finding herself in a derelict room with broken wares and cracks in the floor. A faint glow reached her from the far end, the beginnings of a portal crafted by the mur.

Satjan spun around at the sound of her steps. The portal was not yet ready, taking longer to come to life without the aid of his staff. Asja stared into his eyes, her first encounter with the head morlock. Her hand trembled as it gripped the staff. She steadied it with the force of will, bringing it aglow with the energy of the stone. His hands responded in kind, draining energy from the vortex behind him, abandoning any hope of a quick escape in a desperate attempt to throw the first strike.

Hungry flames shot out from the palms of his hands, licking the walls and the ceiling on their passage through the room. Asja instinctively set to wrap herself with a shield, then thought better of it, her prior defence against a morlock's fury having left her with a defective hip.

The blaze scorched everything in her path. Wooden utensils ignited at her touch. Candles and potions, ropes and fabric, all sat burning in her scorching wake. The flames sped towards the dwarf figure standing at the door. They engulfed the space she had filled moments before, searing the stale air with their blistering breath.

Asja's solid form dissolved into the floor before she could be devoured by the ferocious flames. She flowed beneath the stone, the bulky rock shielding her from the blaze. Only cracks in the floor failed to restrain the heat, scorching her hair and skin as she passed beneath them, letting her move on engulfed in pain but with no means to voice her torment.

Satjan stared at the burning room, fire and smoke clouding his view, searching for a dwarf body overcome by the flames. When he didn't see one, he moved his hands to motion the flames away, seeking to clear his sight. But the entrance stood empty, filled with nothing but smouldering embers and deviant smoke.

A solid form took shape where the portal had just been. An anguished cry escaped from her lips, her body still burning from the rapacious heat. Satjan spun around at the tortured sound, fear and panic flashing across his face, standing an arm's length from the renegade mur. Hatred for his kind poured from her eyes, her arcing staff radiant and ready.

She lunged forward, the blinding tip pressing into his chest. The fuming discharge seared his flesh, his elegant robe scorched at first touch, his spent hands too slow to put up a fight. He screamed in agony as his body withered away, but Asja pressed on, charge pouring from her staff until all that remained of the head of the Circle was a burned-out husk.

There she saw him, shining through the wasted body of the dead mur, soothing rays emanating from a deep ocean core. A dream of what the mur nation could be, a vision clear enough to withstand being razed by human hand, like a phoenix rising from the ashes of their homeland and flourishing anew upon the isles of the reef.

She felt the gentle embrace of his light on her face, soothing and healing with his velvety touch. She saw the strength of the dream's essence, his authentic mastery, his commanding presence. She sensed the indomitable spirit who burgeoned within, ready to lift up the most wretched soul. And she felt completely at home, as if the very spirit of her birth people stood there before her, vibrant and strong. In his presence, Pariah was not needed.

The dream's yearning touched her – to be the soothing rock in the lives of the mur, to carry them to their new homeland and sustain them there until they could flourish. A budding hope arose within him as the people gathered around, distraught and lost, desperately in need of help. Hope led to elation as Satjan took up the mantle of their leader, offering a new vision for them to enact. The dream's optimism grew, the reality of his existence within the mur's reach.

Asja tasted his bewilderment as Satjan stopped there, never following through on the promise he held, but keeping the people dependent on his aid, and himself in charge. The disbelief at watching him seek to break others instead of working to make his own people whole. And the surrender at seeing the leader of the Circle brought down by those he sought to destroy.

The mur gone, the dream had no way of acting in this world, no way to remedy past mistakes, to change course and start anew. He rose to leave, the promise of what the mur nation could be seeping away with him. Asja watched him go, her heart crying out for the wonderous dream she had expelled from this land, forced to return to the place of his birth without ever having come to be.

Asja stood in the open space of her tent, confused and distraught, as if the head of the Circle had just left her side.

The sharing of her memory disarmed the witch further. She stared at the ground, silent and trembling. When she did speak, her lamenting words held none of the malice or hubris Asja recalled from their first encounter in the sylvan wood.

"He's always been the strongest of us. The one the people looked up to. When he told us that we needed to let our people be, that they couldn't deal with the danger that the humans posed, we believed him. When he hatched a plan to destroy those who'd harmed us as well as their friends, we went along."

She grew more distraught as she spoke, as if facing Satjan's dream from Asja's memory had brought the old misgivings to the fore, and shone light on what she'd always suspected was true and could no longer deny. She collapsed on the floor, her face in her hands, weeping.

"How... did we... end up here?"

Asja stared at the broken witch on the floor of her tent, a sight she never expected after their first encounter. A dream beneath the fractured exterior reached out to her, a vision of an ambassador to the peoples of the land who showcased the greatness of her nation to them. A hope shattered by the human rejection of her gift, learning to subject them to the new mur ways. A dream failed by her people after she had failed them first.

Centane looked up at the noise of leather flapping in the wind. She gasped as the tent walls closed in around her, pushed inexorably closer by the raging gust. But Asja stopped the display there, ending any likeness to the ordeal she'd endured at the witch's hands in the Kritall Wood.

"Imagine where we'd be had you welcomed me instead," she said to Centane.

"We welcomed humans, and they destroyed us!"

"You provoked them."

"We were trying to help them!"

"They didn't know that."

"True." Centane nodded, taking a deep breath. "True. Lyra made a mistake. Humans were new to the plains. We didn't know them then."

"You do now. You know just how differently your neighbours see the world, and you're better able to protect your people... our people... from them."

"Our people?" the witch repeated the words, the scales on her face contorting in confusion. She closed her eyes, standing in the girl's presence with no sight of her dwarven look. When she opened them again, they widened with surprise, her mouth hanging open with them.

"Ama changed me," Asja explained.

Centane nodded, as if there was nothing unusual about the goddess intervening in someone's life. Her gaze shifted inward, looking at the girl but not seeing her, when her head started to shake. "I can't replace Satjan. I don't have his strength. I can't lead our people."

Asja understood, knowing that Centane's path led somewhere else, seeing herself in the elderly witch at the start of her training, having far too much to learn to lead anyone else.

Her face brightened nonetheless. "I know someone who can."

The witch stared at her blankly before a knowing flash sparkled from her eyes. "Rangorr?"

Asja nodded with a smile. "I'd met him after he was set free. He's a remarkable man, with a dream as bold as Satjan's."

Centane avoided her gaze, diverting her eyes to the ground. "I can't face him again. Not after what we've done to him."

"He's no longer in Tyrant's grip, but is wiser for it."

Centane nodded, forcing herself to look up again. She picked up her staff, getting ready to leave, but lingered by the girl, having more to say.

"I will join you," Asja pre-empted the question, "but first I must end this war before it begins, or our people might never find peace again."

WAR COUNCIL

Asja stepped out of her tent. A song of tribal drums reverberated through the air. She turned at the haunting sound to gaze at the river and the forest beyond. Dwellers of the desert filled her, a goblin war camp joined by ogres, only visible in the few clearings where the trees had failed to tame the sands, leaving merely grass to serve as cover for the ground.

A handful of goblins emerged from the shadows to take station on the eastern bank. Ogres soon joined them, called to arms by the beating drums, wielding their clubs as if in defiance. A troop of dwarves assembled on the western bank, brandishing their weapons and shouting from their side, spontaneously gathered by the shallow water with no leader or battle line.

Asja cursed under her breath. A stray arrow might be all it takes for the warring sides to enter the ford and the carnage to begin. She set forth, hobbling hurriedly with the aid of her staff, down the sloping path into the heart of the camp. Dwarf warriors milled about, their weapons leaning against wooden stands arrayed along the ground. Armour partially covered their bodies, with more to come, their actions hurried by the shouts coming from the ford. The smell of meat filled the air, along with smoke and the crackling of fires burning throughout the camp.

Tribal heads and clan leaders had already gathered, accompanied by runemages and master druids, animated in conversation around the centre of the group – a crystalline rock growing from the knoll. Asja wondered whether they'd even waited for the skylights to rise, or whether this day had weighed on them too heavily for sleep to come.

Their talk ceased as she approached. People stepped aside to let her through. Her stature had risen in the eyes of the clans, her otherworldly companions inspiring awe and fear, her sacrifice to end the morlock threat now widely known.

"I have important news," she spoke as she entered the circle assembled around the rock, taking full advantage of the attention she received. "Morlocks have been inciting the desert people against us. They were going to come and stand with goblins in battle."

She waited for her words to sink in, a quiet murmur confirming the effect.

"Now only one morlock remains. I spoke with her last night. She has abandoned the war effort and will not be taking part."

"You let her live?" Recha was aghast.

"I did," Asja acknowledged. "She's no longer a threat."

The murmur grew, dwarves and elves looking at each other and shaking their heads.

"I've also spoken with Urc," Asja continued, "a goblin hunter from—"

The murmur exploded into an uproar, drawing the attention of other warriors in the camp.

"Why?" pleaded Galen, the leader of the Garnet clan, a cry of betrayal rippling through his voice.

Asja stopped her announcement, taken aback by the intensity of the question. She looked around the assembly, at faces mirroring Galen's, sharing his distress. She was lost for words, unable to comprehend how her mere interaction with a goblin could provoke such an outcry.

"To know our enemies," she finally uttered.

"They are savages," spat Aorar.

"They will stand down if we do," she continued, alarmed by the venom in the archon's voice, sidestepping the merits of their desert foes. "They will leave this ford if we do the same."

"What, disband so they can go back to raiding?" Aorar asked with an exasperated sigh.

"Goblins can't be trusted!" Galen insisted.

"Yes, they can!" Asja fired back. "I have met them. I've travelled deep into their lands, beyond the Pyrenees, where they live free from our threat. They know of us, they've adopted some of our ways, and they've welcomed me with none of the hate and disgust that we have for them!"

Her voice rose in confidence as she spoke, drawing courage from her own words, increasingly convinced of the valour of her cause. Until she heard Uronam's deep tone rumble through the camp.

"Stop this foolishness!" he glared at her, no longer the supportive elder whom she'd looked up to since she was a child, but the leader of her clan on whom it fell to set straight a member who had strayed. "So many of our people have died in goblin raids. So distraught were you by this that you'd brought the matter before the clans. A cause I supported you in. We all did. And now you want to turn your back on us? Your own people?"

His glare remained after his words had left, as if his look alone could sway her to his side. She shuddered from the fierceness of his demand, made with the stature of the leader of her clan, and nearly caved to it as she had before.

But a power to match rose from her belly, filling her with rage until it found a voice. A power dredged up from the depths of the Underworld, Asja finally ready to call him her own.

"I will not support this war!" The young woman stood her ground, leaning on Tyrant, rooted in him, projecting his strength back at the assembly. They stepped back, unfamiliar with her, reluctant to insist again.

"Whose side is she on?" a murmur spread, moving from one warrior to the next, speaking to each other rather than to her, until the crowd turned hostile to her attempt to undermine their stand against their age-old enemies from the desert lands.

Recha broke from the crowd and cautiously stepped forward, slow to speak until she had their attention. "Asja, your skills are invaluable to us. You know that," she began, her conciliatory tone at odds with the mood of the camp. "We need you on our side, or many of us will die needlessly today. If being with us means anything to you, please, help us win this battle. Help us strike dread into the hearts of our enemies and end the goblin threat once and for all."

The soft words moved the young woman, the grimace on her face betraying her turmoil. Recha's plea touched her, as they had before, even as she saw through it to sense the agenda unfolding behind the scenes. Only this time she would not go along, doubting the wisdom of the runemages' guidance, their acceptance no longer her coveted reward.

"This battle won't do that," she replied in a sorrowful voice. "Neither will your lust for crystals from their lands."

The head runemage recoiled from her words, her eyes filling with trepidation, but not of the enemy from across the ford.

"Then you are against us!" she hissed, her body shaking, and turned her back on the defiant woman.

One by one, the other mages and clan leaders followed suit and shunned Asja from their midst. Then came the warriors and the elves assembled there, all following their example, turning their backs on the middle of the assembly and the sorceress standing there, denying her presence, banishing her from their group.

Silently, Asja watched it unfold. The rejection of the people whose favour she'd worked for since she was a child. She gripped her staff firmly, to steady her trembling feet. Each freshly turned back hurt her anew, as if a piece of her had been ripped away, a fragment of her childhood she wasn't ready to discard. She breathed in deeply, drawing on every ounce of Pariah's grit. Without her resilience, she would have been shattered there and then.

She understood the reasons the runemages had for ejecting her from their fold, but why did the warriors follow their lead? She looked into their eyes as they started to turn and saw only a desire to stand with their people in the common cause, with no understanding of how that cause had even come about.

Was this how the War of Inheritance started? The memory of Kinrum Hall resurfaced in her mind, and the rising of the common dwarves to follow their heroes and drive the flying beasts from the Peruvius Range. Beasts who continued to thrive atop the Pyrenees even as the desert folk lived beneath them.

She had come to think of it as the turning point in the history of her people, the moment when they chose to chart their course together instead of leaving it to be carried on the shoulders of a few. Now she wondered what use it was to add their own voice but not their own sense of what that course ought to be.

She saw herself in them, before the wizard training, before her journey to get to know her birth people and the desertfolk. Nothing would have convinced her to change her mind then. Certainly not the voice of a lonely outsider who'd never been accepted by the people among whom she lived. But she did know of an outsider whom they looked up to, who might be able to sway them where she could not.

A swooshing sound of a portal stirred the dwarves. They looked to see the young sorceress melt from their sight and turn to mist swallowed by churning air. And then the portal vanished and the air grew still, leaving the crowd to stare in open-mouthed wonder at the empty space where the child of the mountain had just been.

THE LAST HOPE

Asja knelt on the jutting cliff overlooking Delden Ford, facing the broad river as she flowed peacefully between the war camps. Her closed eyes took in none of the preparations for the upcoming clash, helping her instead seek help of a different kind.

A figure appeared in the space behind her, dressed in the grass of the meadow beyond the cliff, her presence felt in the whisper of the wind. Asja turned around with trembling hands to embrace the goddess in her hour of need. She held on tightly, reluctant to let go, as if her last hope of staving off the war might slip from her grasp.

"What is it, Asja?"

The young woman pulled away to gaze at the eyes that held the entire land in their view. She missed those eyes and the strength that peered through them, even if her melody had changed, shifted to a harsher tone than Asja recalled.

"Surely you know?"

Ama nodded gently. "You are troubled by the course of action your people have taken."

"I've tried to convince them to stand down," her distress poured out, "but they won't listen to me! I... I spoke with goblins too, tried to reason with them... They won't pull back either." Her eyes glistened with tears, staring straight at the goddess, a rock of support from the days of her childhood. "I really need your help!"

"My help?"

The surprise in Ama's voice unnerved her. "Yes! Tell them to stand down and stop this madness before it's too late!"

The goddess' silence puzzled the young woman, as did the sharper edges to the contours of Ama's face. They gave her a harsher look, one that Asja couldn't associate with her childhood friend.

"Don't you hear me?" she pressed.

Ama returned her gaze, but with a shaking head resigned to her fate. "Yours is but a lone voice in the wilderness, a soothing drop in a wave raging with fury." She shrugged her shoulders. "Much too faint to act upon."

Asja stared at the goddess, the memory of her moulting playing on her mind. *Who is this stranger standing before me?*

She peered deeply – with her inner sense as her eyes blurred – gazing at layer upon layer of seething and despair, extending further than her vision could reach. A tranquil tone did touch her from afar, barely audible beneath the rising clamour, reminding her of the task Ama had given her, a mission she never knew but whose import she now understood.

"What about the dream you once had? You sent me to the wizards, remember? You needed my help?"

Ama stood pensively for a moment when her face suddenly brightened, as if she recalled a radiant memory in a sea of gloom, a fleeting hope that once dared rise amongst the turmoil and offer the promise of who her world might be.

"It was a good dream."

RIVER OF BLOOD

Dwarf warriors stood facing the river, axes in hand, arrayed in jagged lines following the contours of the bank. Each man wore the armour he had at hand, some passed down from the War of Inheritance, made by blacksmiths from Peruvius' metal peaks, enchanted by the mages to withstand fire and charge. Mages and runemages walked between the lines, short in number but still offering words of encouragement before the looming clash.

Elves stood behind them, lacking the protection of their stockier friends, never having fought against beasts of their own. Their bows stood at the ready, short and nimble to aid them in the hunt, made of yew trees who grew aplenty in the forests to the west. Their hunting knives rested in the scabbards, for hand-to-hand fray should there be a need. Druids held back, far too few to be of any help.

They looked down with disgust at the scrawny creatures who faced them from the other side, seemingly imitating them in their battle order. But they did eye the towering brutes with great unease, even if their wooden clubs lacked the sharpness or utility of a dwarven axe.

Aorar swung his axe over his head and stepped into the water, sounding a rallying cry. His compatriots responded, following him forward, keeping their line and chanting in unison. The line broke as they waded in waist-deep, bogged down in the silt carried by the river, their weapons and armour weighing them down.

Seeing the line falter, the ogres lurched forward, barging into the shallows with their clubs held high. A barrage of arrows flew at them from across the bank, launched by elven bows held safely behind the lines. They flew over the advancing dwarves, their crystalline tips sharp and forged with runes, piercing rock and flesh wherever they struck. Ogres growled in pain, the first few falling where they stood, others turning in retreat, their large feet dragging in the sand, arrow shafts protruding from their hulking frames.

Seeing their demise, the dwarves pressed forward, catching straggling brutes with blades to their backs. Goblins aimed their bows as the ogre line cleared, but their arrows glanced off the armoured mountainfolk, the wood unable to pierce their garb, only a handful finding gaps through which to maim.

Ogres charged again as the first dwarves reached solid ground, their heavy clubs denting the armour, the force of the impact throwing the attackers back into the river. Their compatriots stumbled over them, struggling for footing in the shifting mud.

Lightly armed goblins jumped in to join them, their lithe bodies moving swiftly through the flowing stream, their daggers made of stone, crystal and bone looking for exposed skin to pierce and hack.

Drawing his hunting knife from its sheath, Ilyasah led the elves to join the fray, their bows of little use facing an entangled mass of friends and foes stumbling through the ford.

Dwarves held their axes high, striking the goblins from above, slashing flesh and hacking limbs, leather coverings offering little shelter from the metal blades. Goblins danced and contorted in the water waist-deep, tripping their adversaries and wrestling them from behind, seeking to unbalance them until they fell, unable to get up from the weight of their armour and the mass of bodies pressing upon them. Those who rose for air fell down again, stabbed through any opening goblin daggers could find.

Cries of pain filled the air, the clank of weapons and splashes of water, strained exertions and gurgling cut short. Blood splashed from fresh wounds. Severed arms floated freely. Heads cut off stuck with tortured frowns from the severing blow.

The water level rose, held back by the mass of bodies clogging up the ford. The two armies kept adding to that number, changing the river colour from rust to crimson red.

Then Ilyasah plunged his knife into a nimble goblin whose movements he barely matched, and Aorar slashed a towering ogre who surpassed his own strength.

A cry escaped the desert dwellers' lips when they witnessed the scene. They stared in disbelief as their champions sank beneath the tide. The westerners cried too, a shrill rallying call, sensing that victory was near.

The goblins broke and ran through the water towards their bank. Ogres tried to follow, their broad feet struggling to move through the churning mud, until they were brought down by elves in close pursuit, delaying the forest dwellers and blocking their path.

Elves set foot on the eastern bank, knives in hand, their exposed bodies bleeding from countless cuts, cutting down anyone too slow to escape. Dwarves came after, drenched with water and blood, their exhausted legs barely carrying them. They gave in as they reached the camp, leaving elves to pursue the fleeing goblins past the abandoned tents and into the forest beyond.

The elves returned to find dwarf mages rummaging through the camp. They claimed the rare crystals they found and set fire to the rest. The victorious troop stood at the edge of the forest and watched flames devour the enemy tents, a hundred courageous souls from the force of a thousand. They left as the fire took to the trees, wading back into the river and over the bodies of their enemies and kin, on their way to their own camp to recover from the ordeal. They stopped to pull up anyone who still breathed, helping them across the bleeding water to the refuge of the western bank and into the hands of healers who did what they could to stave off death.

The victors watched the blaze devour the woods of the eastern bank, lighting up the sky over the battlefield, until only charred trunks remained. Thinner branches and leaves were lost to the flames, goblin livelihood along the river burning away with them.

A sorceress descended upon the cooling bank in the fading light of the day. She staggered through the hacked corpses soaked with blood, her body shaking, struggling to walk. She collapsed on the ground, her face buried in her hands, weeping.

The last fragment of the Mount Granat skylight breathed his final breath, leaving the night to spread and shadow to take hold of the land.

The day of darkness had come.

UNITY

Asja lay down to rest in the shallow waters of the Mirrordon Plane. The stillness of the sea enveloped her, calming her from the turmoil of the world at war. Her touch sent ripples across the tranquil surface, needing more water than usual to wash away her distress.

The sea teased out images of the battle, adding to the water's image of her and of the world in whom she lived. Despite her dread, she let herself relive the tortured scenes of severed limbs colouring the rusty channel and cries of anguish filling the fervid air. She released the memories into the sea to make the burden of carrying them easier to bear.

The sea received each one gently and completely, letting it imprint itself into the receptive liquid, giving it life within the fluid form. They added to the vast knowledge of Asja's world that the plane already had. It let the soothing waters provide her with comfort and solace, making it her favourite refuge from a brutal and senseless world.

How could this have happened? The question kept running through Asja's mind, though she knew the answer she wanted to forget. She herself went on a warpath not so long ago, against some of her own people. It held no surprise for her that dwarves and goblins would do the same after all the carnage that had amassed from cross-border raids.

Asja doubted her ability to steer their course, something she'd thought that – as an aspiring wizard – she would be able to do. Worse, it brought into question the most profound insights she'd acquired in her training, especially those that had come from this plane.

But the plane would not be brushed aside so lightly.

The sea assembled the memories she'd received from Asja's very first visit up to now, but as a single watery whole, joined them together until each scene bled into the next. They enveloped Asja with their pervasive presence, all of which she experienced first-hand.

She stood on the floor of Obalin's study and looked up at the runemage, apprehensive of being in such prestigious company, but eager to receive instruction in the art of runes. And she looked down at the little girl standing before her, mildly annoyed to be stuck with an obscure peasant from a remote corner of the dwarf lands.

She looked at the fallen goblin with distrust, pointing her staff at him, his figure basking in the light of Chromatic Hills. She opened her wings to rise at the commotion, fearful for her childhood friend, only to be told by her to stay back and not frighten the goblin. And she lay on the ground at the foot of the cliff, her leg broken, unable to run, staring at the two intruders in her land, startled by the thunderoc and terrified of the mage.

She felt the energy course through her three-stranded staff, released with abandon, the enchanted ground of Sentinel Grove furnishing aplenty. She felt it pass through the crystalline staff held by each dwarf hand, though more subdued, her rune magic no match for that of a mur. She felt it in each wooden staff held by her elf hand, and even the composite staves in her morlock hands, all the magicians doing their utmost to feed the barrier erected to protect them, or break through it in the tense stalemate at Sentinel Grove.

She watched in distress as dwarves and elves turned their backs on her in the open space of their war camp. She breathed in relief as her attempts to undermine Asja's dissent resonated with the dwarves. And she turned away in disgust at Asja's betrayal of the dwarf cause, her decision cascading through the war camp until she shunned the traitor to the last man.

The memories washed over Asja, leaving nothing hidden, no other to add something unknown to each scene, as if she were every person she'd encountered in her life, as if only Amana were there in her many forms.

The warring no longer made any sense, with no one there to fight but herself.

A renewed drive to end the war arose within Asja. But as she rose from the ocean to depart from the plane, she realised she was no closer to a course of action that would achieve this aim. Like Lyra before her, her methods had failed, and she had no novel ones to try in their place.

As she descended through the interior of the Algalash tree, she heard faint whispers falling into disarray. Colourful patterns spilled beyond their room to fill other chambers with their playful display.

The Chaos Plane had something to tell her.

SYMPHONY OF LIFE

The Chaos Plane was the last place Asja would have chosen to be at a time like this. She had no patience left for its mischievous quirks. But the plane invited her in and didn't seek to test it. The colourful visage soon dissolved into a dusky backdrop, making her wonder whether she'd mistakenly ventured into Primogenus instead.

A violet speck of light appeared directly ahead, shining brightly against the black canvas, announcing its presence with a soothing monotone. The familiarity of the sound gnawed at her, but she couldn't quite place where from. She touched it with her hand, but pulled back startled when she felt her fingers press upon something deep beneath her skin.

The speck sprouted into a faint strand whose stem rose as it grew, checked immediately by a broad rainbow thread of the most intricate design that had sprung up all around. Its azure and emerald tones Asja did know, alongside its symphonic hum that seemed to absorb the speck's own note. The goddess transformed the strand with her deft touch, dulling its violet hue and prompting a change of route.

Two more threads appeared thereafter and chose to stay, intertwining with Asja's own to keep it safe. Their warmth and nourishment brought tears to her eyes when she recognised in them Erna and Tor. In their loving embrace her strand steadily grew, appreciated and cared for if not quite understood.

Her heart rushed a beat when a sapphire spot appeared in her path, its fibre soon growing on her like a conjoined twin. It shone the brightest of all the threads in her view, but also with the least intricacy, its beautiful note not deviating from its starting tone, making her wonder whether he was even aware of it, or whether it came to him as naturally as lightning. Their union gave her own strand a boost, drawing her wildness out from beneath its shell, so it could flourish in the land of dwarves, among people where wildness was no longer welcome. Convulsing with sobs, she reached out to touch the essence of her friend, thanking him for his companionship and the gift he'd given her, saying goodbye to him one more time.

As the strand continued to grow, new fibres came into its life – other people, places of uncommon presence, events conjured up by the land herself. Each one imprinted upon her ever so slightly, causing her strand to twist and twirl as it veered from its path, radiating a fresh blend of violet and mauve and sounding a note more melodious than the one before.

She saw the first glimpse she'd caught of Florella's dream while recovering from Shar's wounds in her bed of flowing stone, and the encounter in the garden where it had revealed itself fully. She hadn't understood it then, yet still admired her teacher's uncommon beauty that both inspired her and soothed her distress. She'd wondered how the plant could develop such depth of feeling – a capacity lacking in many people she knew – despite all the hardships she had endured. In fact, her beauty only grew, as if each painful event unlocked new depths of feeling to explore and enlarged her capacity to love.

She saw the thread of Obalin, whose rejection made her acutely aware of her own power more than any of his compliments ever could. Lyra, who taught her to remain true to her dream even when her methods backfired, but to own those failures lest she suffer the same fate. Rangorr, who taught her to love the Tyrant within her and embrace his potent gifts lest her disowning of him provoke his wrath. Empyrean, whose brief appearance taught her to welcome home her inner demons no matter how long they'd been wandering and lost. Centane, who showed her the beauty of such a homecoming. Dimotai, who revealed to her what life amounted to in the absence of a dream. Tenaya, whose dream nursery opened her eyes to the nature of the world in whom she lived. Hloim, who showed her the wonder of a dream fleetingly fulfilled. And the dark thread of Death who awoke in her the magic of life.

A strand conspicuous by its absence was the stone wizard's one. She used to wonder why her gift never worked on him, how he was able to conceal his dream from her so skilfully and for so long, and why he would even want to. Looking at the tapestry before her eyes, she realised now that he had nothing to hide. Forged in a desperate struggle for survival when the world was young, before people like her existed and long before they dared to dream. He encountered dreams in other worlds and sought to bring them to his own, admiring the wonder of what he himself lacked, nurturing it in the end with his own life.

His death marked the end of an age – of fighting for the bare necessities of life, of merely going through the motions of living, of being content to simply be. Dreams were starting to shine through the layers of tradition and duty, inviting people to move beyond well-worn habits and paths well-walked.

Satjan and Lyra had answered the call before abandoning it or losing their way. Hloim and Rangorr were ready to try anew. Asja had even imagined in the mages' brief acceptance of her that they, too, might soon be swayed.

Now she understood that enough strength lingered in the age of old to suffocate the new in its dying grip. Dwarves resisted the call of their dreams – to become more than their ancestors had been. Their struggle for survival had to go on no matter how much the dreams ached for more.

As if on cue, Asja's own life tapestry receded into the distance to make space for the tapestries of others – strands of singular colour dancing to a shrill monotone, proudly played, drowning out the melody of dreams too concealed from the world to really be heard. But there was familiarity to the sound that she did recall – the kaleidoscopic tone of the dwarf archon Aorar.

She understood now that dwarf cries for war gave him physical form as they reached fever pitch. She appreciated the source of his strength, even as she now opposed it with every fibre of her being. She recognised again that desert people had archons of their own, the fall of whom must have shattered their resolve to continue with the war.

As the dwarven strands of life receded into space, those of other people came into view. Elves and humans, her own birth people, goblins and ogres and other desert dwellers, creatures of frost, of lakes, rivers and seas, of marshes and swamps in the far reaches of the land. They all came together, each people with their own song.

But the Plane of Chaos didn't stop there. The strands rebelled, bringing out the dreams hereto hidden, honouring their song with their every breath. In an instant, the tapestry transformed into a colourful mosaic of unimaginable complexity and indescribable beauty, each dream shining with full splendour, playing a part distinct from the others yet coming together in harmonious accord. A world come alive, born of imagination, a land having become all that she could be, unconstrained by the established order in the space of the plane.

For a sublime moment, Asja had borne witness to Ama's dream.

A dream who felt... sacred.

She wondered what it would take to make it real beyond the imagined reality of the Chaos Plane. What would cause the dwarf warriors who had turned their backs on her to awaken to their dreams and let them flourish?

Her own gift whispered the answer, having stirred Hloim to the wonder of his dream during their chance encounter in the enchanted grove.

She finally knew why the goddess had interfered in her life, invested in having her trained as a wizard, wanted the girl to be in her service. Only now did she understand what it truly meant. Only now was she finally ready to heed the call.

CHRYSALIS

Asja stood in a smouldering haze, her gaze transfixed on an enormous burning eye staring back at her. She'd almost forgotten how intimidated she felt being in his presence. The scars from her prior visit still lingered – the residual views he'd mercilessly sheared off her – despite being the better for it.

But the beholder looked different somehow. For all his fiery heat, she remembered him as a cold arbiter of facts on a relentless pursuit of truth. This Watcher felt warm, passionate even, as if logic and reason were no longer his favoured tools.

He hovered closer, creeping tentatively through the churning air, his tentacles flailing about him in slow motion, as if to test the strength of her resolve, her desire to face him again. It took all of her willpower to resist the urge to run. But she stood her ground. She'd endured the intensity of his flame once before and came back for more.

The warmth from the giant eye grew as he approached. The life-sized iris commanded her attention until it took over her entire view. The sweltering heat permeated every pore of her body, draining drops of sweat through her parched skin that evaporated before they could touch the ground. And when she was certain she couldn't withstand any more, the Watcher's tentacles coiled around her exposed back, wrapping tightly around her and drawing her closer in a ferocious embrace.

Her ideas of what her life ought to be about were the first to perish in the Watcher's flame, their connections to her seared by the rapacious heat.

Gone was her fantasy of serving her clan as the most capable mage they'd ever had. Gone was her notion of becoming a runemage, a master druid, or even a wizard of great renown. Their edges still burning, they landed with a thud on the floor of the plane. Any thoughts of fame she'd still quietly harboured fell with them.

Gone was her notion of swooping in and ending the goblin war like the dwarf heroes of old, vestiges of which still lingered in her reverence of their historic deeds. Gone was her notion of rallying dwarves and their friends against the war effort. The war itself no longer felt like her concern, despite the frightful devastation that it had wrought.

Next came her knowledge of the world and her place in it. One by one the fragments fell, dislodged by the Watcher's relentless gaze. Her childhood memory of Erna and Tor, her lifelong friendship with Vagran, the teachings of Florella and Shar, her relations with her adoptive people as well as their enemies and friends.

Even her mur heritage couldn't withstand the heat. Her mur presence beneath the dwarven exterior, the rich memories of her accomplished ancestors, her healing talent that was the first to blossom, even the wizardly skills she'd worked most doggedly to develop and most fiercely clung to as her own. None could withstand the Watcher's searing embrace.

The blaze poured from the beholder's eye until all that remained of her was her naked dream. And then he left, vanishing without a trace into the frothing haze of the Purgatory Plane, leaving her standing in the open space surrounded by the scattered pieces of her dismembered self.

Freed and laid bare, the dream gleamed through the seething mist, her hollow hum sounding through the plane. Asja felt the longing of Paradise burn unquenched within her own being, aching to be more than the dream she'd always been, yearning to become real.

Only once did she taste the nourishment she sought – by helping another mage satisfy his own. The nourishment that filled her longing until it overflowed, the excess finding home within the staff she kept by her side. A staff who was nothing other than the realised strands of her own dream.

Now she yearned to find Firmament kin with longing equally unquenched and share in their ecstasy of having it fulfilled. A desire so strong she could see them through their worldly clothes and partake of their rapture as if it were her own.

She bent down to gather the fragments of her worldly self, as she had at the moment of her birth. Some she left lying on the floor, seeing no way for them to engender the experience she sought. All thoughts of popular success, of recognition for her talent and skill – she left on the ground where they had dropped, seeing them as distractions from her goal, not worthy of her attention or time. The thoughts of ending the war and remedying the world's ills she also left untouched, recognising this important work as a less meaningful way for her to be, leaving it for other dreams who sought fulfilment in it, knowing her place in the world, that this was not it.

She picked up all the talents she'd inherited at birth, and all the skills she'd developed thereafter, and tried to clothe herself with them, lining them up as she used to do, thinking how best they might serve her goal. But each time she laid down a path, it seemed to diminish where she sought to go. Her dream agreed, rejecting her plans, scattering them back across the ground.

Thinking her planning faulty, she tried again, arranging her fragments in a new pattern, only to have it rejected time and time again. In the end, she gave in, seeing that she couldn't chart her path from the start. She'd have to wear her worldly self lightly and wield her freely, mindful of the needs of the moment she found herself in. She'd have to walk a path to see where it led, and see it anew with each step she made. She'd know the way by how deeply it moved her, by how meaningful her life became for her being on it.

Her metamorphosis complete, she ran her hands all over her body, getting to know herself again having been born anew. She gazed at the remnants of her old self, grateful to them for where they had brought her, but no longer recognising them as her own.

And then the new wizard stepped away from the scene of her birth and departed from the Purgatory Plane.

BELUGA

The full weight of a porous fin came down upon the water. She receded in response, pushed out by the mass of rock, only to come back with a vengeance and wash over the earth who grew upon the stone. The hefty wave covered the coastal belt, feeding the lakes at the tip of his reach before receding into the Primal Ocean from whom he had emerged.

Another fin made of primeval rock splashed into the sea, provoking a surge and a flood at the other end of the land. The creatures living there left and then returned, familiar with the earthly cycle retold in their myths. The plants could not, but learned to welcome their communion with the sea, drinking her thirstily while she frolicked in their midst.

A massive fin at the back of the land rose next, dwarfing the others with his enormous reach. He came down hard on top of the water, submerging his surface in the rising tide, a covering of enormous trees hardened by the waves. The water gushed to his joint with the mainland, but could advance no further, the sturdy mountains standing in her way. With nowhere to go, she pushed against the range, propelling the land on her journey across the sea.

The land swam across the Primordial Ocean, searching, exploring, her fins moving the floating bulk with their rhythmic dance. When the people living upon her came of age, they joined the search in their wooden ships, sailing into the darkness far from her shores, but always returning to her sky-bound lights, not finding another place where they could live.

The mariners' song carried across the waters, speaking of their world with poetic words, inviting anyone who could hear them to come. It joined the melody of their land on her search for others of her kind. They mingled, playing in harmony, their pitch rising through the eons, until the land and her people became their song, a pure resonance radiating from the core of their being. The lower tones of earth and stone gave off a cloudlike glow that filled the space with motley textures and vibrant colours. Quivering flesh shone more brightly, each creature becoming a dazzling point of light, bursting through the nebula in whom they resided to spread their rays to other regions of their world.

The powerful tailfin came down once more, but instead of moving the land forward, she lifted up, leaving the familiar surface of the Primal Waters upon whom she had lived all her life, never having encountered another land, not knowing whether she ever would. She rose over the water and beyond the sky, no longer bound to them, moving freely through Aia's cosmic reach.

She spied countless lands from her new vantage, burgeoning worlds filled with life, kept apart by an endless expanse of water. She visited each one in turn, her motion swift, her path not confined to the surface of Aia. Some of their dreams joined her, awed by the spectacle of a universe filled with stars. Some of hers chose to remain, nostalgic for a world as theirs used to be, wanting to feel the pull of Primal Waters and undertake that journey one more time.

She left a myth in her wake with each land she touched, imprinted in the dreams who decided to stay. A myth of a land beyond their present sorrows, waiting for them somewhere in the Heavens.

THE FIRST STEP

A young sunflower moved to track the motion of the sun. His head turned, but his face remained hidden, wrapped with interlocking layers of overprotective leaves. He remained safe from the skylight's gaze until his leaves felt the tender touch of a young woman's hand. The warmth stayed with them, as did the message she impressed upon them. With a sudden burst of courage, the flower opened to bare his face and absorb the rays of light the skylight freely shared.

The sight brought a smile to the woman's face. She stood up, staff in hand, her scaled body slender and smooth, still getting used to her taller frame, still hobbling as she had before.

Her face darkened as the field of flowers brought on a memory of her Mount Edars home and of the dwarf people who'd raised her as their own. The people who now ravaged the goblin lands under the watchful guidance of clan leaders and runemages. The people who no longer counted her among them.

Elves accompanied them in this quest, spurred on by both archons who lived and breathed war. Even humans had offered their aid, seemingly not content with their command of the plains, the lamias having perished long ago and with them any chance of learning from felines and finding common ground.

She swallowed hard to hold back tears.

This was not the world she wished to live in. Her influence over it had not kept pace with her magic skill. She watched it slip away even as she formally became a wizard and took up residence in the Algalash tree. She understood Shar now more than ever, treasuring the teaching he was trying to convey, mindful of her gift and the promise it held, the one beacon of hope in a world gone astray.

She looked down at Bioluminescent Bay, the mur town bustling with motion, the people who'd made a new life for themselves on the eastern islands of the archipelago. She didn't know what she was going to do when she appeared among them. What she'd say. Whether she'd seek out Centane or watch from the sidelines, observing the dreams reveal themselves to her, waiting for the opportune moment to help them become real.

Her heart pounded in her chest. Her fingers gripped the staff. The bronze strands pulsated in her hand, centring her thoughts on the task ahead. She breathed in the hushed scent of wild marigolds whose slender stems saturated the field. Her eyes focused on the beckoning path, her dream attuned to the moment's grace.

She took the first step...

EPILOGUE

Silence descended upon the class.

Rukha's voice, deep and melodic, had ceased telling the tale. The children leaned forward in their seats as if to soak up the next adventure that she had to share.

"And then?" asked a little boy seated in the front, his gaze fixed on the storyteller, his face filled with anticipation.

Rukha smiled. She loved this part of her work, seeing the students completely absorbed in the tale she was there to tell, spellbound and thirsting for the next morsel of the story.

"To find out what happened after, you can listen to the many legends about the life of Asja the Dream Seer that have been preserved. They talk of her heroic deeds in a time of great upheaval. While embellished, they will give you some sense of what she has been able to accomplish.

"Some people treat those deeds as the true highlights of her life. They point to her mur origins, as if every mur is destined to accomplish great things. They talk of her magic skills, as if every shaman's had a profound effect on the lives of their people from that time and beyond.

"Only a few people from her time have thought to capture her early life in a tale. I think we owe them a profound debt, for they have shown us what it took for her to perform the feats described in the legends, what she's had to learn and live through to become a person worthy of their mention.

"If there's one thing about her life that stays with you from this moment on, let it be that."

Silence followed her words again. When it became clear that Rukha had nothing more to say, the children got up from their seats, followed by a low murmur and the rustling of leaves. No commotion accompanied their departure. Soon they would return to their customary games, but for now, the tale held them in its grip, enticing them to continue living in its world even as they walked away from the scene of its retelling.

Rukha would leave soon, too, to another village in the Kalhar Desert that had not yet heard the tale, after she was done answering the questions the children and even adults would undoubtedly have. For now, she stayed in the park, unhurried and alone, enjoying the shade of the palm trees and the shelter they furnished from the desert wind.

Whenever she told a story from that bygone time, the reality of her ancestors' savageness struck her anew.

Ogres had merely been a footnote in her story, labouring away and protecting goblins from harm in return for being looked after by a people better adapted to the desert's ways. She could scarcely believe that such primitive people could learn to live as they do now, flourishing in a bountiful garden crafted by their own hands, attracting students from regions steeped in history far more illustrious than their own.

Her gaze fell on a solitary tree beyond the clearing, plaited from thin stems to grow wide and strong, and better withstand the harsh desert winds. She'd never been to Kritall Wood, but this was how she imagined her trees to be. Legend had it that Asja herself had blessed the tree with a potent spell. A plaque above the roots attested to this event. True or not, Rukha loved the place regardless, and could easily have stayed were it not for her commitment to the work of keeping the story alive lest it be reduced to heroic deeds with no backstory of how they'd come about.

A knowing smile spread across her face. She was the opposite of Asja in so many ways. Born an ogre, with no magical talent to call her own, she should have no inkling of what a dream seer's life was truly like, how it felt to make full use of her wizardly skills. And yet, when she spun her tale and held listeners enraptured, she felt like a wizard too, crafting whole worlds in their imagination. In those moments, she touched the core of their being as much as any dream seer who had ever lived.

She turned to leave when she saw a celestial being standing at the edge of the park, his eyes locked with hers, his body glowing as if a furnace had been lit from within.

She gasped at the sight. Her heart skipped a beat. Meeting celestials was rare even in this time. She bowed in deference, her body shaking with excitement, daring to believe that he really did gaze in her direction, that she really was the object of his concern.

His features softened. Warmth and affection permeated his being. He bowed in response, as if to give credence to her work, his flowing movements the epitome of elegance and grace, light pouring from the deep lines etched into his face.

About Me

Asja's dream from the story is my dream, too.

It crystallised on the pages of this novel in the final years of writing.

I hope it inspires you to pursue your own dream, and gives you some tools that can help you along the way.

That would mean the world to me.

If you wish to know more about this novel, you can find it on the Fandom wiki: *A Wizard's Dream*. You can also connect with me there.

https://a-wizards-dream.fandom.com

Till then...

Hrvoje Butković

www.ingramcontent.com/pod-product-compliance
Lightning Source LLC
Chambersburg PA
CBHW071151020726
47502CB00002B/364